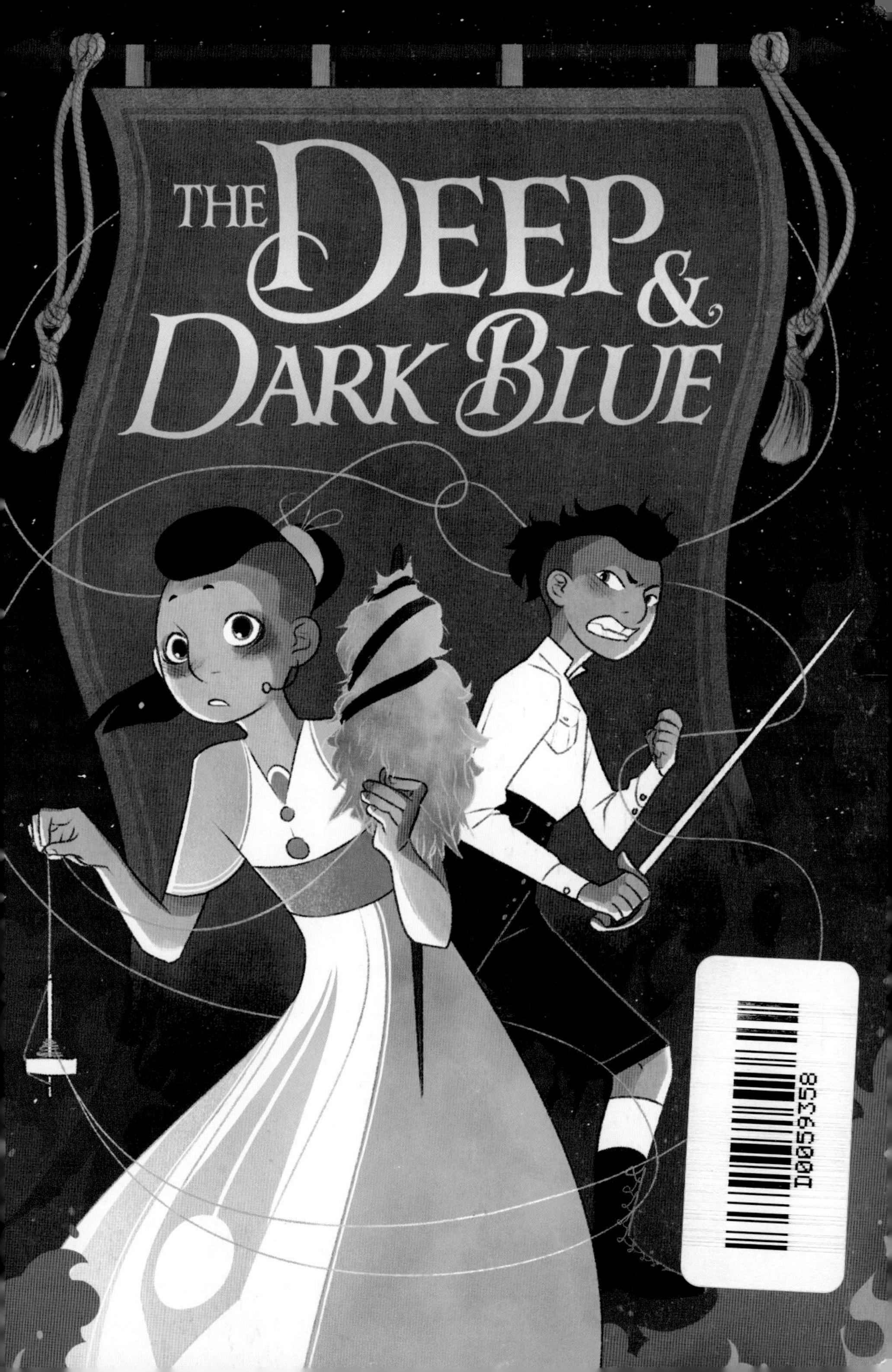
THE DEEP & DARK BLUE

About This Book

The illustrations for this book were done in Clip Studio Paint and Adobe Photoshop. This book was edited by Rex Ogle and designed by Ching Chan. The production was supervised by Erika Schwartz, and the production editor was Annie McDonnell. The text was set in Claire Hand, and the display type is Yana B.

Little, Brown and Company
Hachette Book Group
1290 Avenue of the Americas, New York, NY 10104
Visit us at LBYR.com

First Edition: January 2020

Little, Brown and Company is a division of Hachette Book Group, Inc. The Little, Brown name and logo are trademarks of Hachette Book Group, Inc.

The publisher is not responsible for websites (or their content) that are not owned by the publisher.

Library of Congress Control Number: 2019941622

ISBNs: 978-0-316-48598-2 (hardcover), 978-0-316-48601-9 (paperback), 978-0-316-48602-6 (ebook), 978-0-316-48599-9 (ebook), 978-0-316-48597-5 (ebook)

PRINTED IN CHINA

1010

Hardcover: 10 9 8 7 6 5 4 3 2 1

Paperback: 10 9 8 7 6 5 4 3 2 1

THE DEEP & DARK BLUE

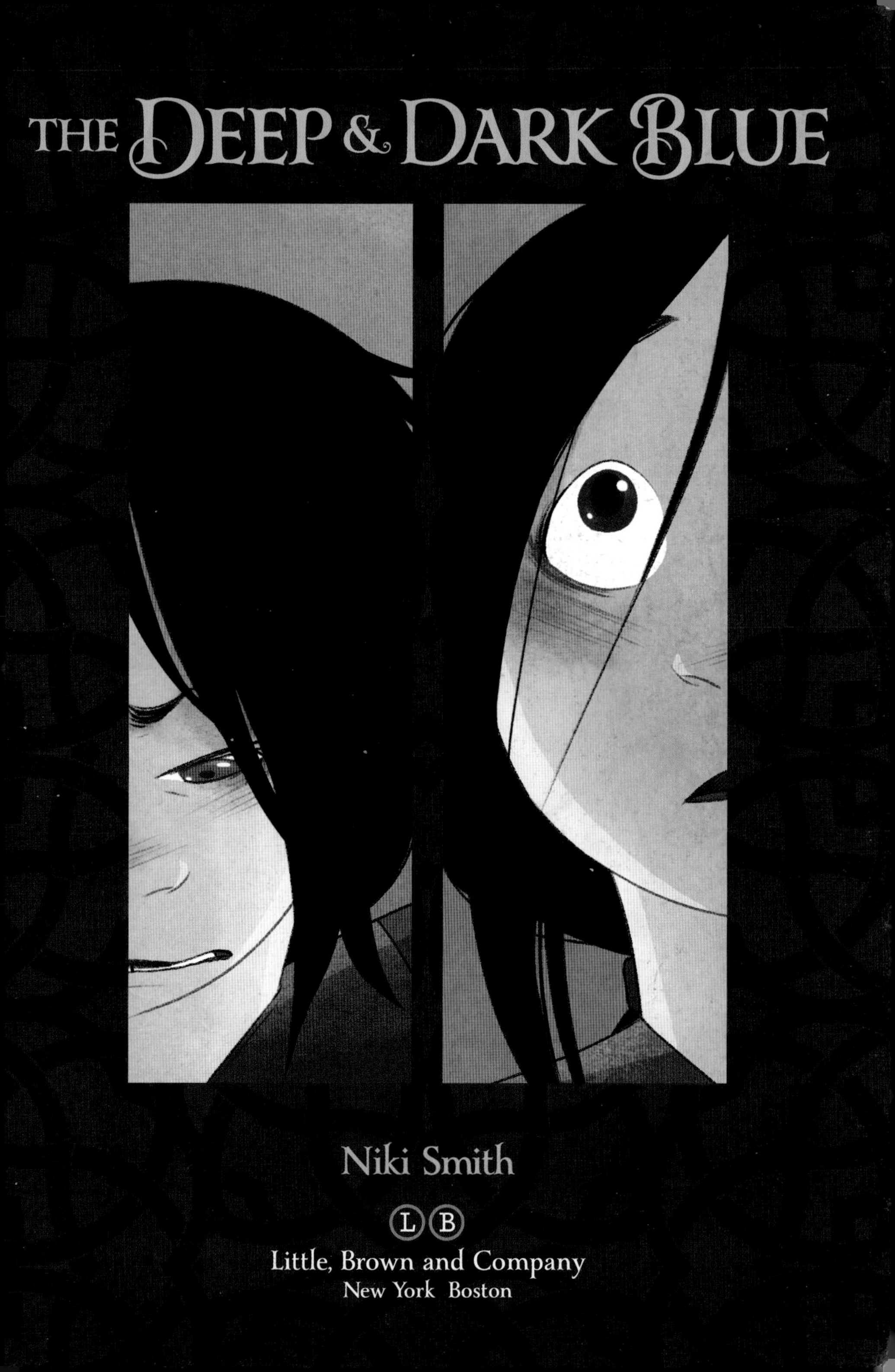

Niki Smith

LB
Little, Brown and Company
New York Boston

For my dad, who loved to dream.

Thank you to Mey Rude, Jo Kreil, and
Sarah W. Searle, for all your help and guidance.
And thank you, Kiri, for everything.

CHAPTER I
COUP

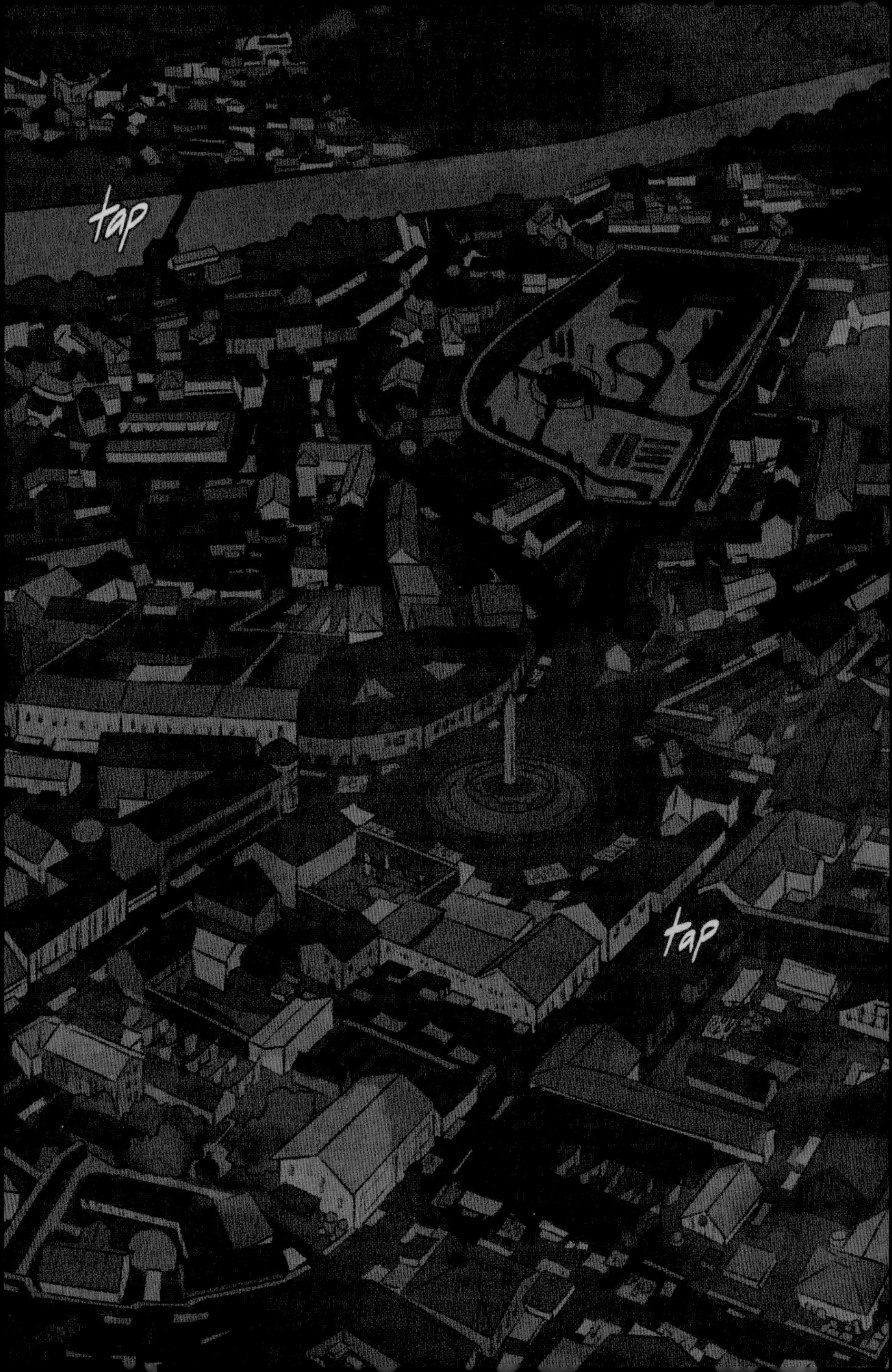
tap
tap

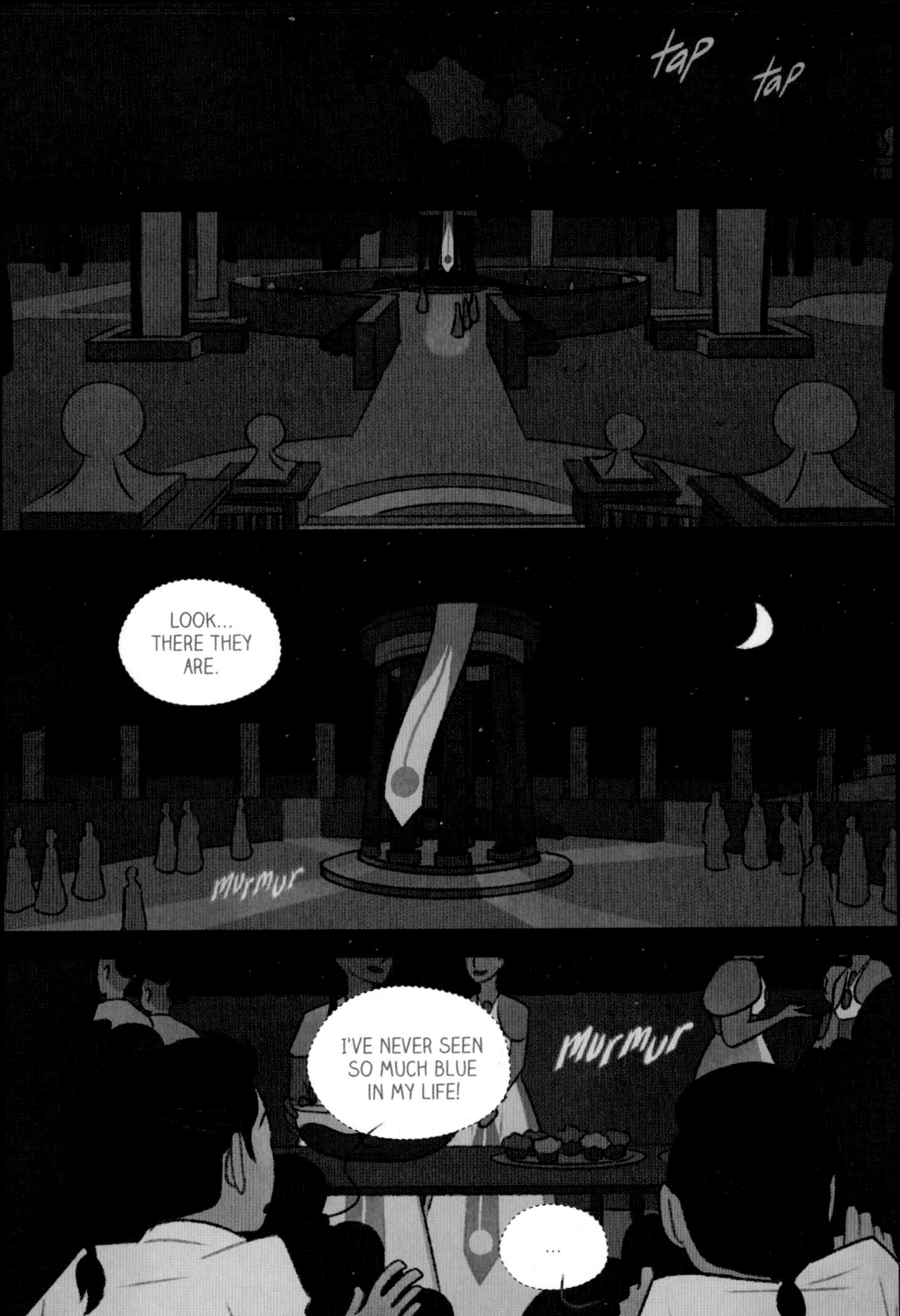
tap
tap
LOOK... THERE THEY ARE.
murmur
I'VE NEVER SEEN SO MUCH BLUE IN MY LIFE!
murmur
...

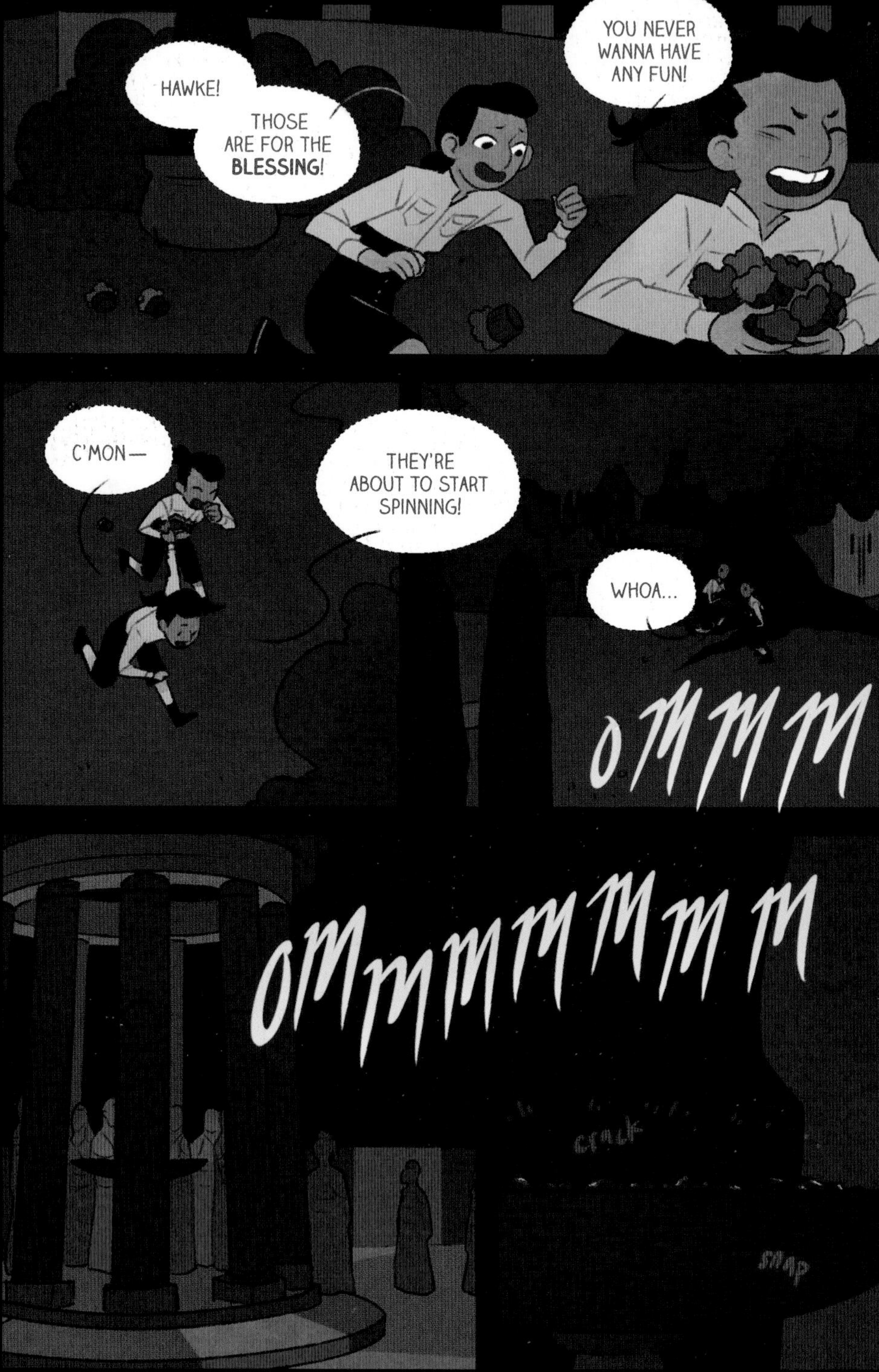
HAWKE!
THOSE ARE FOR THE **BLESSING**!
YOU NEVER WANNA HAVE ANY FUN!
C'MON—
THEY'RE ABOUT TO START SPINNING!
WHOA...
OMMMM
OMMMMMMMM
crack
SNAP

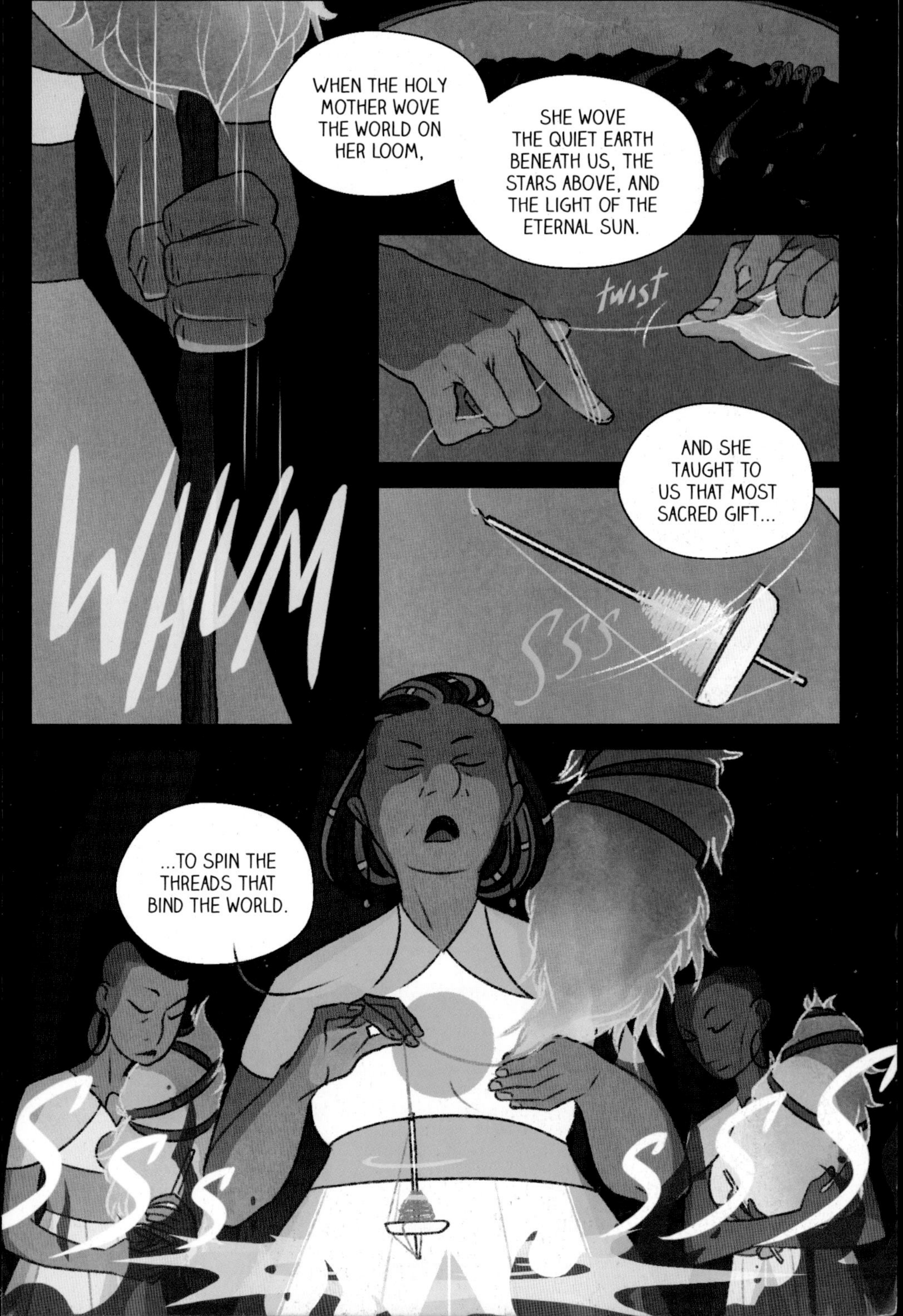
WHEN THE HOLY MOTHER WOVE THE WORLD ON HER LOOM,
SHE WOVE THE QUIET EARTH BENEATH US, THE STARS ABOVE, AND THE LIGHT OF THE ETERNAL SUN.
twist
WHUM
AND SHE TAUGHT TO US THAT MOST SACRED GIFT...
SSS
...TO SPIN THE THREADS THAT BIND THE WORLD.
SSS
SSS

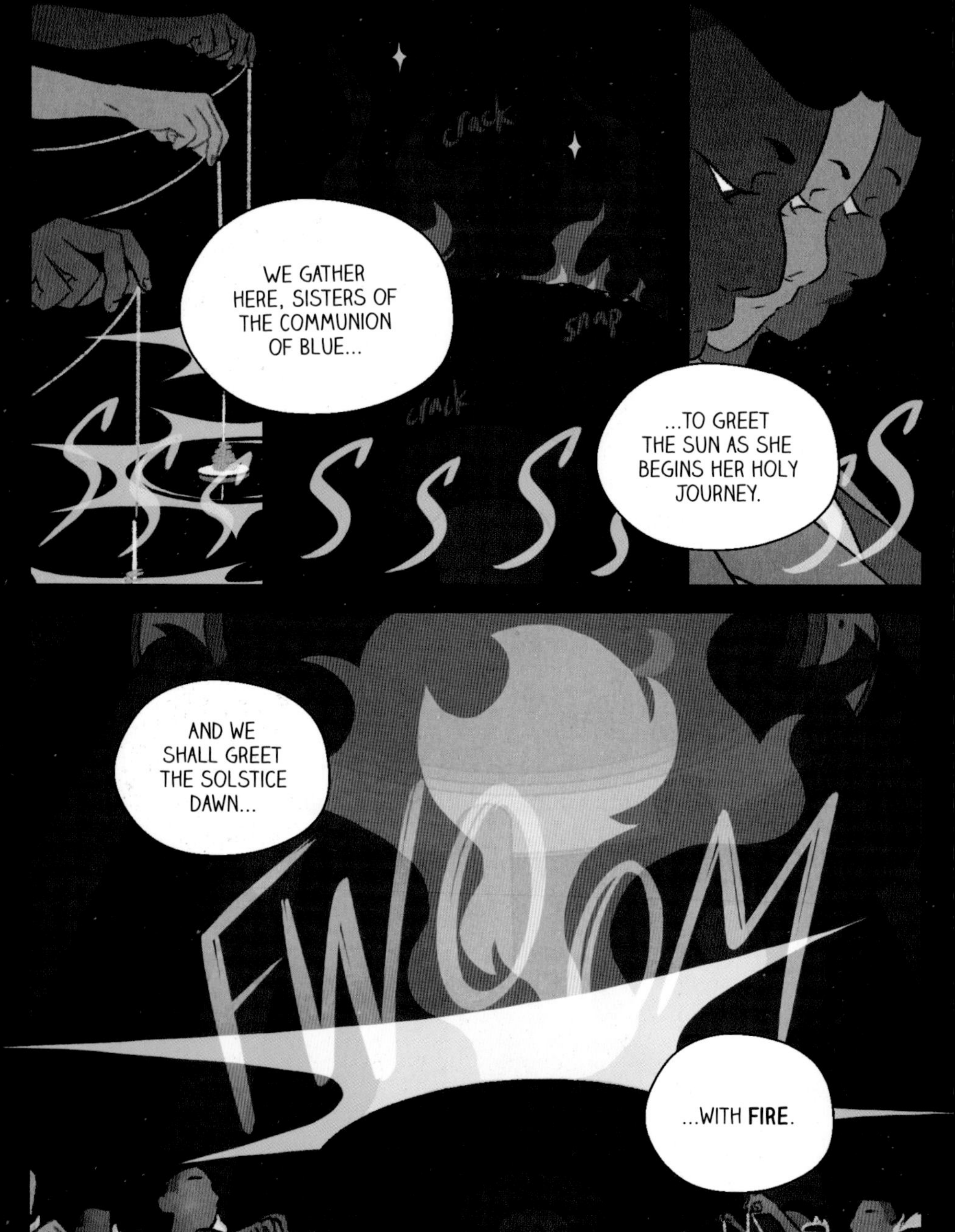

CRACK
SNAP
CRACK
WE GATHER HERE, SISTERS OF THE COMMUNION OF BLUE...
...TO GREET THE SUN AS SHE BEGINS HER HOLY JOURNEY.
SSSSSS
AND WE SHALL GREET THE SOLSTICE DAWN...
FWOOM
...WITH **FIRE**.

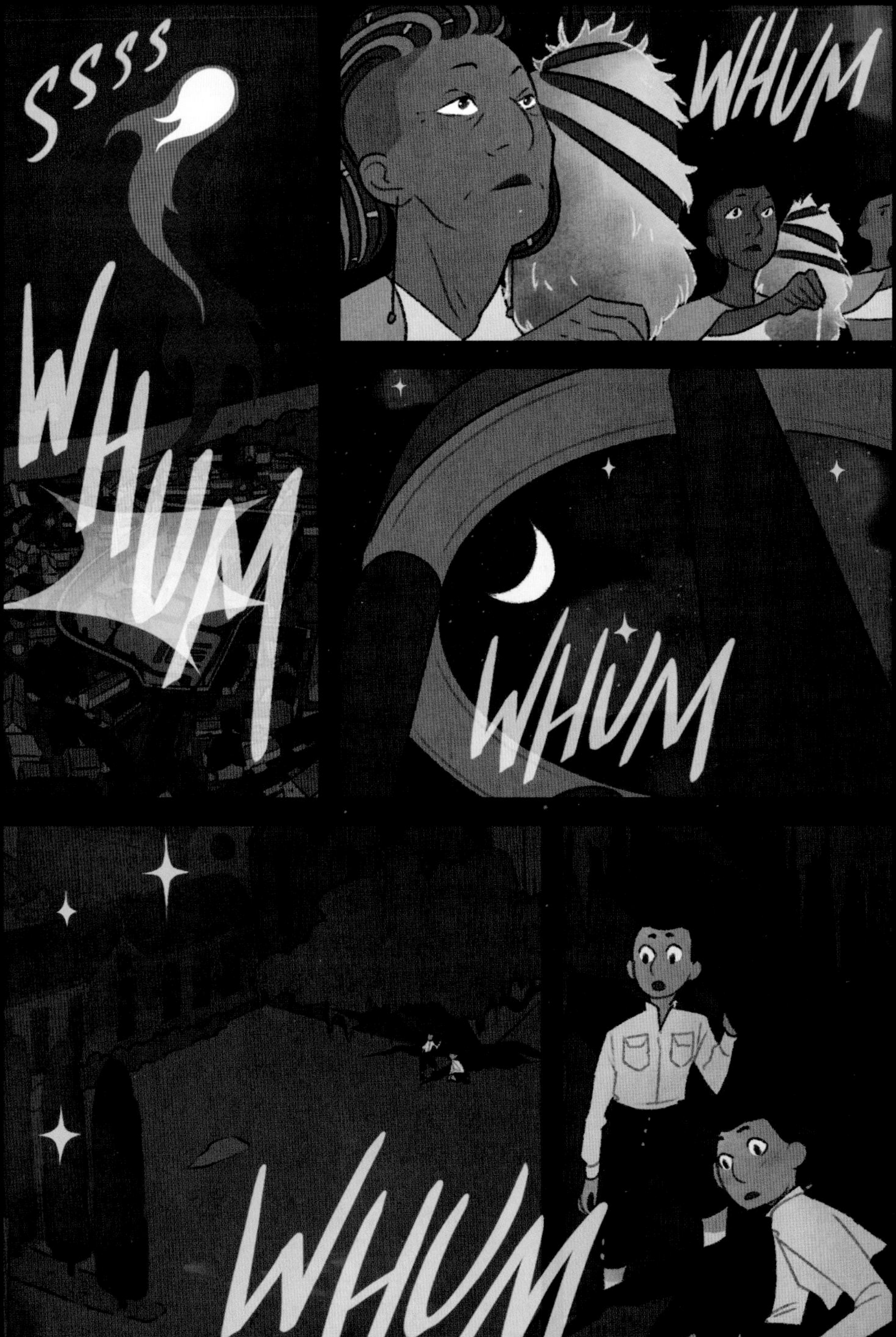
SSSS
WHUM
WHUM
WHUM
WHUM

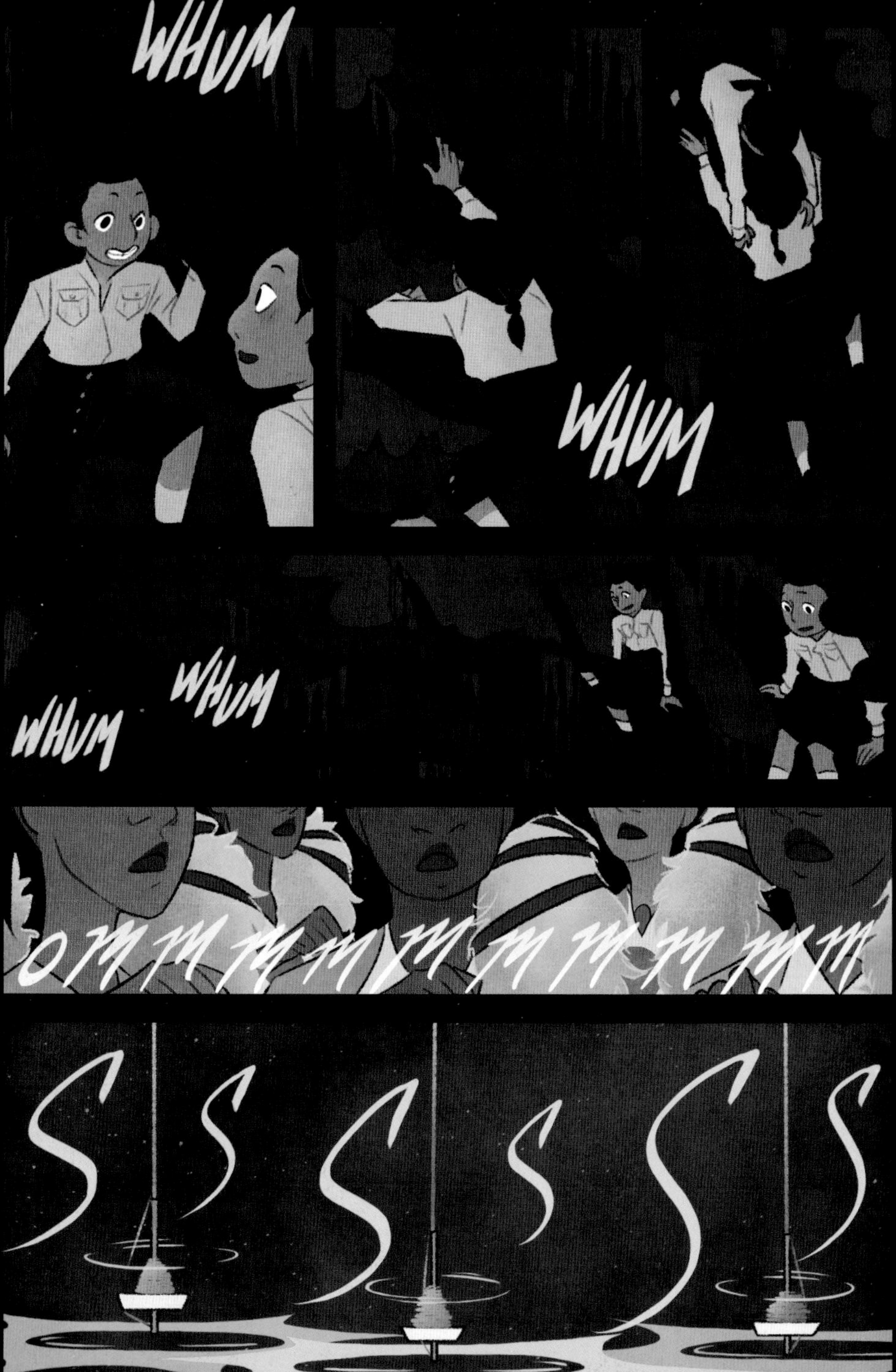
WHUM
WHUM
WHUM
WHUM
OMMMMMMMMMMMM
SSSSSSS

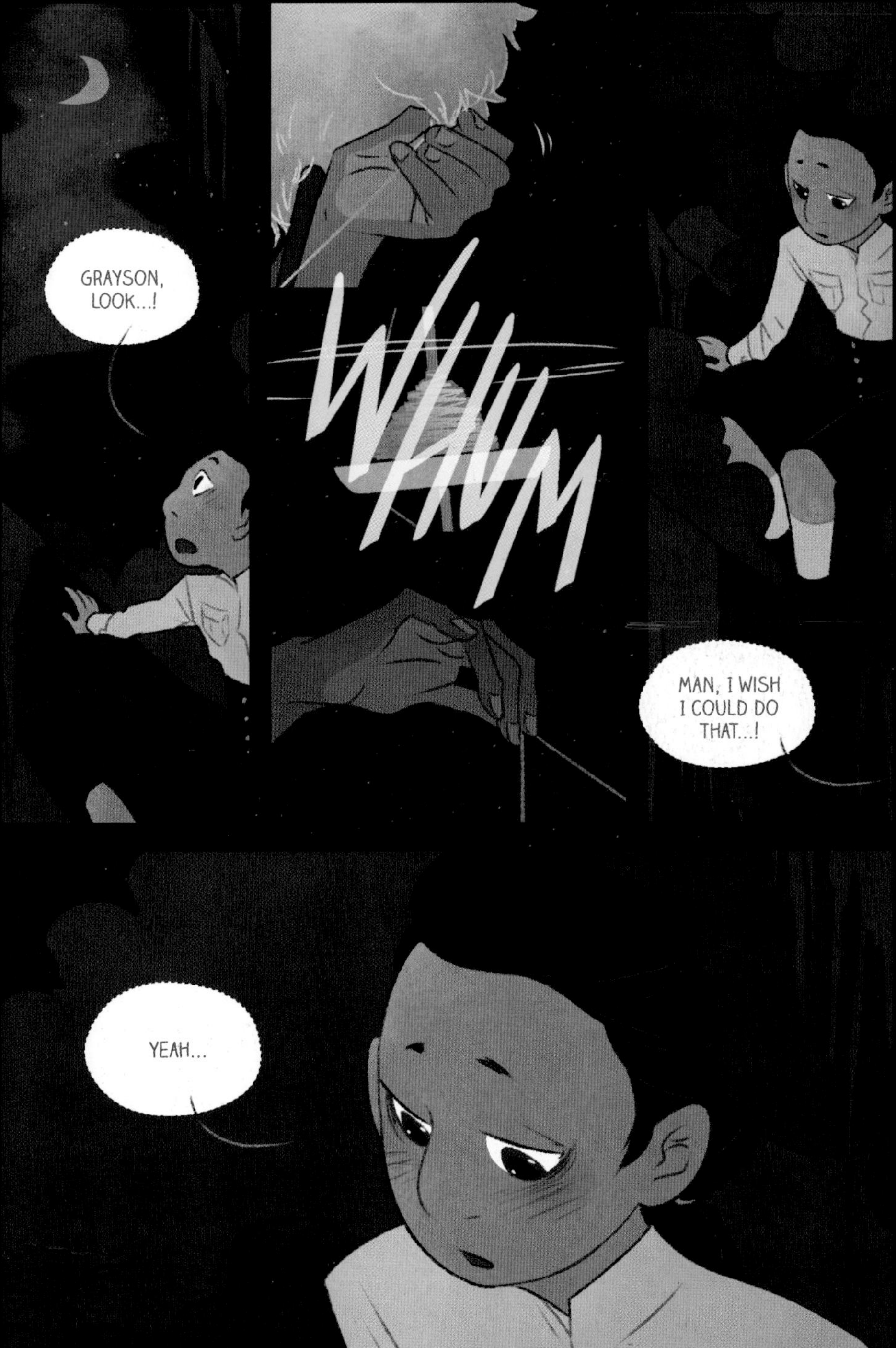

GRAYSON, LOOK...!
WHUM
MAN, I WISH I COULD DO THAT...!
YEAH...

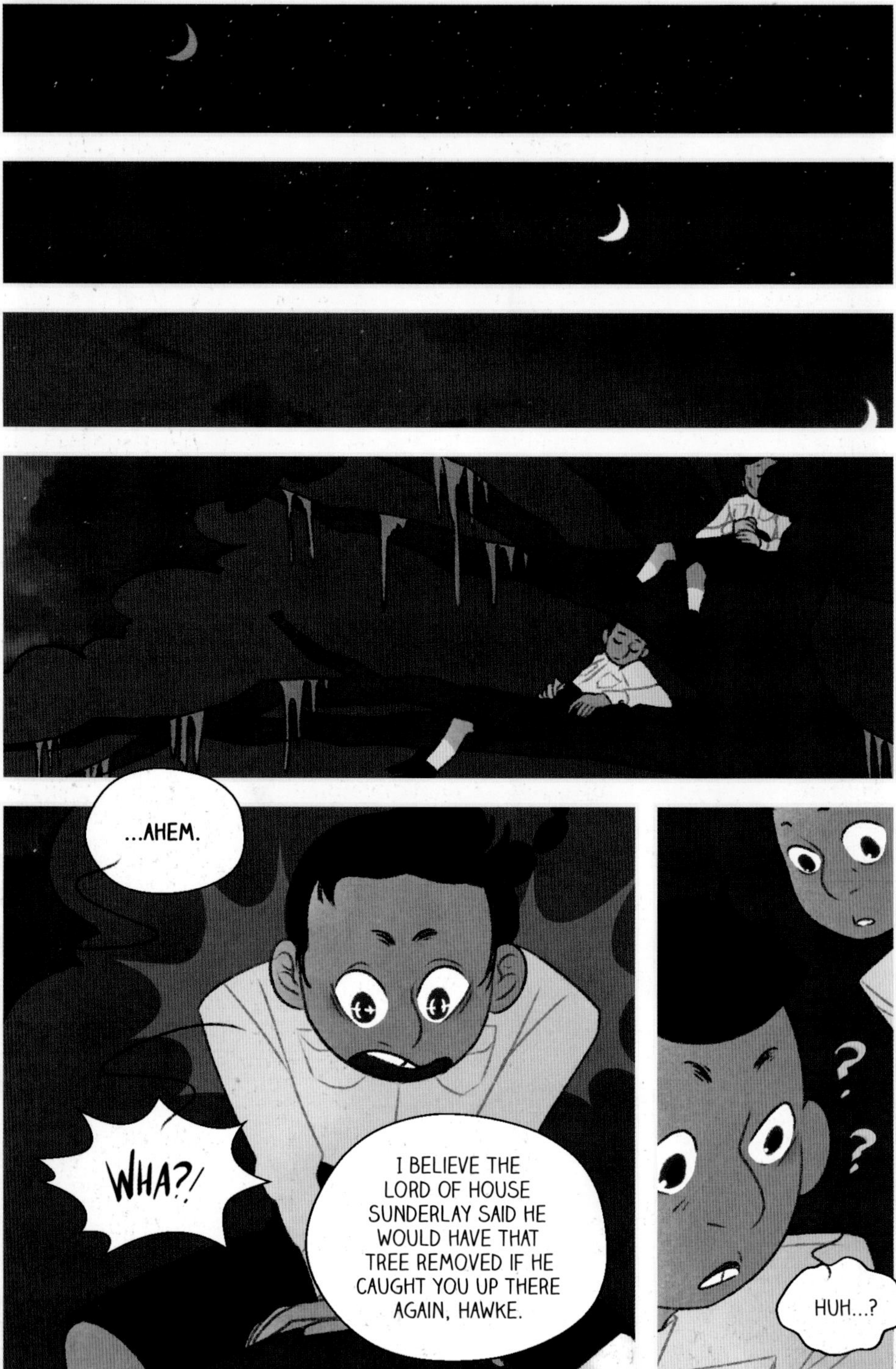
...AHEM.
WHA?!
I BELIEVE THE LORD OF HOUSE SUNDERLAY SAID HE WOULD HAVE THAT TREE REMOVED IF HE CAUGHT YOU UP THERE AGAIN, HAWKE.
HUH...?

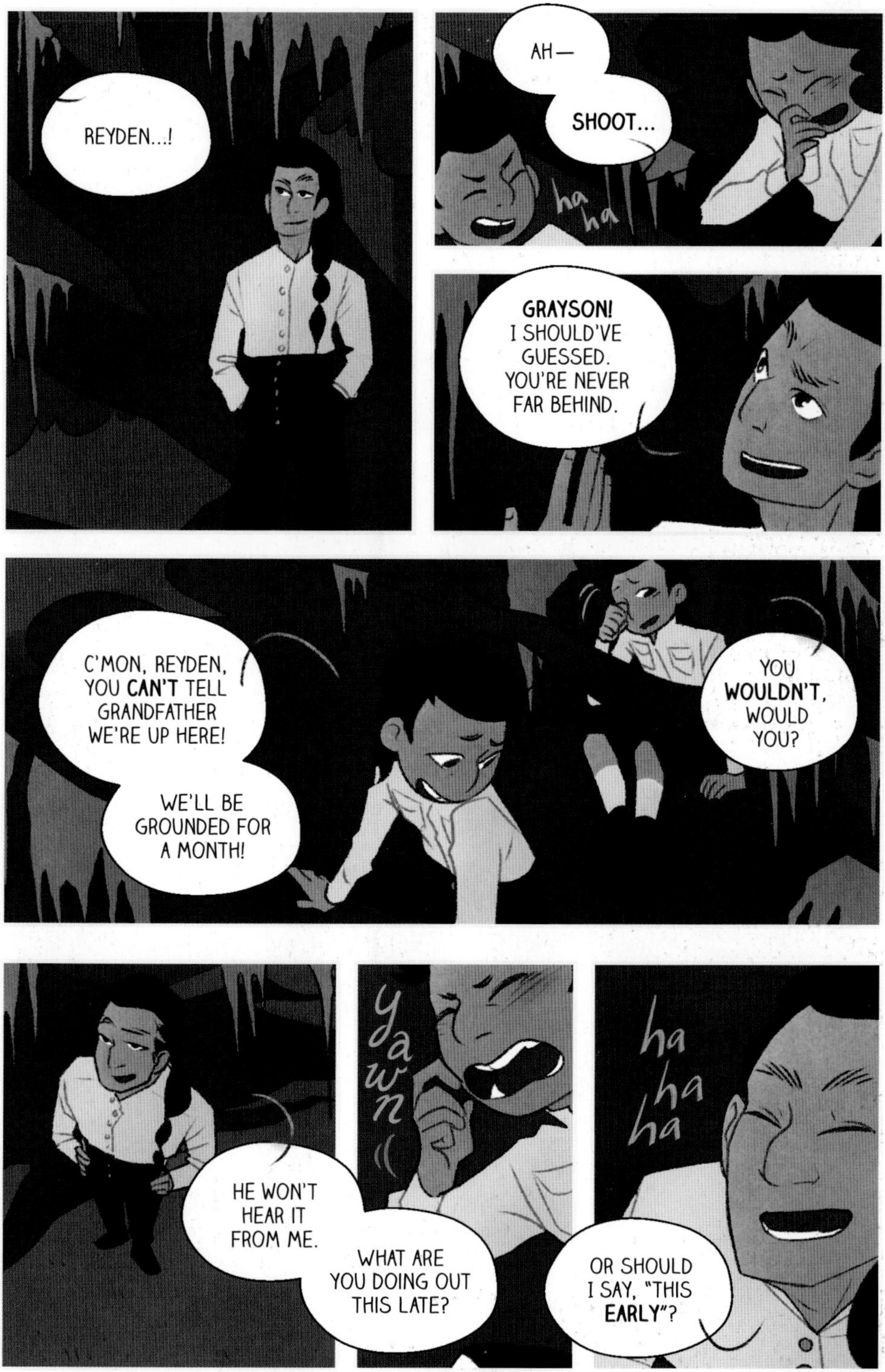
REYDEN...!
AH—
SHOOT...
ha ha
GRAYSON! I SHOULD'VE GUESSED. YOU'RE NEVER FAR BEHIND.
C'MON, REYDEN, YOU CAN'T TELL GRANDFATHER WE'RE UP HERE!
WE'LL BE GROUNDED FOR A MONTH!
YOU WOULDN'T, WOULD YOU?
HE WON'T HEAR IT FROM ME.
yawn
WHAT ARE YOU DOING OUT THIS LATE?
ha ha ha
OR SHOULD I SAY, "THIS EARLY"?

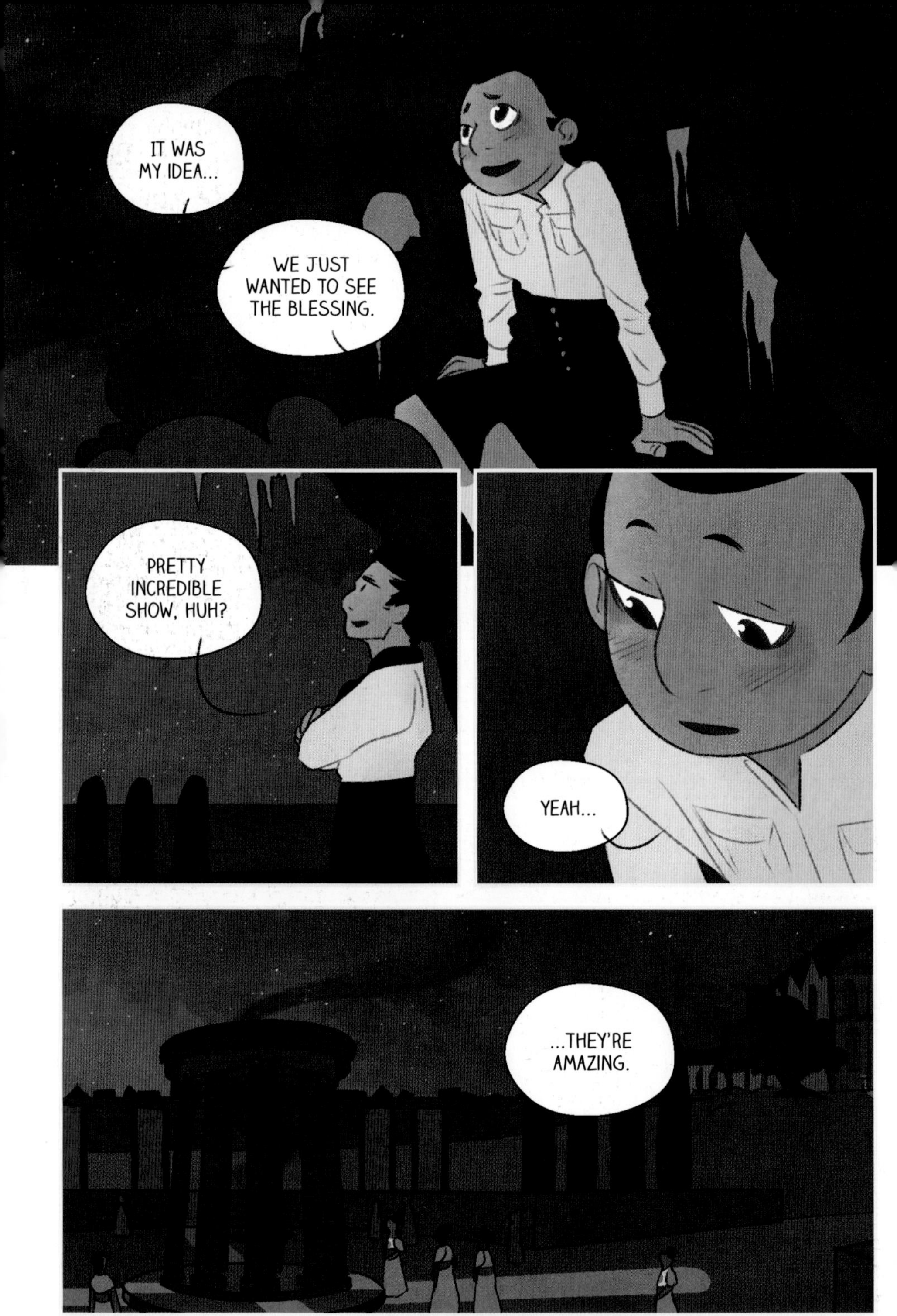
IT WAS MY IDEA...
WE JUST WANTED TO SEE THE BLESSING.
PRETTY INCREDIBLE SHOW, HUH?
YEAH...
...THEY'RE AMAZING.

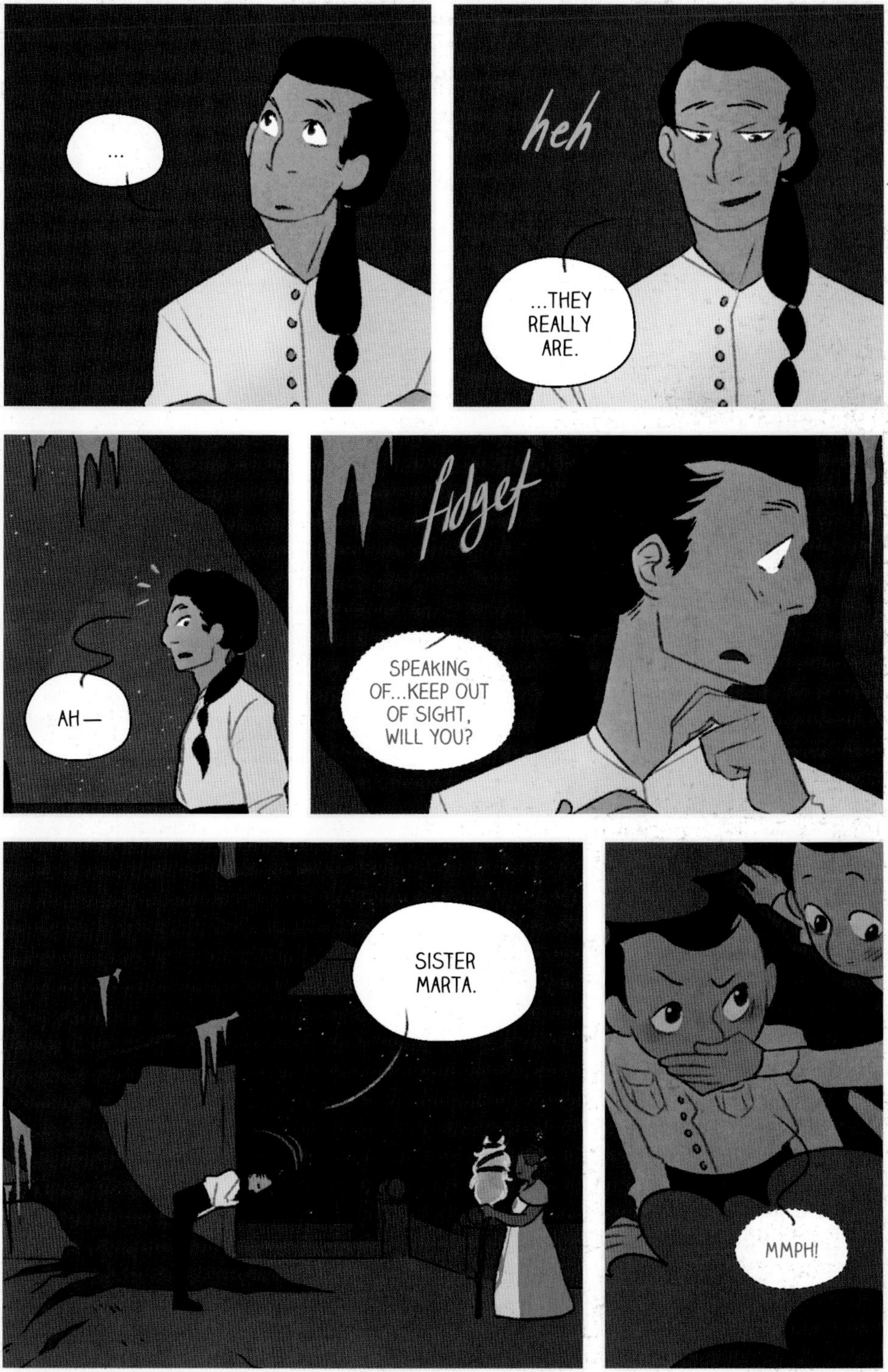
...
heh
...THEY REALLY ARE.
AH—
fidget
SPEAKING OF...KEEP OUT OF SIGHT, WILL YOU?
SISTER MARTA.
MMPH!

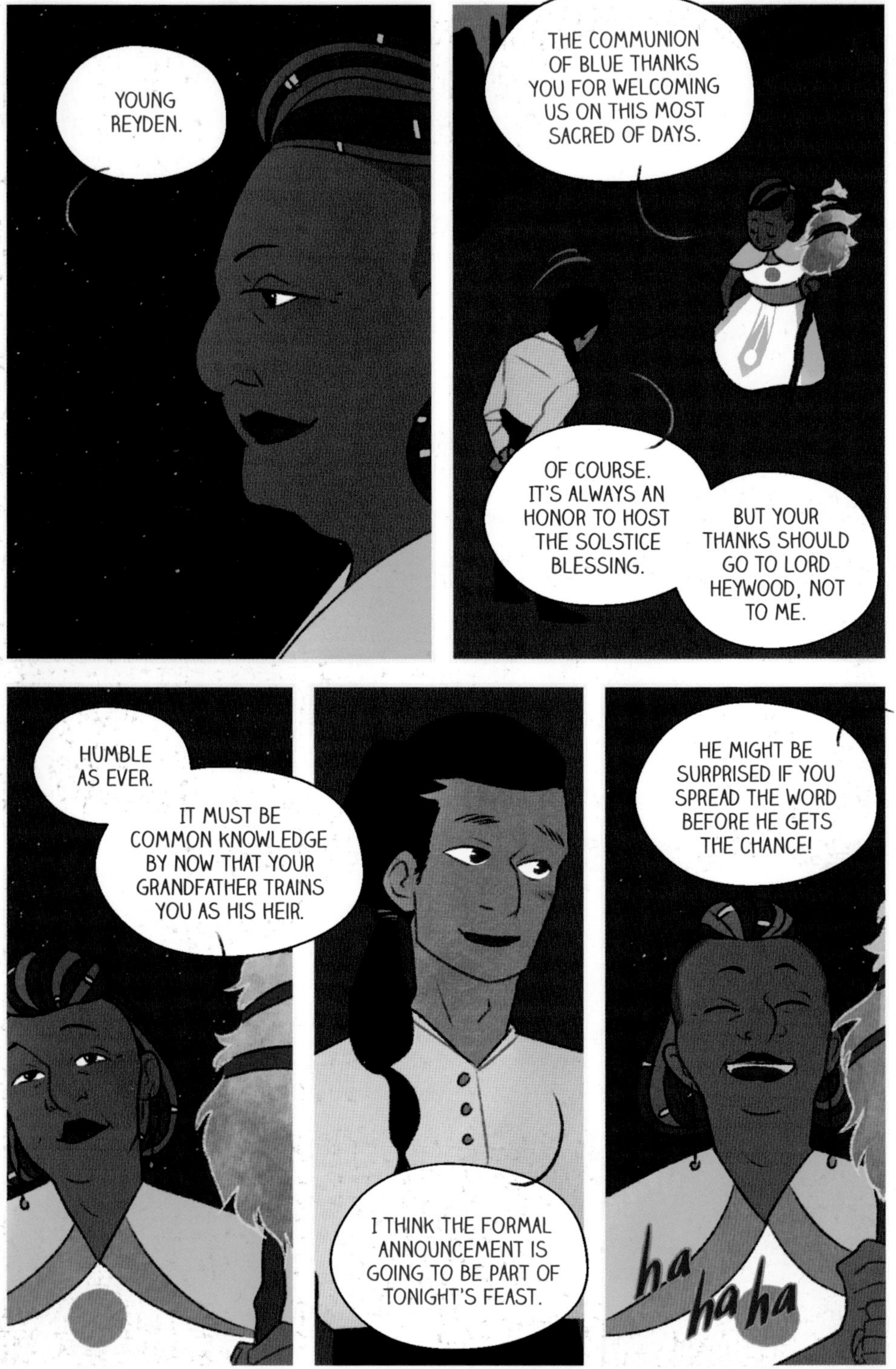

YOUNG REYDEN.
THE COMMUNION OF BLUE THANKS YOU FOR WELCOMING US ON THIS MOST SACRED OF DAYS.
OF COURSE. IT'S ALWAYS AN HONOR TO HOST THE SOLSTICE BLESSING.
BUT YOUR THANKS SHOULD GO TO LORD HEYWOOD, NOT TO ME.
HUMBLE AS EVER.
IT MUST BE COMMON KNOWLEDGE BY NOW THAT YOUR GRANDFATHER TRAINS YOU AS HIS HEIR.
I THINK THE FORMAL ANNOUNCEMENT IS GOING TO BE PART OF TONIGHT'S FEAST.
HE MIGHT BE SURPRISED IF YOU SPREAD THE WORD BEFORE HE GETS THE CHANCE!
ha ha ha ha

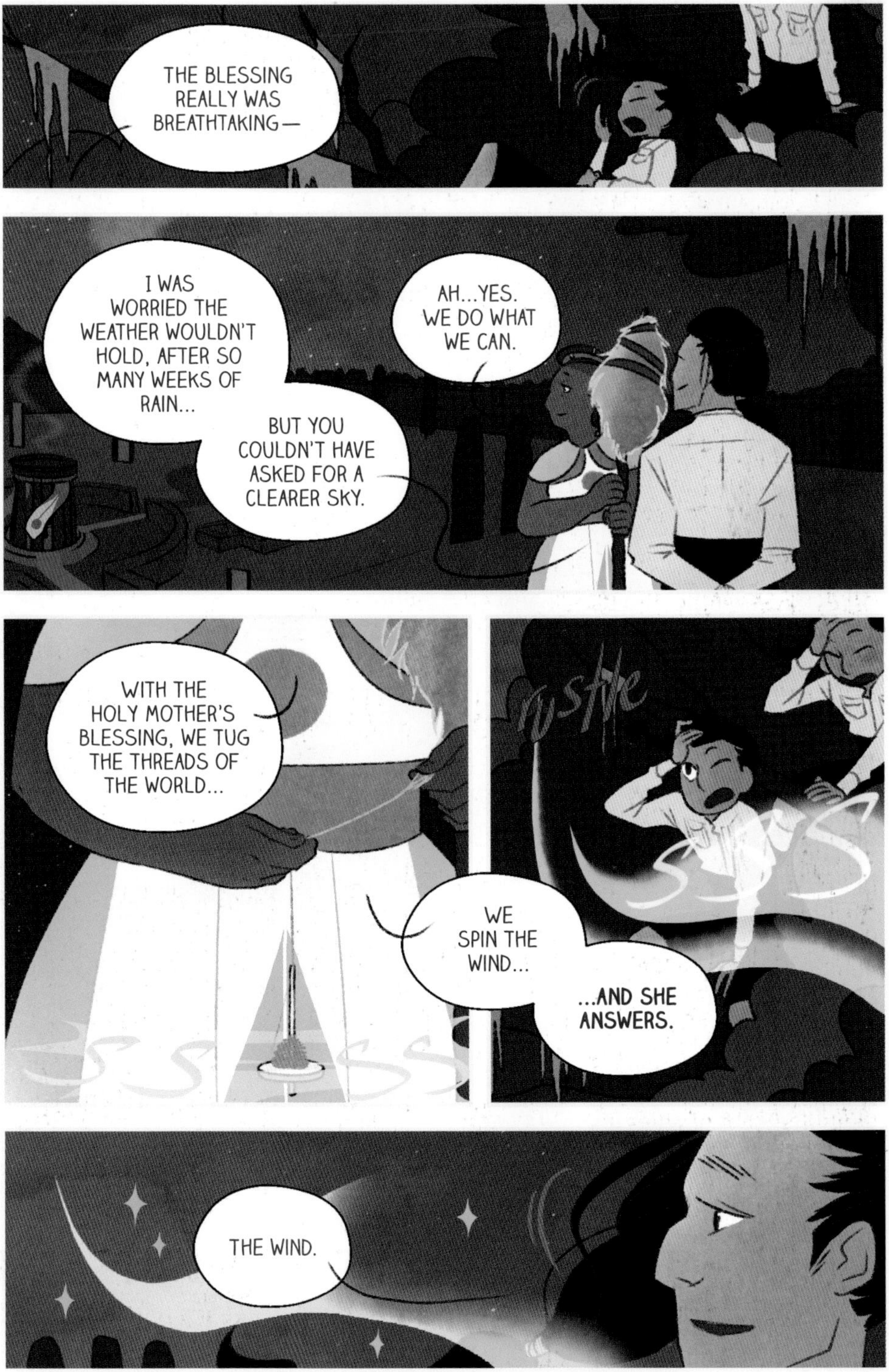
THE BLESSING REALLY WAS BREATHTAKING—
I WAS WORRIED THE WEATHER WOULDN'T HOLD, AFTER SO MANY WEEKS OF RAIN...
BUT YOU COULDN'T HAVE ASKED FOR A CLEARER SKY.
AH...YES. WE DO WHAT WE CAN.
WITH THE HOLY MOTHER'S BLESSING, WE TUG THE THREADS OF THE WORLD...
rustle
WE SPIN THE WIND...
...AND SHE ANSWERS.
THE WIND.

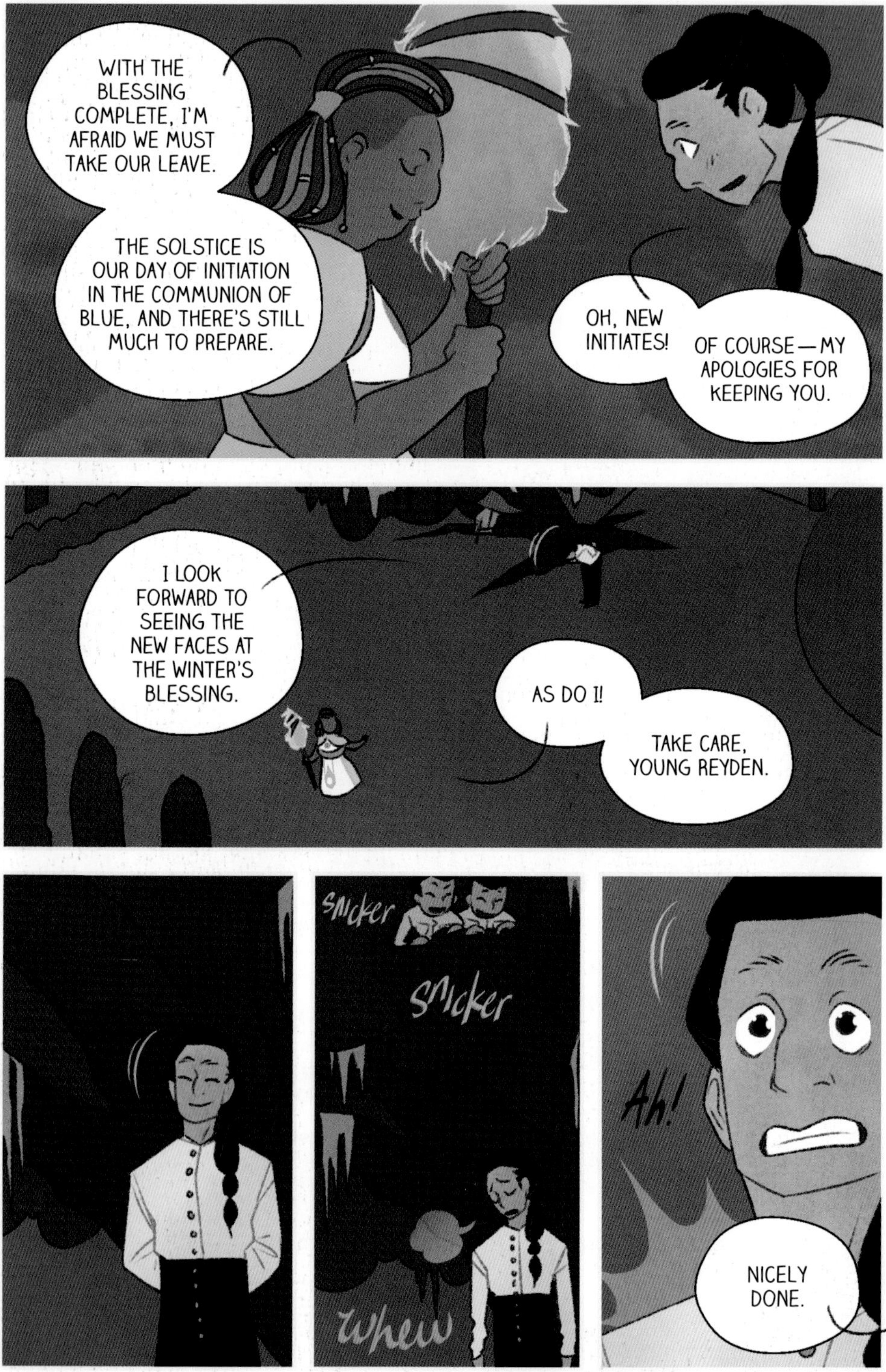
WITH THE BLESSING COMPLETE, I'M AFRAID WE MUST TAKE OUR LEAVE.
THE SOLSTICE IS OUR DAY OF INITIATION IN THE COMMUNION OF BLUE, AND THERE'S STILL MUCH TO PREPARE.
OH, NEW INITIATES!
OF COURSE—MY APOLOGIES FOR KEEPING YOU.
I LOOK FORWARD TO SEEING THE NEW FACES AT THE WINTER'S BLESSING.
AS DO I!
TAKE CARE, YOUNG REYDEN.
snicker
snicker
whew
Ah!
NICELY DONE.

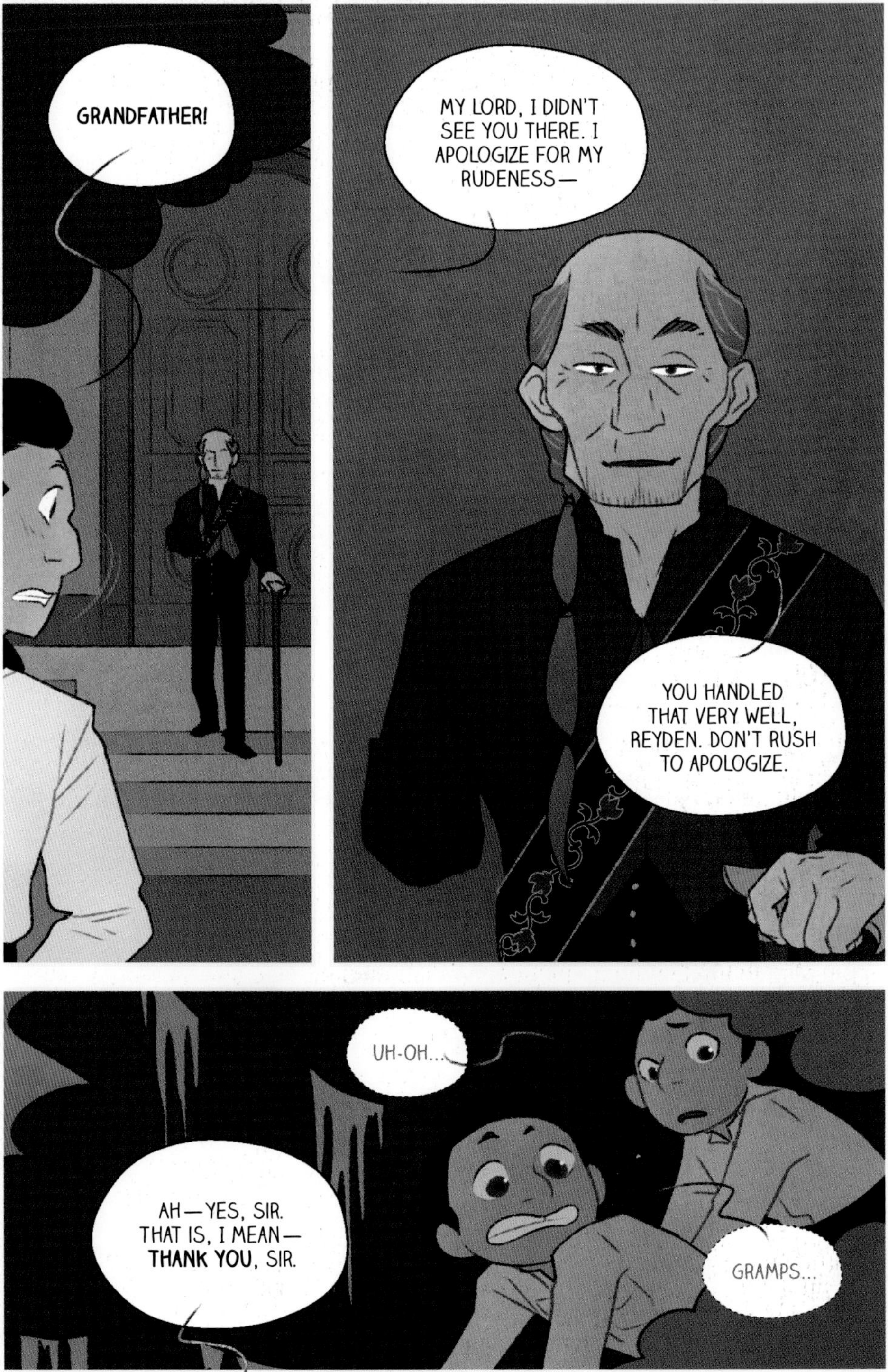
GRANDFATHER!
MY LORD, I DIDN'T SEE YOU THERE. I APOLOGIZE FOR MY RUDENESS—
YOU HANDLED THAT VERY WELL, REYDEN. DON'T RUSH TO APOLOGIZE.
UH-OH...
AH—YES, SIR. THAT IS, I MEAN—**THANK YOU**, SIR.
GRAMPS...

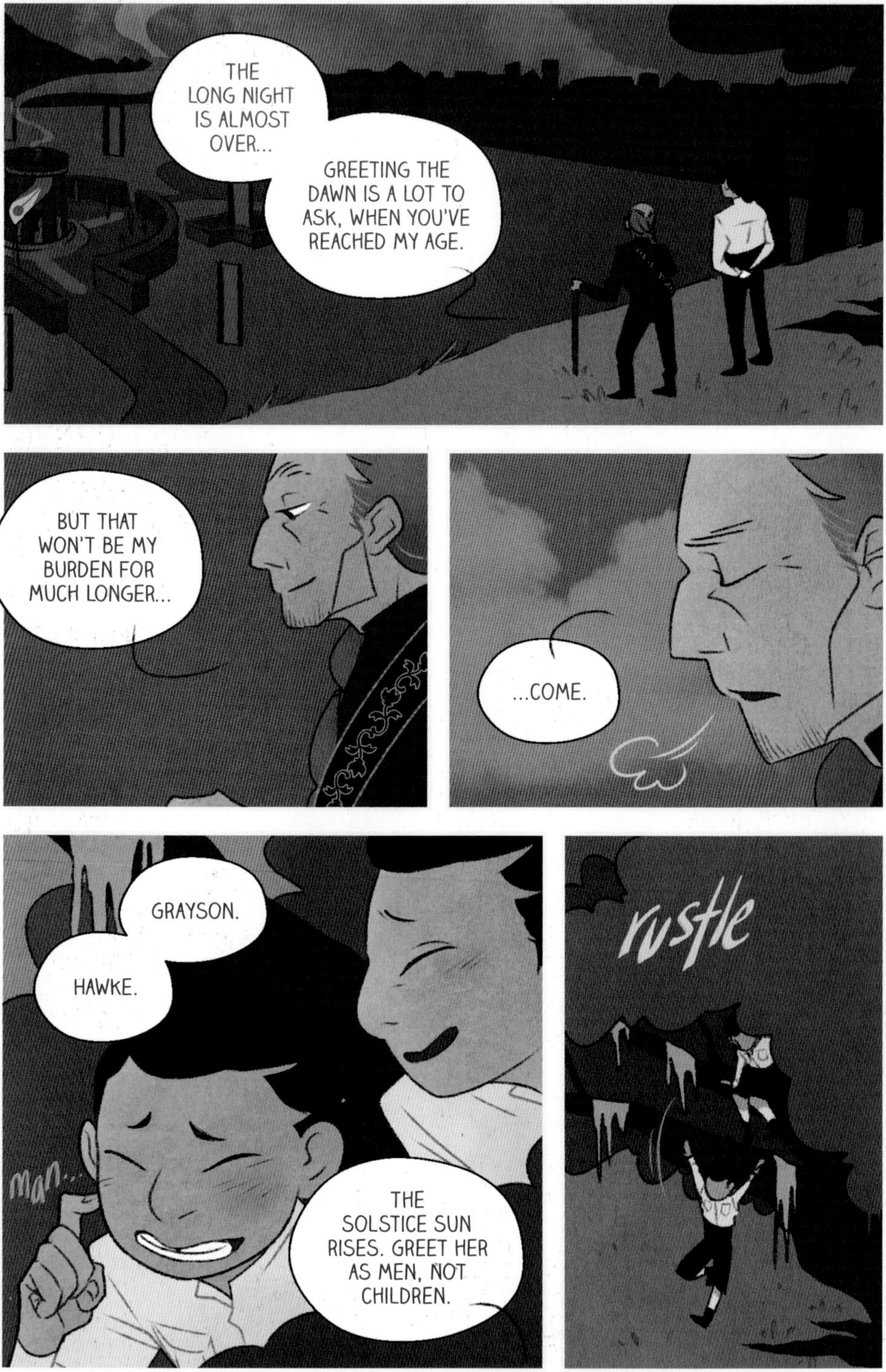
THE LONG NIGHT IS ALMOST OVER...
GREETING THE DAWN IS A LOT TO ASK, WHEN YOU'VE REACHED MY AGE.
BUT THAT WON'T BE MY BURDEN FOR MUCH LONGER...
...COME.
GRAYSON.
HAWKE.
man...
THE SOLSTICE SUN RISES. GREET HER AS MEN, NOT CHILDREN.
rustle

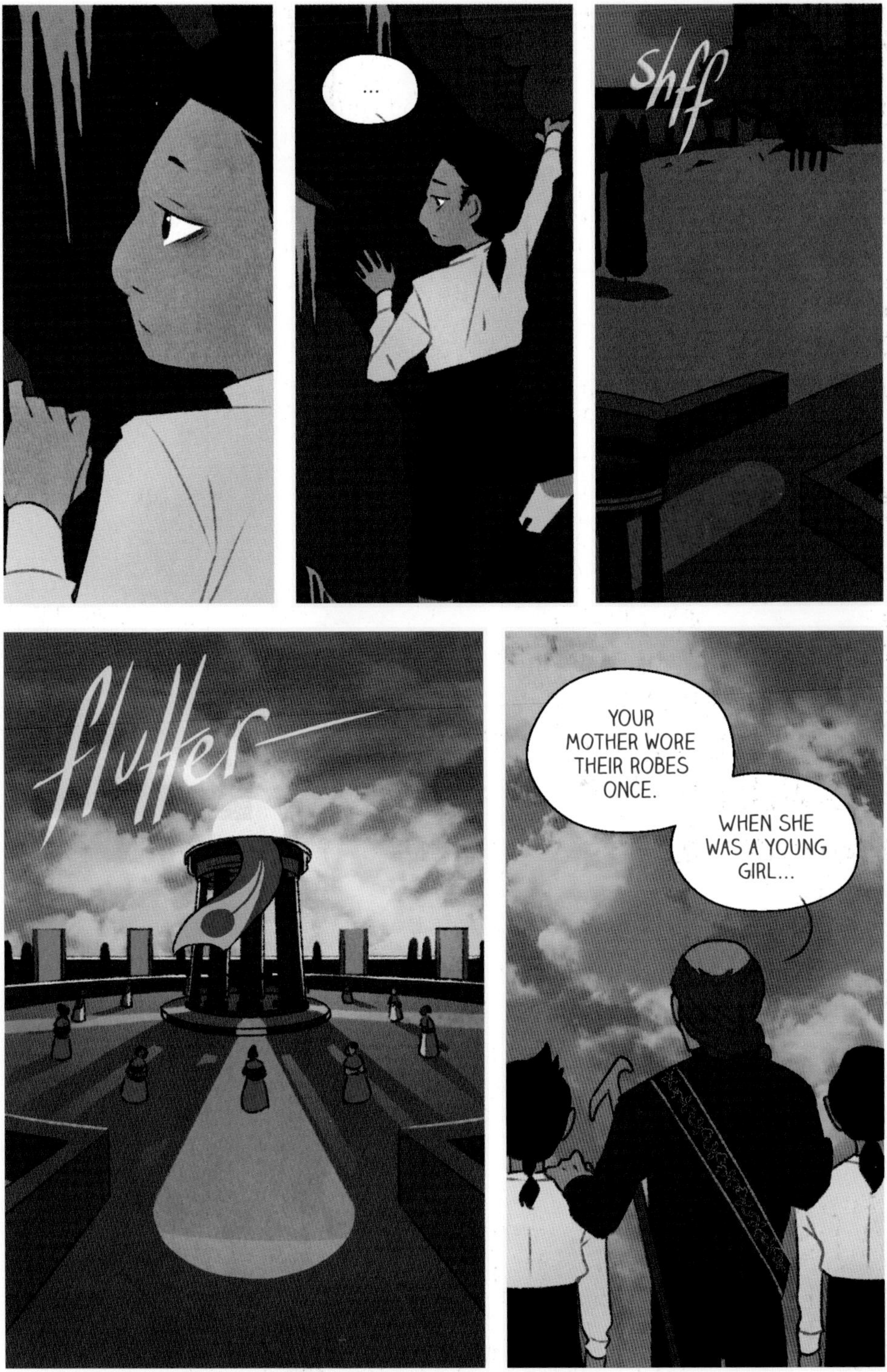
...
shff
flutter
YOUR MOTHER WORE THEIR ROBES ONCE.
WHEN SHE WAS A YOUNG GIRL...

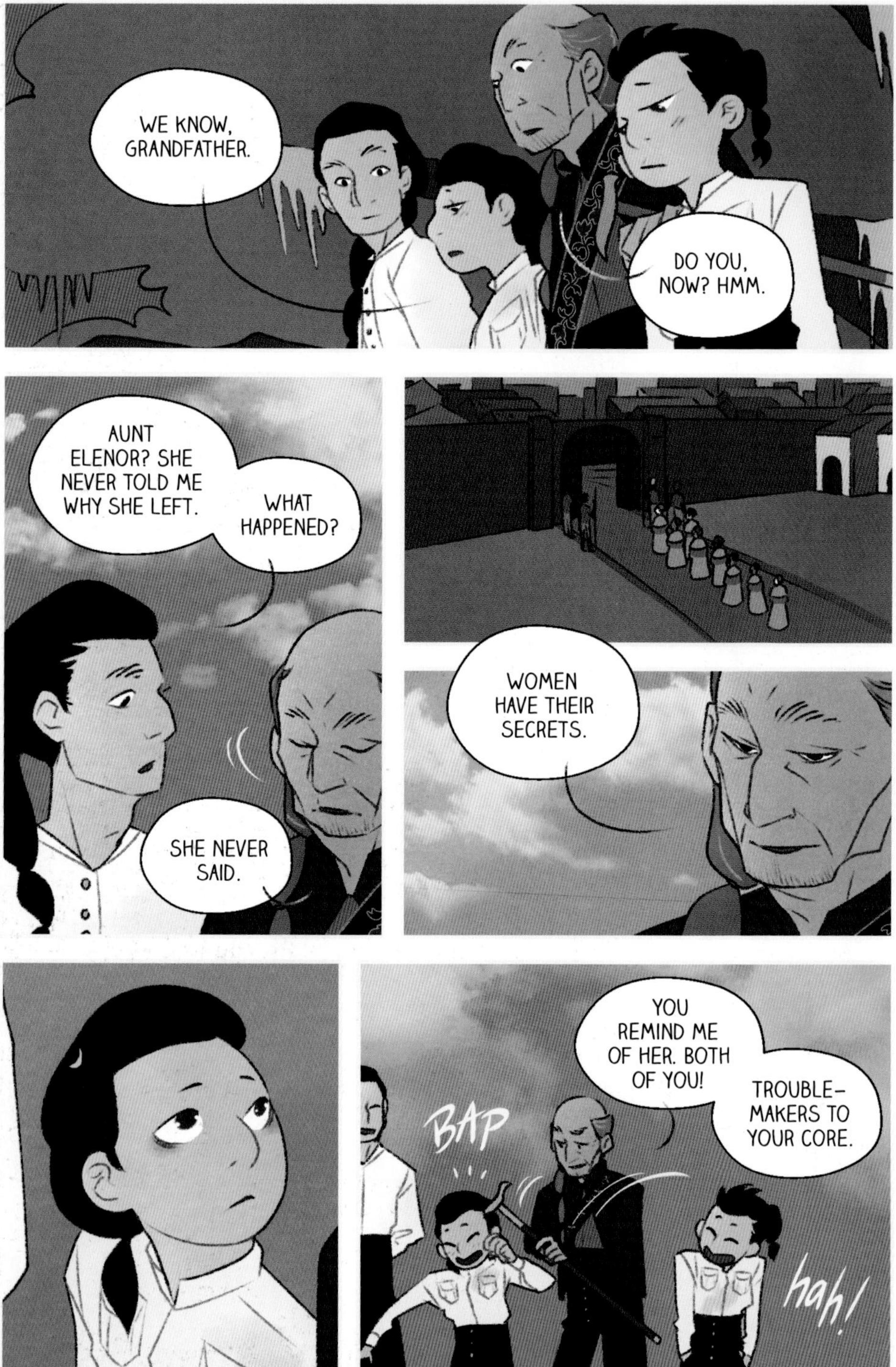
WE KNOW, GRANDFATHER.
DO YOU, NOW? HMM.
AUNT ELENOR? SHE NEVER TOLD ME WHY SHE LEFT.
WHAT HAPPENED?
SHE NEVER SAID.
WOMEN HAVE THEIR SECRETS.
YOU REMIND ME OF HER. BOTH OF YOU!
TROUBLE-MAKERS TO YOUR CORE.
BAP
hah!

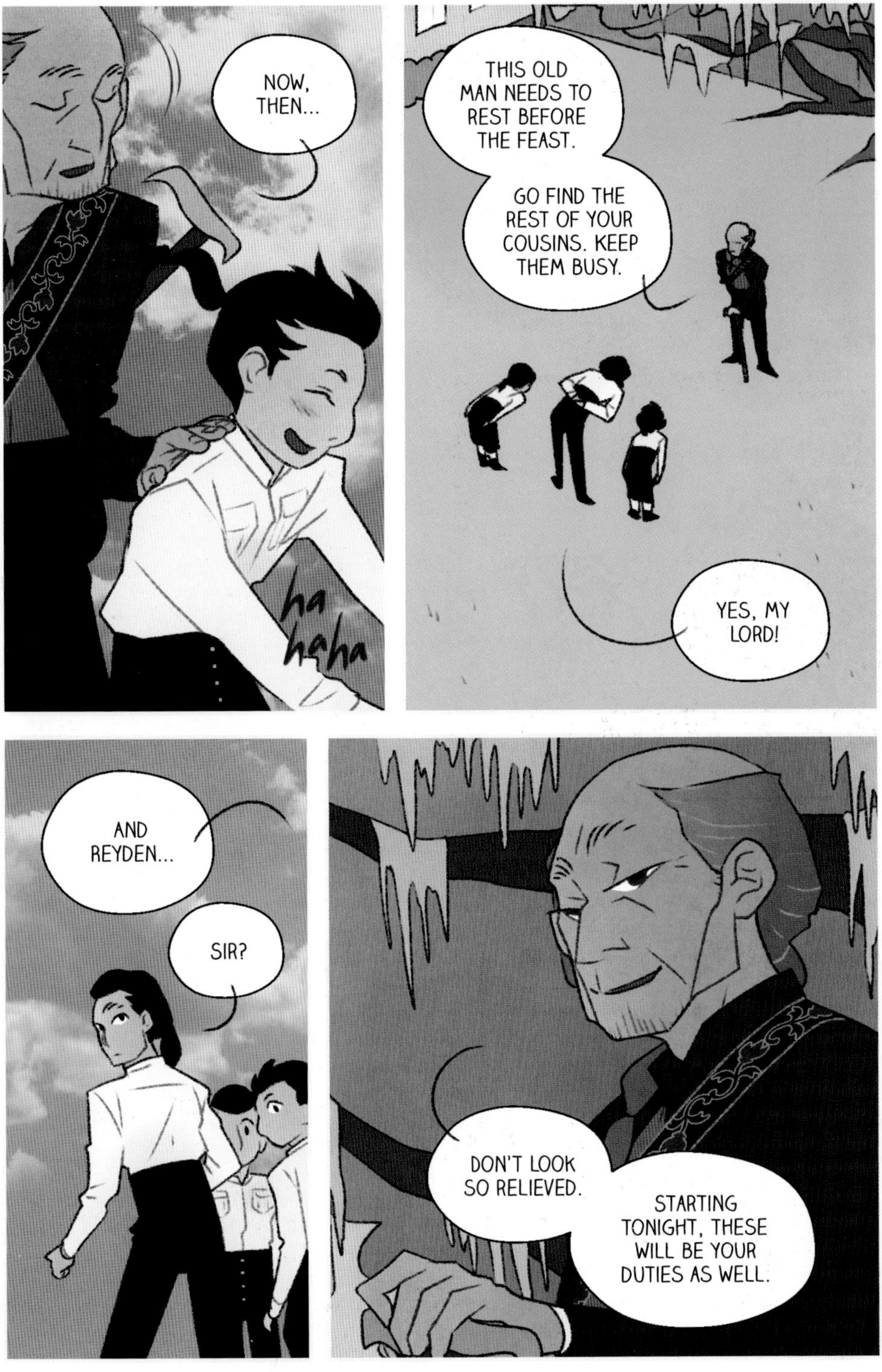
NOW, THEN...
ha haha
THIS OLD MAN NEEDS TO REST BEFORE THE FEAST.
GO FIND THE REST OF YOUR COUSINS. KEEP THEM BUSY.
YES, MY LORD!
AND REYDEN...
SIR?
DON'T LOOK SO RELIEVED.
STARTING TONIGHT, THESE WILL BE YOUR DUTIES AS WELL.

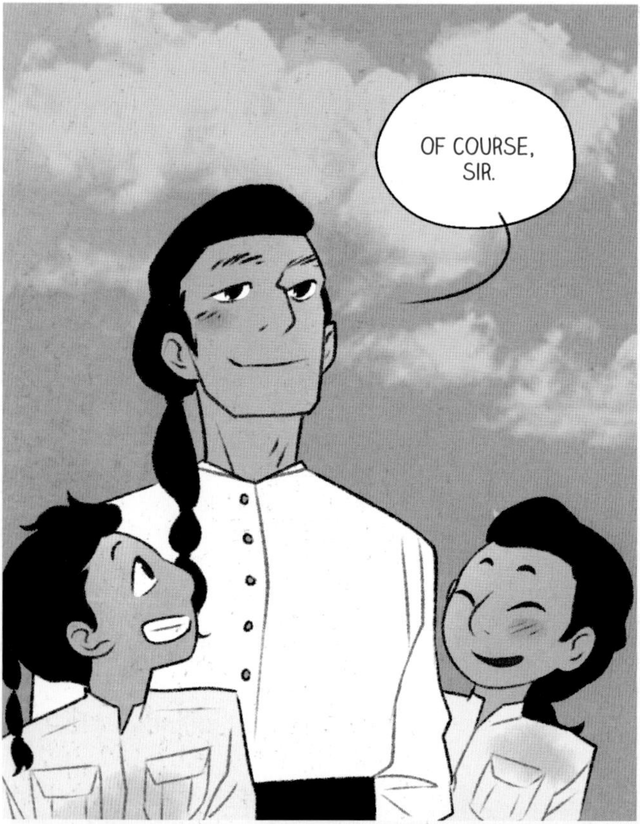
OF COURSE, SIR.

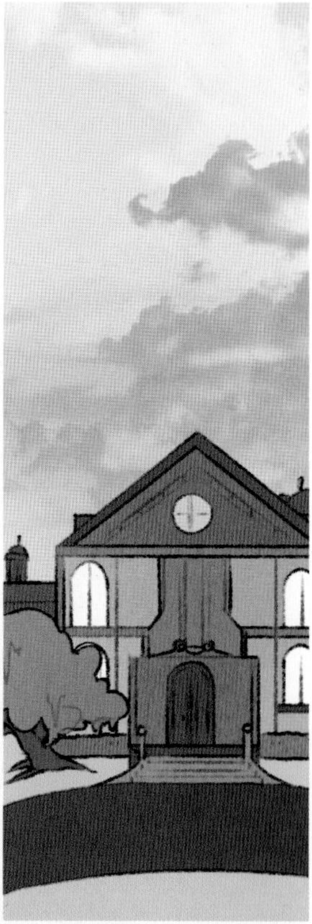

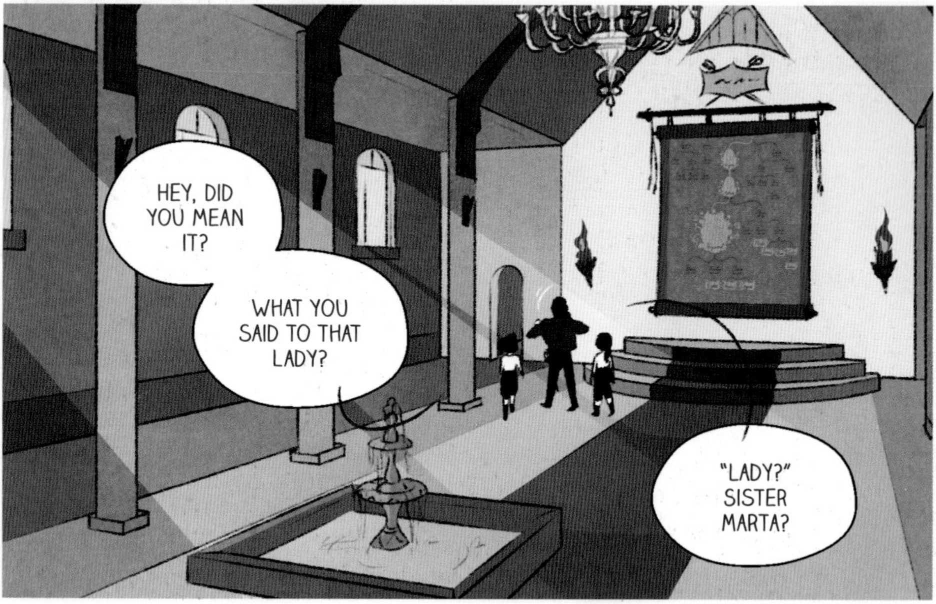
HEY, DID YOU MEAN IT?
WHAT YOU SAID TO THAT LADY?
"LADY?" SISTER MARTA?

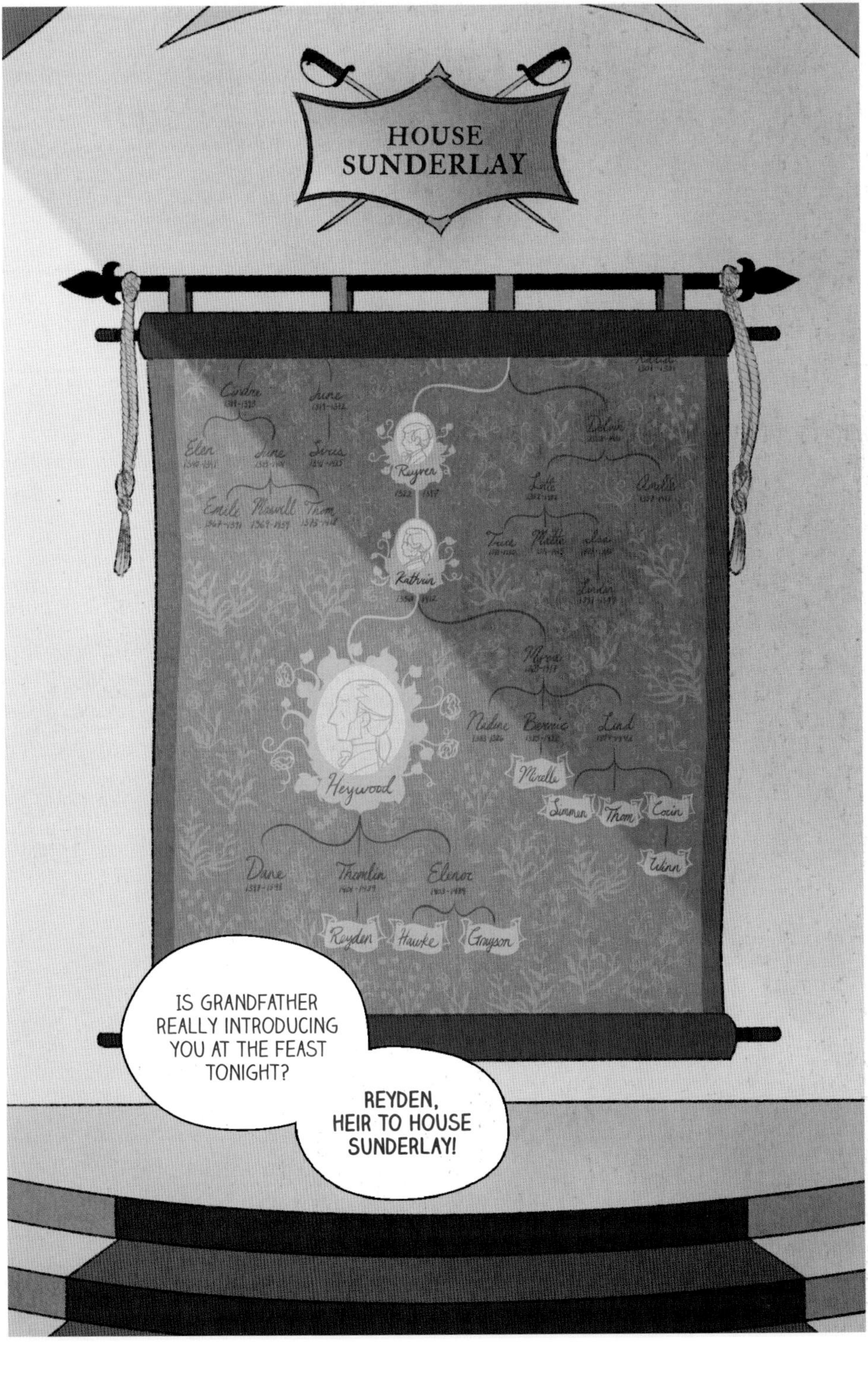
HOUSE SUNDERLAY
Heywood
Dane
Thomlin
Elenor
Reyden
Hawke
Grayson
IS GRANDFATHER REALLY INTRODUCING YOU AT THE FEAST TONIGHT?
REYDEN, HEIR TO HOUSE SUNDERLAY!

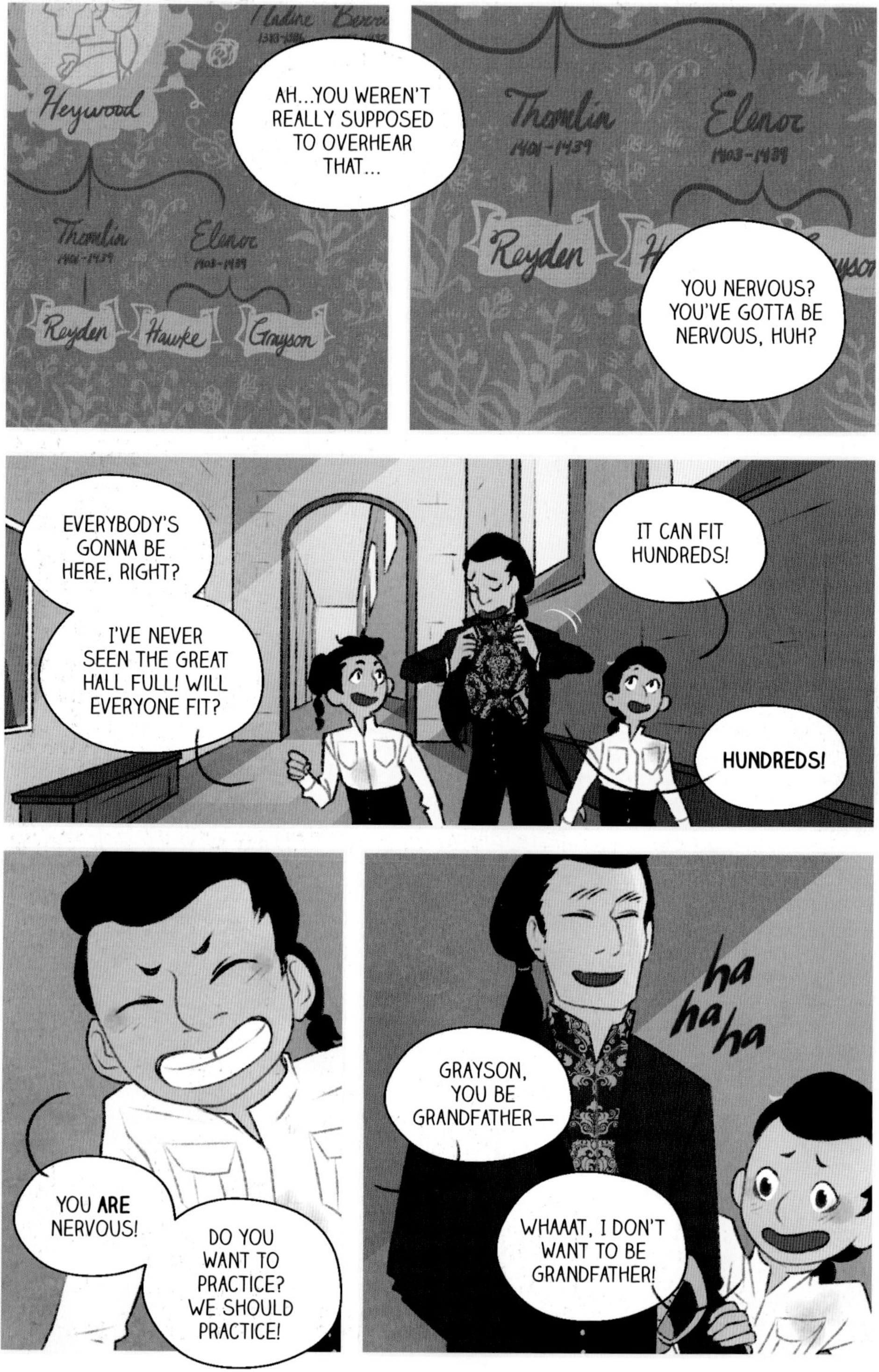
Heywood
Thomlin
1401-1439
Elenor
1403-1439
Reyden
Hawke
Grayson
AH...YOU WEREN'T REALLY SUPPOSED TO OVERHEAR THAT...
Thomlin
1401-1439
Elenor
1403-1439
Reyden
YOU NERVOUS? YOU'VE GOTTA BE NERVOUS, HUH?
EVERYBODY'S GONNA BE HERE, RIGHT?
I'VE NEVER SEEN THE GREAT HALL FULL! WILL EVERYONE FIT?
IT CAN FIT HUNDREDS!
HUNDREDS!
YOU **ARE** NERVOUS!
DO YOU WANT TO PRACTICE? WE SHOULD PRACTICE!
ha ha ha
GRAYSON, YOU BE GRANDFATHER—
WHAAAT, I DON'T WANT TO BE GRANDFATHER!

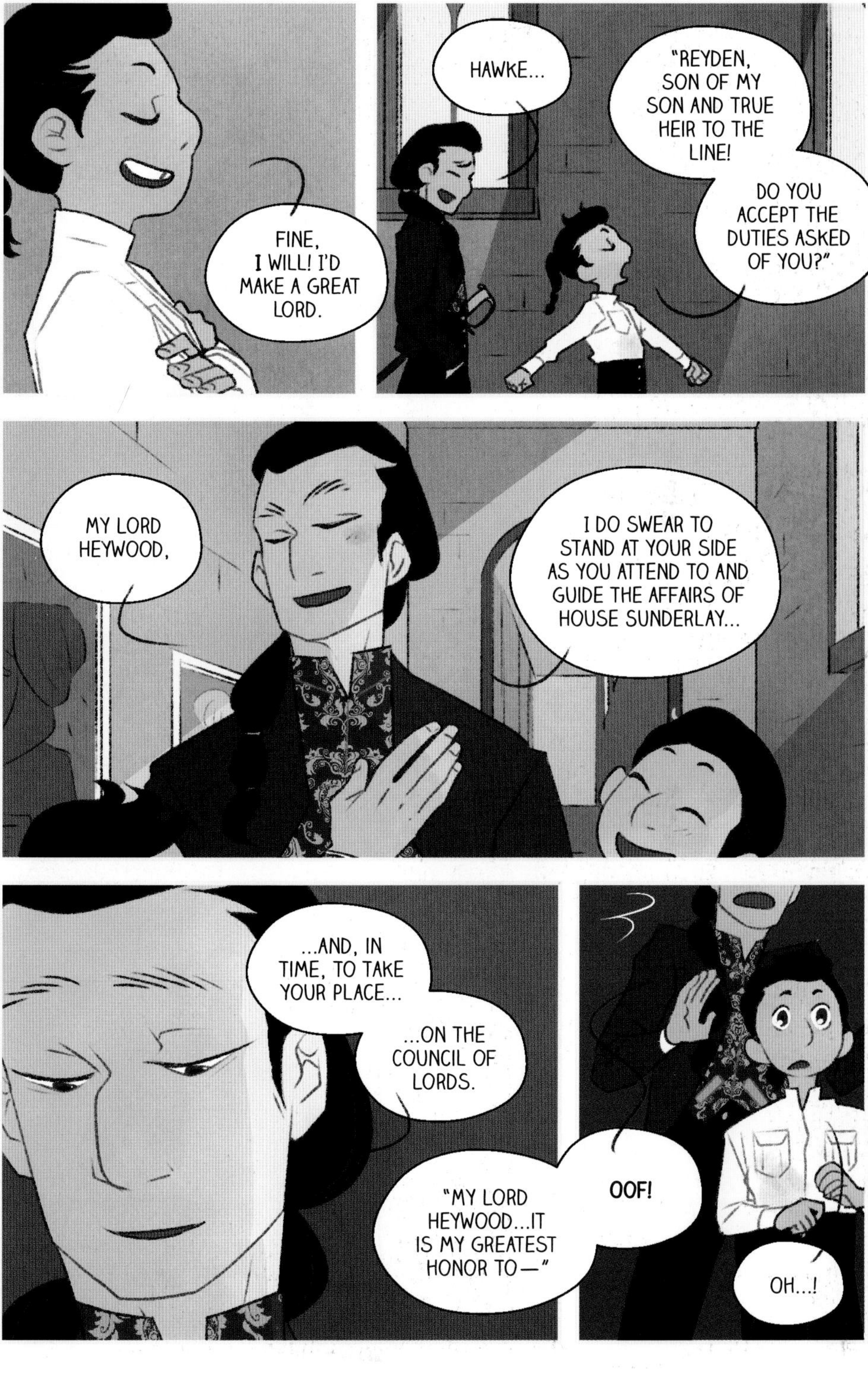
FINE, I WILL! I'D MAKE A GREAT LORD.
HAWKE...
"REYDEN, SON OF MY SON AND TRUE HEIR TO THE LINE!
DO YOU ACCEPT THE DUTIES ASKED OF YOU?"
MY LORD HEYWOOD,
I DO SWEAR TO STAND AT YOUR SIDE AS YOU ATTEND TO AND GUIDE THE AFFAIRS OF HOUSE SUNDERLAY...
...AND, IN TIME, TO TAKE YOUR PLACE...
...ON THE COUNCIL OF LORDS.
"MY LORD HEYWOOD...IT IS MY GREATEST HONOR TO—"
OOF!
OH...!

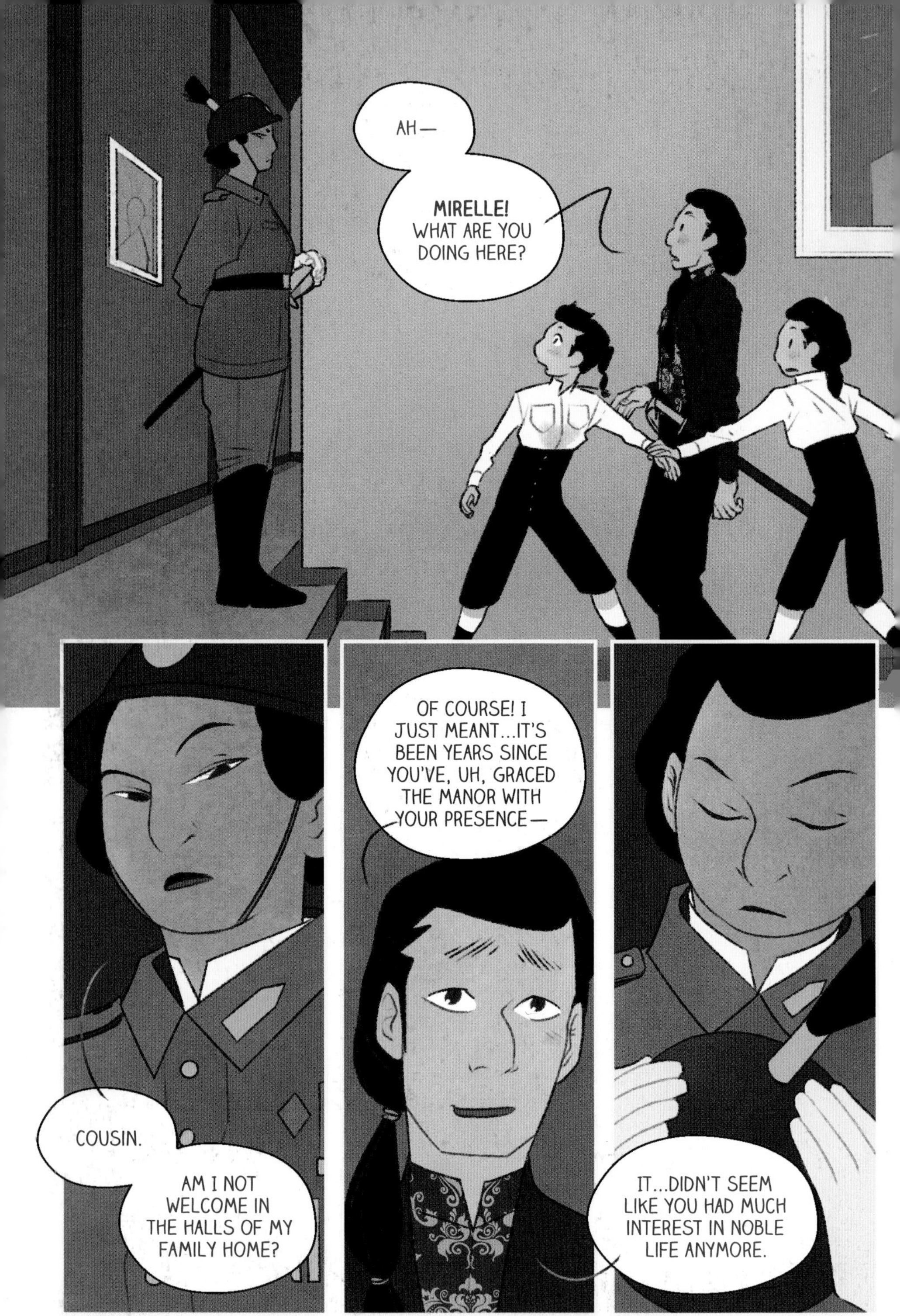
AH—
MIRELLE! WHAT ARE YOU DOING HERE?
COUSIN.
AM I NOT WELCOME IN THE HALLS OF MY FAMILY HOME?
OF COURSE! I JUST MEANT...IT'S BEEN YEARS SINCE YOU'VE, UH, GRACED THE MANOR WITH YOUR PRESENCE—
IT...DIDN'T SEEM LIKE YOU HAD MUCH INTEREST IN NOBLE LIFE ANYMORE.

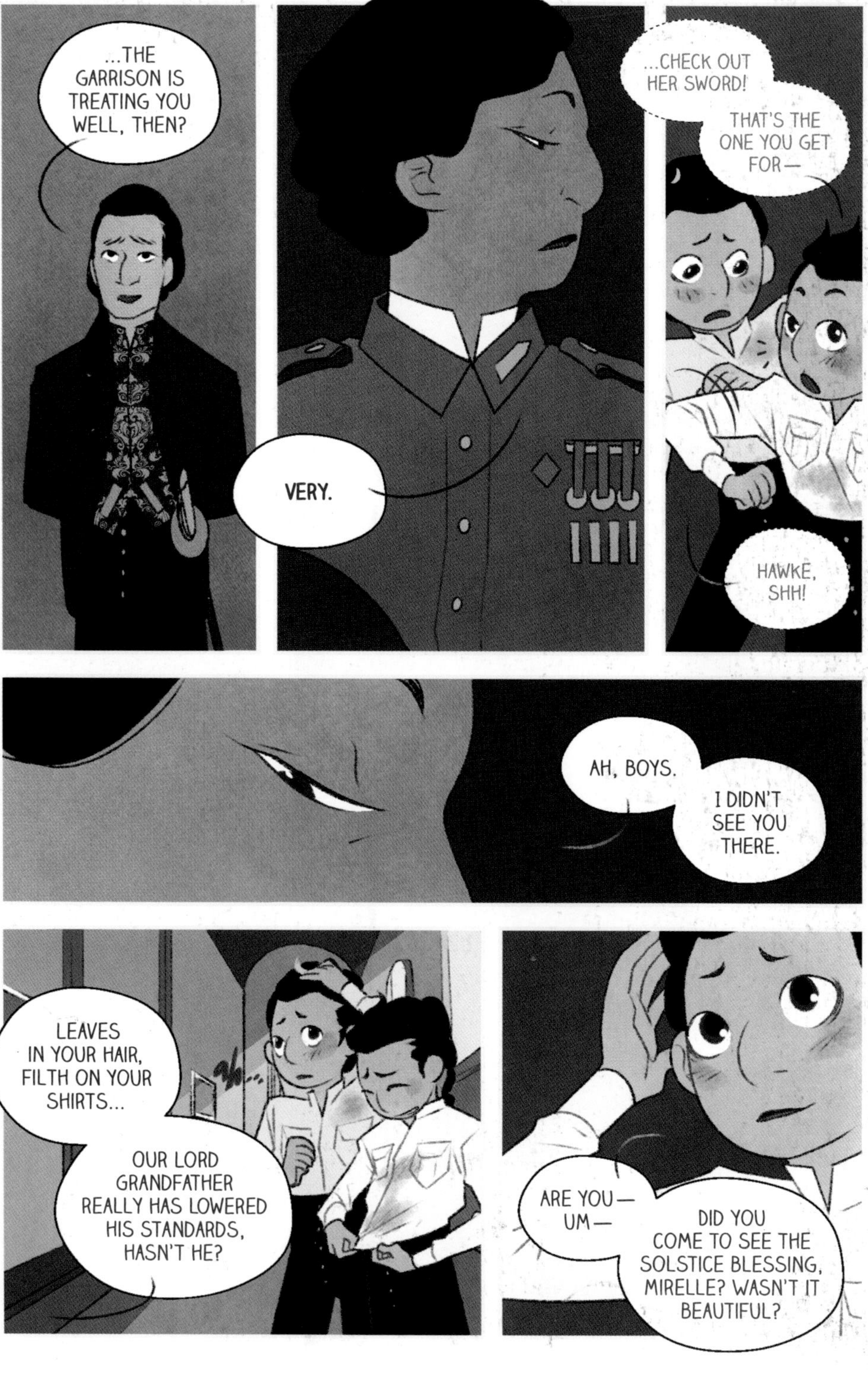
...THE GARRISON IS TREATING YOU WELL, THEN?
VERY.
...CHECK OUT HER SWORD!
THAT'S THE ONE YOU GET FOR—
HAWKE, SHH!
AH, BOYS.
I DIDN'T SEE YOU THERE.
LEAVES IN YOUR HAIR, FILTH ON YOUR SHIRTS...
OUR LORD GRANDFATHER REALLY HAS LOWERED HIS STANDARDS, HASN'T HE?
ARE YOU— UM—
DID YOU COME TO SEE THE SOLSTICE BLESSING, MIRELLE? WASN'T IT BEAUTIFUL?

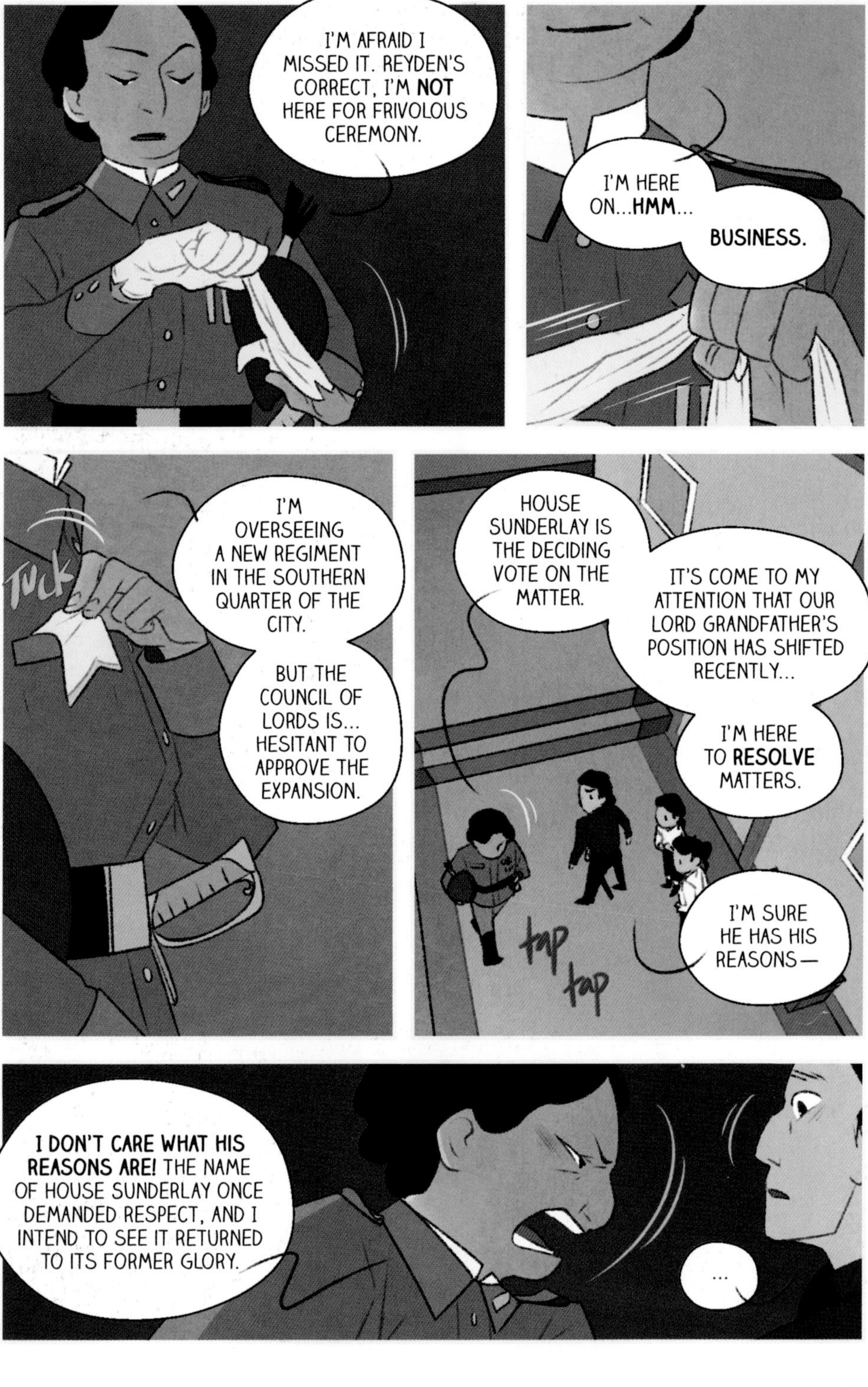
I'M AFRAID I MISSED IT. REYDEN'S CORRECT, I'M **NOT** HERE FOR FRIVOLOUS CEREMONY.
I'M HERE ON...**HMM**...
BUSINESS.
TUCK
I'M OVERSEEING A NEW REGIMENT IN THE SOUTHERN QUARTER OF THE CITY.
BUT THE COUNCIL OF LORDS IS... HESITANT TO APPROVE THE EXPANSION.
HOUSE SUNDERLAY IS THE DECIDING VOTE ON THE MATTER.
IT'S COME TO MY ATTENTION THAT OUR LORD GRANDFATHER'S POSITION HAS SHIFTED RECENTLY...
I'M HERE TO **RESOLVE** MATTERS.
tap
tap
I'M SURE HE HAS HIS REASONS—
I DON'T CARE WHAT HIS REASONS ARE! THE NAME OF HOUSE SUNDERLAY ONCE DEMANDED RESPECT, AND I INTEND TO SEE IT RETURNED TO ITS FORMER GLORY.
...

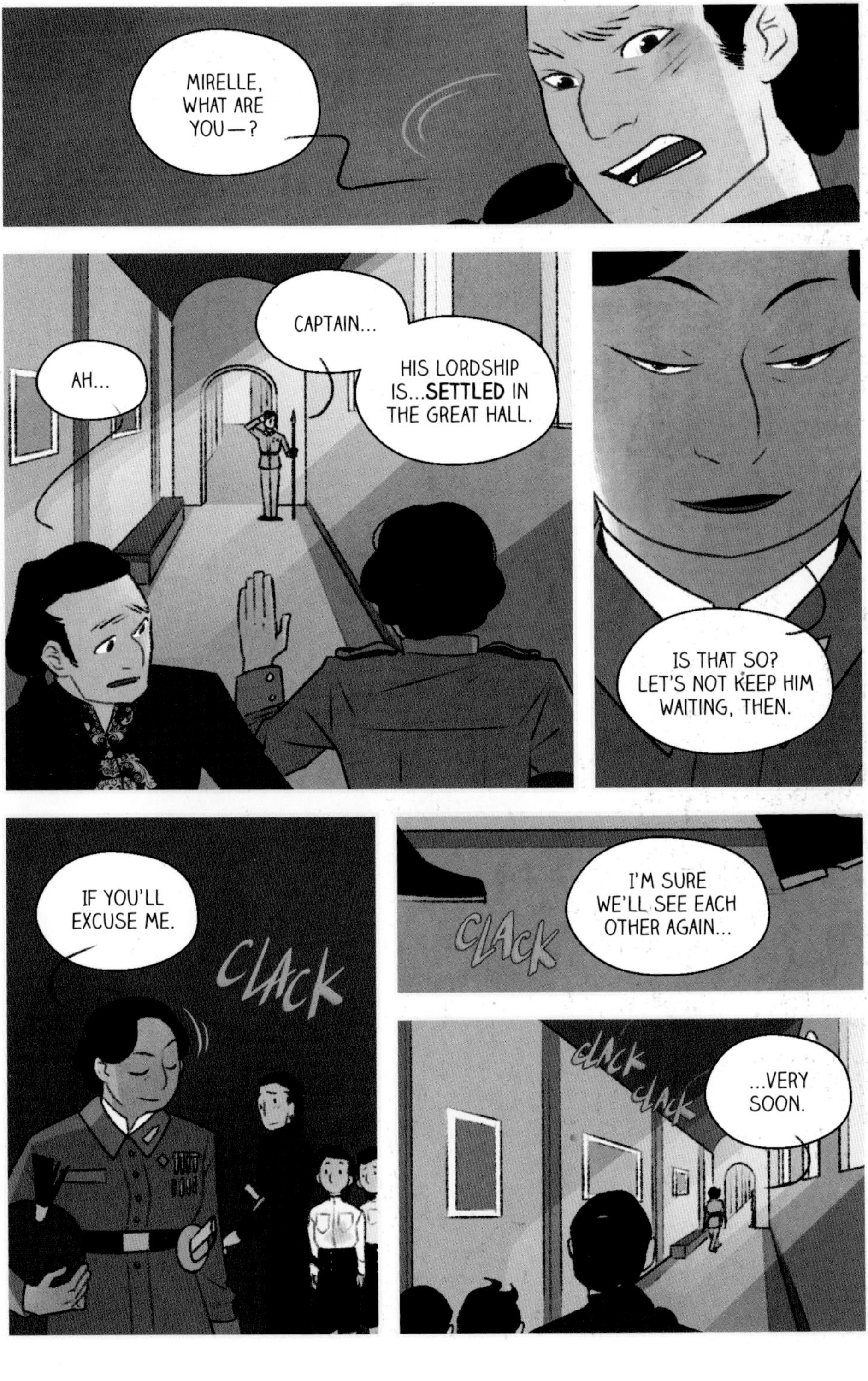
MIRELLE, WHAT ARE YOU—?
CAPTAIN...
AH...
HIS LORDSHIP IS...**SETTLED** IN THE GREAT HALL.
IS THAT SO? LET'S NOT KEEP HIM WAITING, THEN.
IF YOU'LL EXCUSE ME.
CLACK
CLACK
I'M SURE WE'LL SEE EACH OTHER AGAIN...
CLACK
CLACK
...VERY SOON.

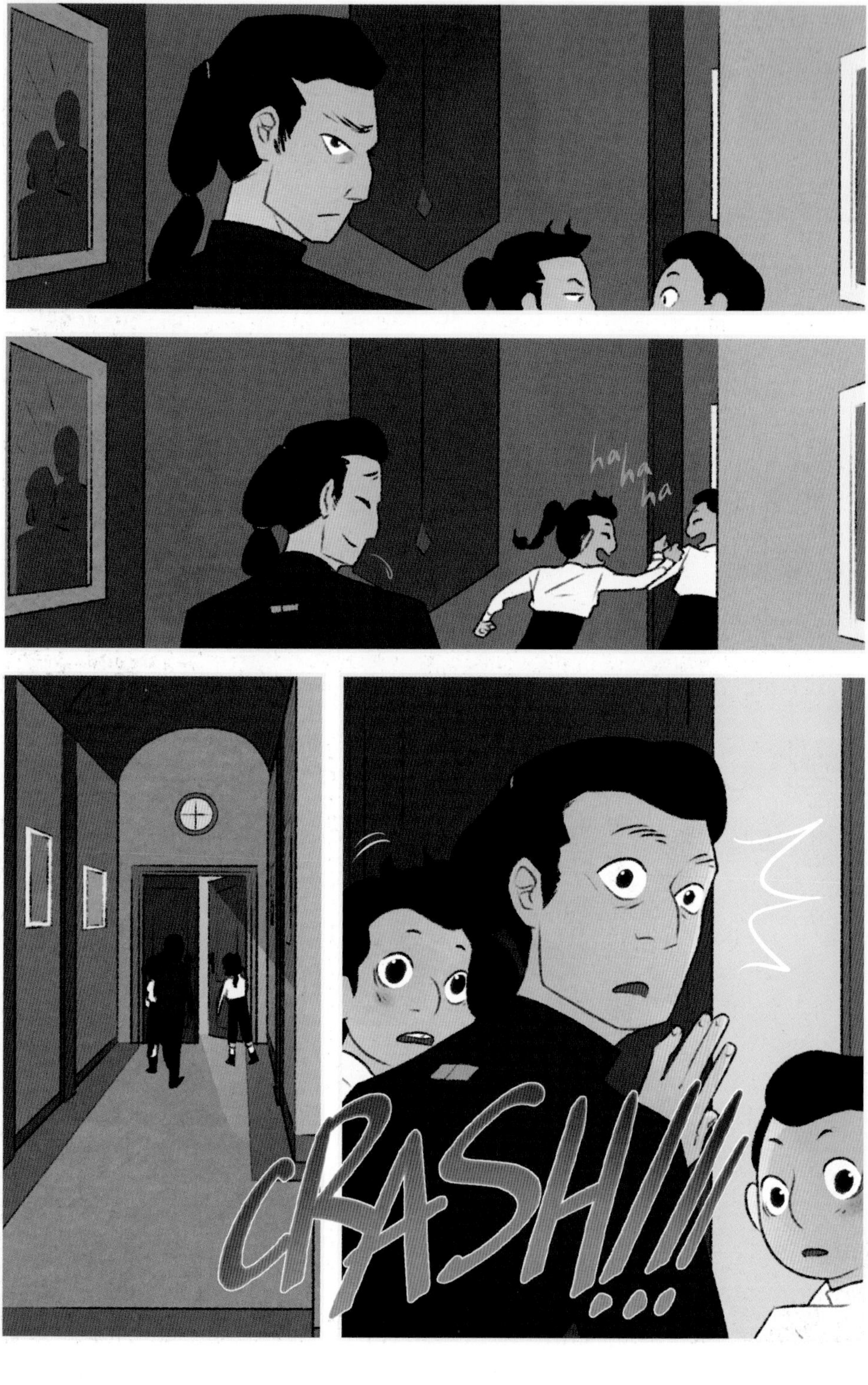
ha ha ha
CRASH!!!

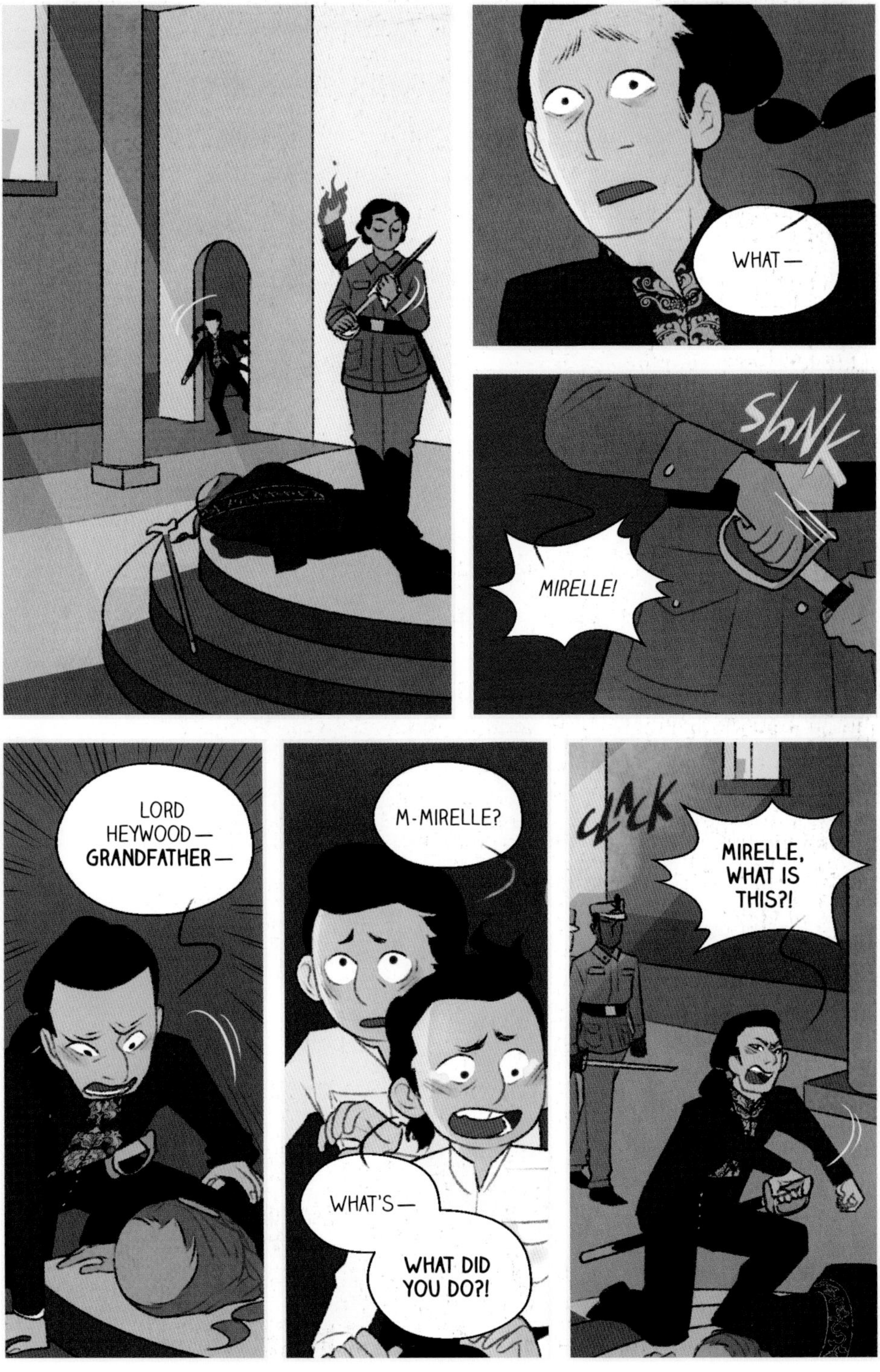
WHAT—
SHNK
MIRELLE!
LORD HEYWOOD—GRANDFATHER—
M-MIRELLE?
WHAT'S—
WHAT DID YOU DO?!
CLACK
MIRELLE, WHAT IS THIS?!

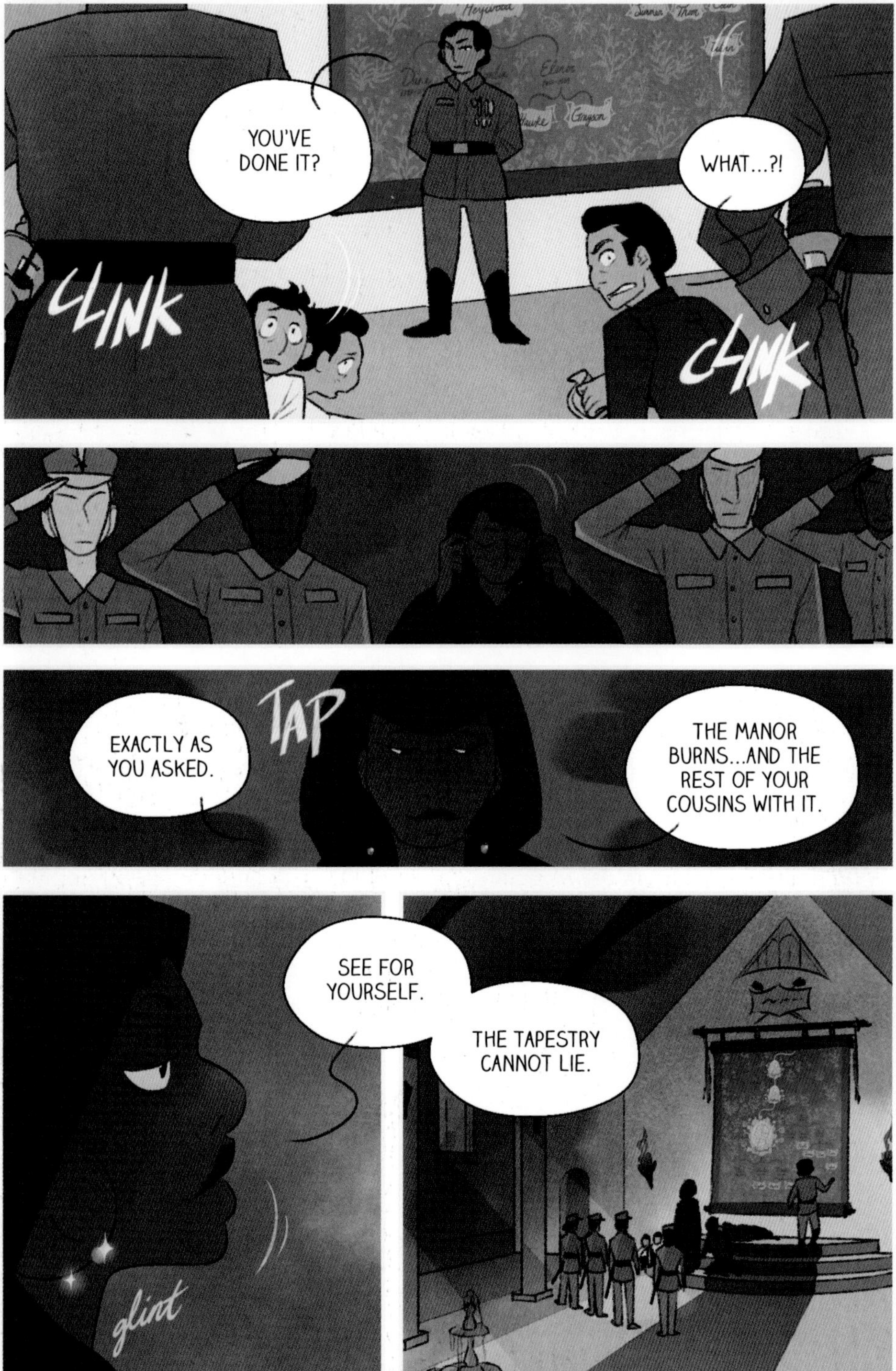
YOU'VE DONE IT?
WHAT...?!
CLINK
CLINK
TAP
EXACTLY AS YOU ASKED.
THE MANOR BURNS...AND THE REST OF YOUR COUSINS WITH IT.
SEE FOR YOURSELF.
THE TAPESTRY CANNOT LIE.
glint

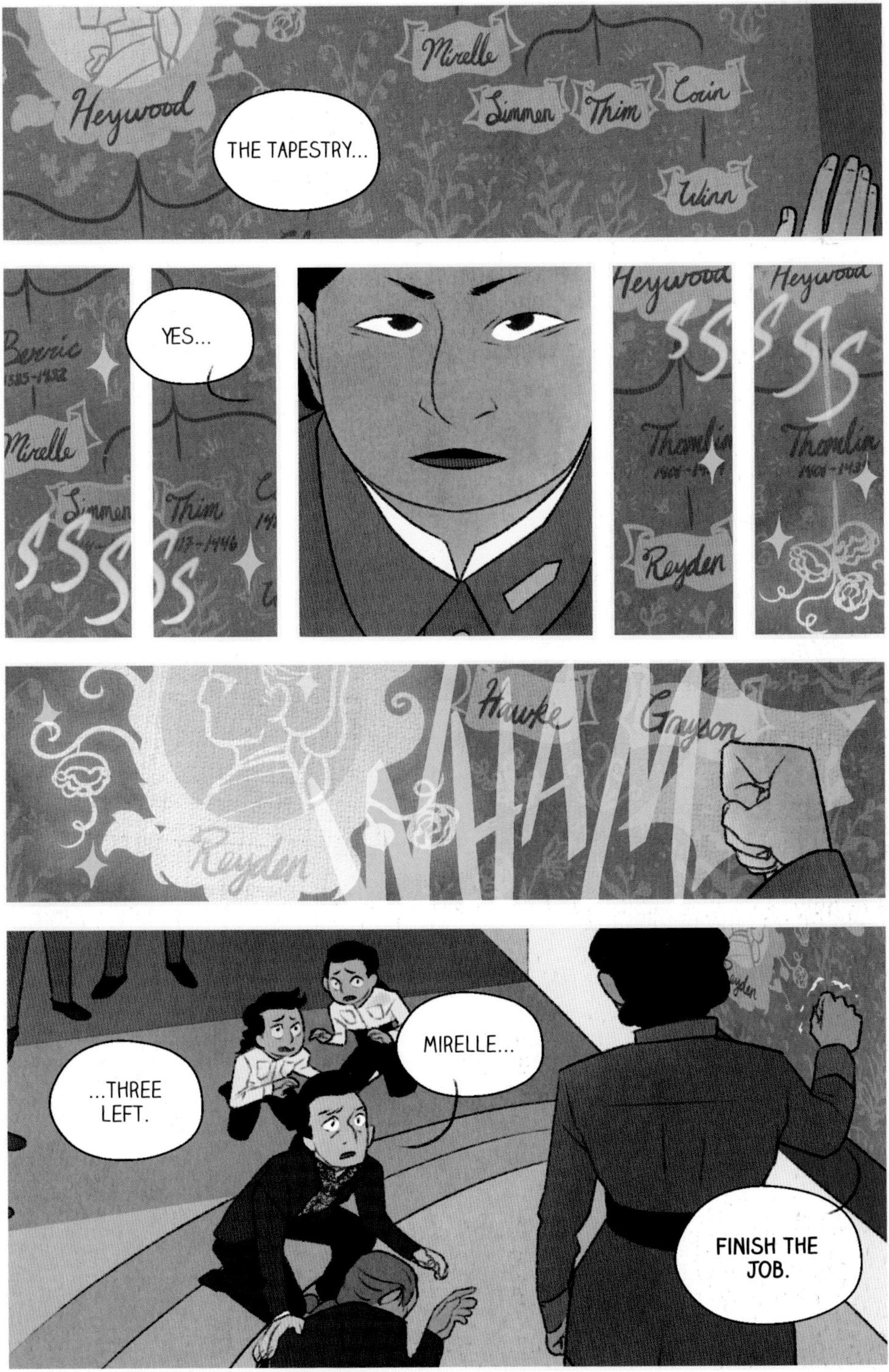
THE TAPESTRY...
YES...
SSSS
SSSS
WHAM
...THREE LEFT.
MIRELLE...
FINISH THE JOB.

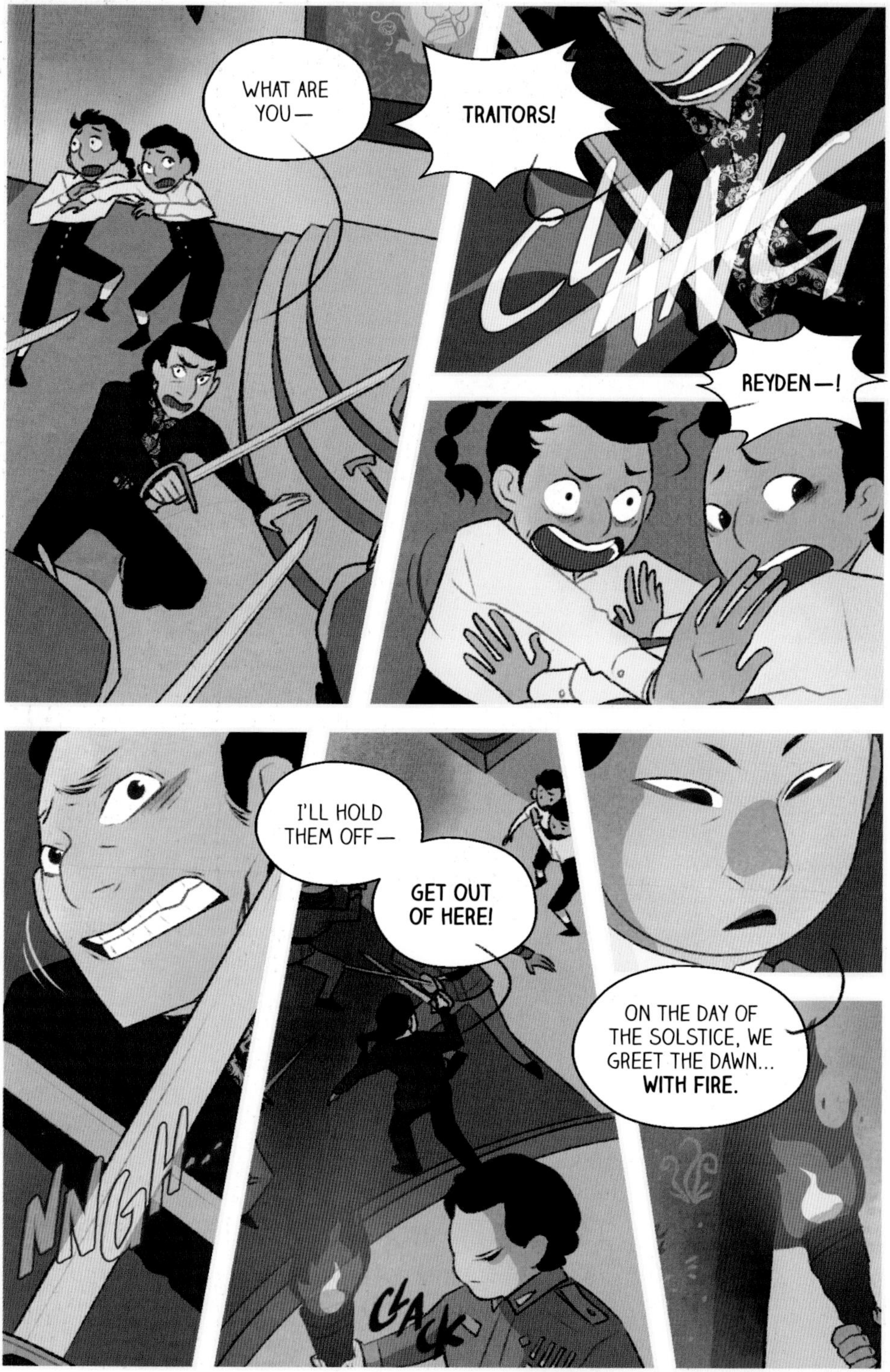
WHAT ARE YOU—
TRAITORS!
CLANG
REYDEN—!
I'LL HOLD THEM OFF—
GET OUT OF HERE!
NNGH
ON THE DAY OF THE SOLSTICE, WE GREET THE DAWN... WITH FIRE.
CLACK

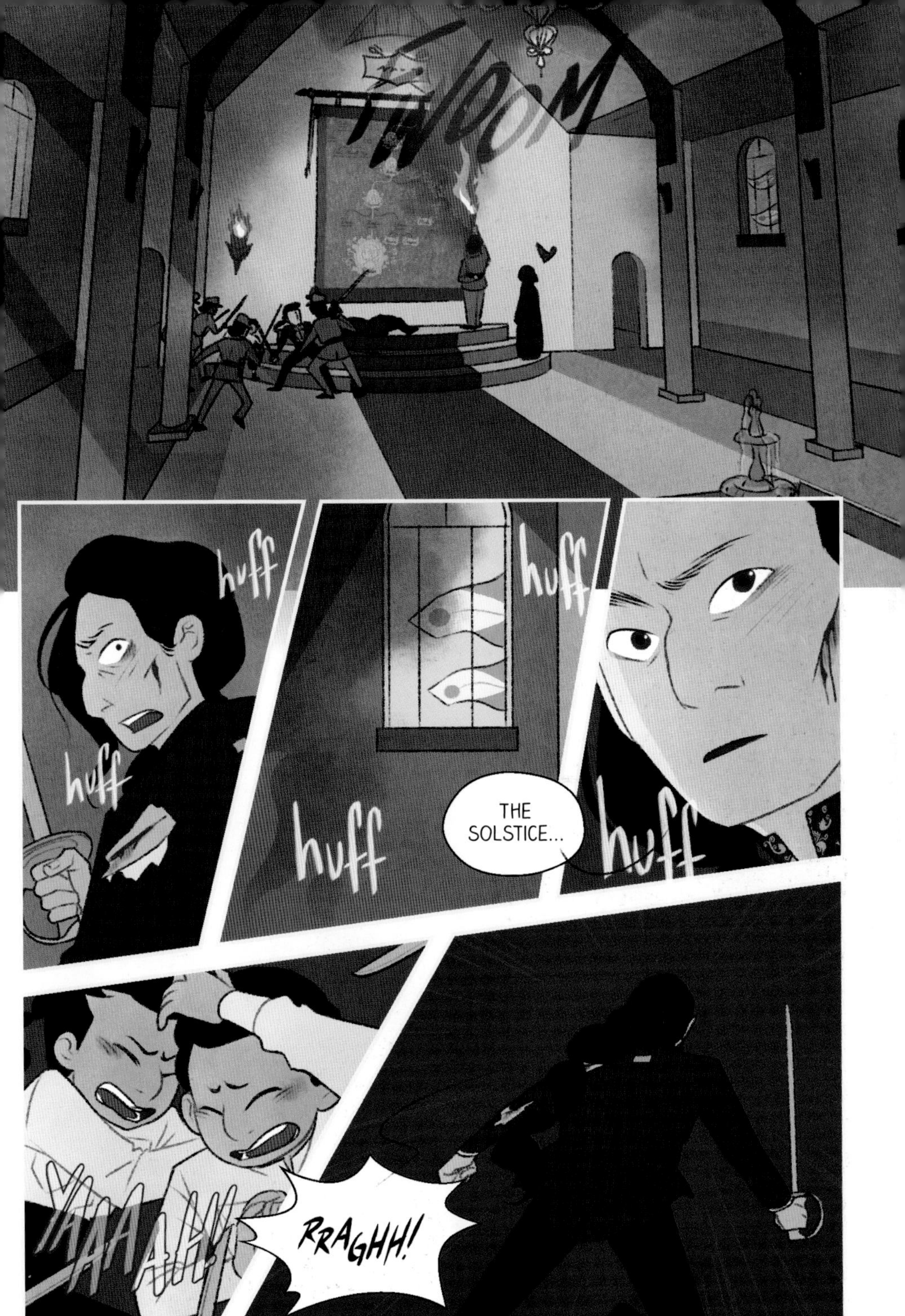
FWOOM
huff
huff
huff
huff
THE SOLSTICE...
huff
YAAAHH
RRAGHH!

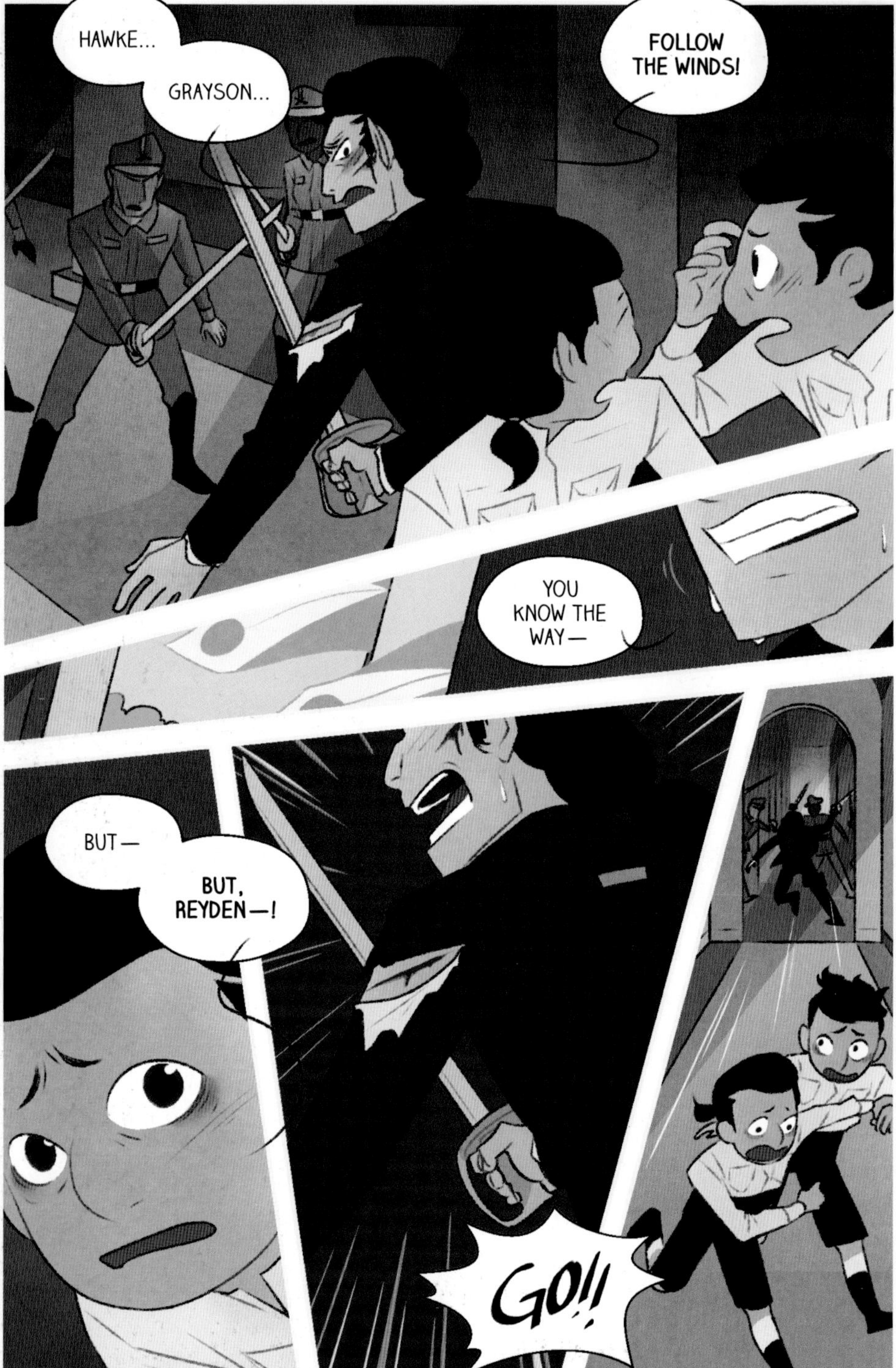
HAWKE...
GRAYSON...
FOLLOW THE WINDS!
YOU KNOW THE WAY—
BUT—
BUT, REYDEN—!
GO!!

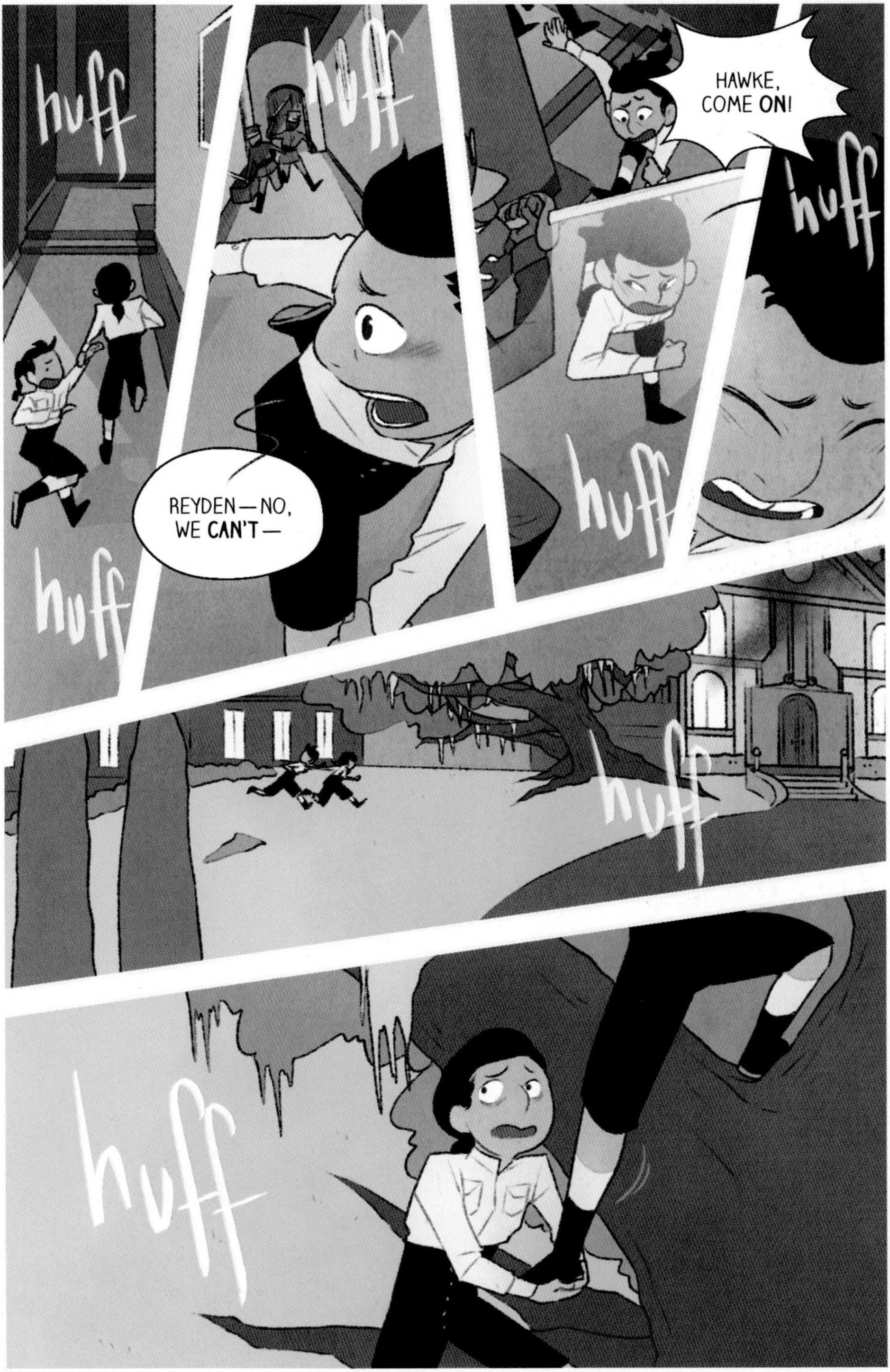
huff
huff
REYDEN—NO,
WE CAN'T—
HAWKE,
COME ON!
huff
huff
huff
huff
huff

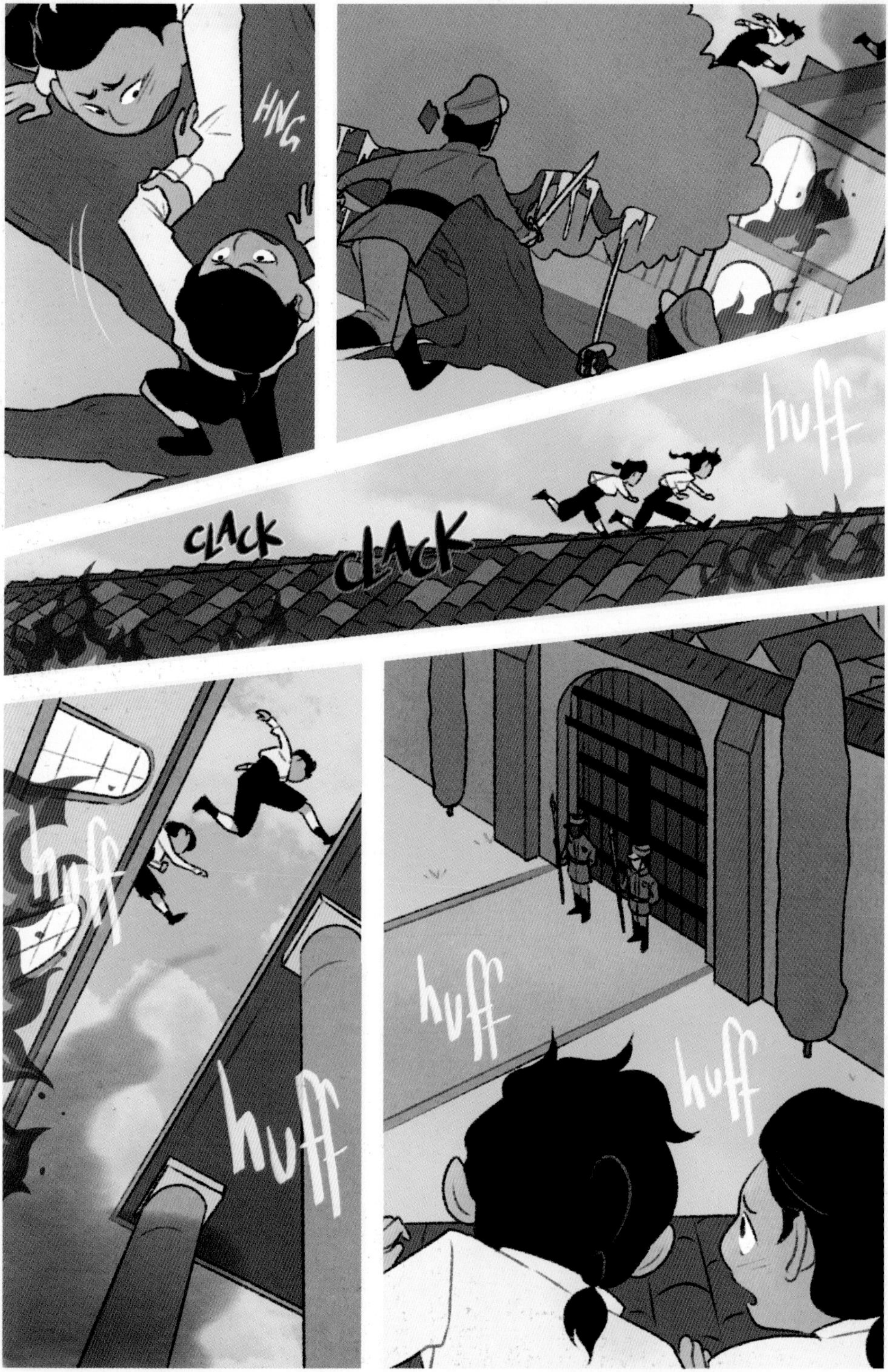
HNG
huff
CLACK
CLACK
huff
huff
huff
huff

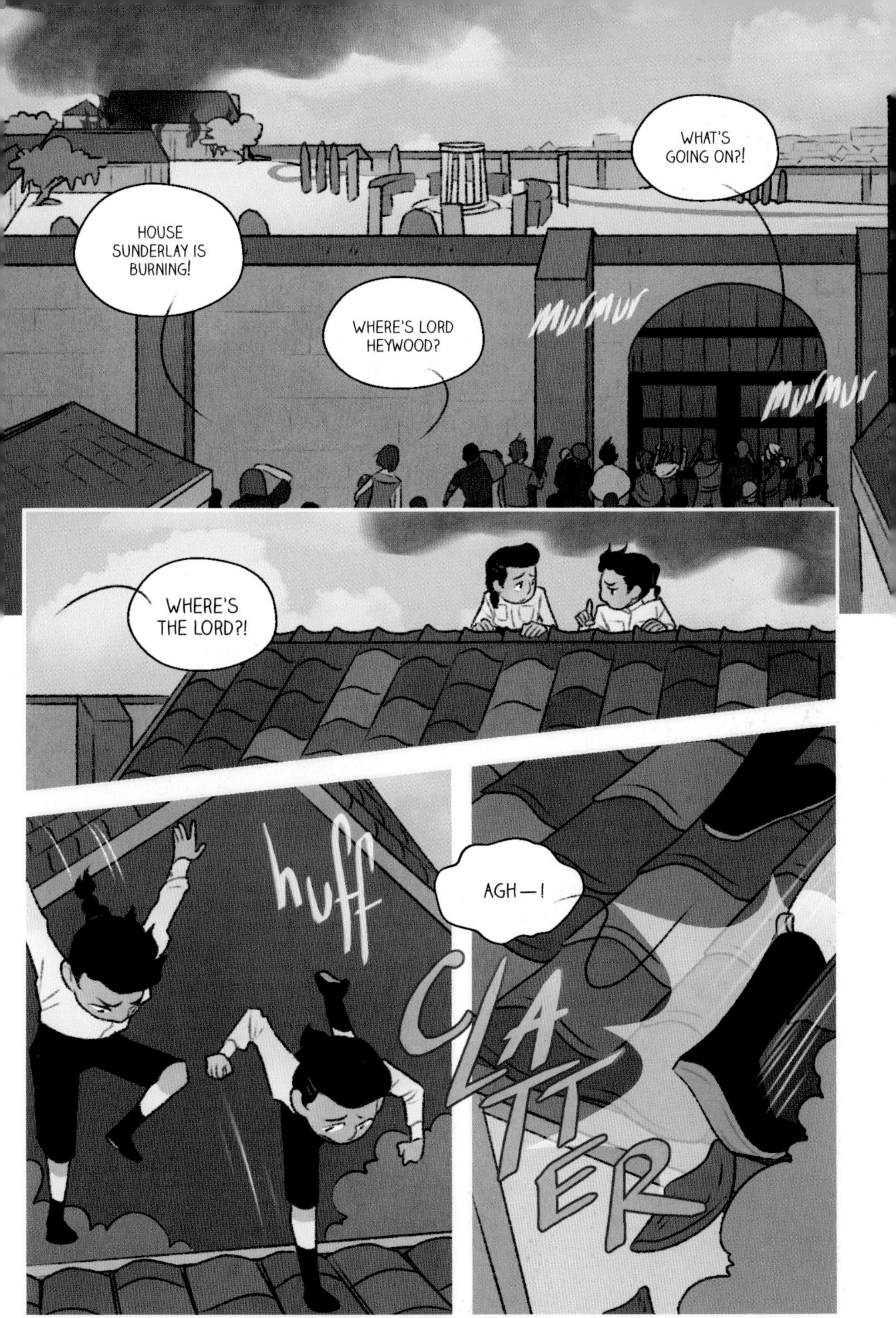

HOUSE SUNDERLAY IS BURNING!
WHERE'S LORD HEYWOOD?
WHAT'S GOING ON?!
MURMUR
MURMUR
WHERE'S THE LORD?!
huff
AGH—!
CLATTER

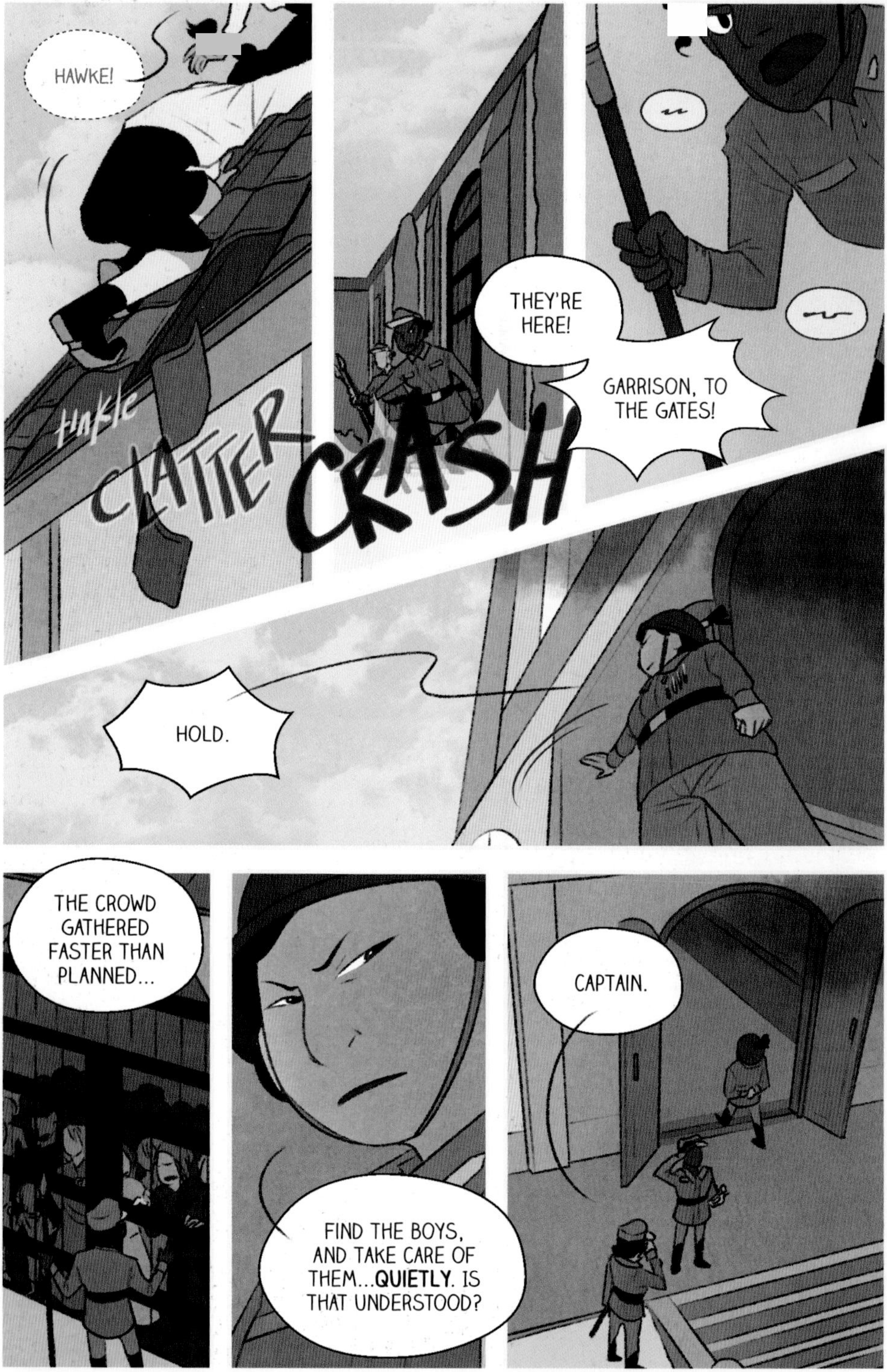
HAWKE!
tinkle
CLATTER
CRASH
THEY'RE HERE!
GARRISON, TO THE GATES!
HOLD.
THE CROWD GATHERED FASTER THAN PLANNED...
FIND THE BOYS, AND TAKE CARE OF THEM...**QUIETLY**. IS THAT UNDERSTOOD?
CAPTAIN.

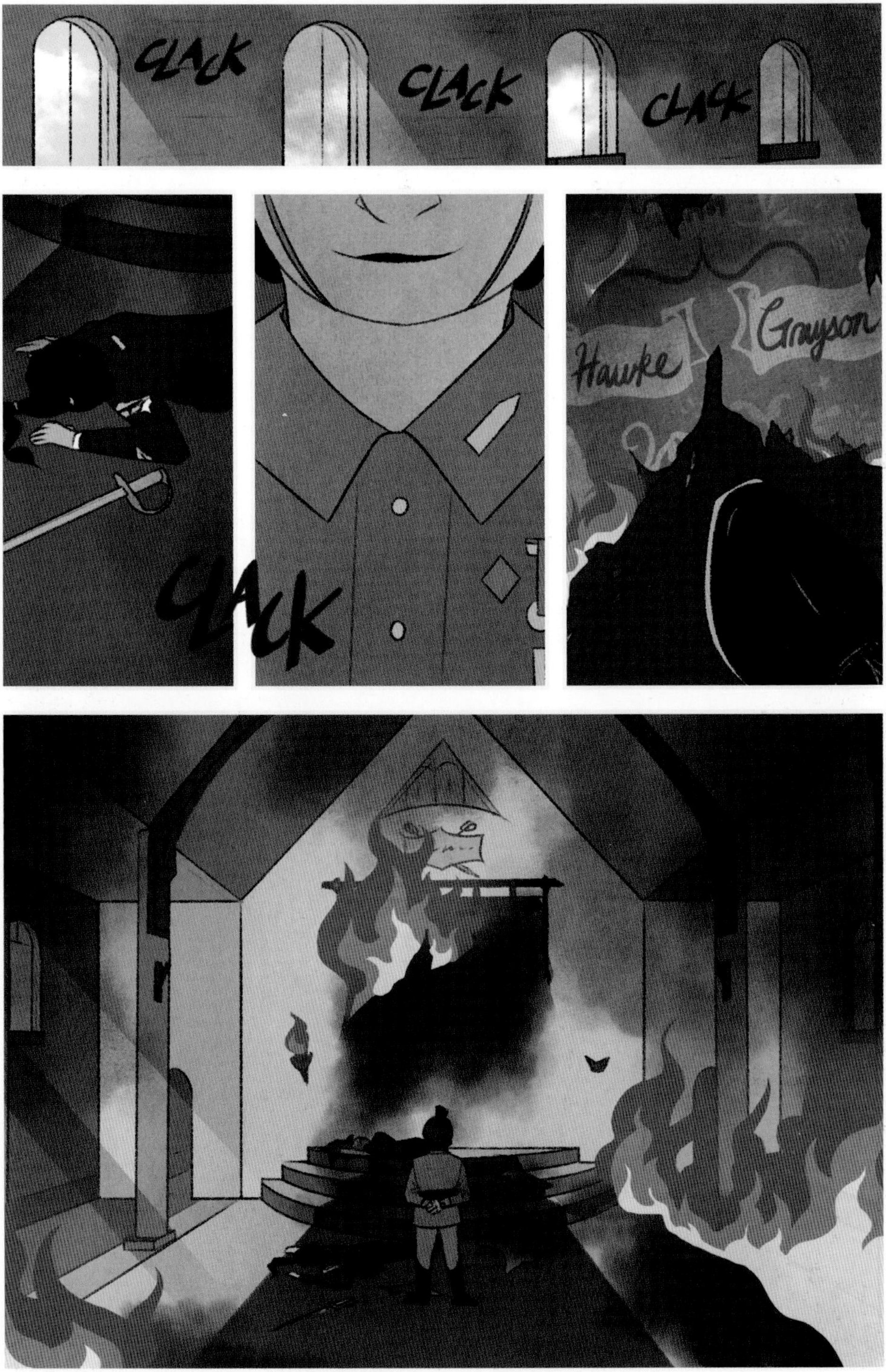
CLACK
CLACK
CLACK
CLACK
Hawke
Grayson

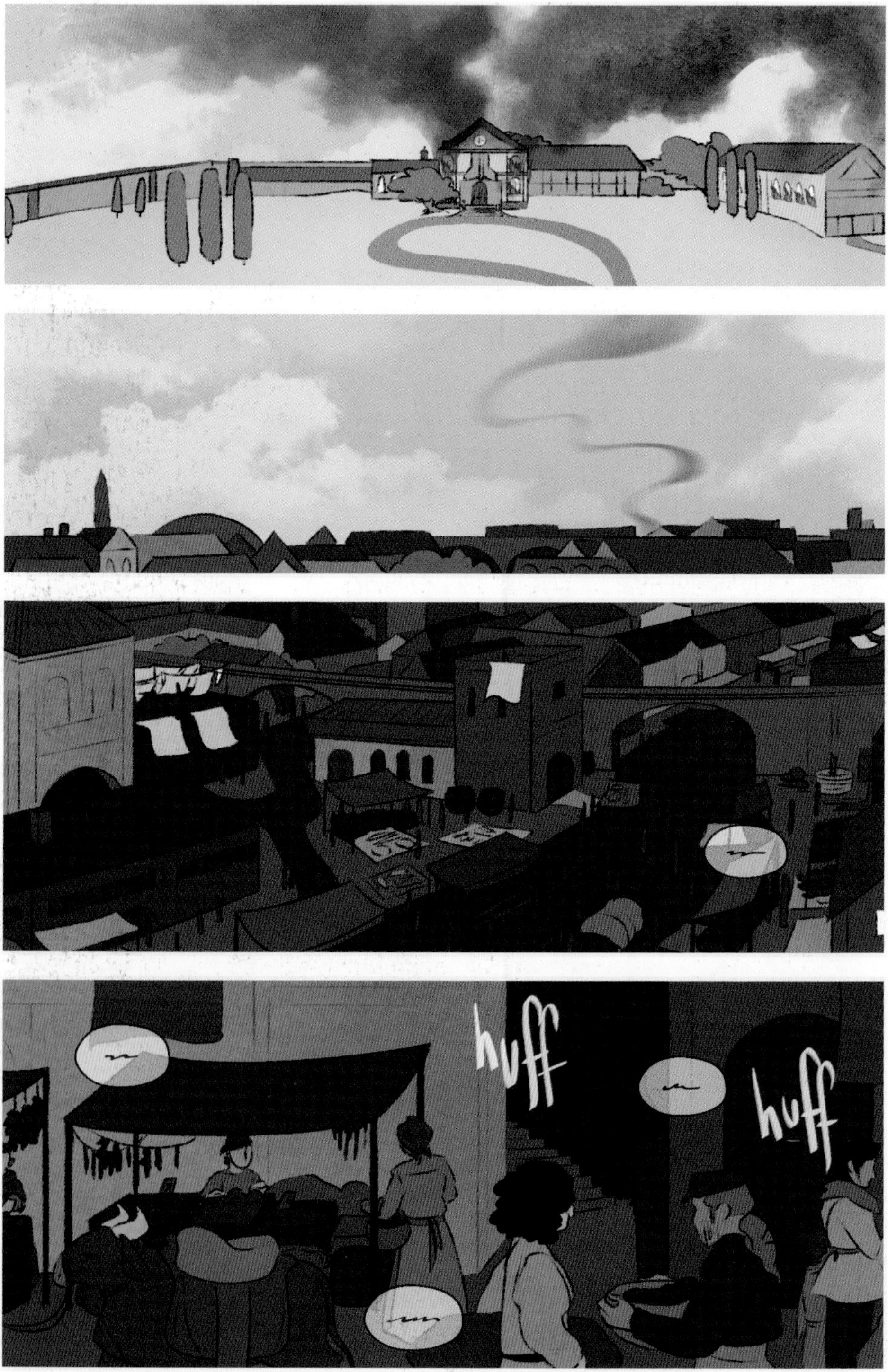
huff
huff

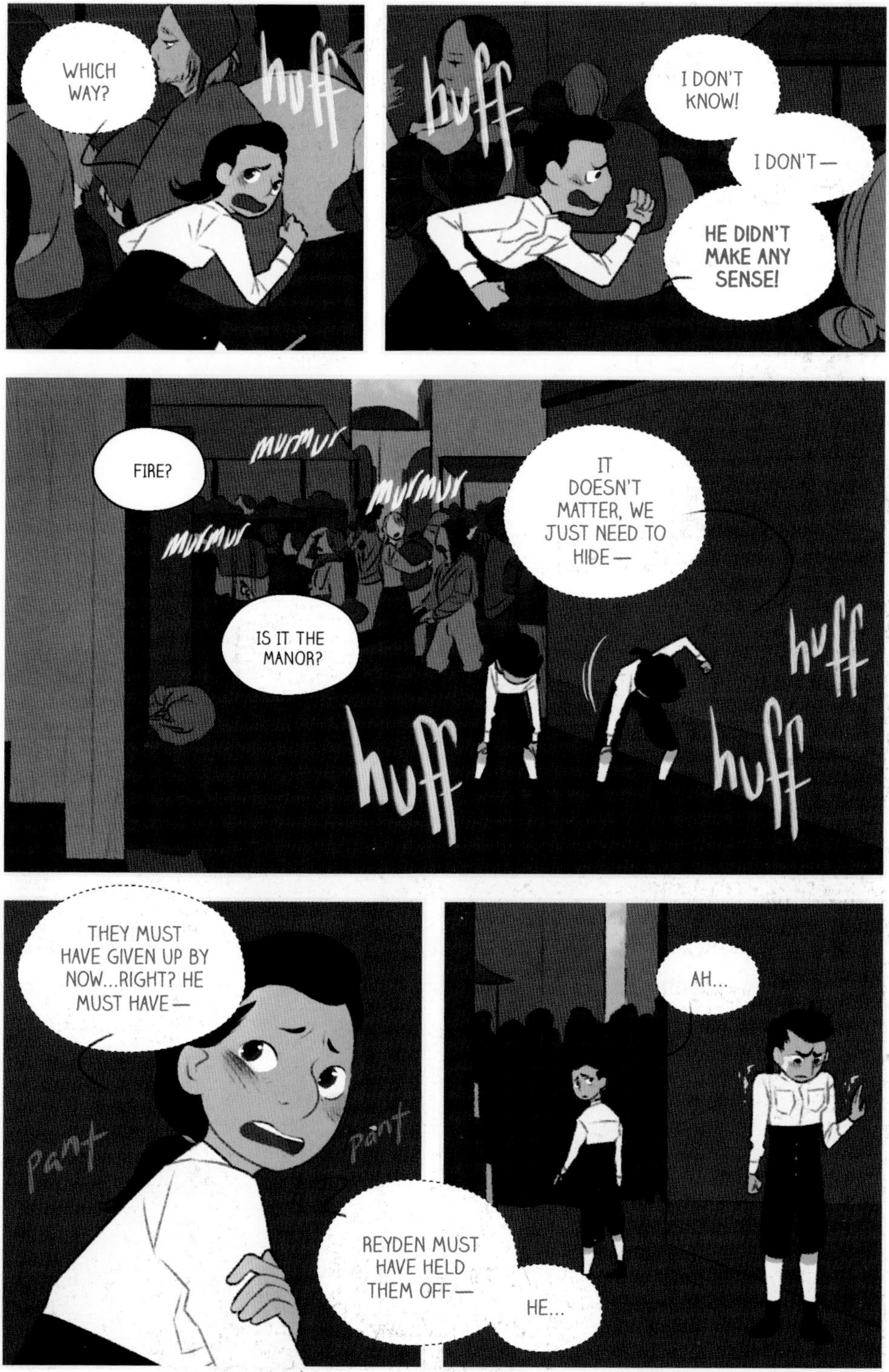
WHICH WAY?
huff
huff
I DON'T KNOW!
I DON'T—
HE DIDN'T MAKE ANY SENSE!
FIRE?
murmur
murmur
murmur
IS IT THE MANOR?
IT DOESN'T MATTER, WE JUST NEED TO HIDE—
huff
huff
huff
THEY MUST HAVE GIVEN UP BY NOW...RIGHT? HE MUST HAVE—
pant
pant
REYDEN MUST HAVE HELD THEM OFF—
HE...
AH...

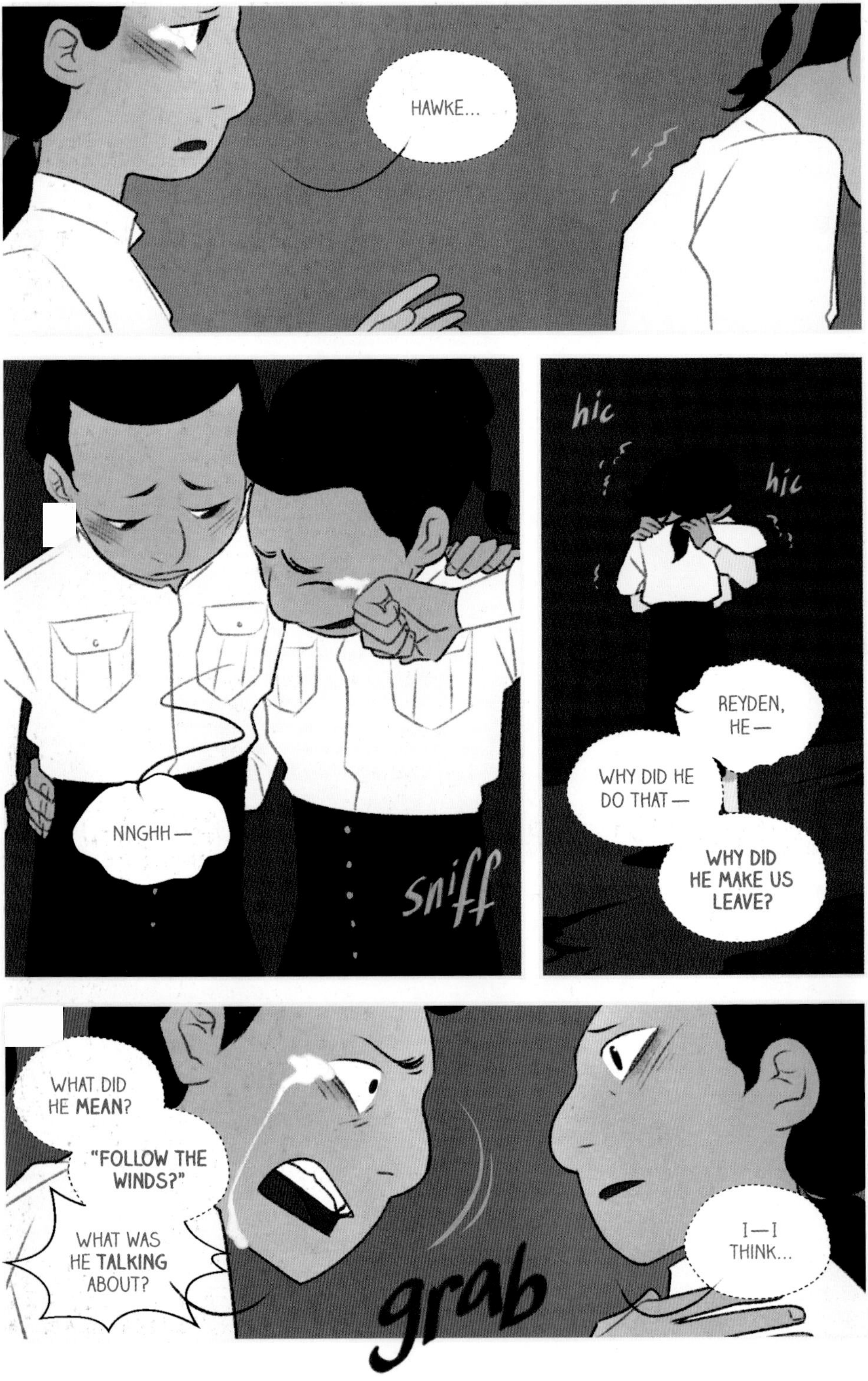
HAWKE...
NNGHH—
sniff
hic
hic
REYDEN, HE—
WHY DID HE DO THAT—
WHY DID HE MAKE US LEAVE?
WHAT DID HE MEAN?
"FOLLOW THE WINDS?"
WHAT WAS HE TALKING ABOUT?
I—I THINK...
grab

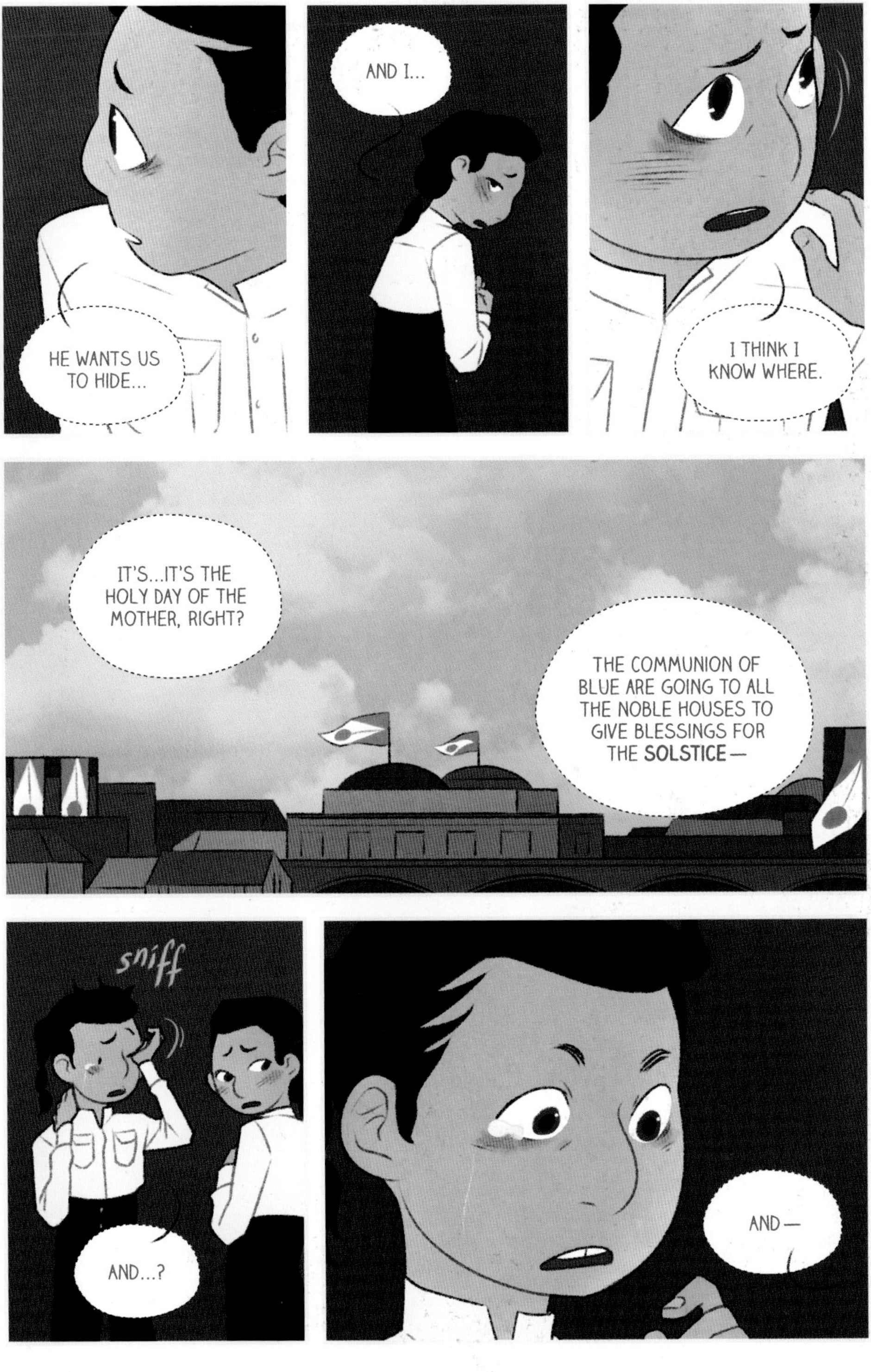
HE WANTS US TO HIDE...
AND I...
I THINK I KNOW WHERE.
IT'S...IT'S THE HOLY DAY OF THE MOTHER, RIGHT?
THE COMMUNION OF BLUE ARE GOING TO ALL THE NOBLE HOUSES TO GIVE BLESSINGS FOR THE **SOLSTICE**—
sniff
AND...?
AND—

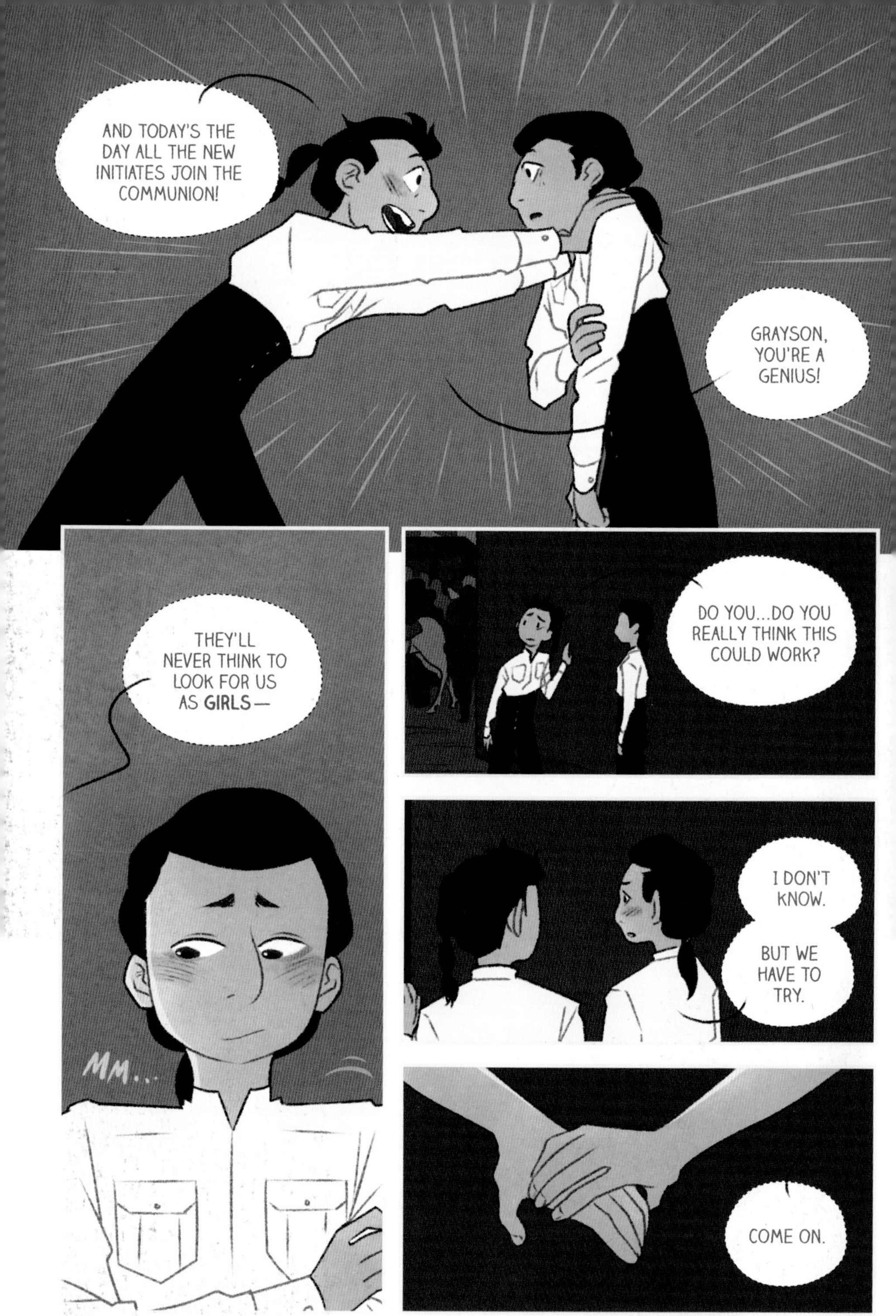
AND TODAY'S THE DAY ALL THE NEW INITIATES JOIN THE COMMUNION!
GRAYSON, YOU'RE A GENIUS!
THEY'LL NEVER THINK TO LOOK FOR US AS GIRLS—
MM...
DO YOU...DO YOU REALLY THINK THIS COULD WORK?
I DON'T KNOW.
BUT WE HAVE TO TRY.
COME ON.

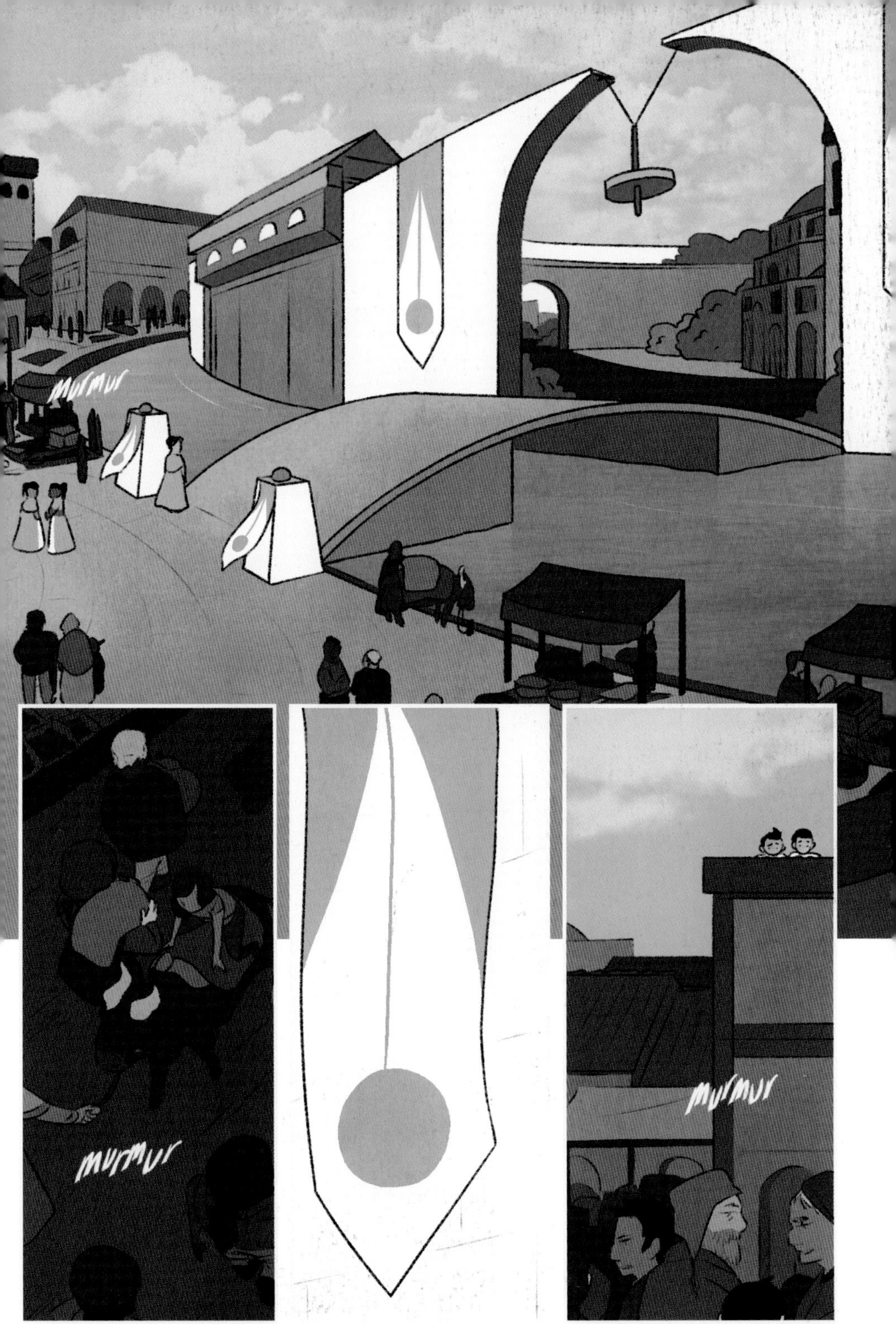
murmur
murmur
murmur

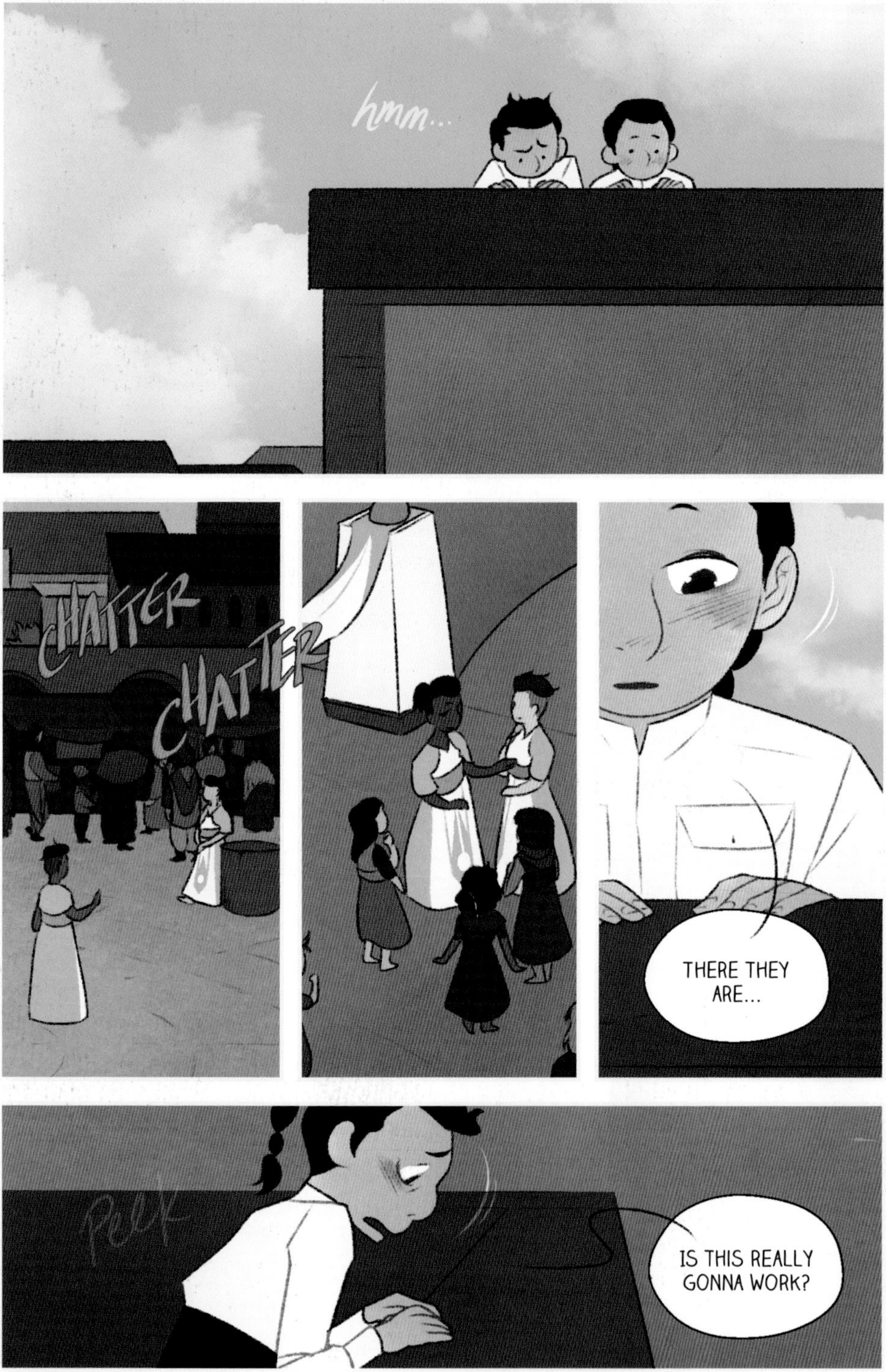
hmm...
CHATTER
CHATTER
THERE THEY ARE...
PEEK
IS THIS REALLY GONNA WORK?

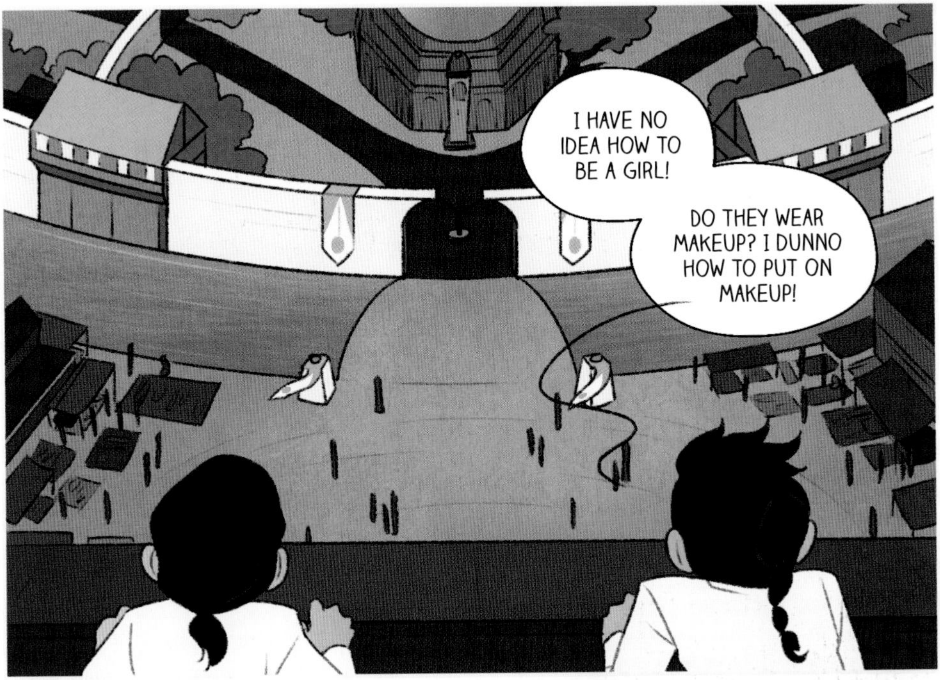
I HAVE NO IDEA HOW TO BE A GIRL!
DO THEY WEAR MAKEUP? I DUNNO HOW TO PUT ON MAKEUP!

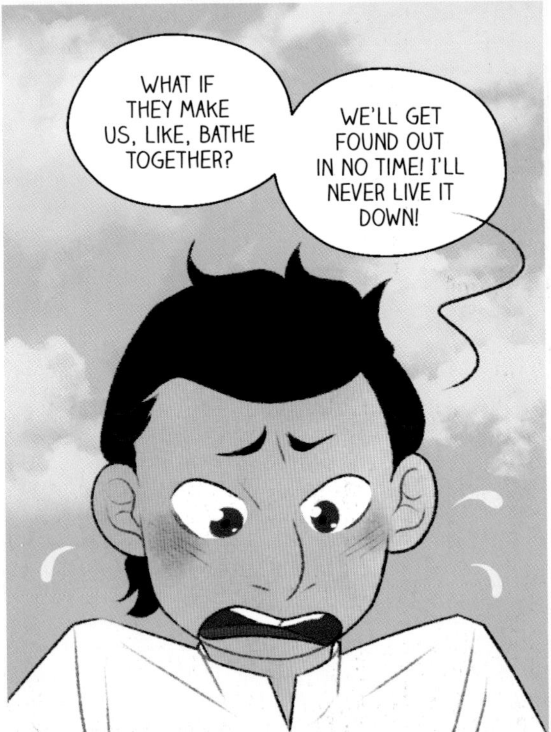
WHAT IF THEY MAKE US, LIKE, BATHE TOGETHER?
WE'LL GET FOUND OUT IN NO TIME! I'LL NEVER LIVE IT DOWN!

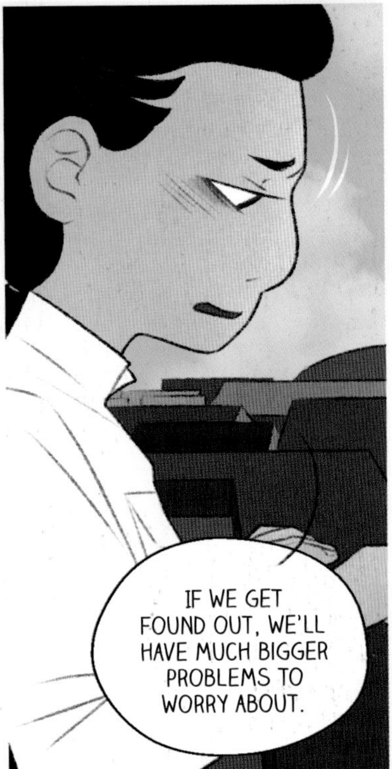
IF WE GET FOUND OUT, WE'LL HAVE MUCH BIGGER PROBLEMS TO WORRY ABOUT.

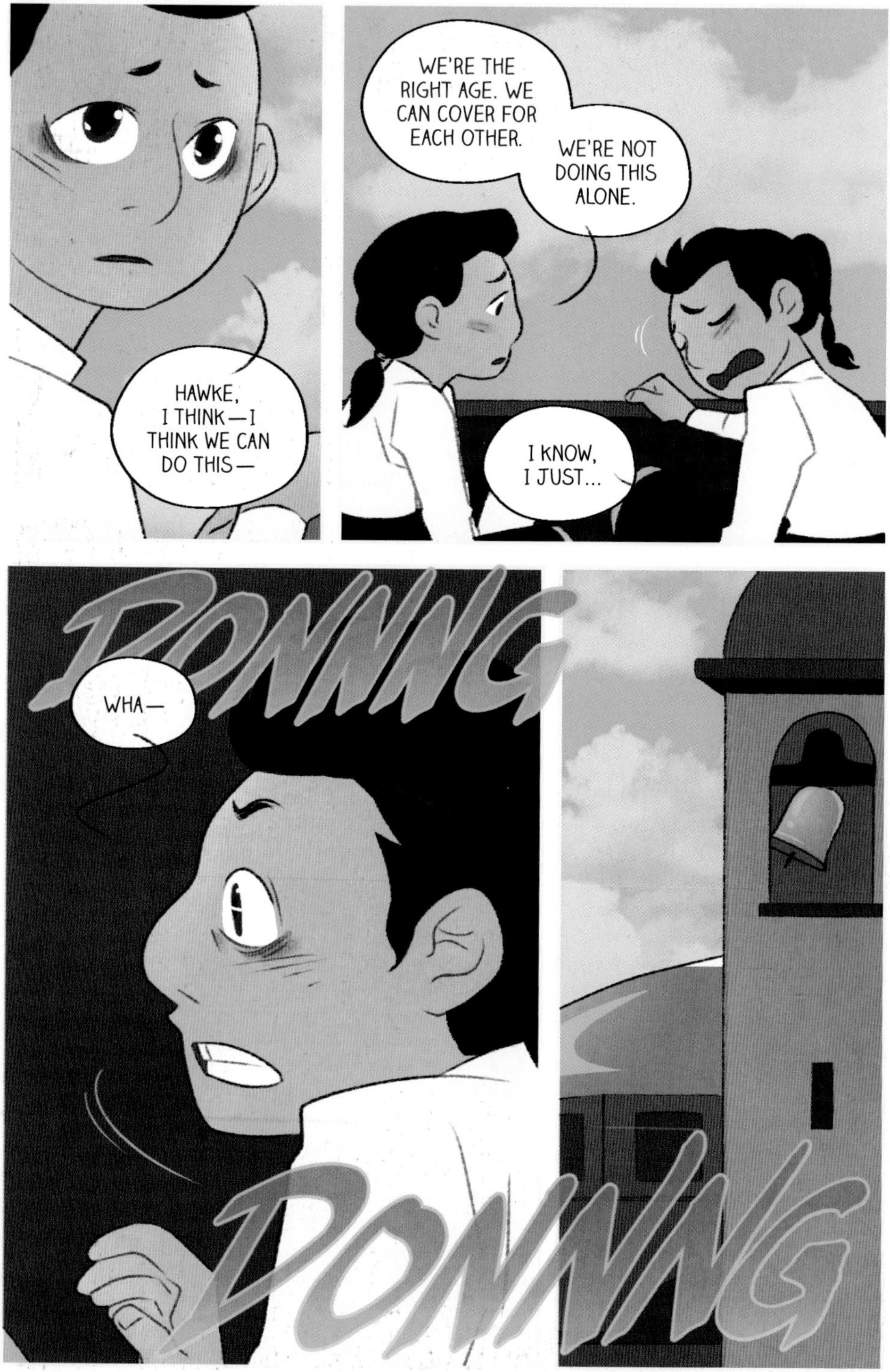
HAWKE, I THINK—I THINK WE CAN DO THIS—
WE'RE THE RIGHT AGE. WE CAN COVER FOR EACH OTHER.
WE'RE NOT DOING THIS ALONE.
I KNOW, I JUST...
DONNG
WHA—
DONNG

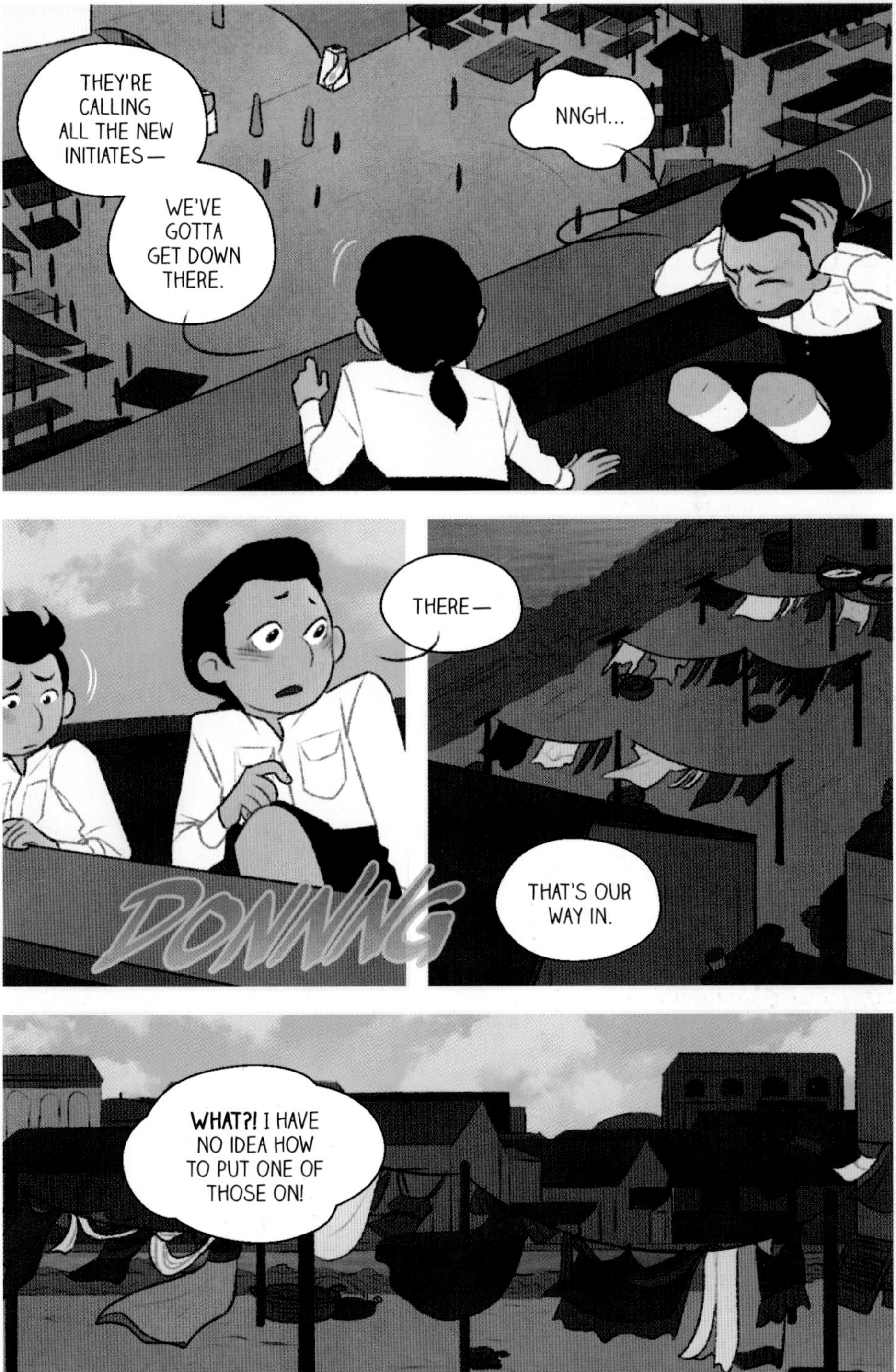
THEY'RE CALLING ALL THE NEW INITIATES—
WE'VE GOTTA GET DOWN THERE.
NNGH...
THERE—
DONNNG
THAT'S OUR WAY IN.
WHAT?! I HAVE NO IDEA HOW TO PUT ONE OF THOSE ON!

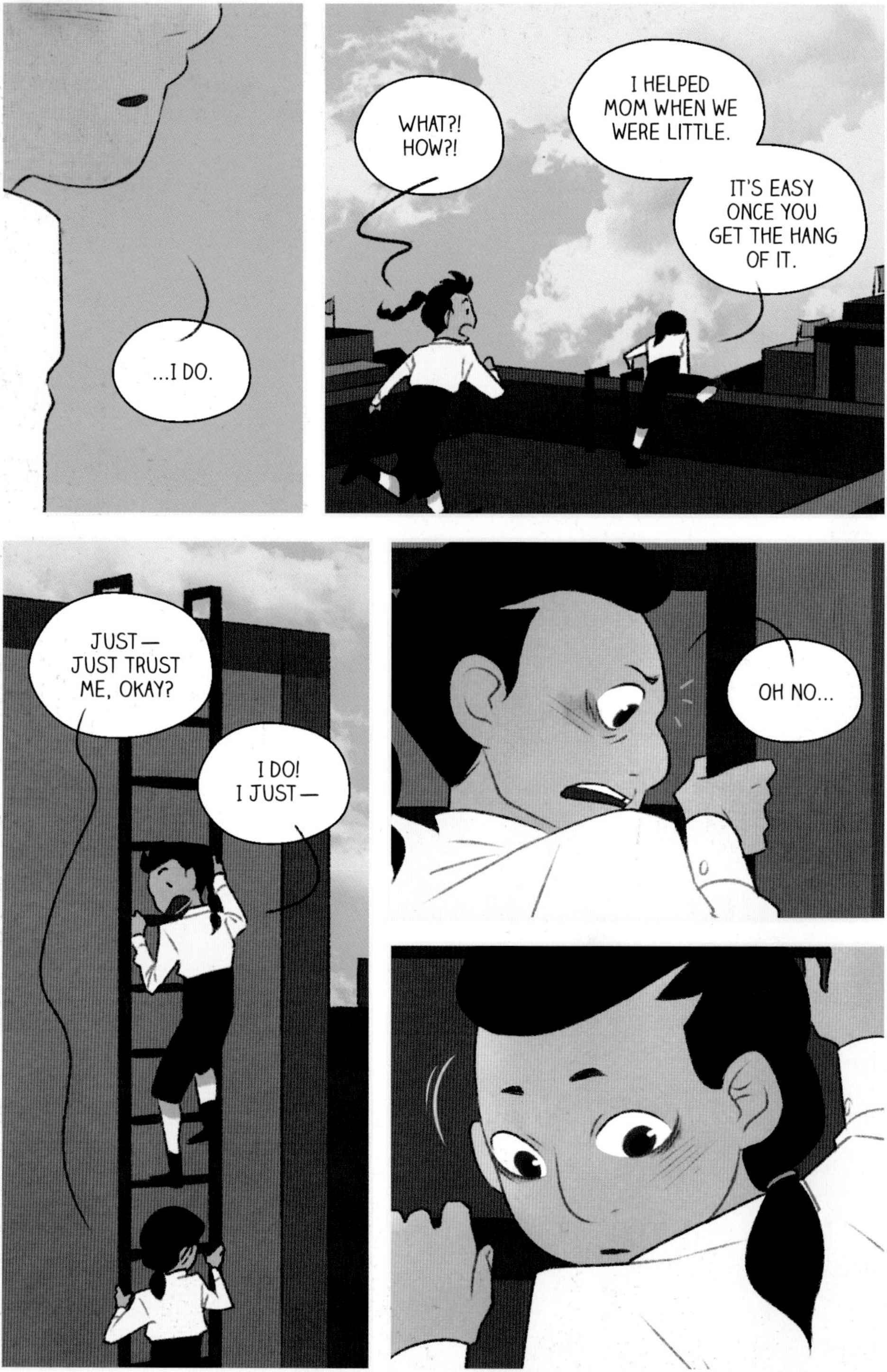
...I DO.
WHAT?! HOW?!
I HELPED MOM WHEN WE WERE LITTLE.
IT'S EASY ONCE YOU GET THE HANG OF IT.
JUST— JUST TRUST ME, OKAY?
I DO! I JUST—
OH NO...

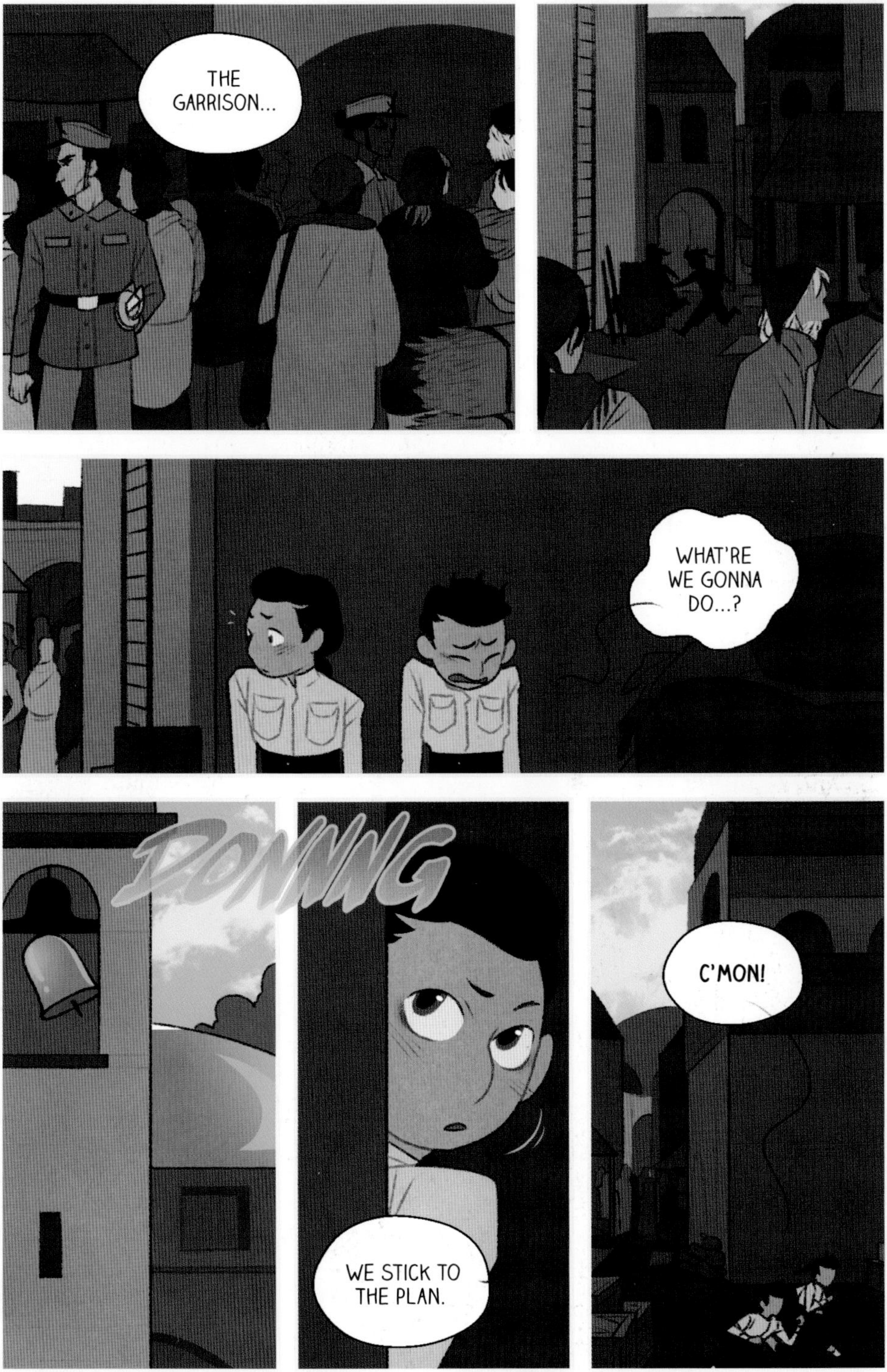
THE GARRISON...
WHAT'RE WE GONNA DO...?
DONNNG
WE STICK TO THE PLAN.
C'MON!

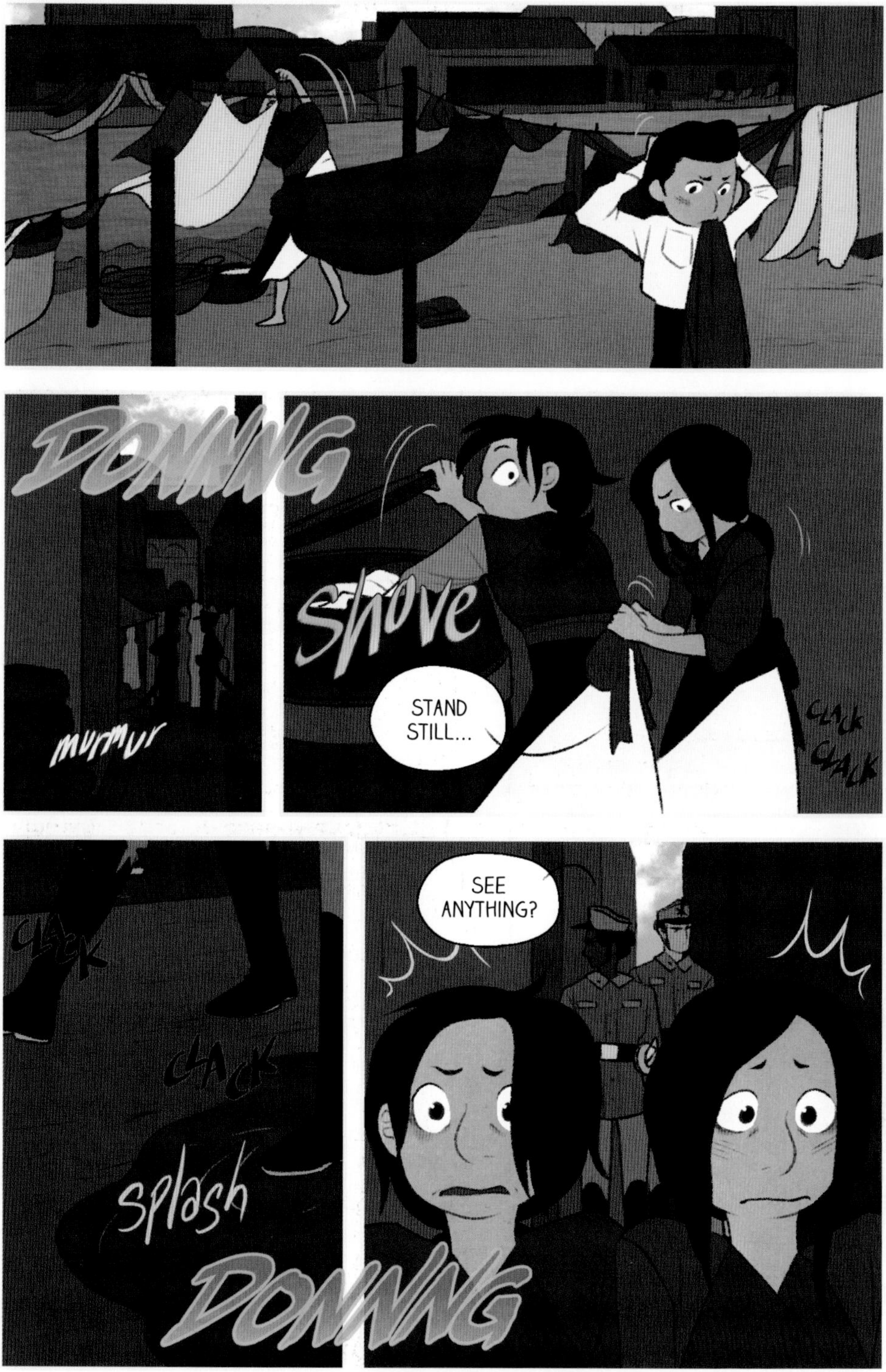
DONNNG
murmur
shove
STAND STILL...
CLACK
CLACK
CLACK
CLACK
SEE ANYTHING?
splash
DONNNG

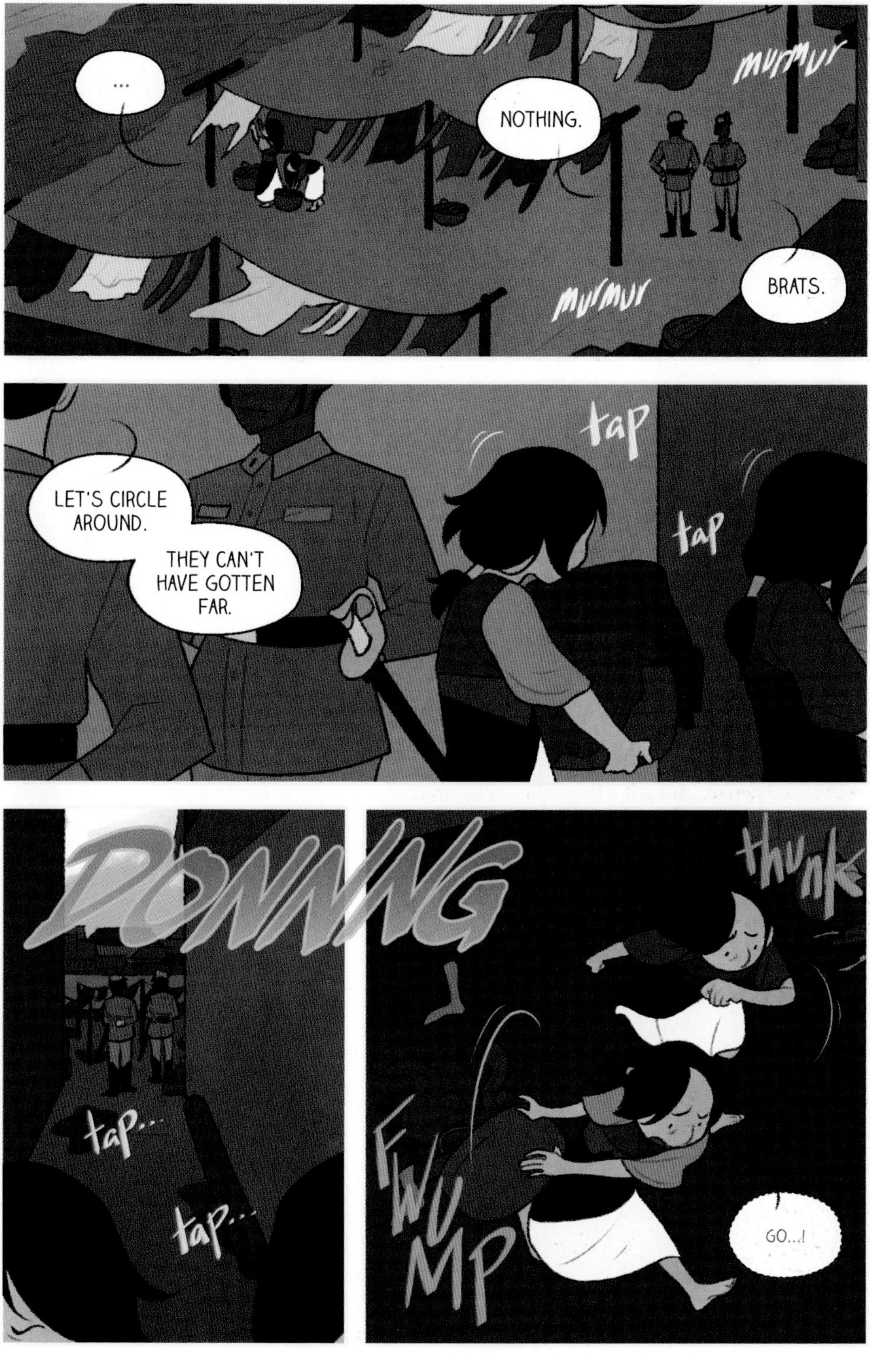
...
NOTHING.
murmur
BRATS.
murmur
LET'S CIRCLE AROUND.
THEY CAN'T HAVE GOTTEN FAR.
tap
tap
DONNNG
tap...
tap...
thunk
FWUMP
GO...!

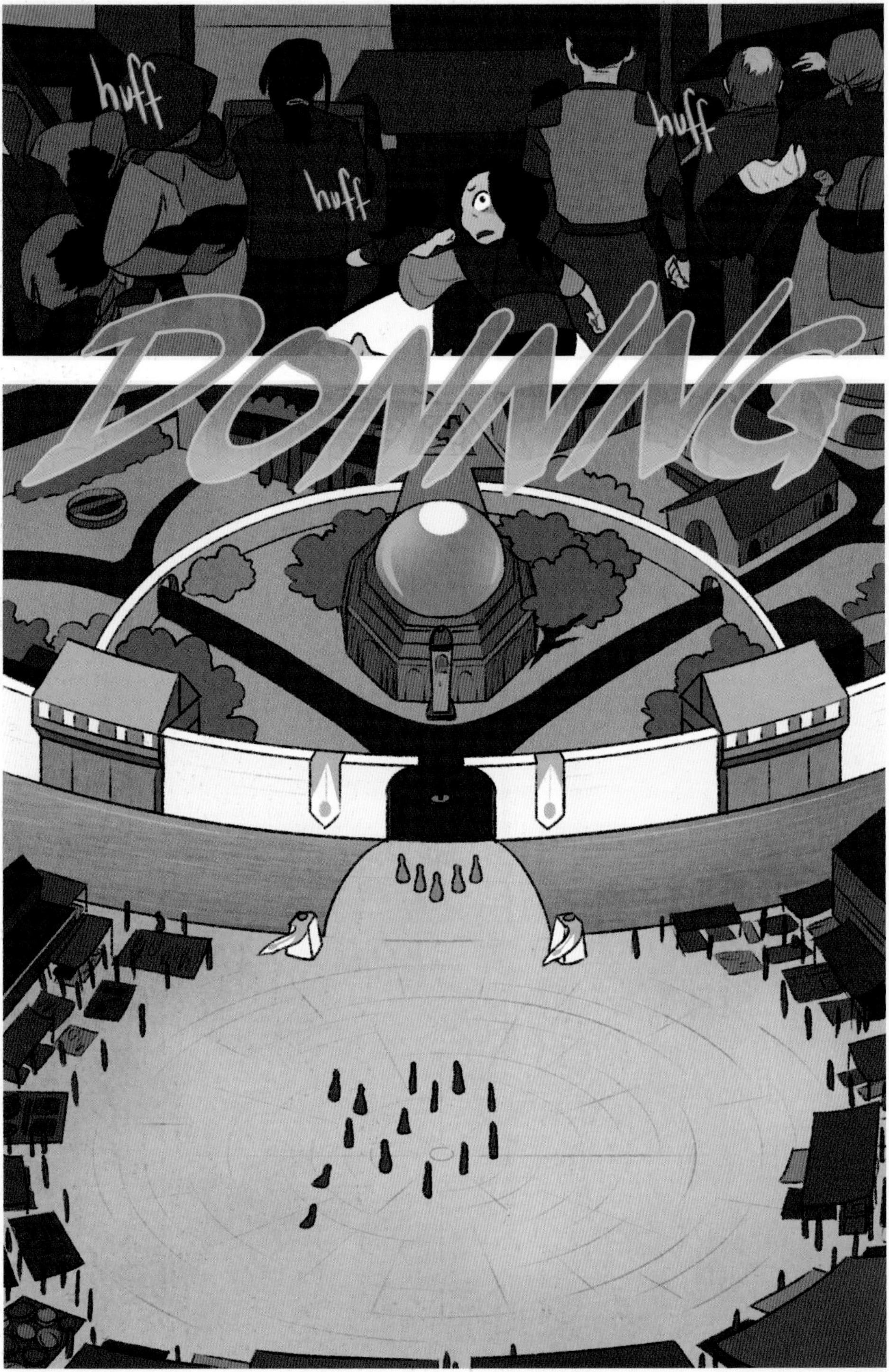
huff
huff
huff
DONNG

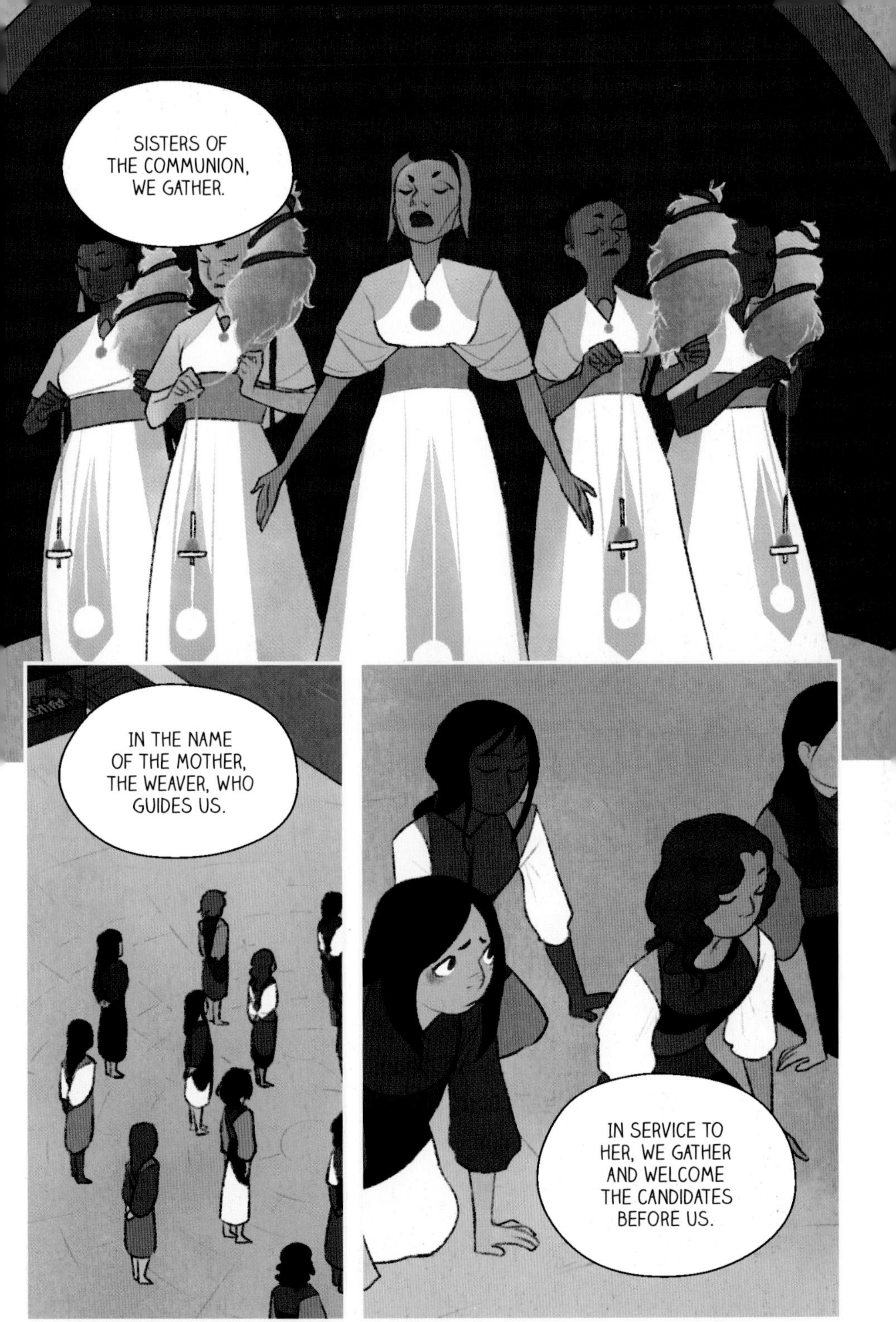
SISTERS OF THE COMMUNION, WE GATHER.
IN THE NAME OF THE MOTHER, THE WEAVER, WHO GUIDES US.
IN SERVICE TO HER, WE GATHER AND WELCOME THE CANDIDATES BEFORE US.

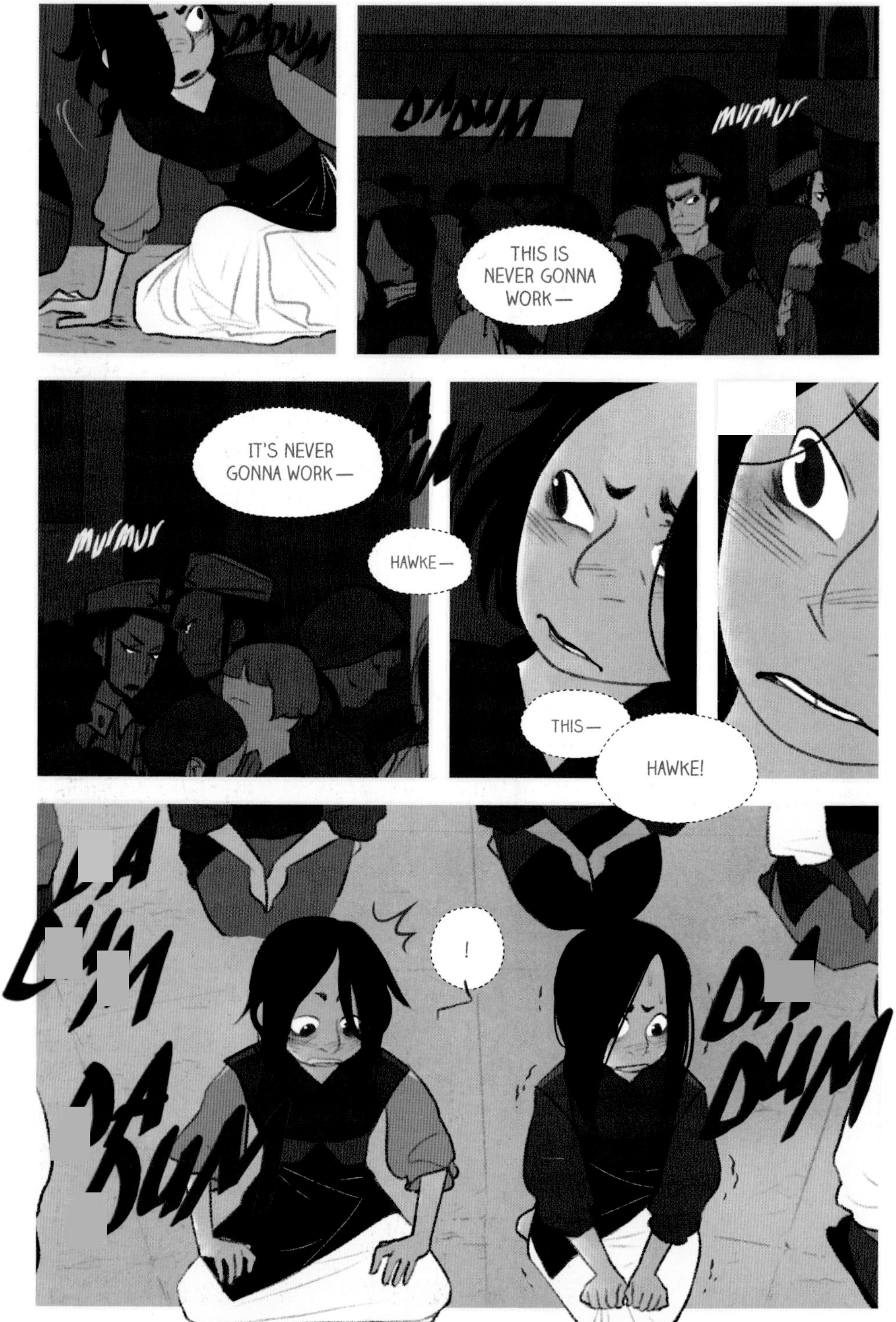
DADUM
DADUM
murmur
THIS IS NEVER GONNA WORK—
IT'S NEVER GONNA WORK—
murmur
HAWKE—
THIS—
HAWKE!
!

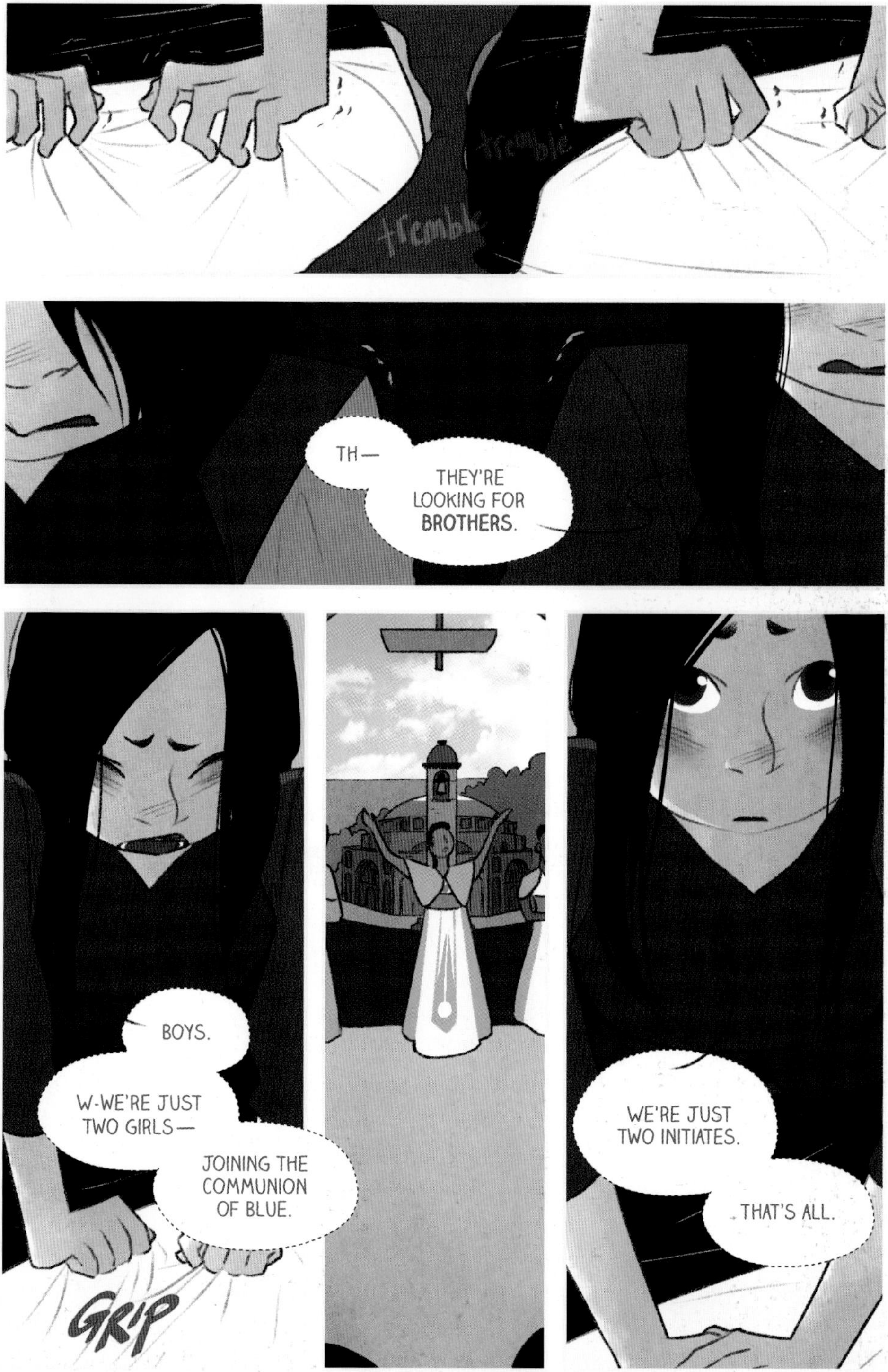
tremble
tremble
TH—
THEY'RE LOOKING FOR **BROTHERS**.
BOYS.
W-WE'RE JUST TWO GIRLS—
JOINING THE COMMUNION OF BLUE.
GRIP
WE'RE JUST TWO INITIATES.
THAT'S ALL.

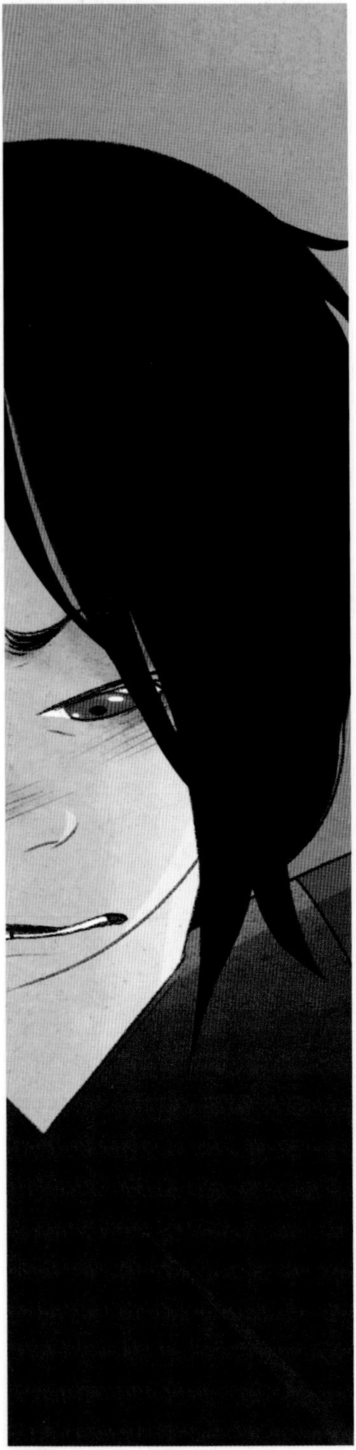

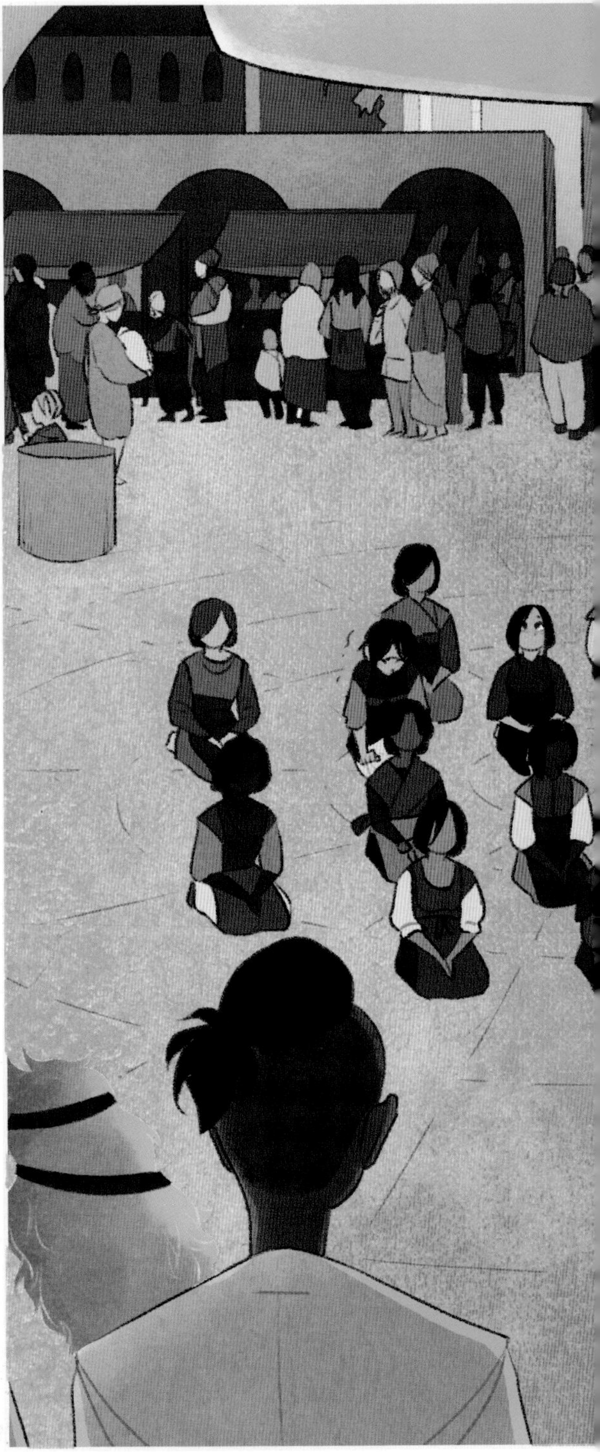

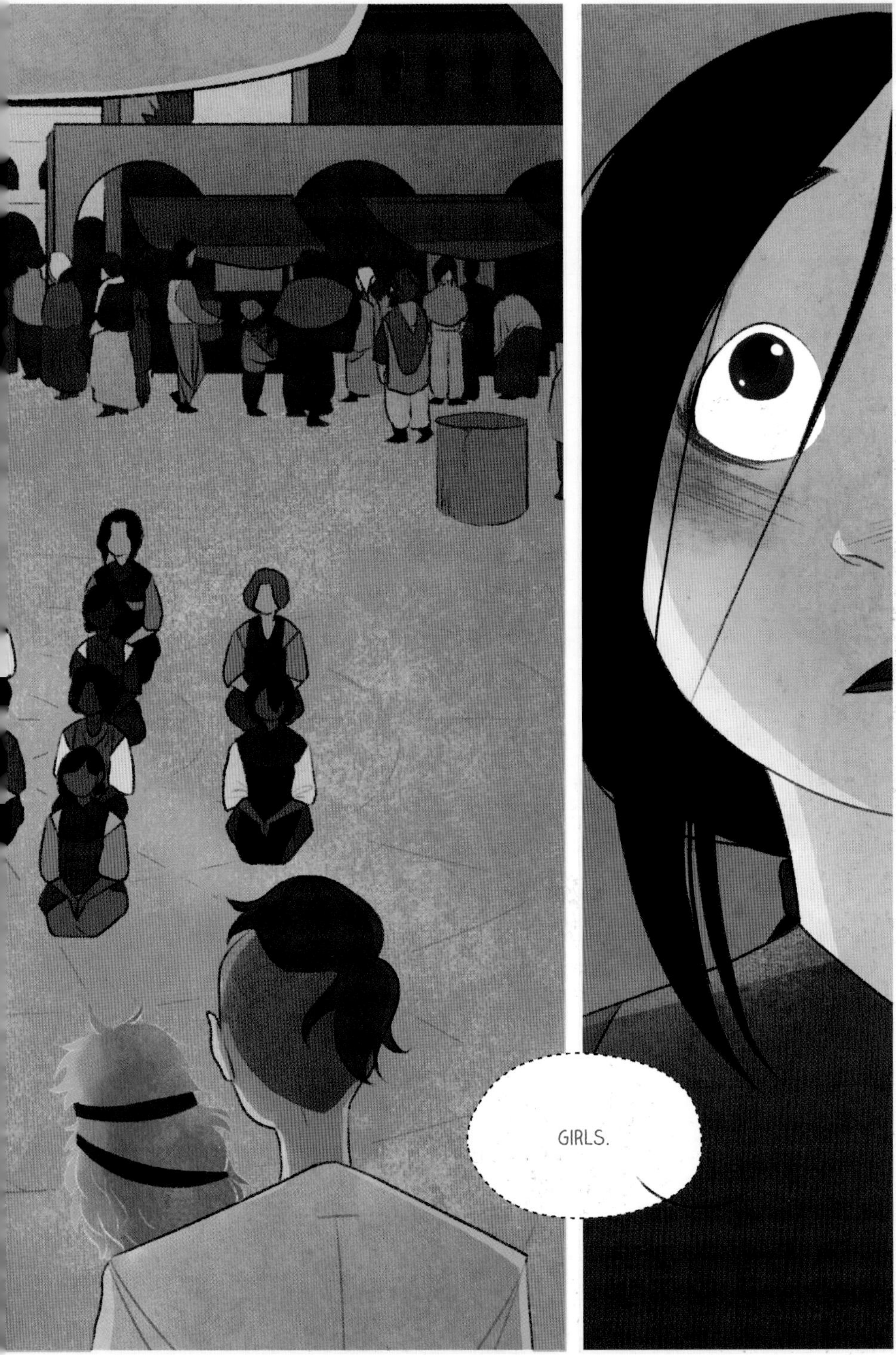
GIRLS.

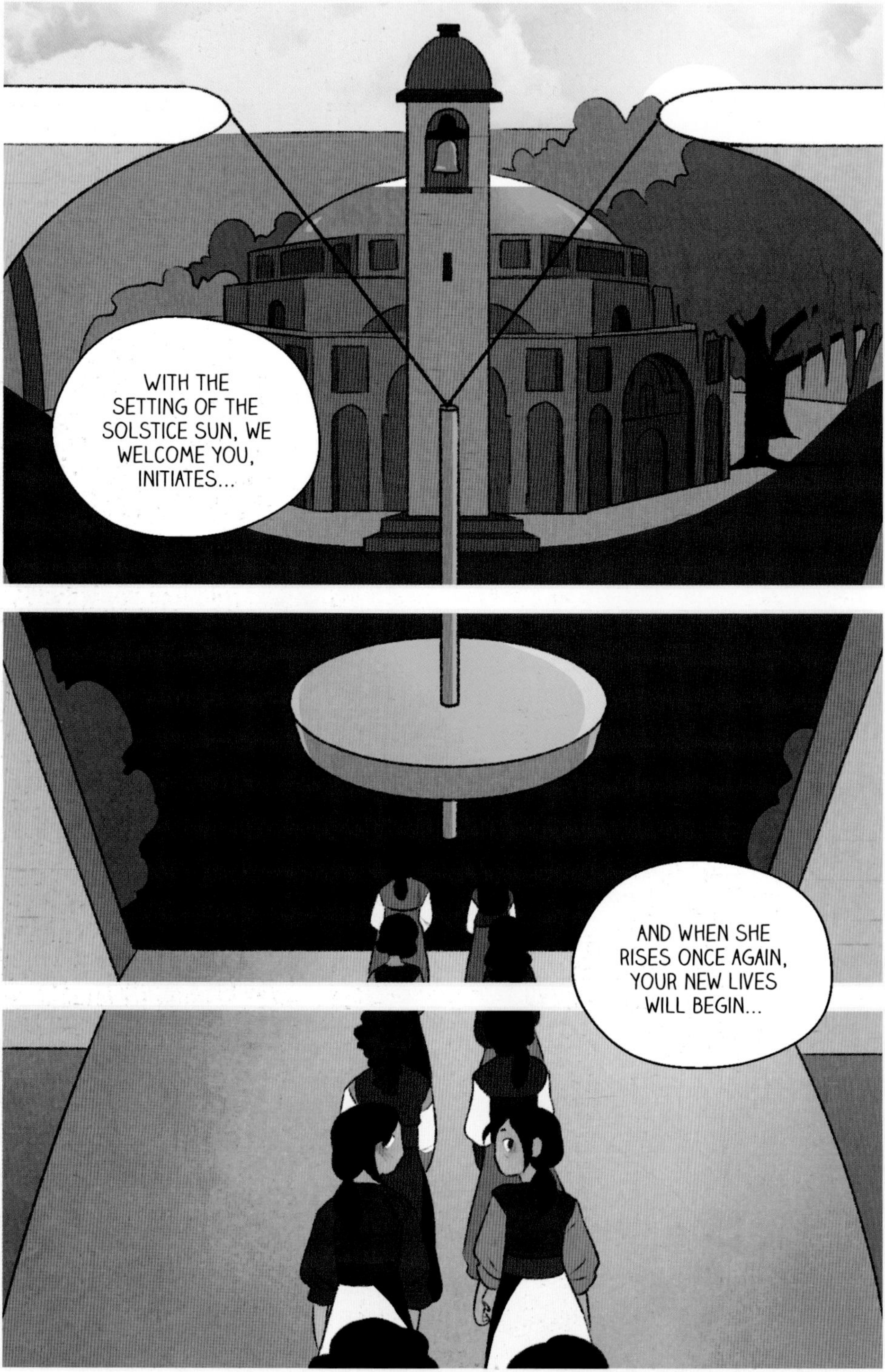
WITH THE SETTING OF THE SOLSTICE SUN, WE WELCOME YOU, INITIATES...
AND WHEN SHE RISES ONCE AGAIN, YOUR NEW LIVES WILL BEGIN...

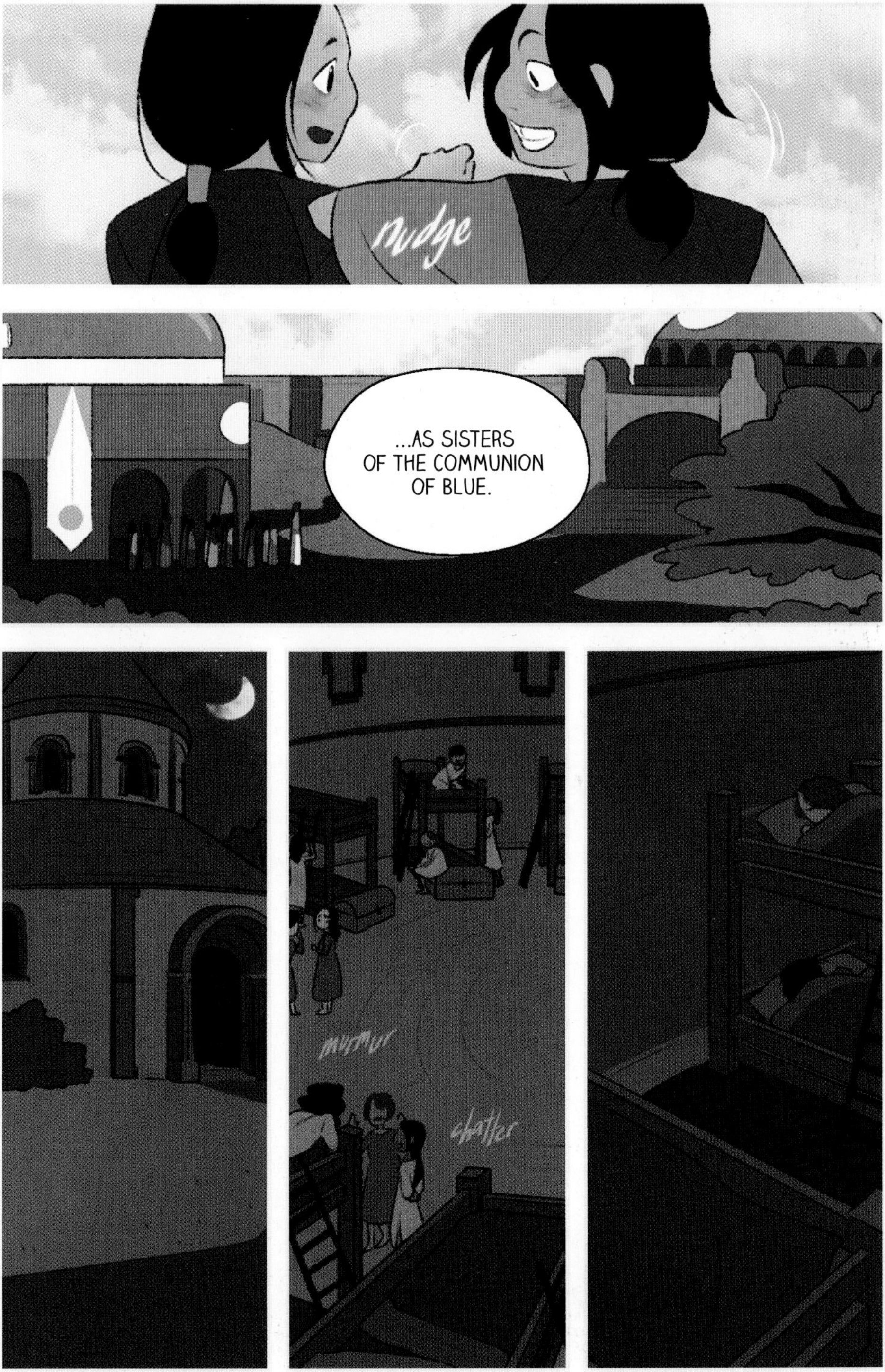
nudge
...AS SISTERS OF THE COMMUNION OF BLUE.
murmur
chatter

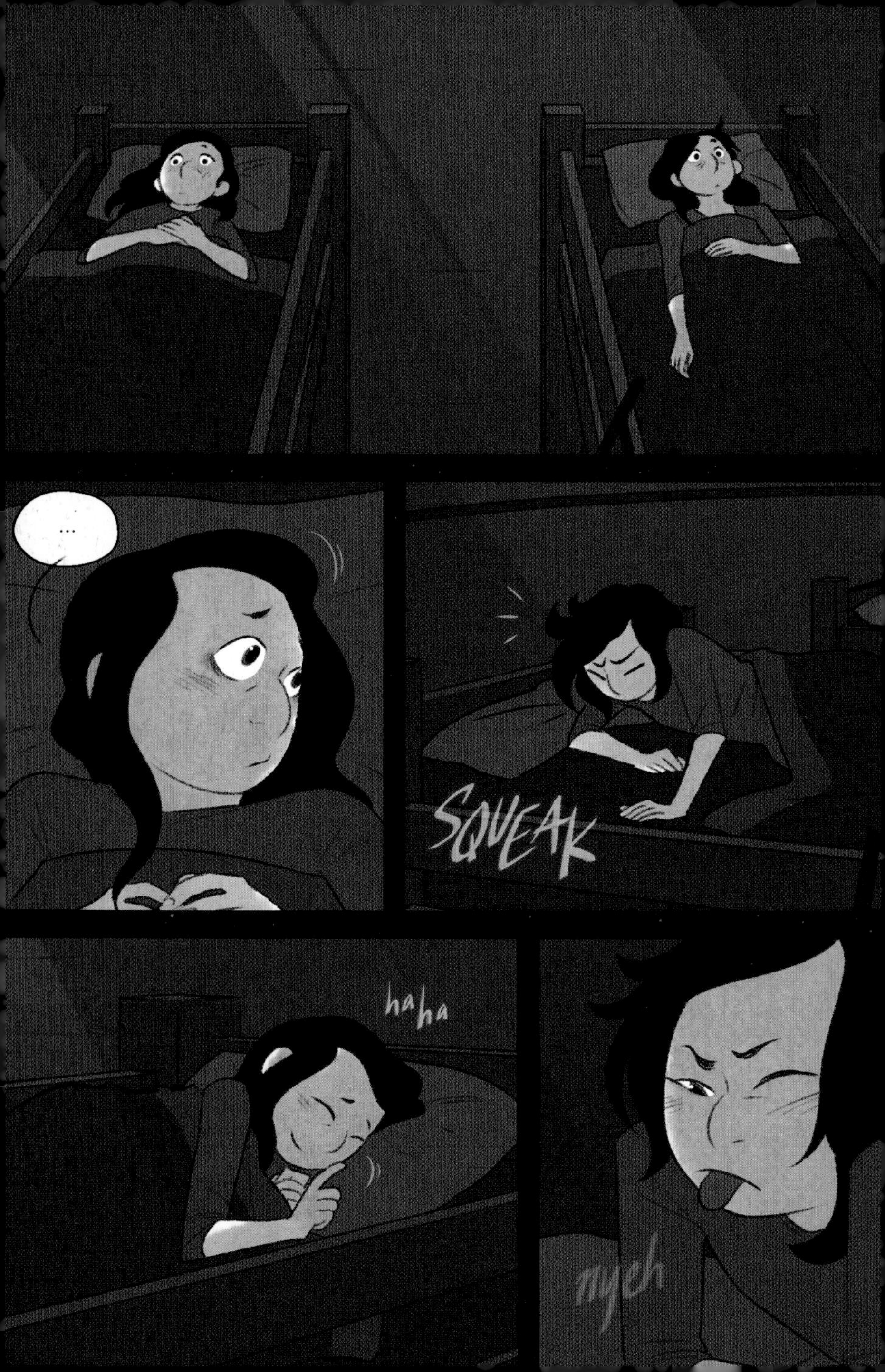
...
SQUEAK
haha
myeh

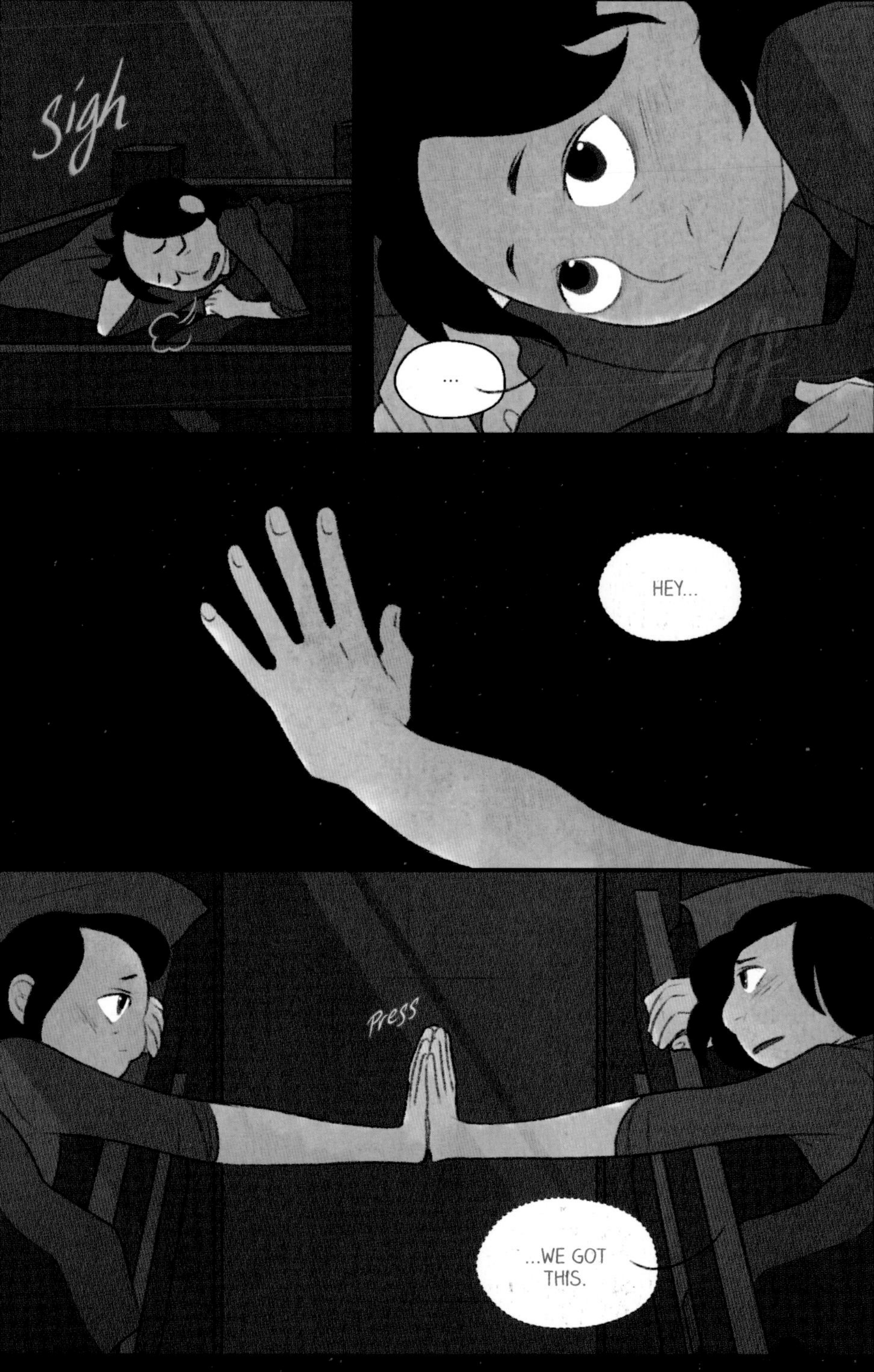
sigh
...
HEY...
Press
...WE GOT THIS.

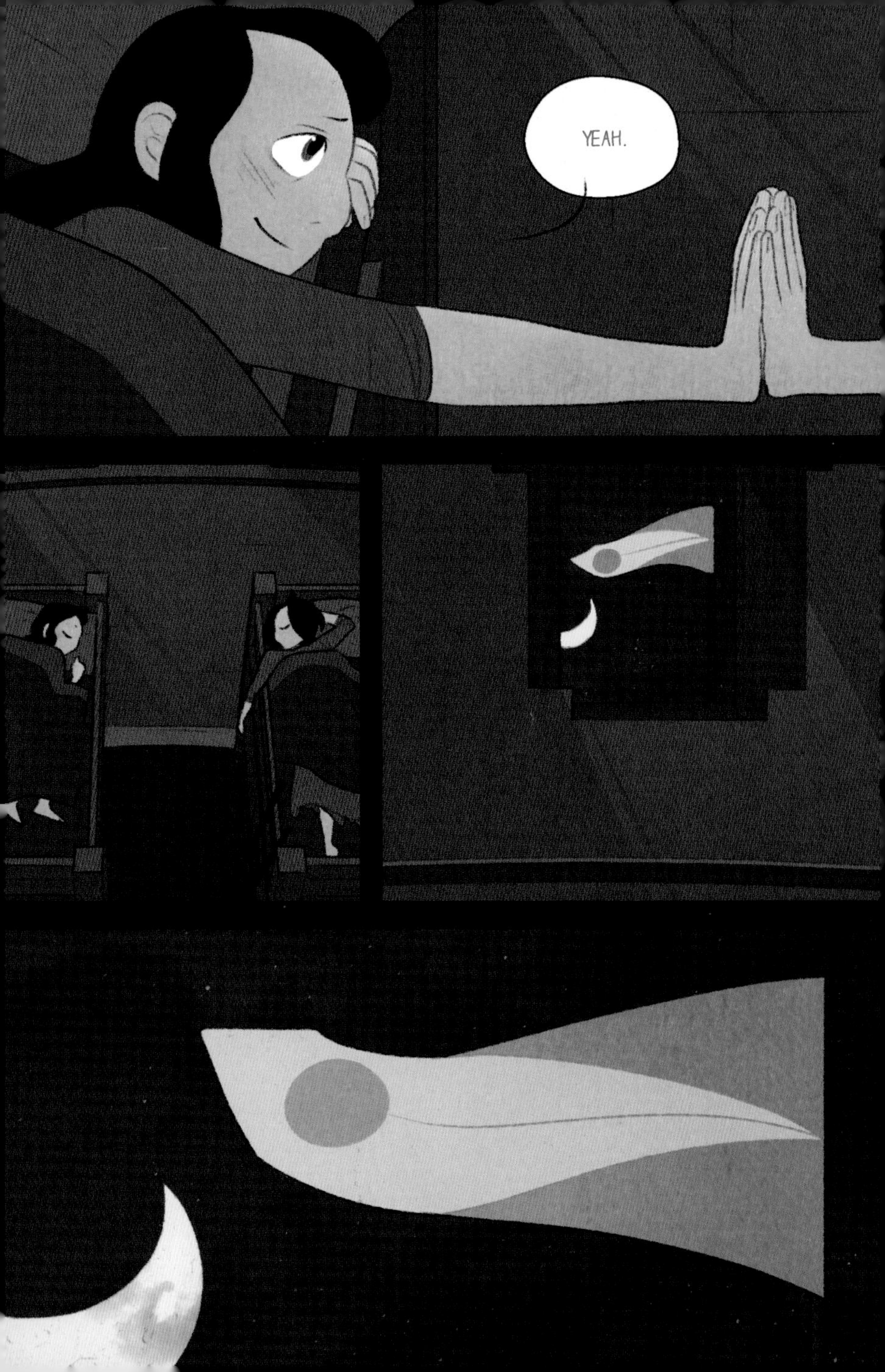
YEAH.

CHAPTER II
THE COMMUNION OF BLUE

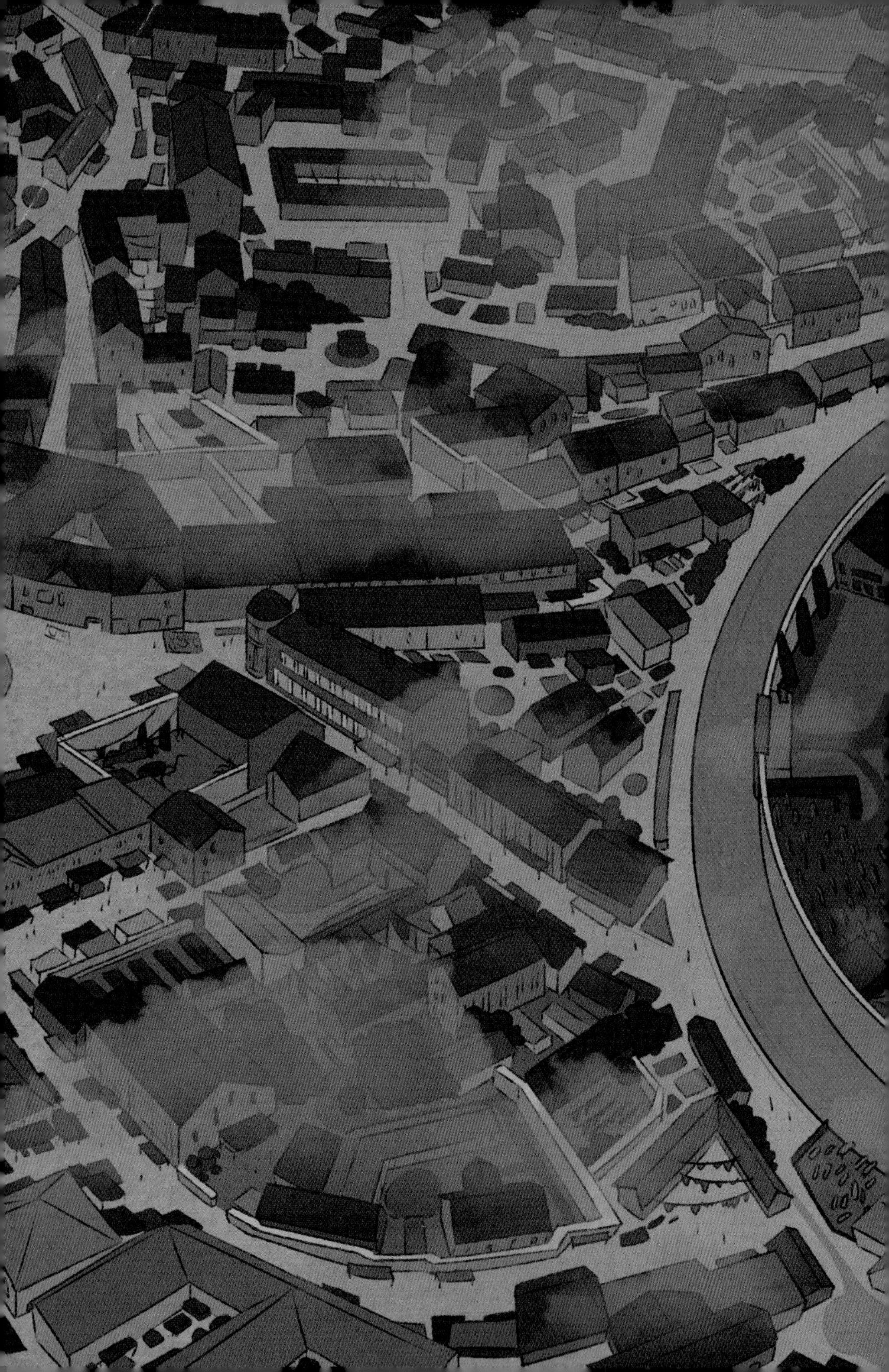

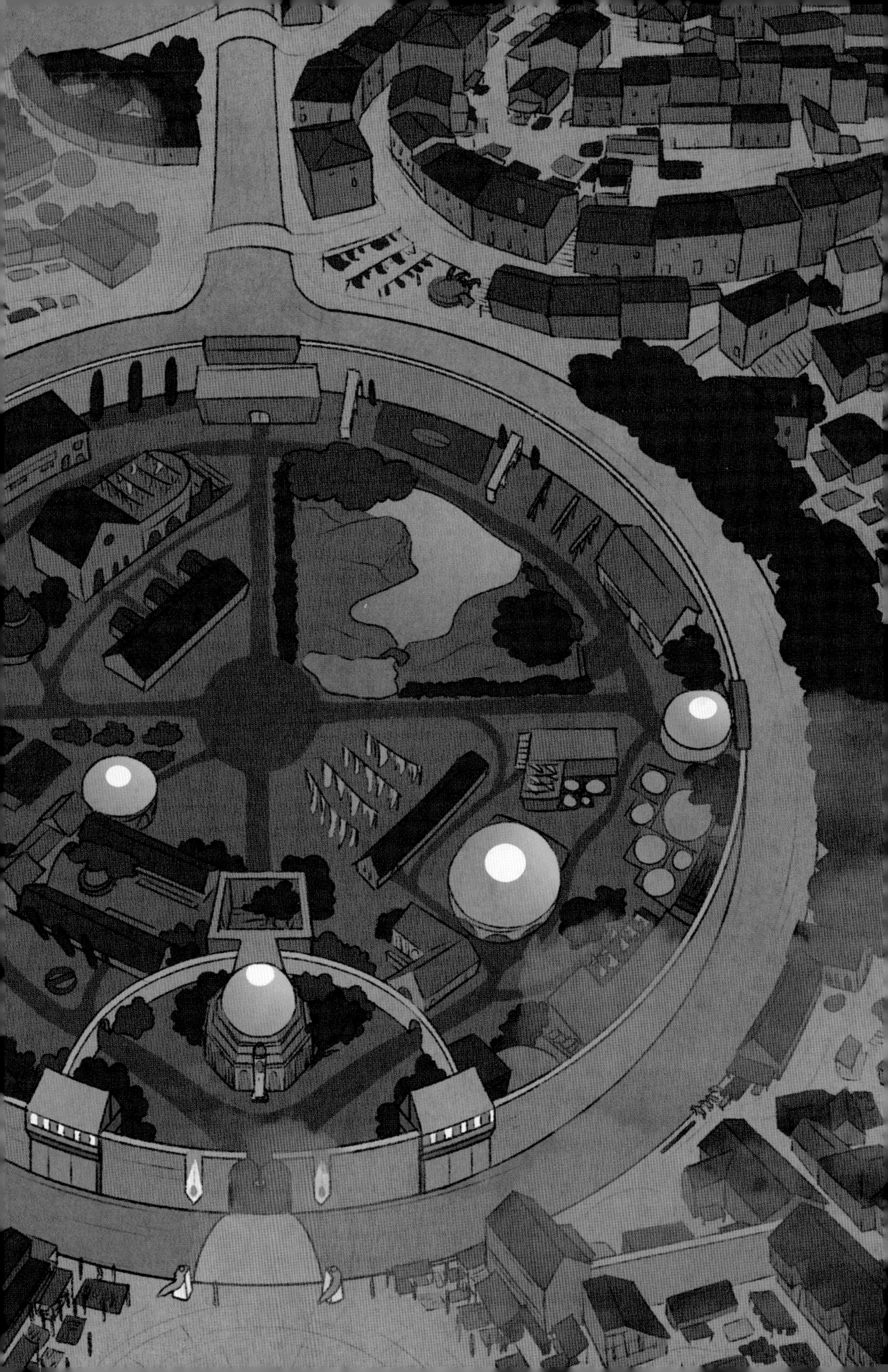

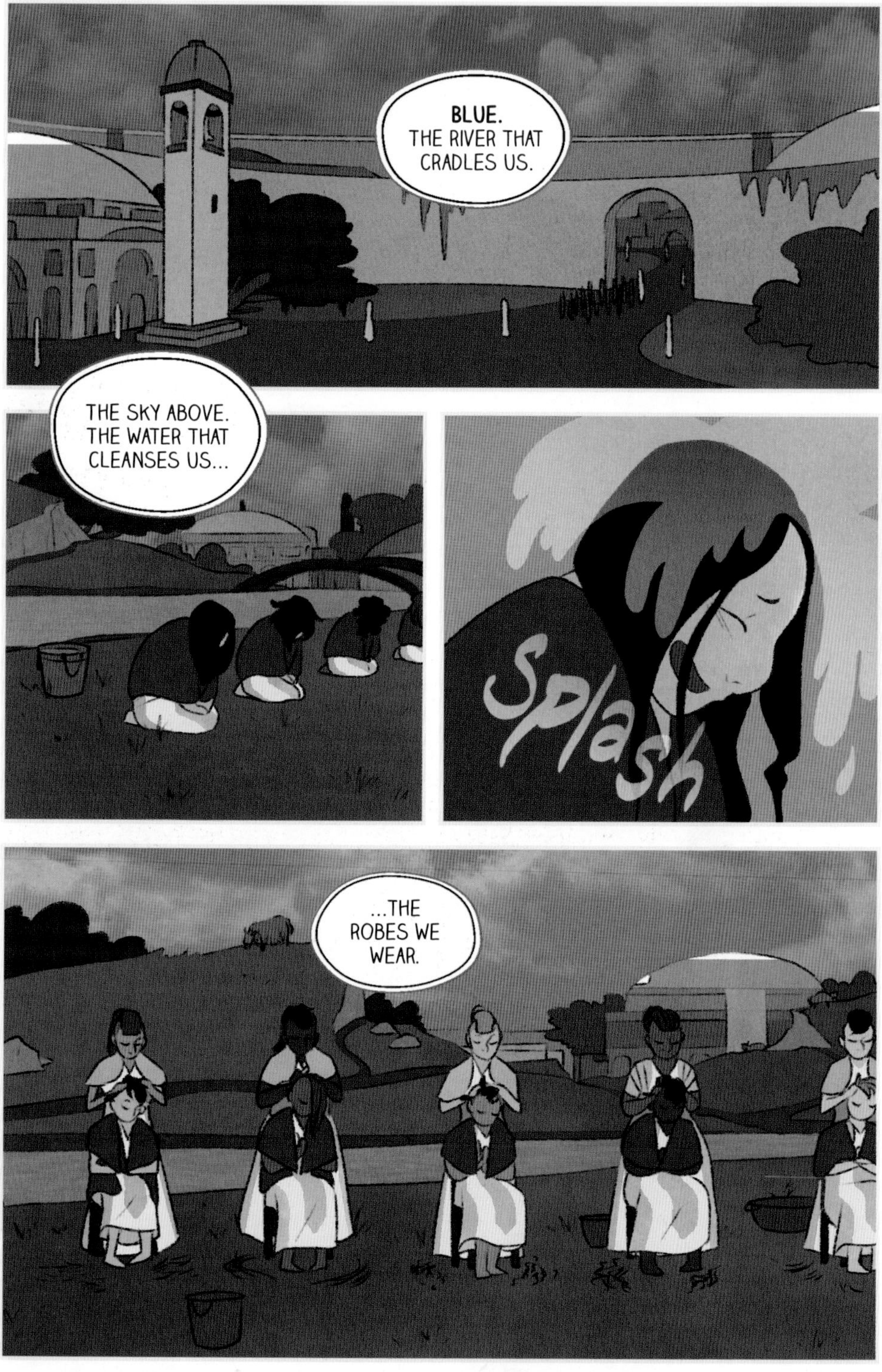
BLUE.
THE RIVER THAT CRADLES US.
THE SKY ABOVE. THE WATER THAT CLEANSES US...
splash
...THE ROBES WE WEAR.

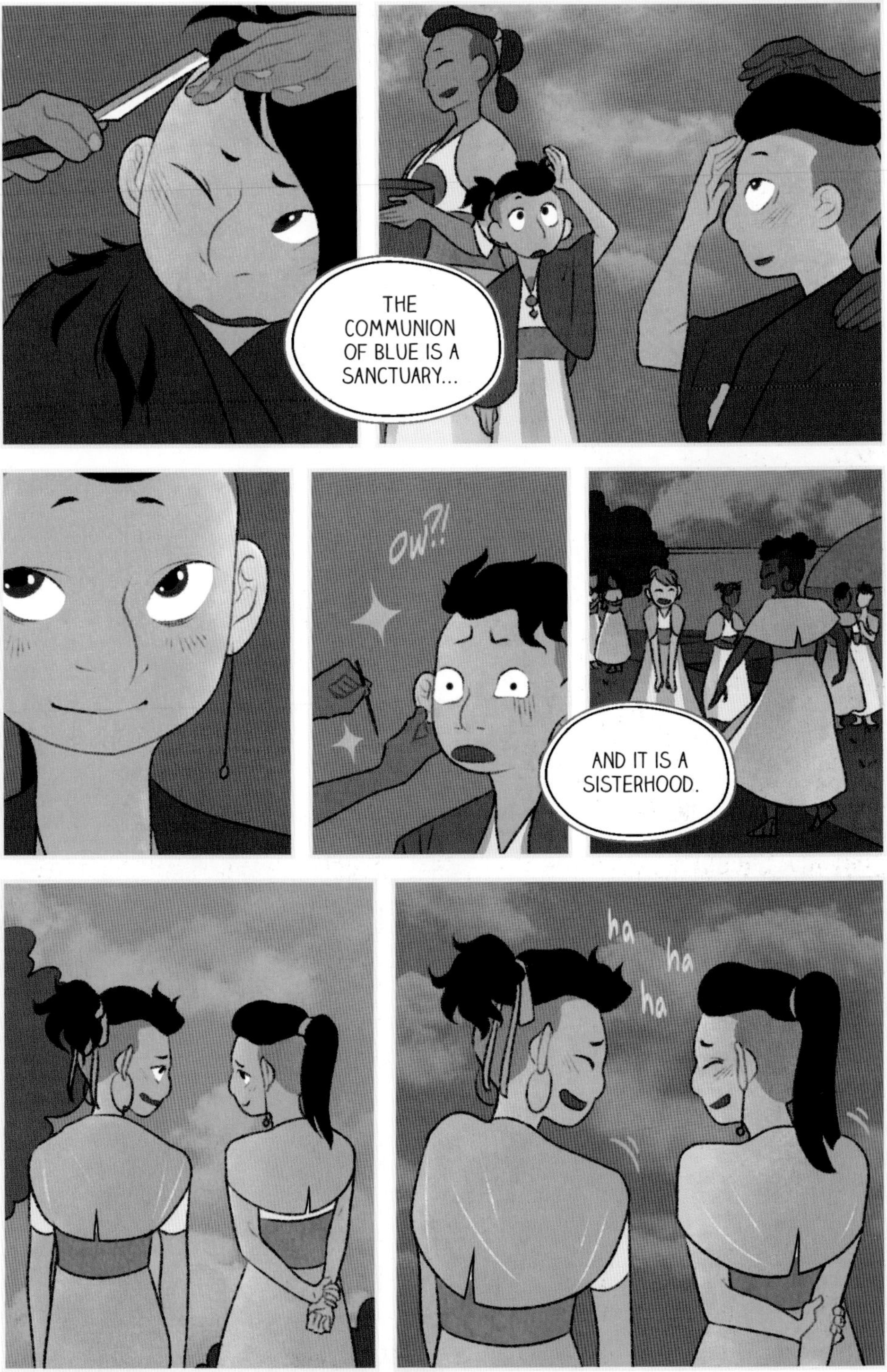
THE COMMUNION OF BLUE IS A SANCTUARY...
OW?!
AND IT IS A SISTERHOOD.
ha ha ha

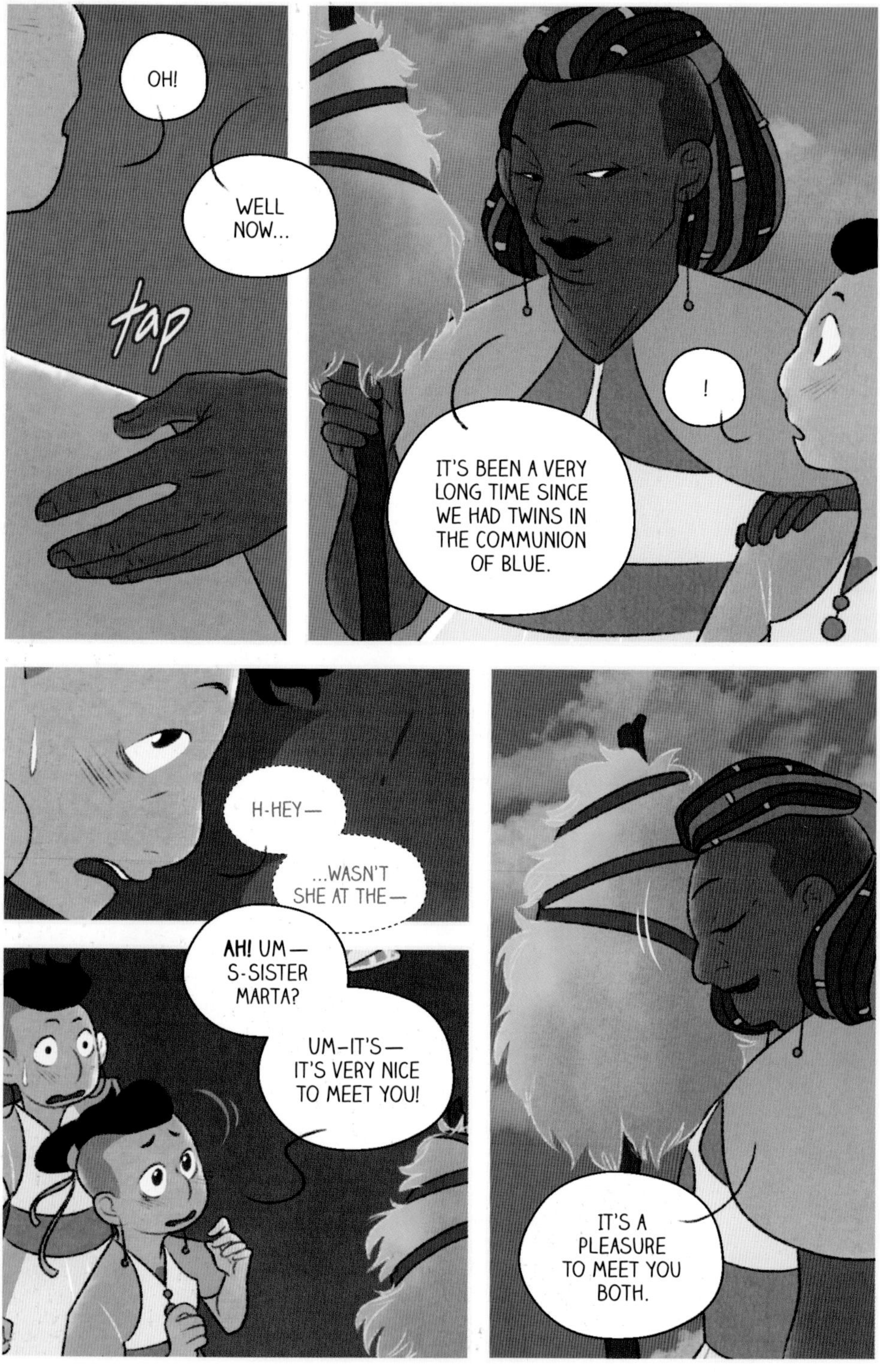
OH!
WELL NOW...
tap
IT'S BEEN A VERY LONG TIME SINCE WE HAD TWINS IN THE COMMUNION OF BLUE.
!
H-HEY—
...WASN'T SHE AT THE—
AH! UM— S-SISTER MARTA?
UM—IT'S— IT'S VERY NICE TO MEET YOU!
IT'S A PLEASURE TO MEET YOU BOTH.

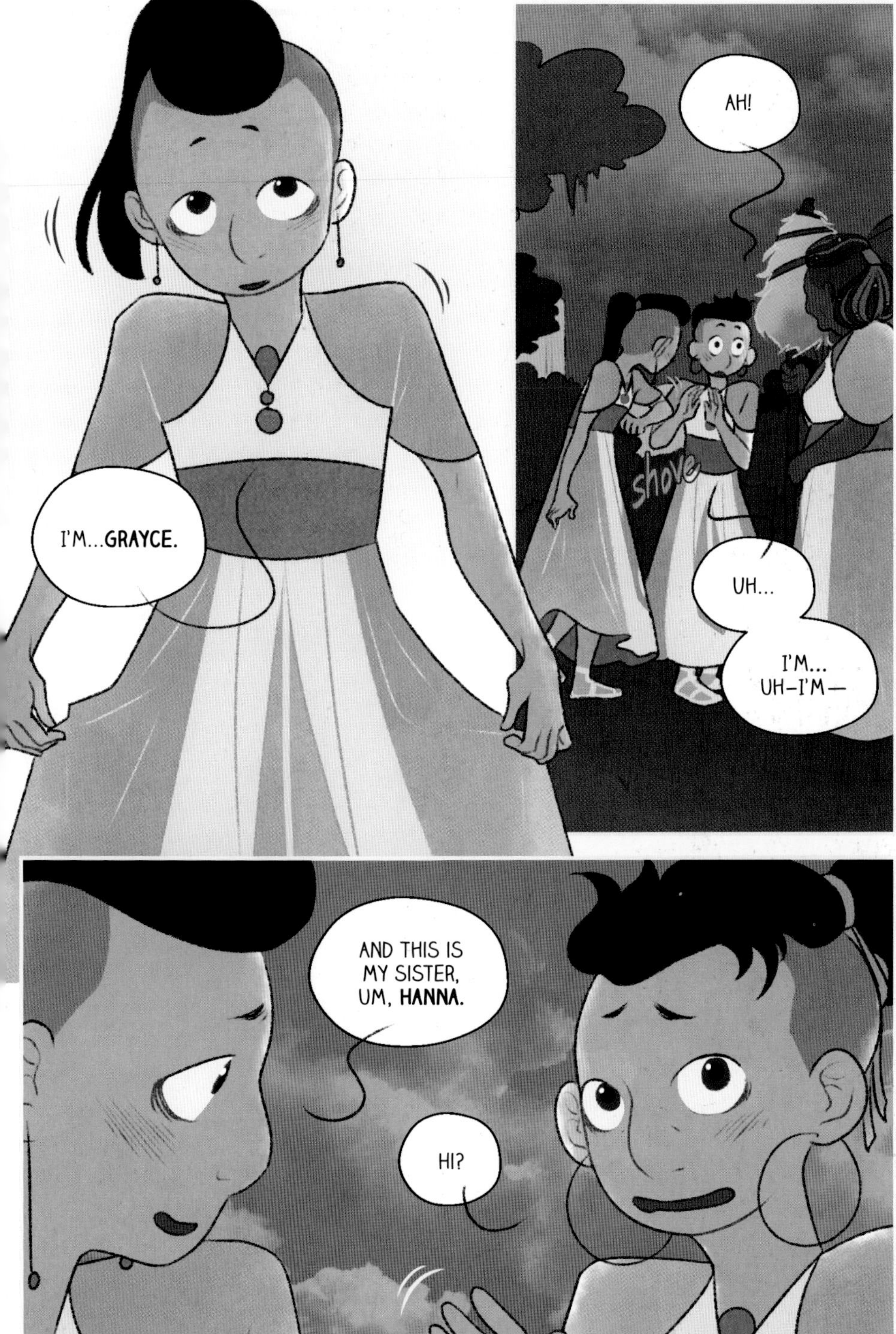
I'M...**GRAYCE.**
AH!
shove
UH...
I'M... UH–I'M—
AND THIS IS MY SISTER, UM, **HANNA.**
HI?

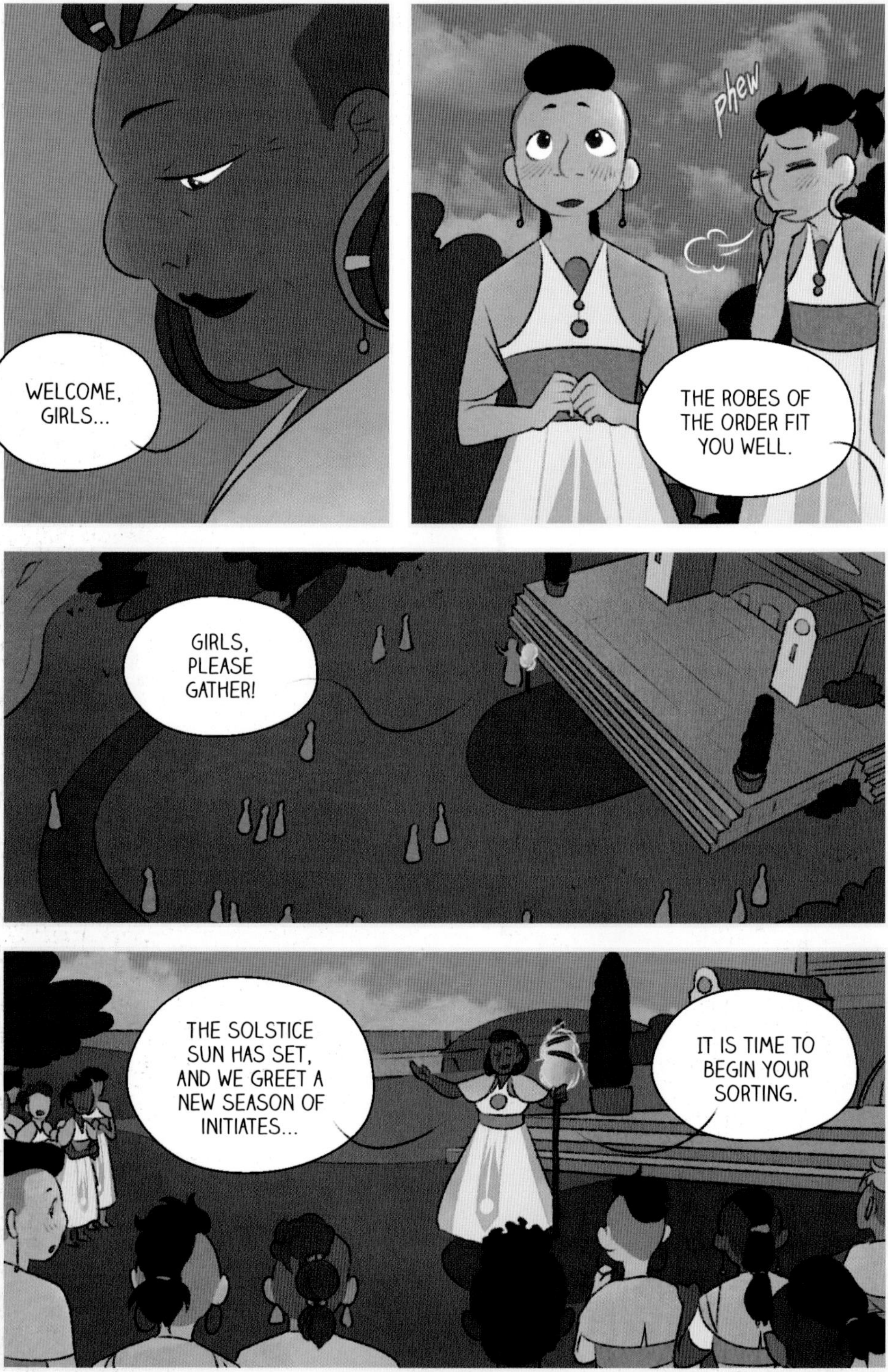
WELCOME, GIRLS...
phew
THE ROBES OF THE ORDER FIT YOU WELL.
GIRLS, PLEASE GATHER!
THE SOLSTICE SUN HAS SET, AND WE GREET A NEW SEASON OF INITIATES...
IT IS TIME TO BEGIN YOUR SORTING.

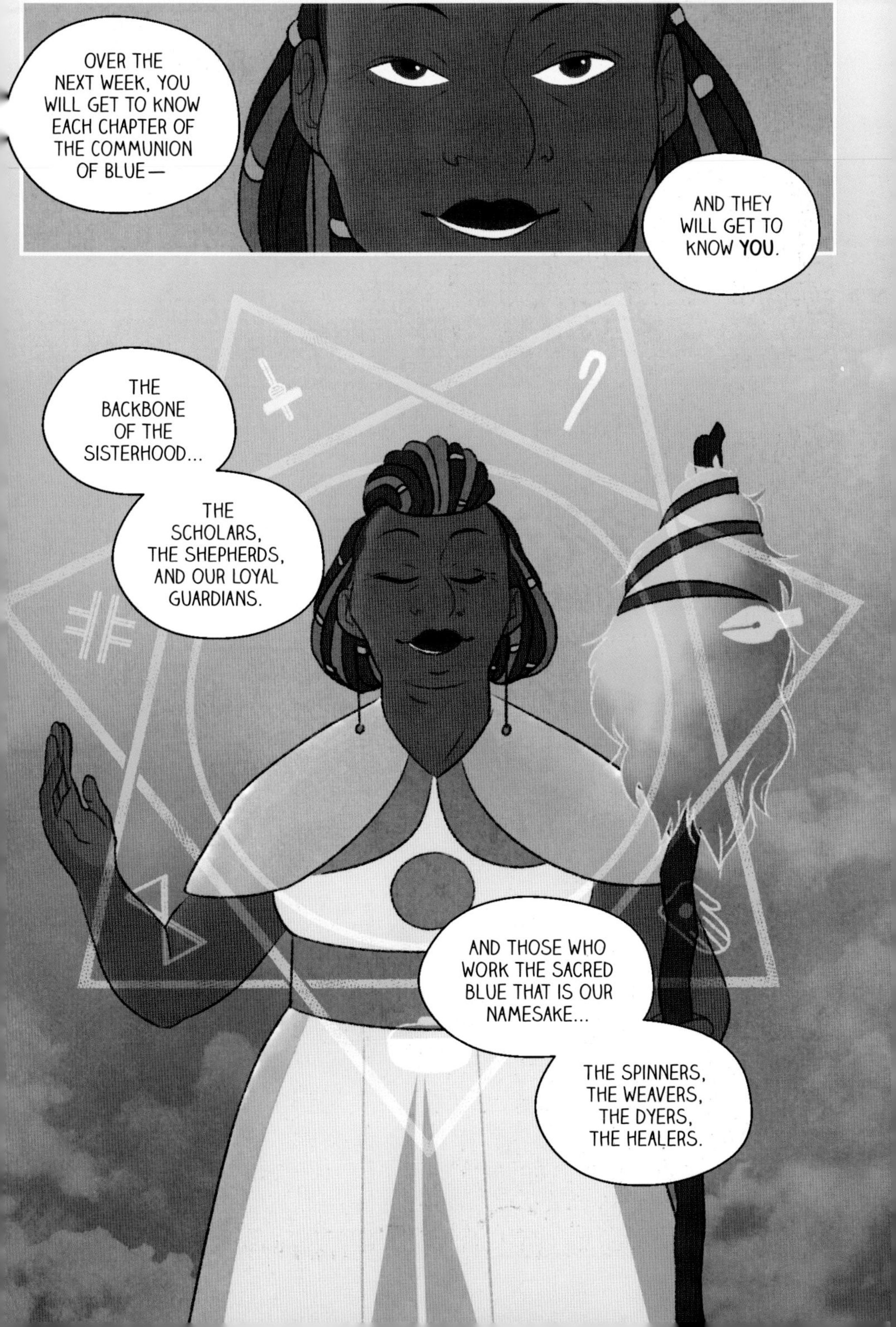
OVER THE NEXT WEEK, YOU WILL GET TO KNOW EACH CHAPTER OF THE COMMUNION OF BLUE—
AND THEY WILL GET TO KNOW **YOU**.
THE BACKBONE OF THE SISTERHOOD...
THE SCHOLARS, THE SHEPHERDS, AND OUR LOYAL GUARDIANS.
AND THOSE WHO WORK THE SACRED BLUE THAT IS OUR NAMESAKE...
THE SPINNERS, THE WEAVERS, THE DYERS, THE HEALERS.

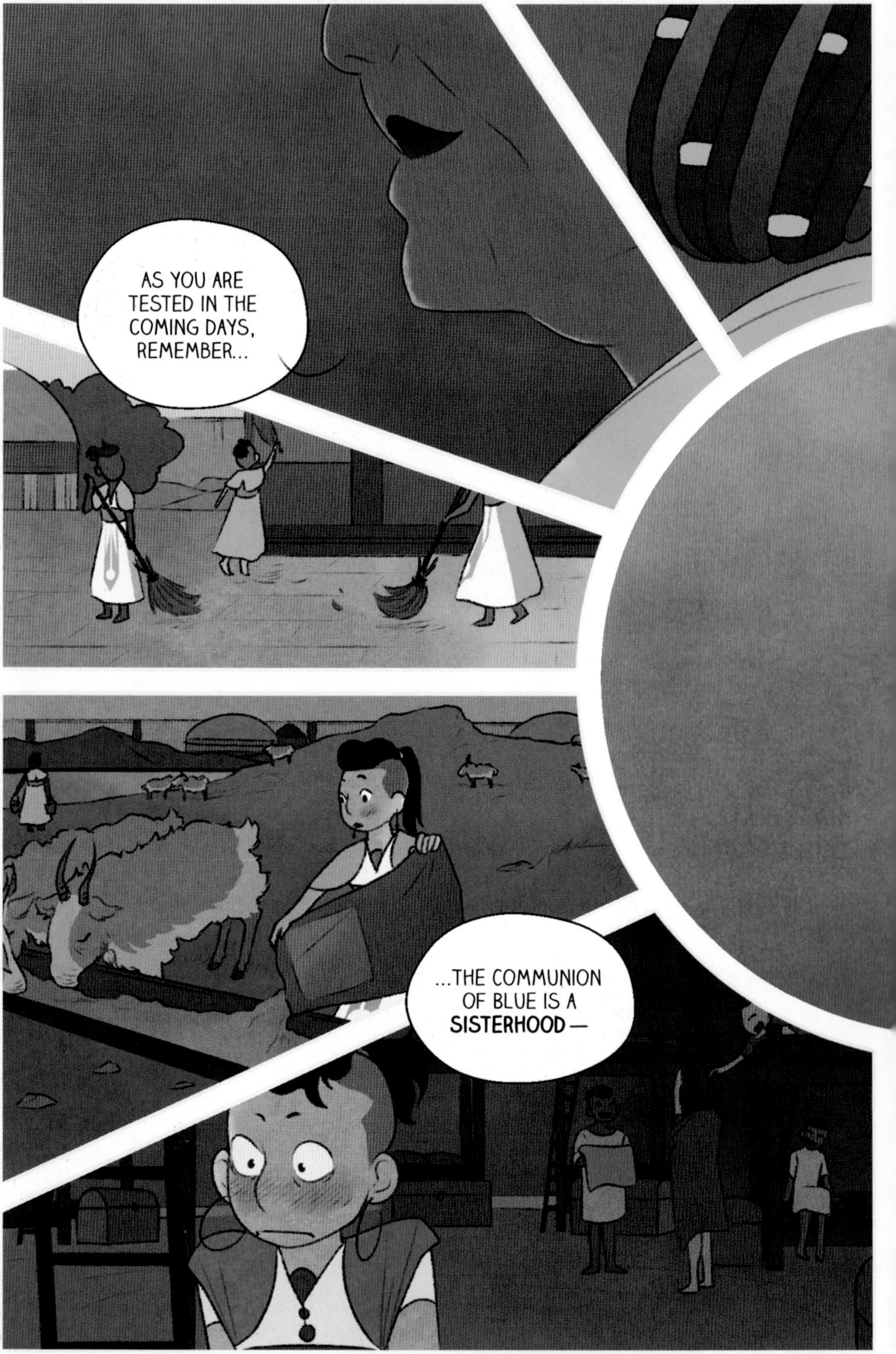
AS YOU ARE TESTED IN THE COMING DAYS, REMEMBER...
...THE COMMUNION OF BLUE IS A **SISTERHOOD**—

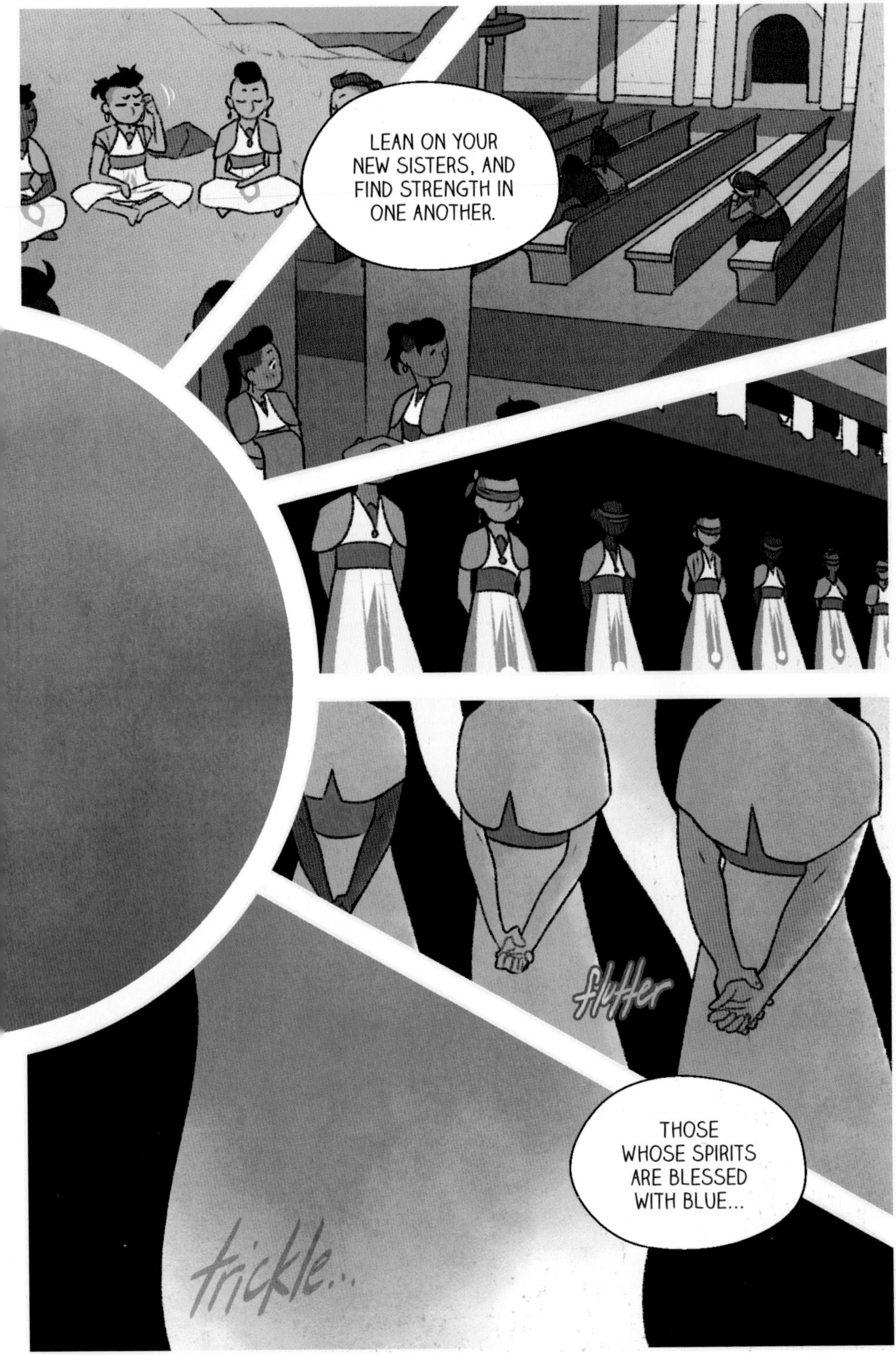
LEAN ON YOUR NEW SISTERS, AND FIND STRENGTH IN ONE ANOTHER.
flutter
THOSE WHOSE SPIRITS ARE BLESSED WITH BLUE...
trickle...

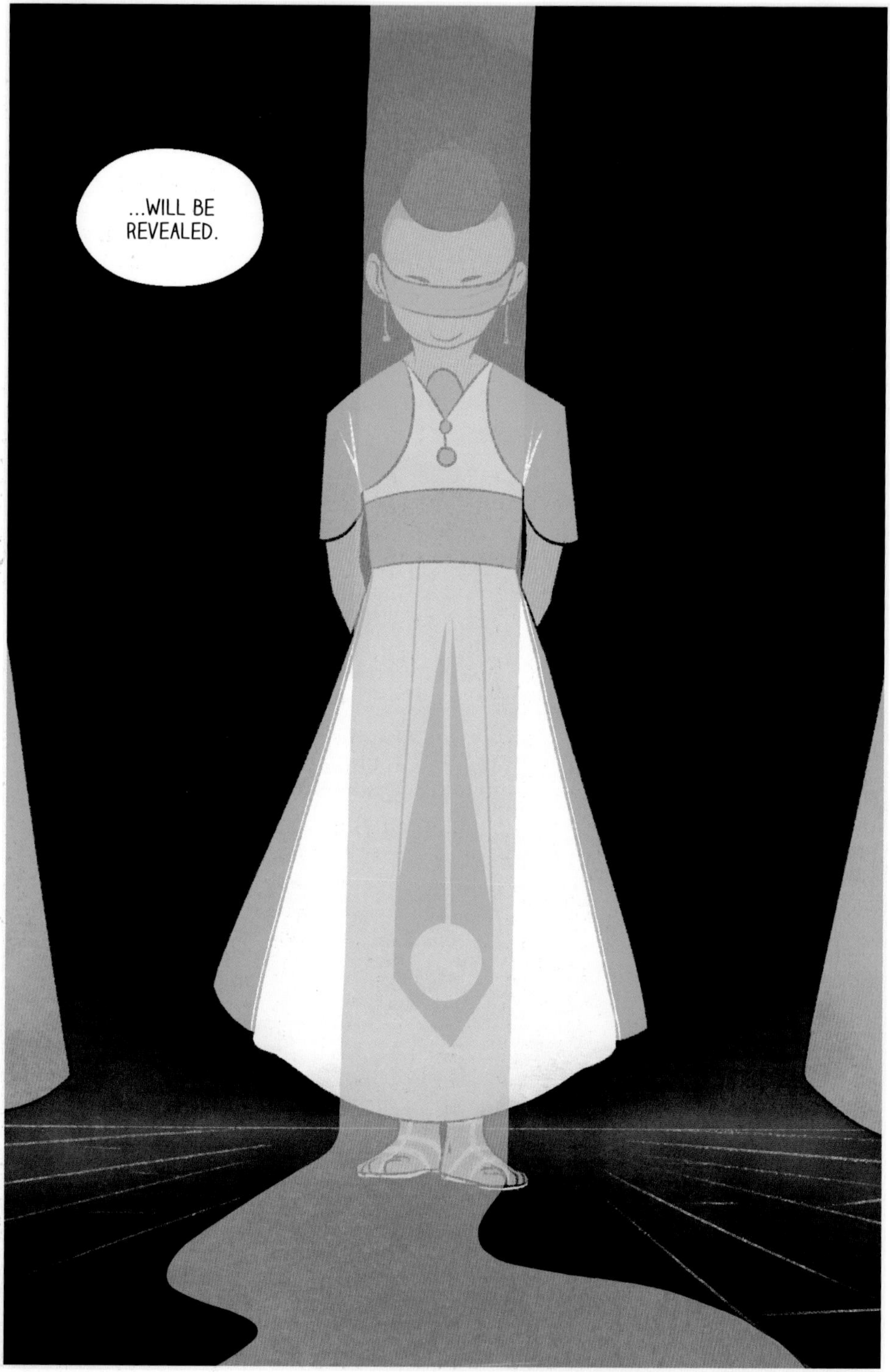
...WILL BE
REVEALED.

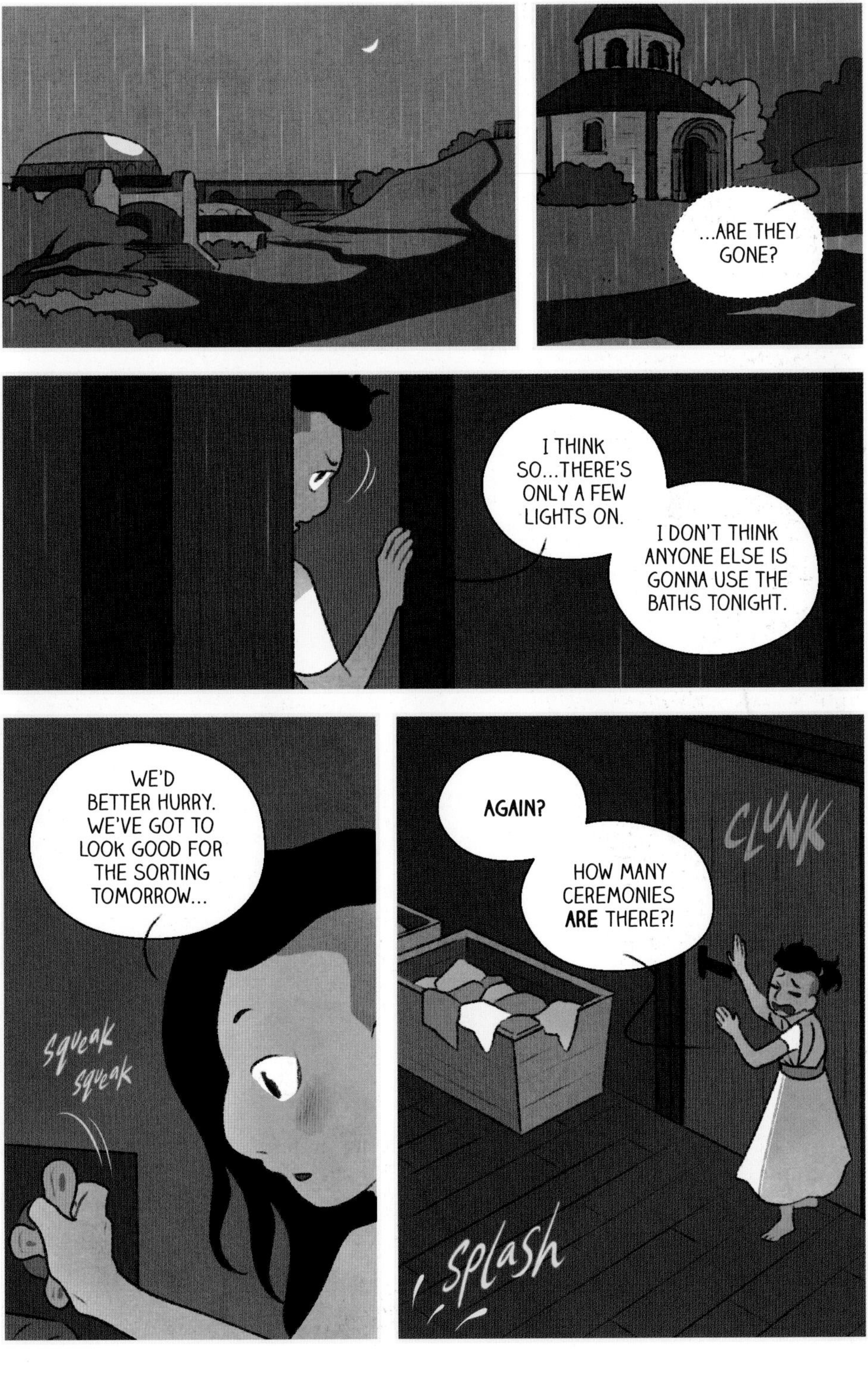
...ARE THEY GONE?
I THINK SO...THERE'S ONLY A FEW LIGHTS ON.
I DON'T THINK ANYONE ELSE IS GONNA USE THE BATHS TONIGHT.
WE'D BETTER HURRY. WE'VE GOT TO LOOK GOOD FOR THE SORTING TOMORROW...
squeak squeak
AGAIN?
HOW MANY CEREMONIES ARE THERE?!
CLUNK
SPLASH

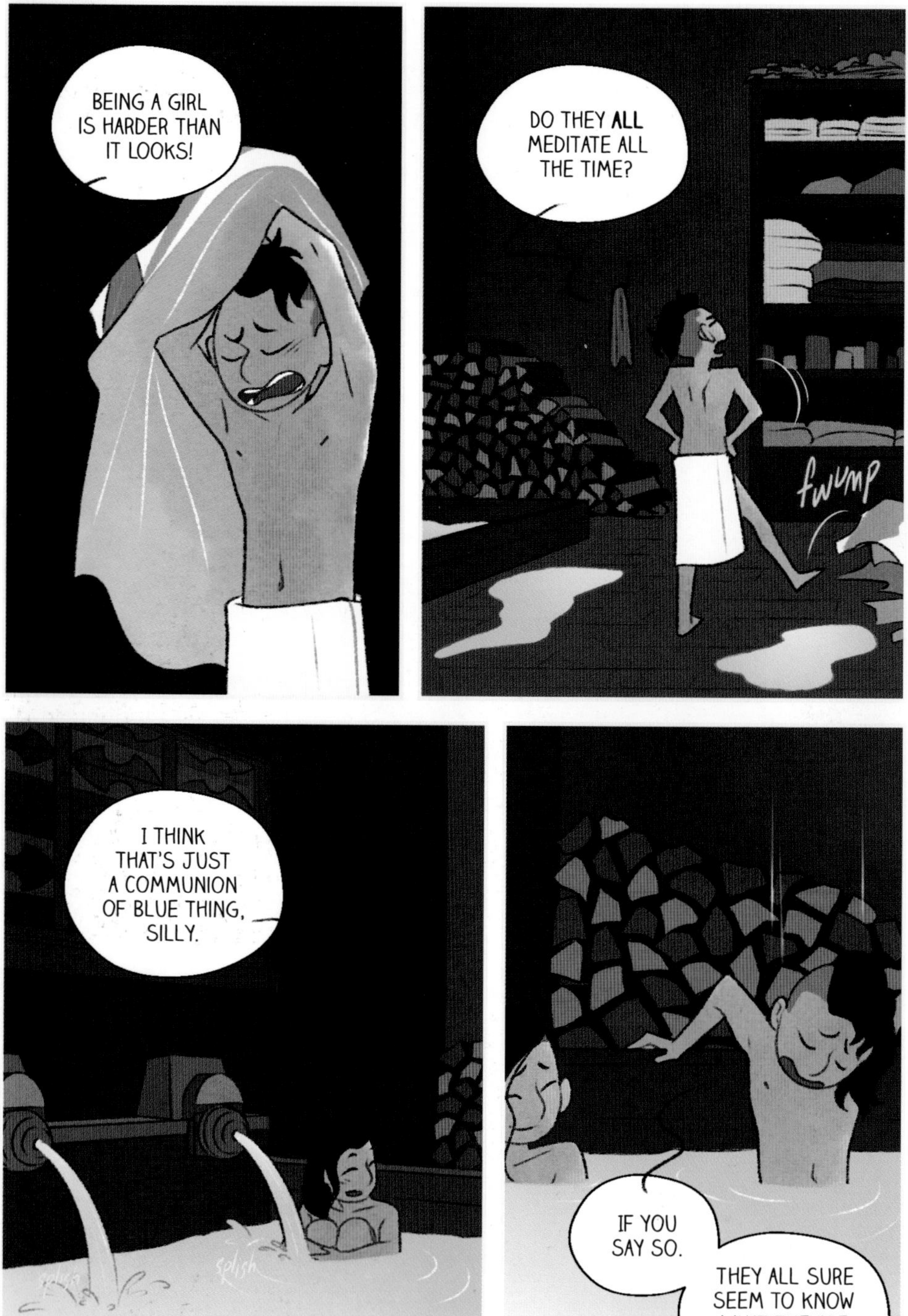
BEING A GIRL IS HARDER THAN IT LOOKS!
DO THEY **ALL** MEDITATE ALL THE TIME?
fwump
I THINK THAT'S JUST A COMMUNION OF BLUE THING, SILLY.
splish
IF YOU SAY SO.
THEY ALL SURE SEEM TO KNOW WHAT THEY'RE DOING.

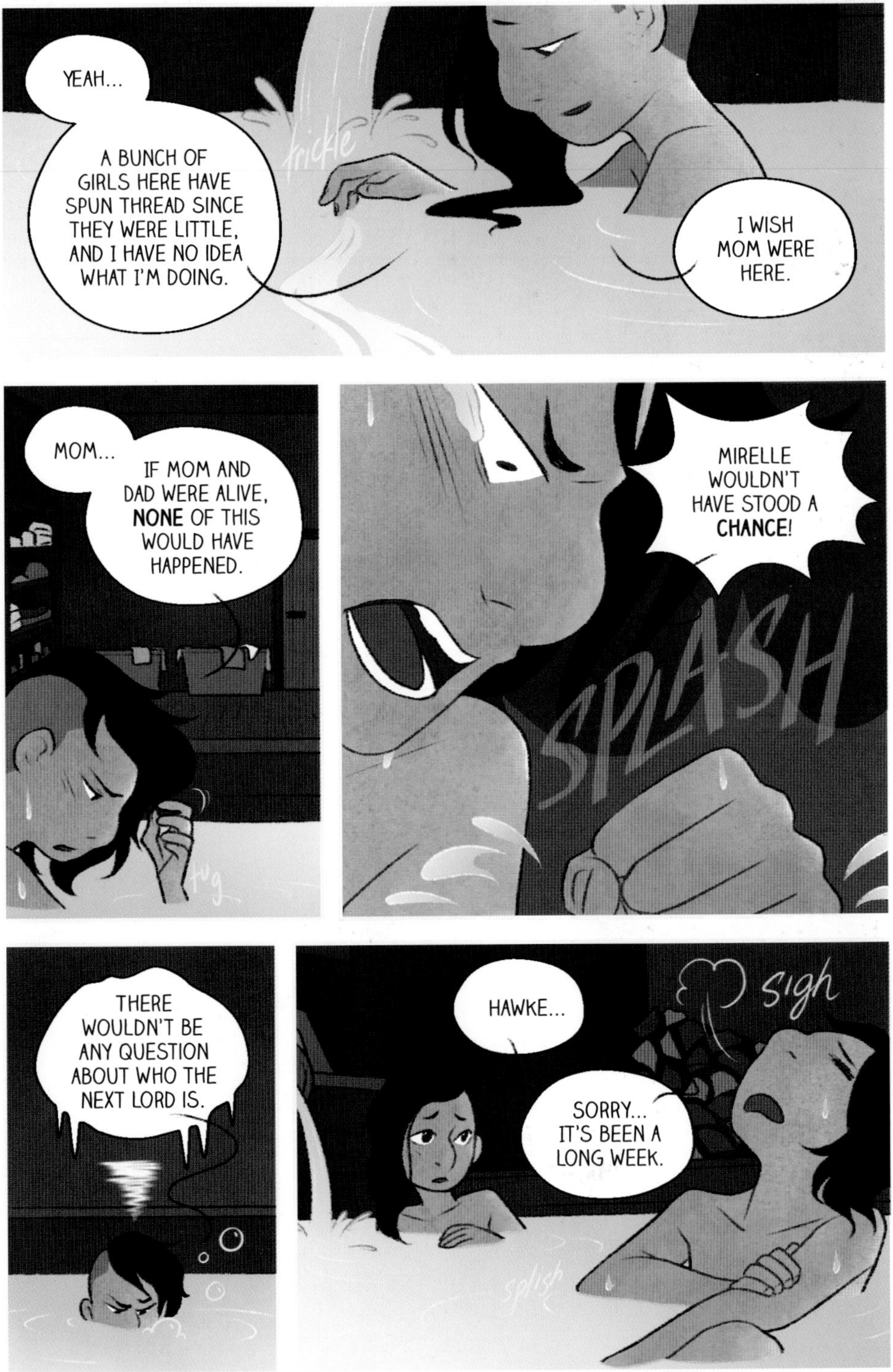
YEAH...
A BUNCH OF GIRLS HERE HAVE SPUN THREAD SINCE THEY WERE LITTLE, AND I HAVE NO IDEA WHAT I'M DOING.
trickle
I WISH MOM WERE HERE.
MOM...
IF MOM AND DAD WERE ALIVE, **NONE** OF THIS WOULD HAVE HAPPENED.
tug
MIRELLE WOULDN'T HAVE STOOD A **CHANCE**!
SPLASH
THERE WOULDN'T BE ANY QUESTION ABOUT WHO THE NEXT LORD IS.
HAWKE...
sigh
SORRY... IT'S BEEN A LONG WEEK.
splish

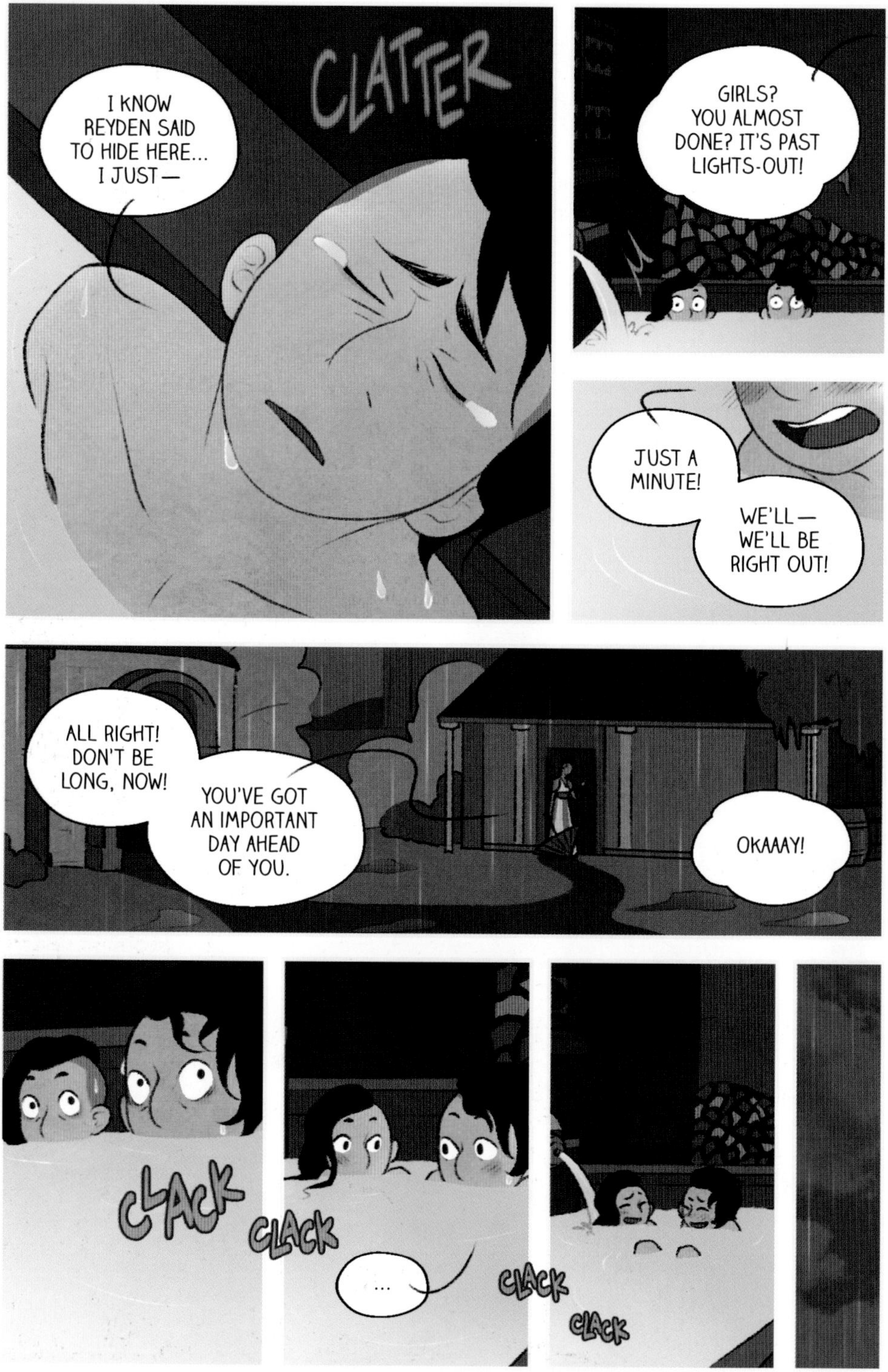
CLATTER
I KNOW REYDEN SAID TO HIDE HERE... I JUST—
GIRLS? YOU ALMOST DONE? IT'S PAST LIGHTS-OUT!
JUST A MINUTE!
WE'LL— WE'LL BE RIGHT OUT!
ALL RIGHT! DON'T BE LONG, NOW!
YOU'VE GOT AN IMPORTANT DAY AHEAD OF YOU.
OKAAAY!
CLACK
CLACK
...
CLACK
CLACK

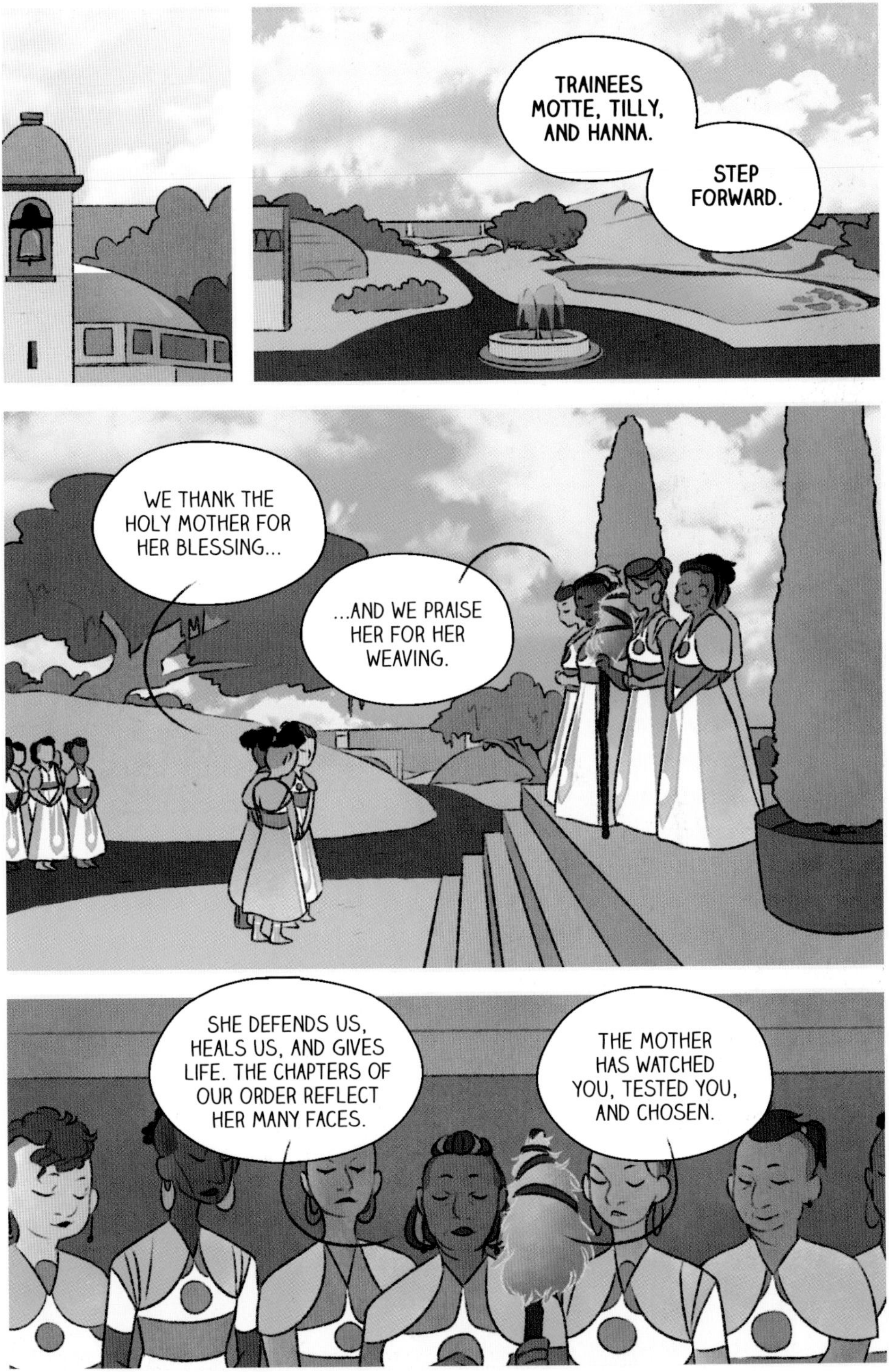
TRAINEES MOTTE, TILLY, AND HANNA.
STEP FORWARD.
WE THANK THE HOLY MOTHER FOR HER BLESSING...
...AND WE PRAISE HER FOR HER WEAVING.
SHE DEFENDS US, HEALS US, AND GIVES LIFE. THE CHAPTERS OF OUR ORDER REFLECT HER MANY FACES.
THE MOTHER HAS WATCHED YOU, TESTED YOU, AND CHOSEN.

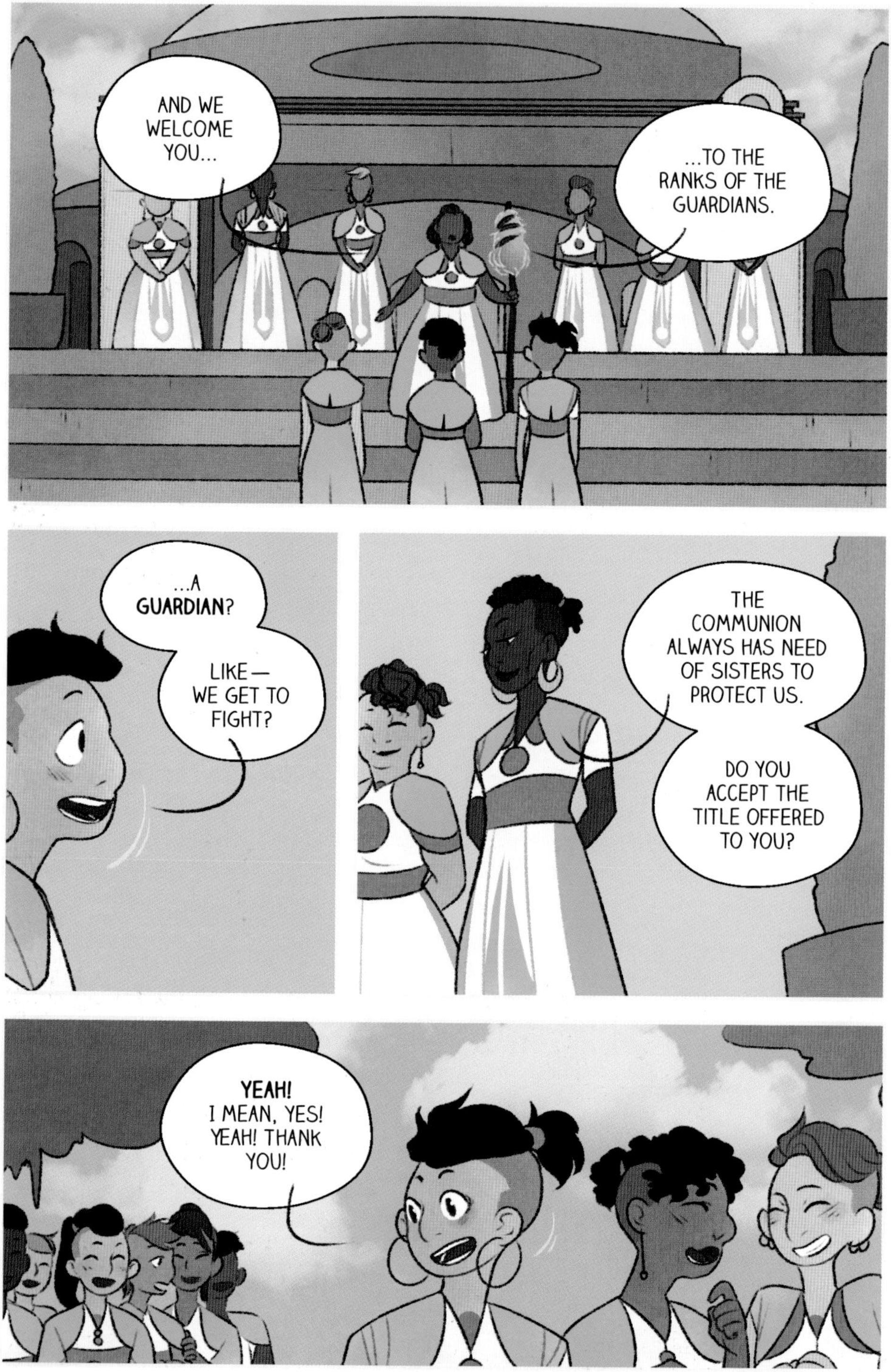
AND WE WELCOME YOU...
...TO THE RANKS OF THE GUARDIANS.
...A GUARDIAN?
LIKE— WE GET TO FIGHT?
THE COMMUNION ALWAYS HAS NEED OF SISTERS TO PROTECT US.
DO YOU ACCEPT THE TITLE OFFERED TO YOU?
YEAH! I MEAN, YES! YEAH! THANK YOU!

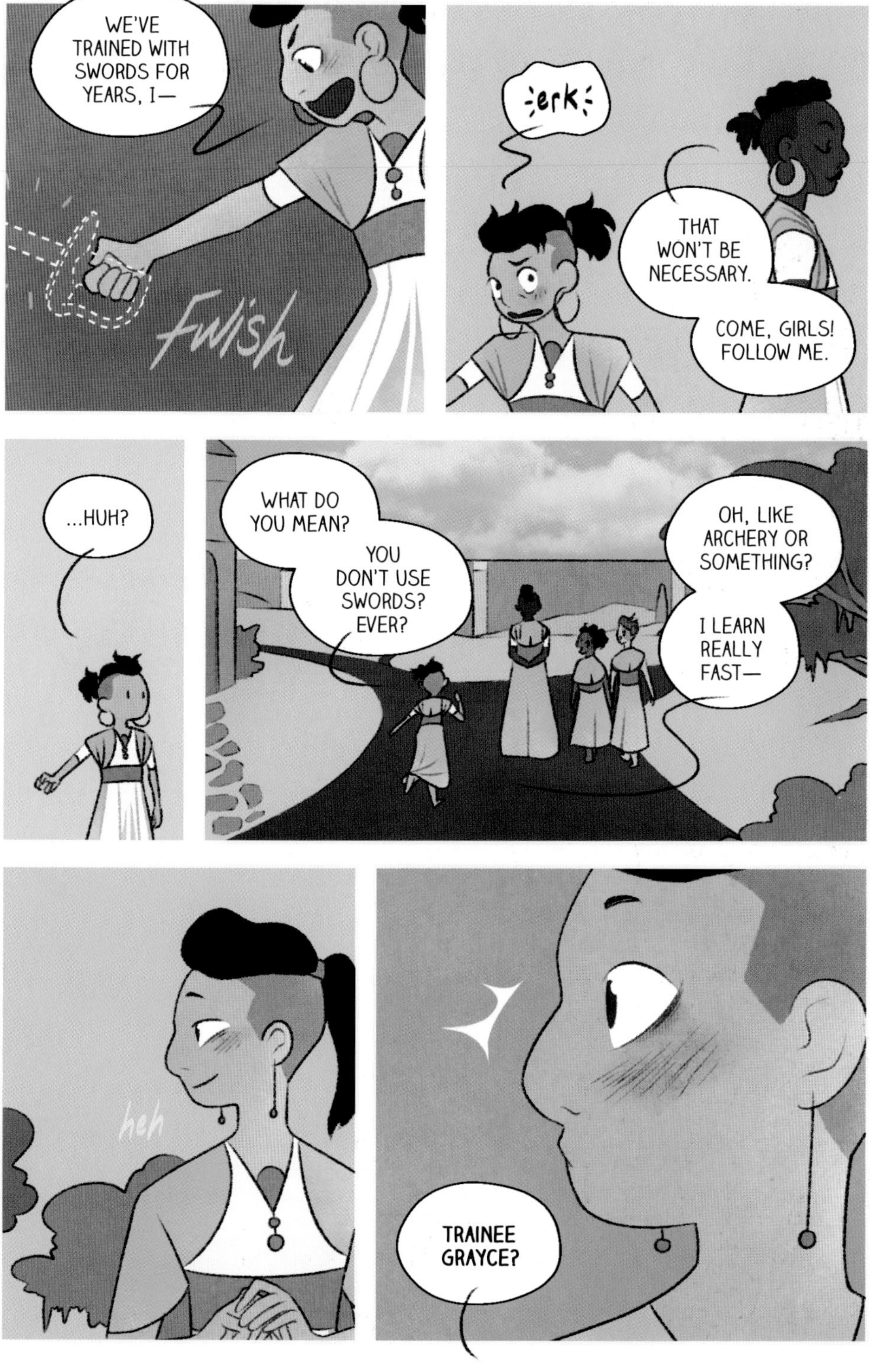
WE'VE TRAINED WITH SWORDS FOR YEARS, I—
fwish
erk
THAT WON'T BE NECESSARY.
COME, GIRLS! FOLLOW ME.
...HUH?
WHAT DO YOU MEAN?
YOU DON'T USE SWORDS? EVER?
OH, LIKE ARCHERY OR SOMETHING?
I LEARN REALLY FAST—
heh
TRAINEE GRAYCE?

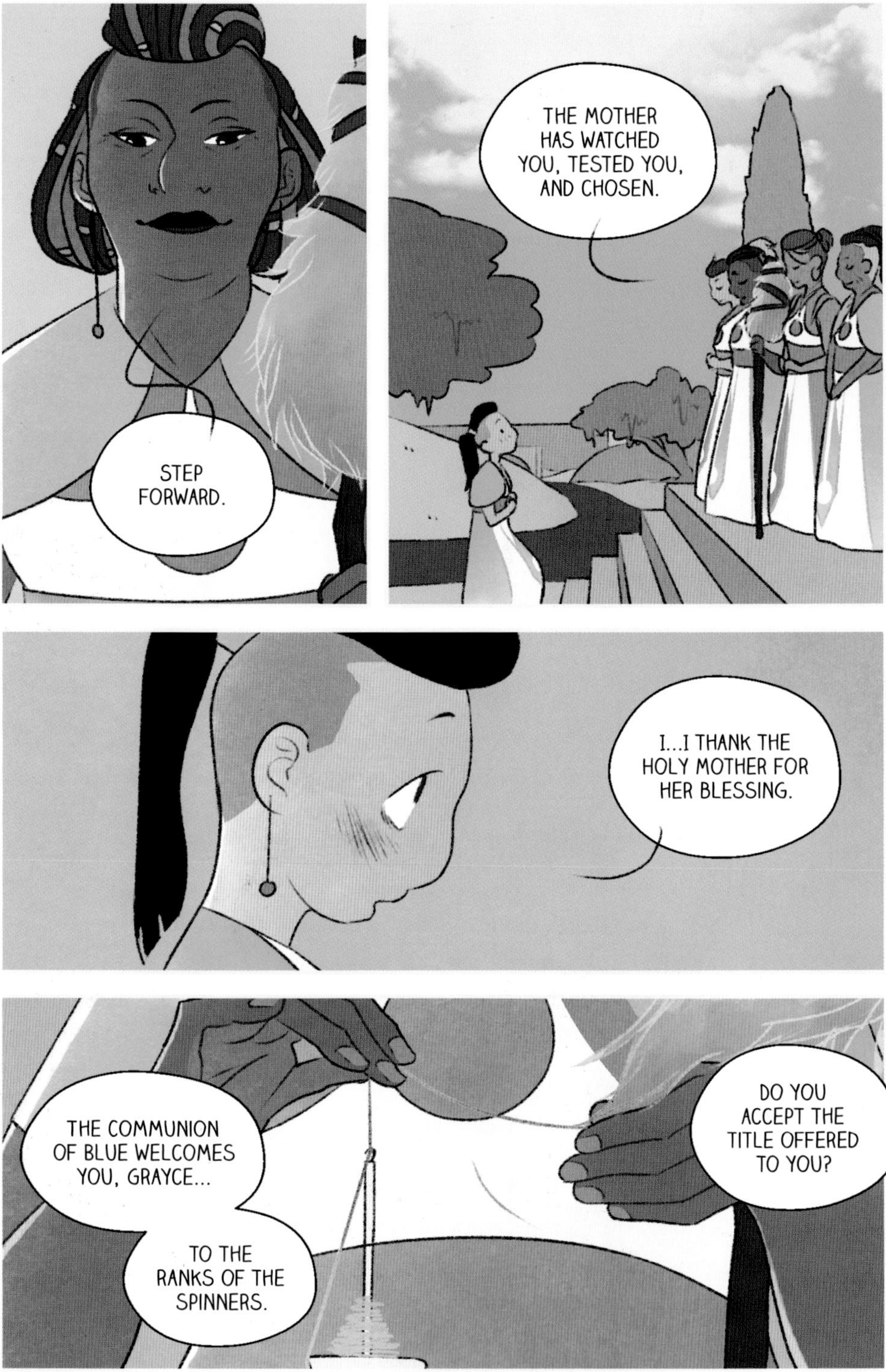
STEP FORWARD.
THE MOTHER HAS WATCHED YOU, TESTED YOU, AND CHOSEN.
I...I THANK THE HOLY MOTHER FOR HER BLESSING.
THE COMMUNION OF BLUE WELCOMES YOU, GRAYCE...
TO THE RANKS OF THE SPINNERS.
DO YOU ACCEPT THE TITLE OFFERED TO YOU?

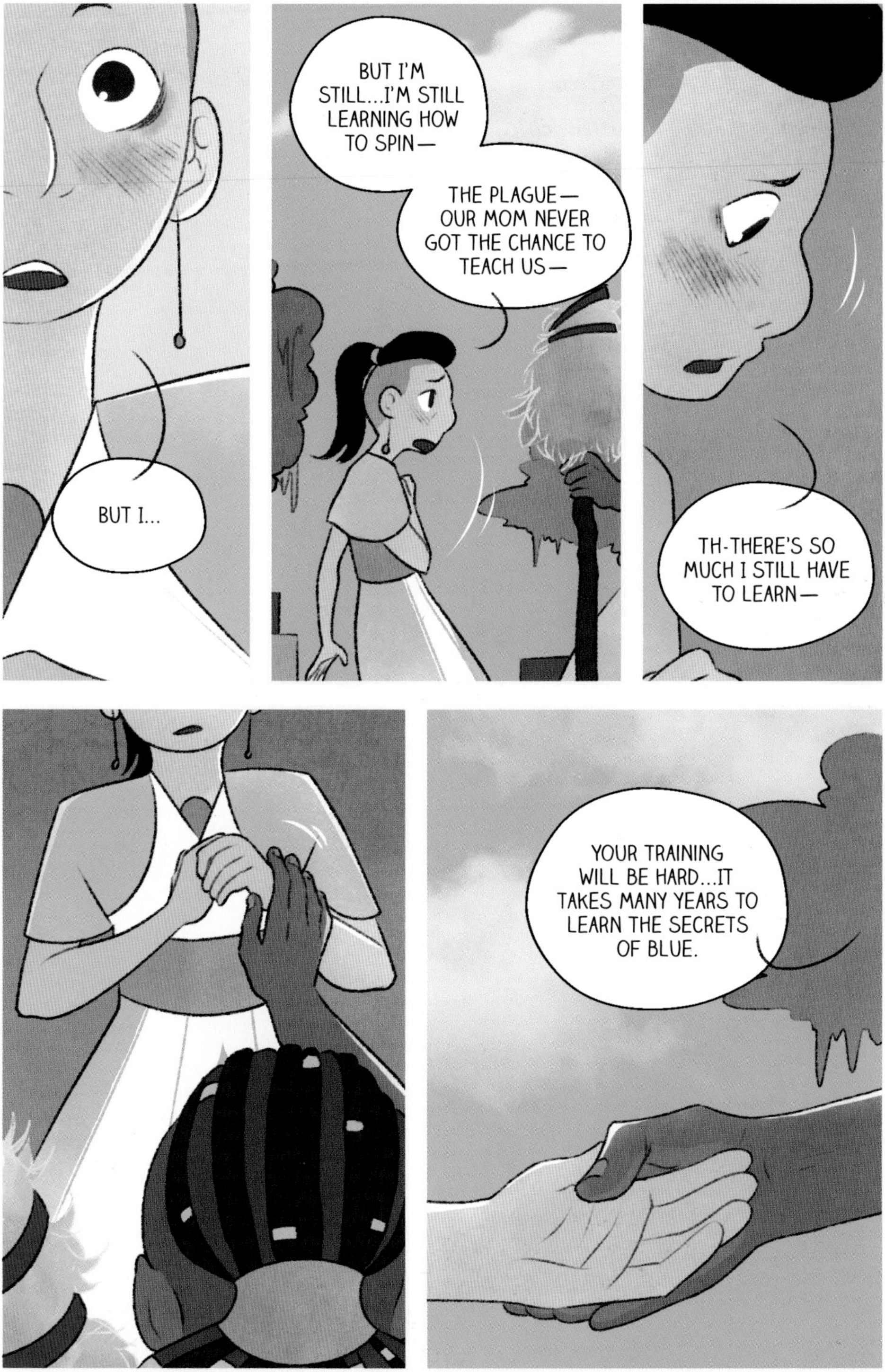
BUT I...
BUT I'M STILL...I'M STILL LEARNING HOW TO SPIN—
THE PLAGUE— OUR MOM NEVER GOT THE CHANCE TO TEACH US—
TH-THERE'S SO MUCH I STILL HAVE TO LEARN—
YOUR TRAINING WILL BE HARD...IT TAKES MANY YEARS TO LEARN THE SECRETS OF BLUE.

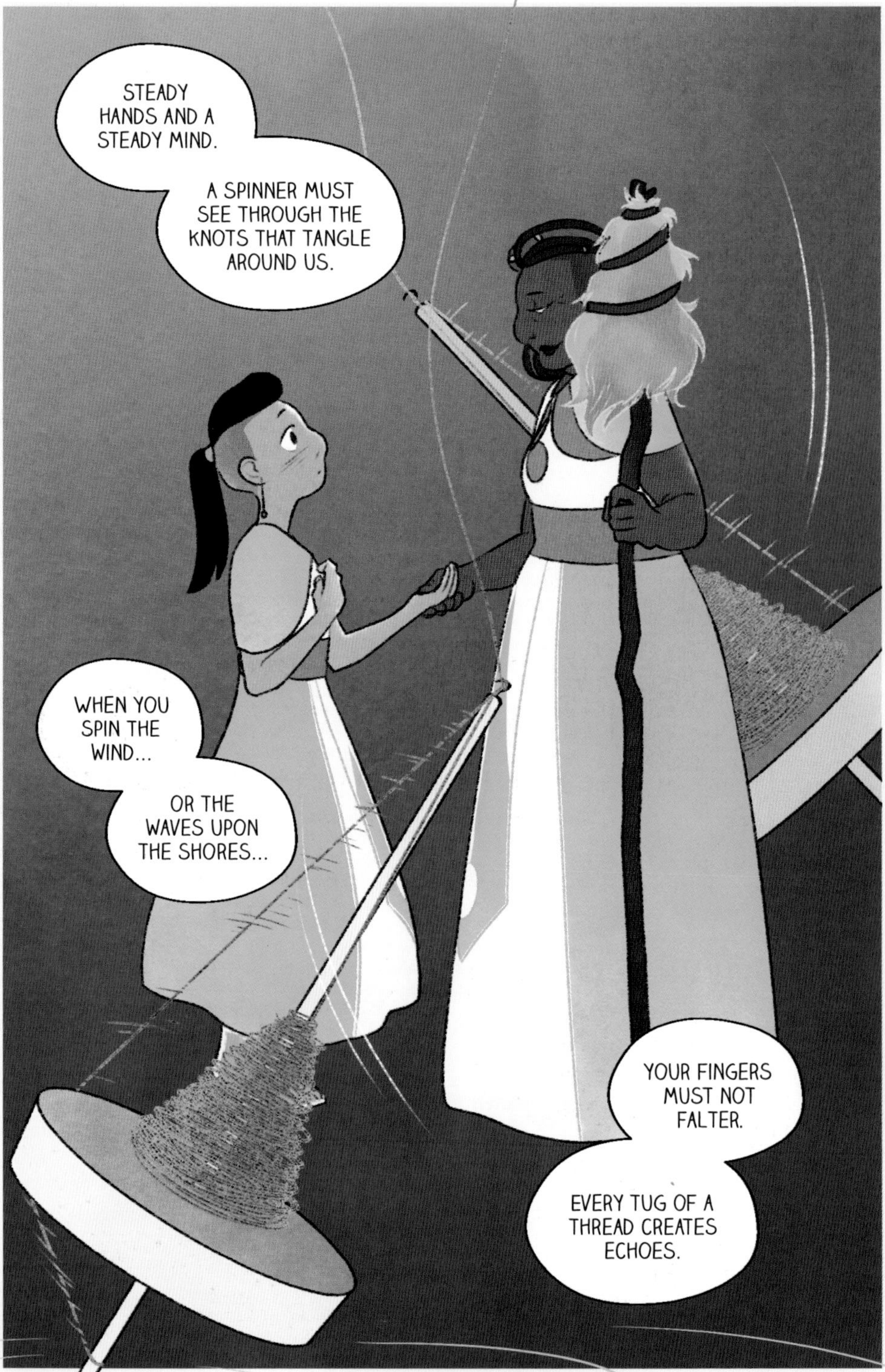
STEADY HANDS AND A STEADY MIND.
A SPINNER MUST SEE THROUGH THE KNOTS THAT TANGLE AROUND US.
WHEN YOU SPIN THE WIND...
OR THE WAVES UPON THE SHORES...
YOUR FINGERS MUST NOT FALTER.
EVERY TUG OF A THREAD CREATES ECHOES.

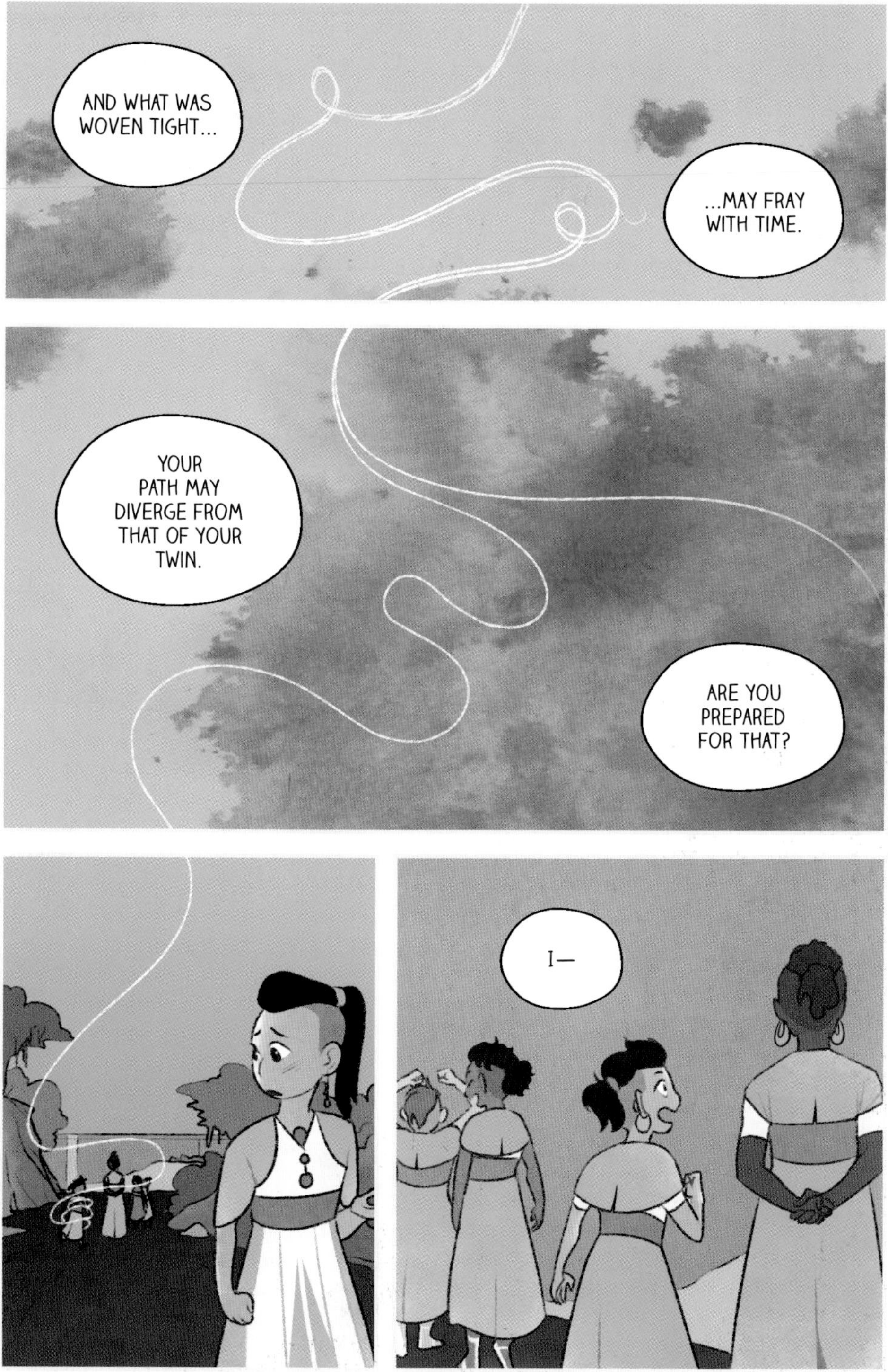
AND WHAT WAS WOVEN TIGHT...
...MAY FRAY WITH TIME.
YOUR PATH MAY DIVERGE FROM THAT OF YOUR TWIN.
ARE YOU PREPARED FOR THAT?
I—

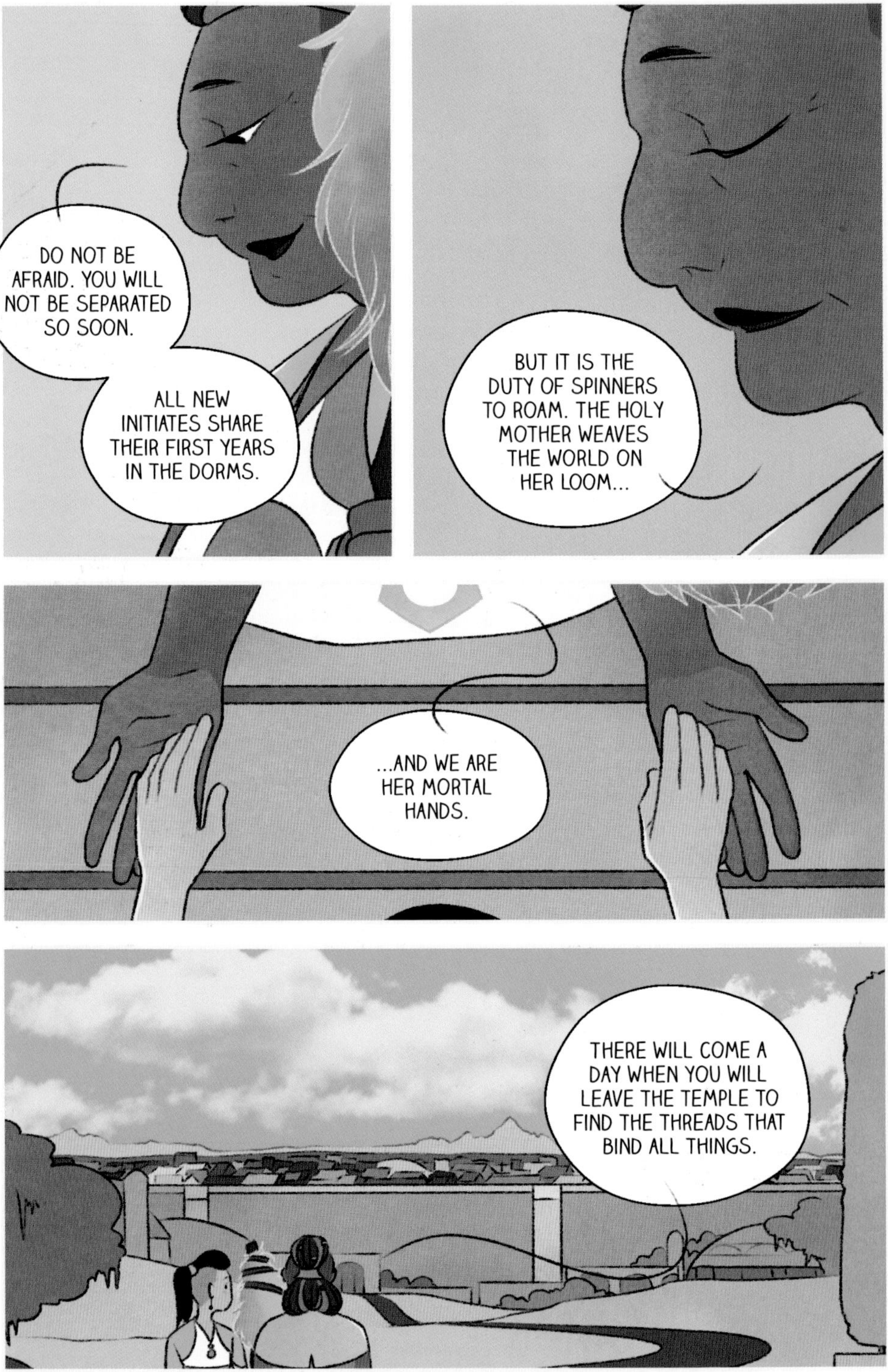
DO NOT BE AFRAID. YOU WILL NOT BE SEPARATED SO SOON.
ALL NEW INITIATES SHARE THEIR FIRST YEARS IN THE DORMS.
BUT IT IS THE DUTY OF SPINNERS TO ROAM. THE HOLY MOTHER WEAVES THE WORLD ON HER LOOM...
...AND WE ARE HER MORTAL HANDS.
THERE WILL COME A DAY WHEN YOU WILL LEAVE THE TEMPLE TO FIND THE THREADS THAT BIND ALL THINGS.

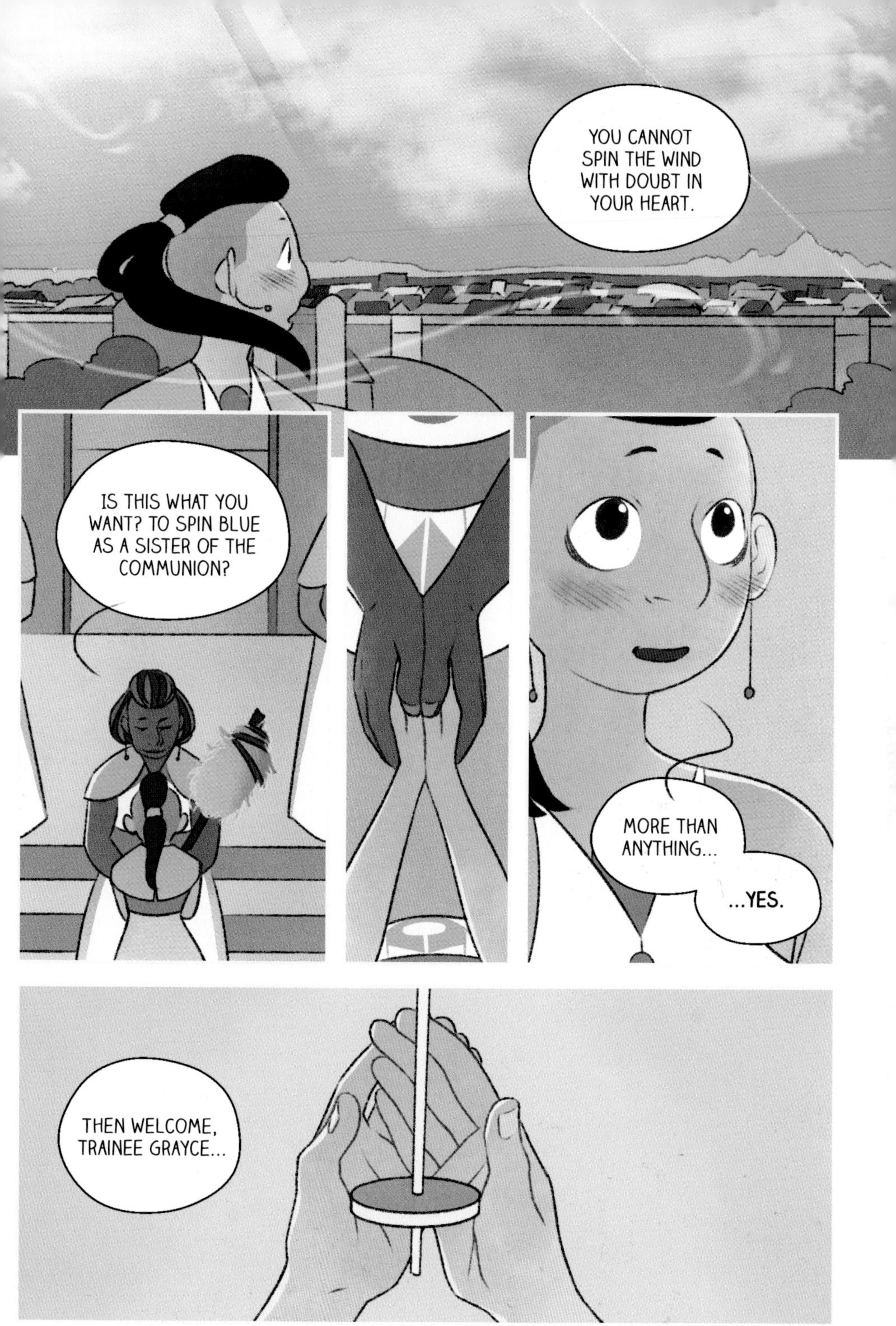

YOU CANNOT SPIN THE WIND WITH DOUBT IN YOUR HEART.
IS THIS WHAT YOU WANT? TO SPIN BLUE AS A SISTER OF THE COMMUNION?
MORE THAN ANYTHING...
...YES.
THEN WELCOME, TRAINEE GRAYCE...

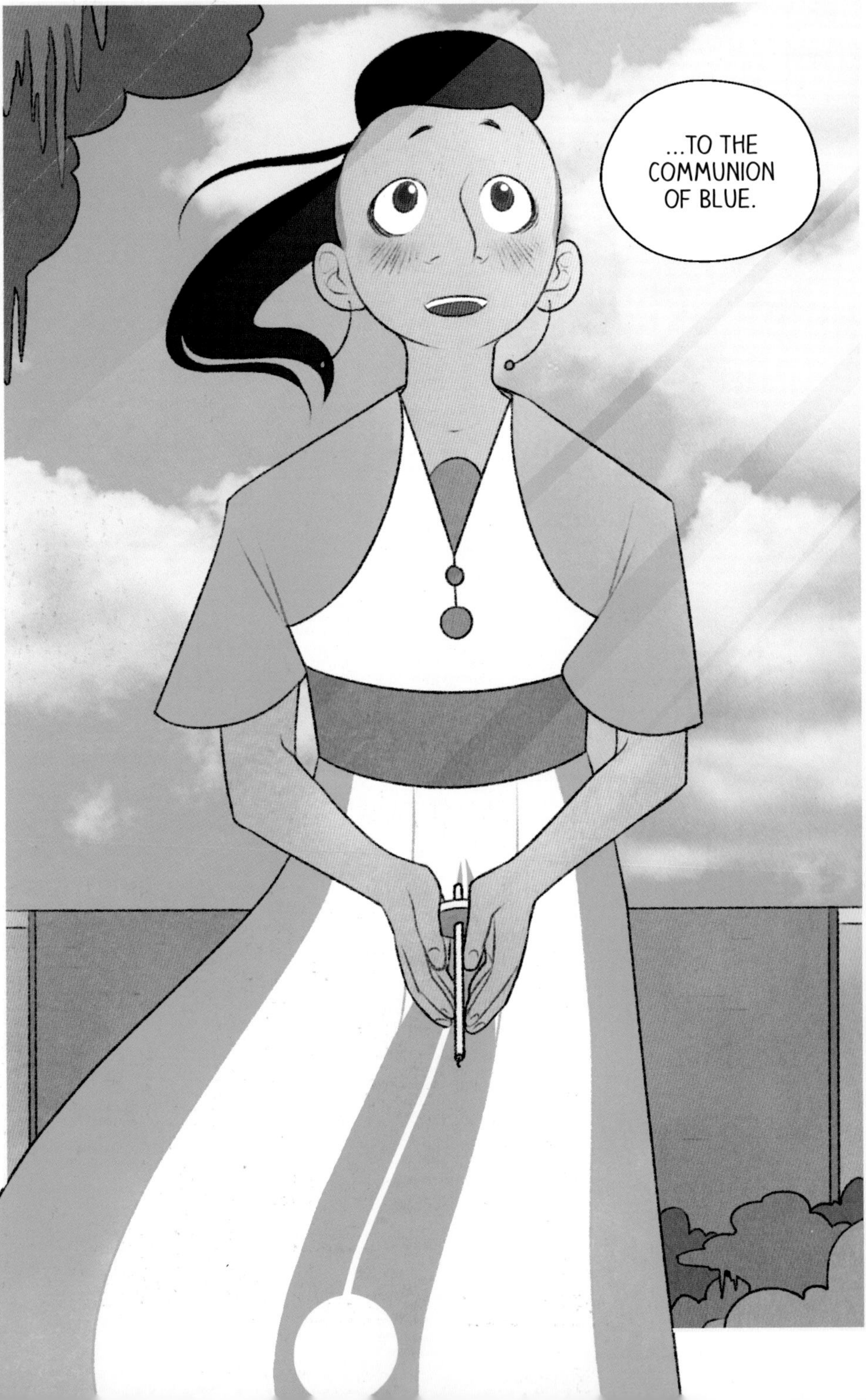
...TO THE COMMUNION OF BLUE.

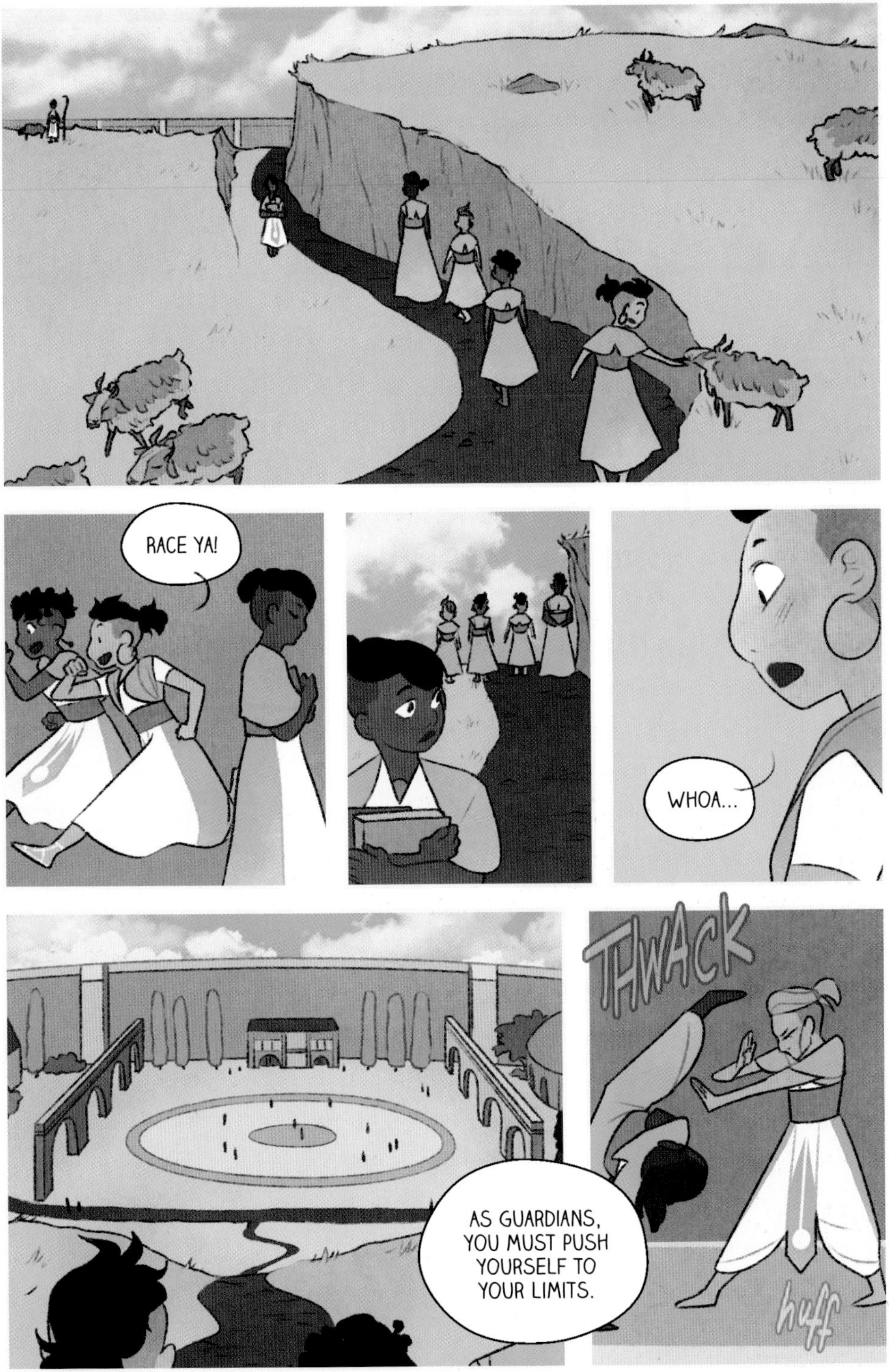
RACE YA!
WHOA...
THWACK
AS GUARDIANS, YOU MUST PUSH YOURSELF TO YOUR LIMITS.
huff

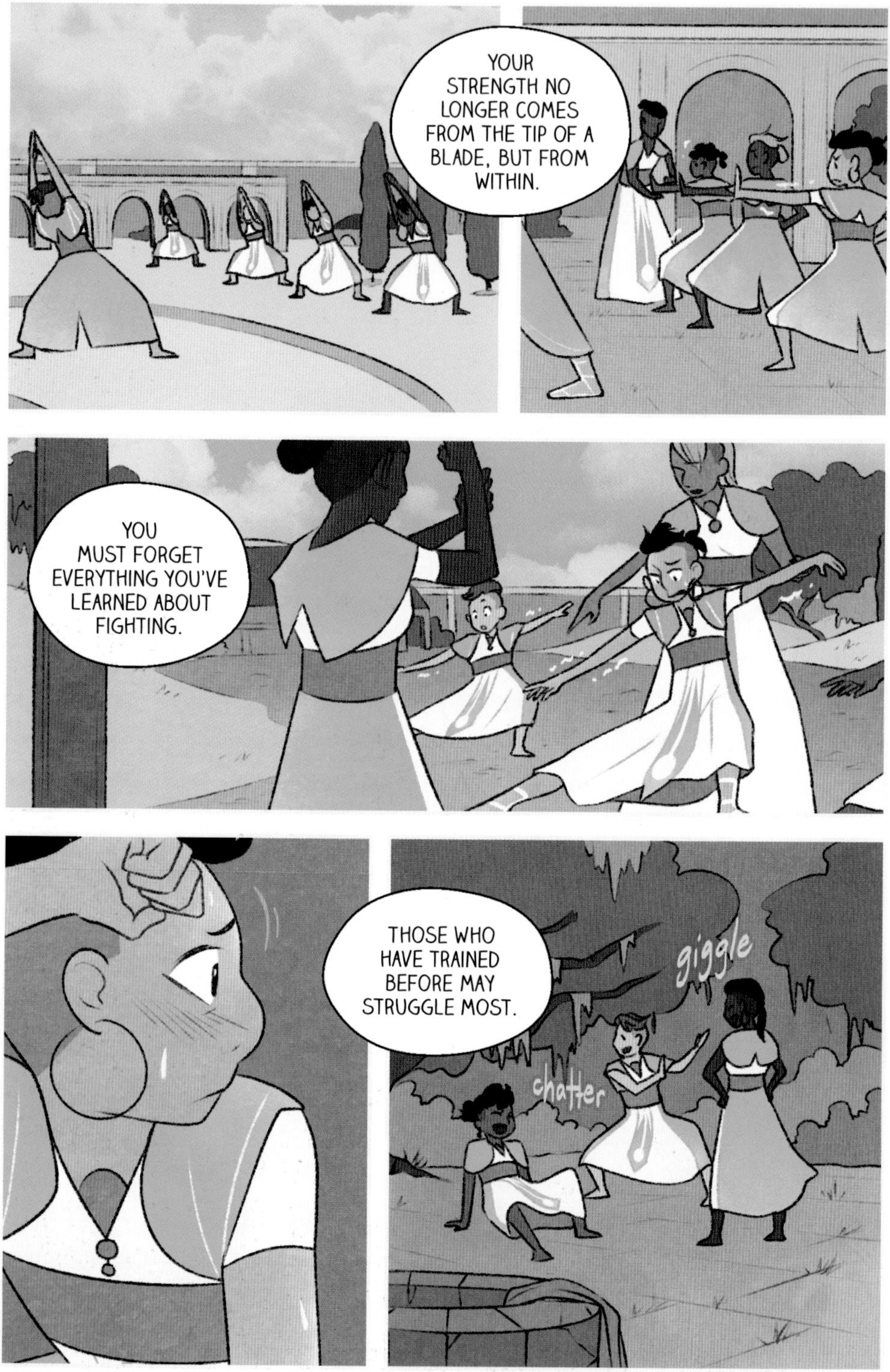
YOUR STRENGTH NO LONGER COMES FROM THE TIP OF A BLADE, BUT FROM WITHIN.
YOU MUST FORGET EVERYTHING YOU'VE LEARNED ABOUT FIGHTING.
THOSE WHO HAVE TRAINED BEFORE MAY STRUGGLE MOST.
giggle
chatter

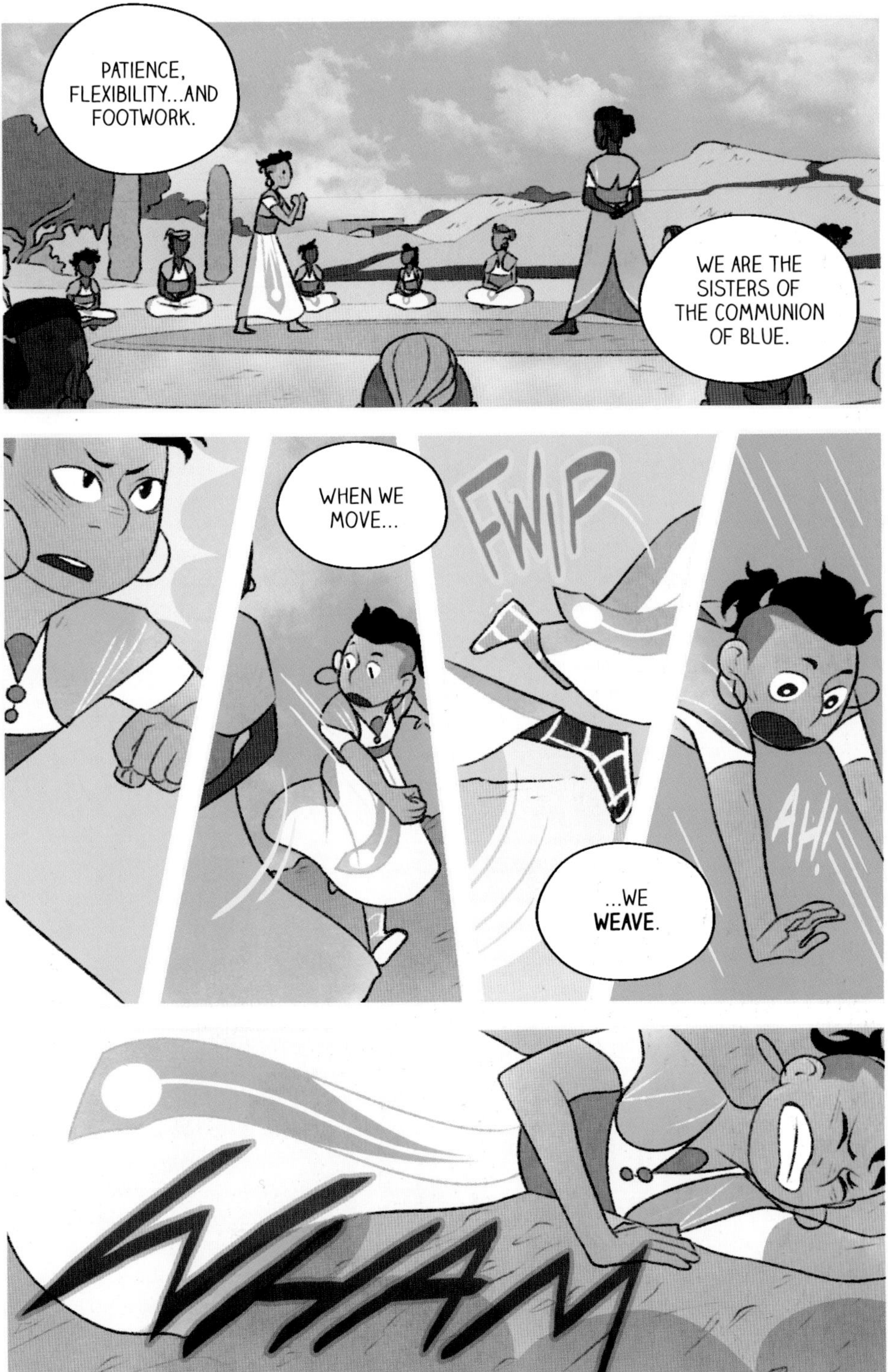
PATIENCE, FLEXIBILITY...AND FOOTWORK.
WE ARE THE SISTERS OF THE COMMUNION OF BLUE.
WHEN WE MOVE...
FWIP
...WE WEAVE.
AH!
WHAM

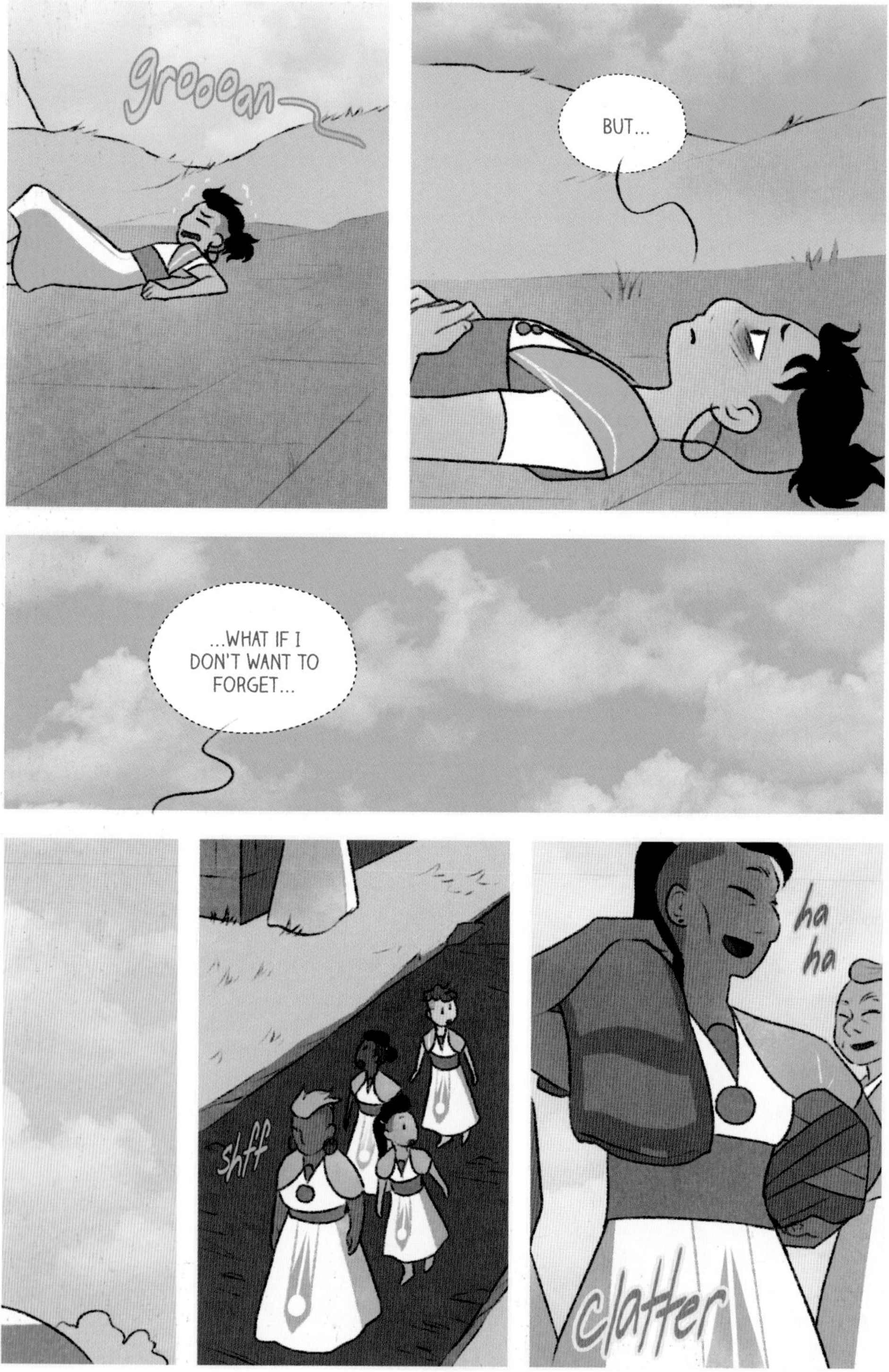
grooooan
BUT...
...WHAT IF I DON'T WANT TO FORGET...
shff
ha ha
clatter

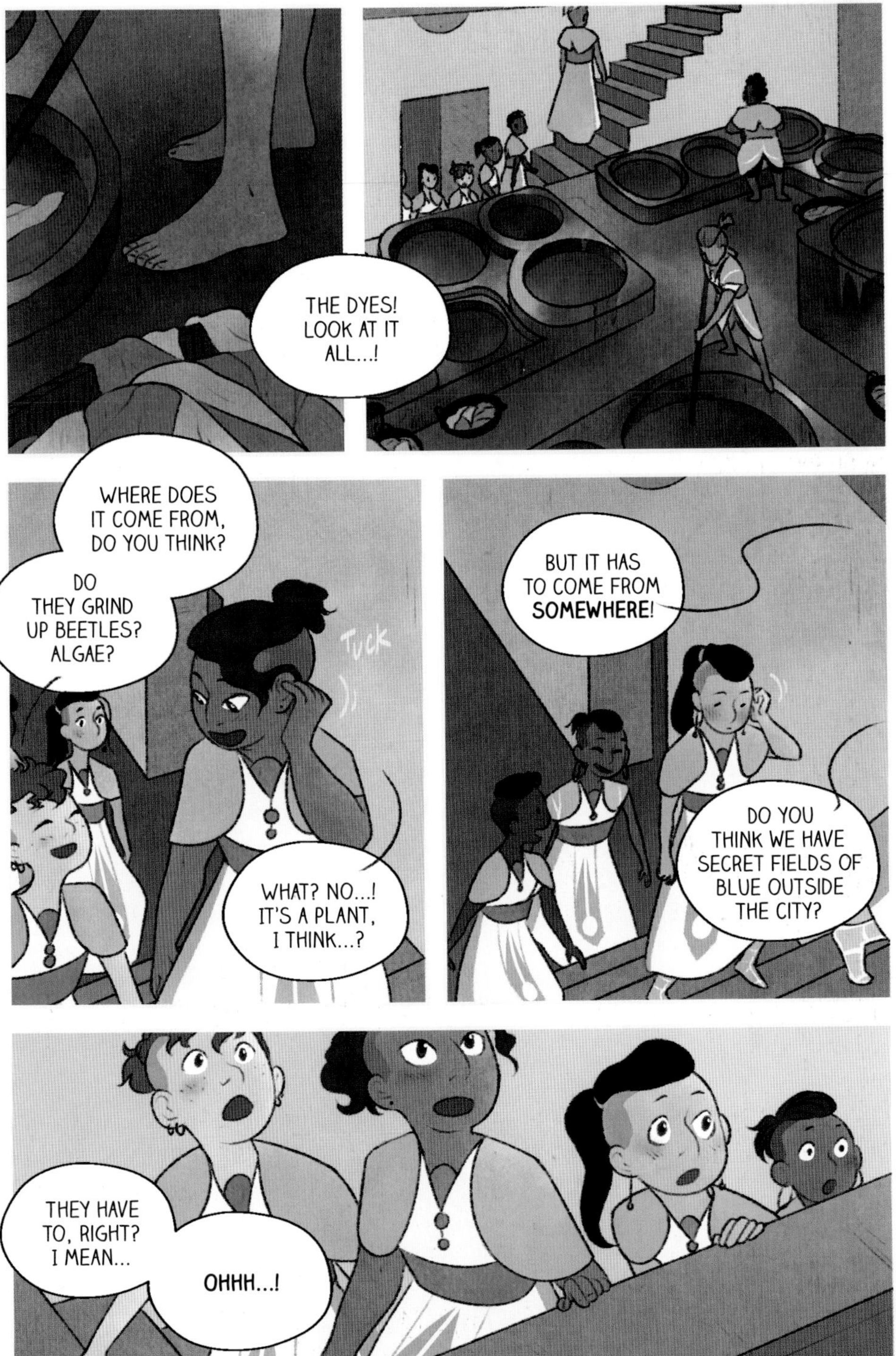
THE DYES! LOOK AT IT ALL...!
WHERE DOES IT COME FROM, DO YOU THINK?
DO THEY GRIND UP BEETLES? ALGAE?
TUCK
WHAT? NO...! IT'S A PLANT, I THINK...?
BUT IT HAS TO COME FROM **SOMEWHERE**!
DO YOU THINK WE HAVE SECRET FIELDS OF BLUE OUTSIDE THE CITY?
THEY HAVE TO, RIGHT? I MEAN...
OHHH...!

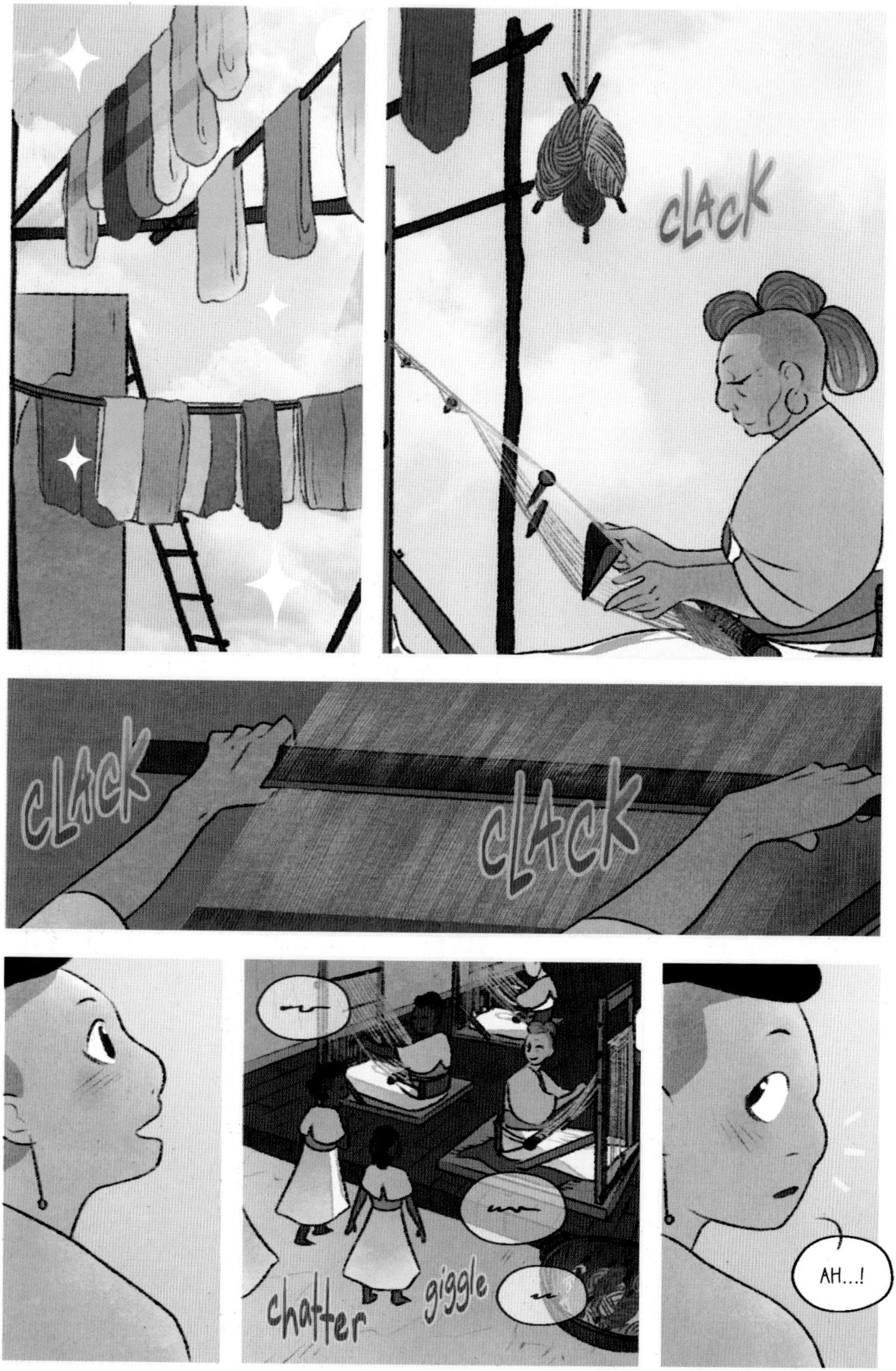
CLACK
CLACK
CLACK
chatter
giggle
AH...!

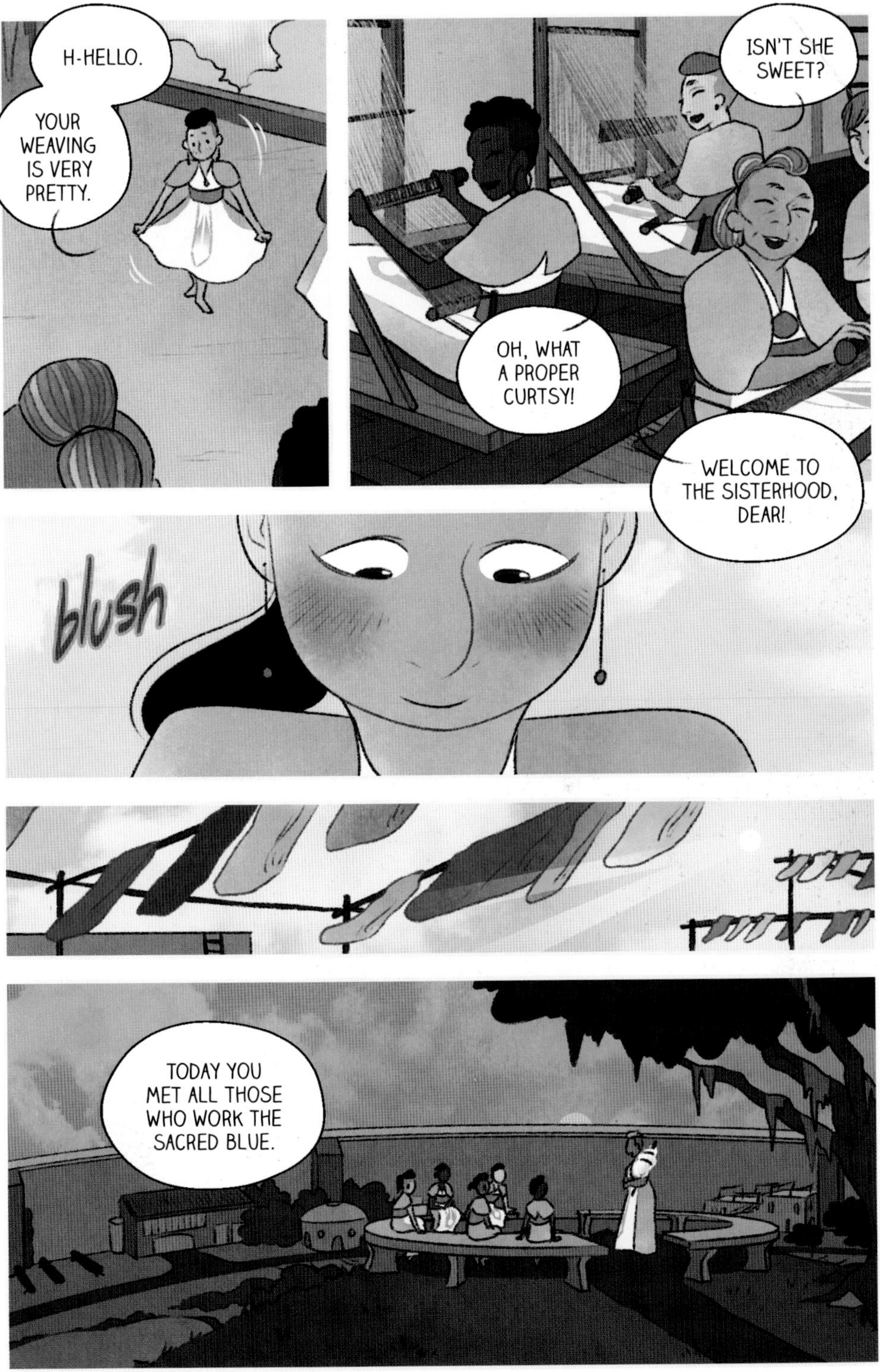
H-HELLO.
YOUR WEAVING IS VERY PRETTY.
ISN'T SHE SWEET?
OH, WHAT A PROPER CURTSY!
WELCOME TO THE SISTERHOOD, DEAR!
blush
TODAY YOU MET ALL THOSE WHO WORK THE SACRED BLUE.

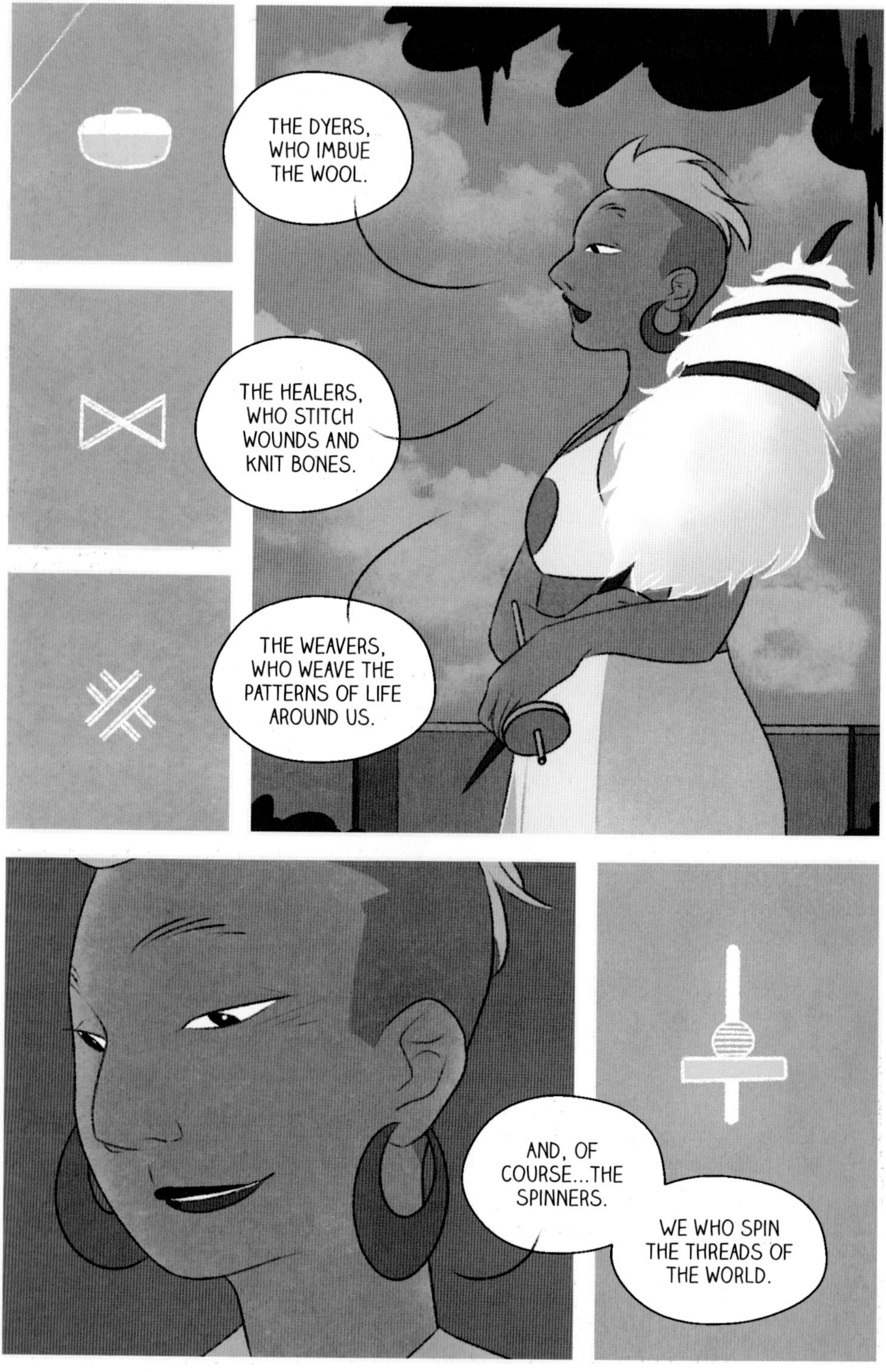
THE DYERS, WHO IMBUE THE WOOL.
THE HEALERS, WHO STITCH WOUNDS AND KNIT BONES.
THE WEAVERS, WHO WEAVE THE PATTERNS OF LIFE AROUND US.
AND, OF COURSE...THE SPINNERS.
WE WHO SPIN THE THREADS OF THE WORLD.

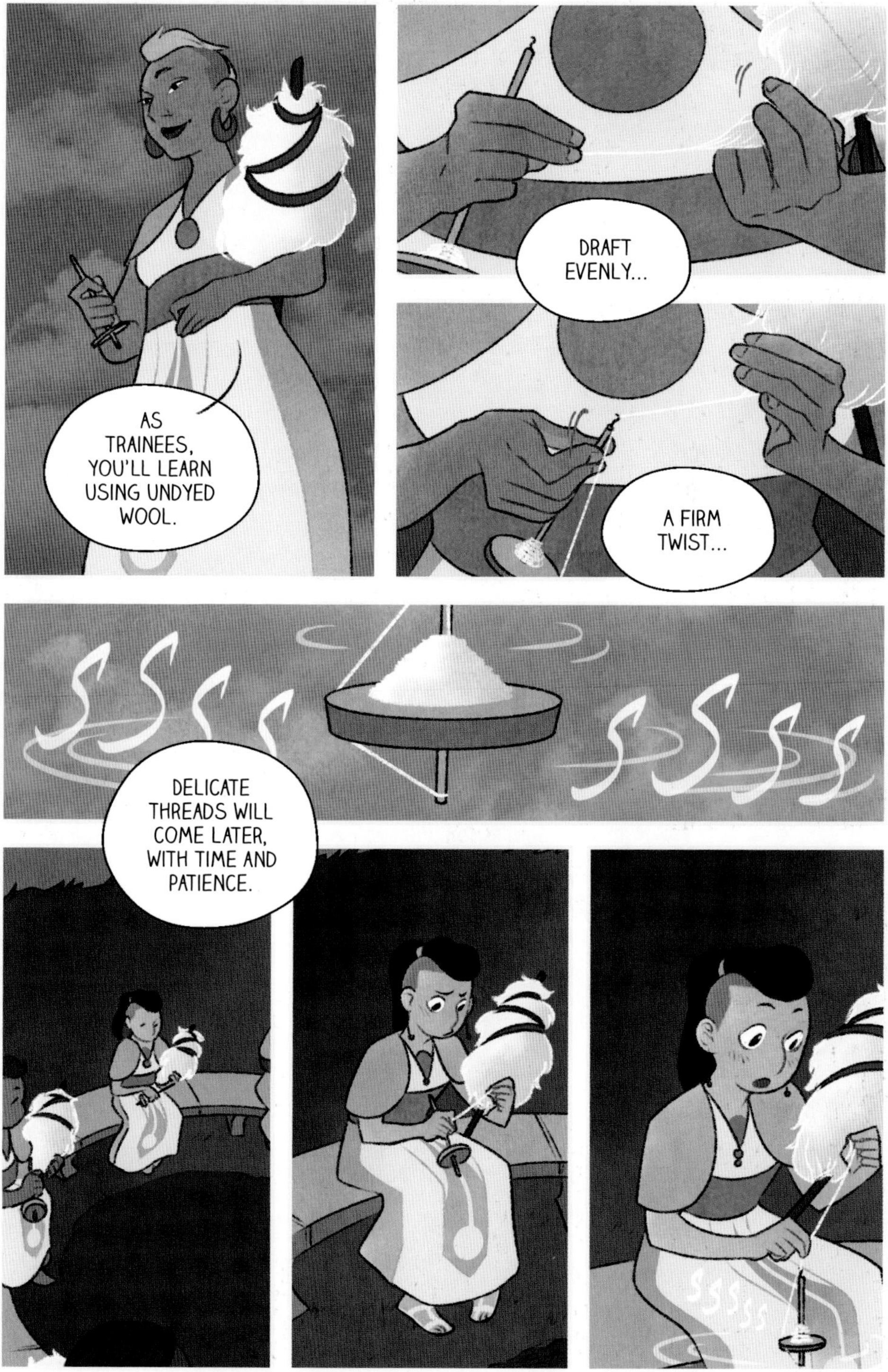

AS TRAINEES, YOU'LL LEARN USING UNDYED WOOL.
DRAFT EVENLY...
A FIRM TWIST...
DELICATE THREADS WILL COME LATER, WITH TIME AND PATIENCE.

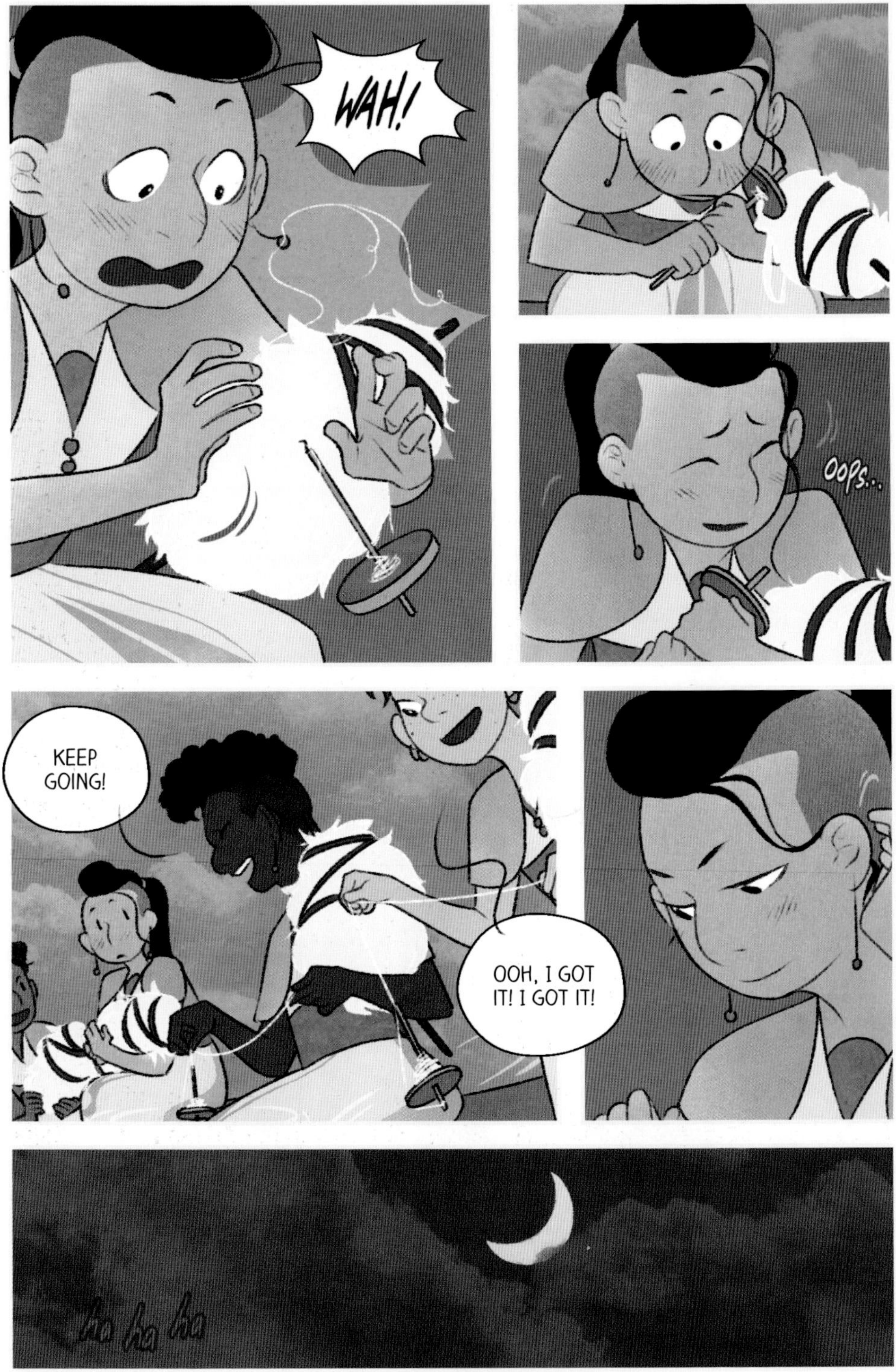
WAH!
OOPS...
KEEP GOING!
OOH, I GOT IT! I GOT IT!
ha ha ha

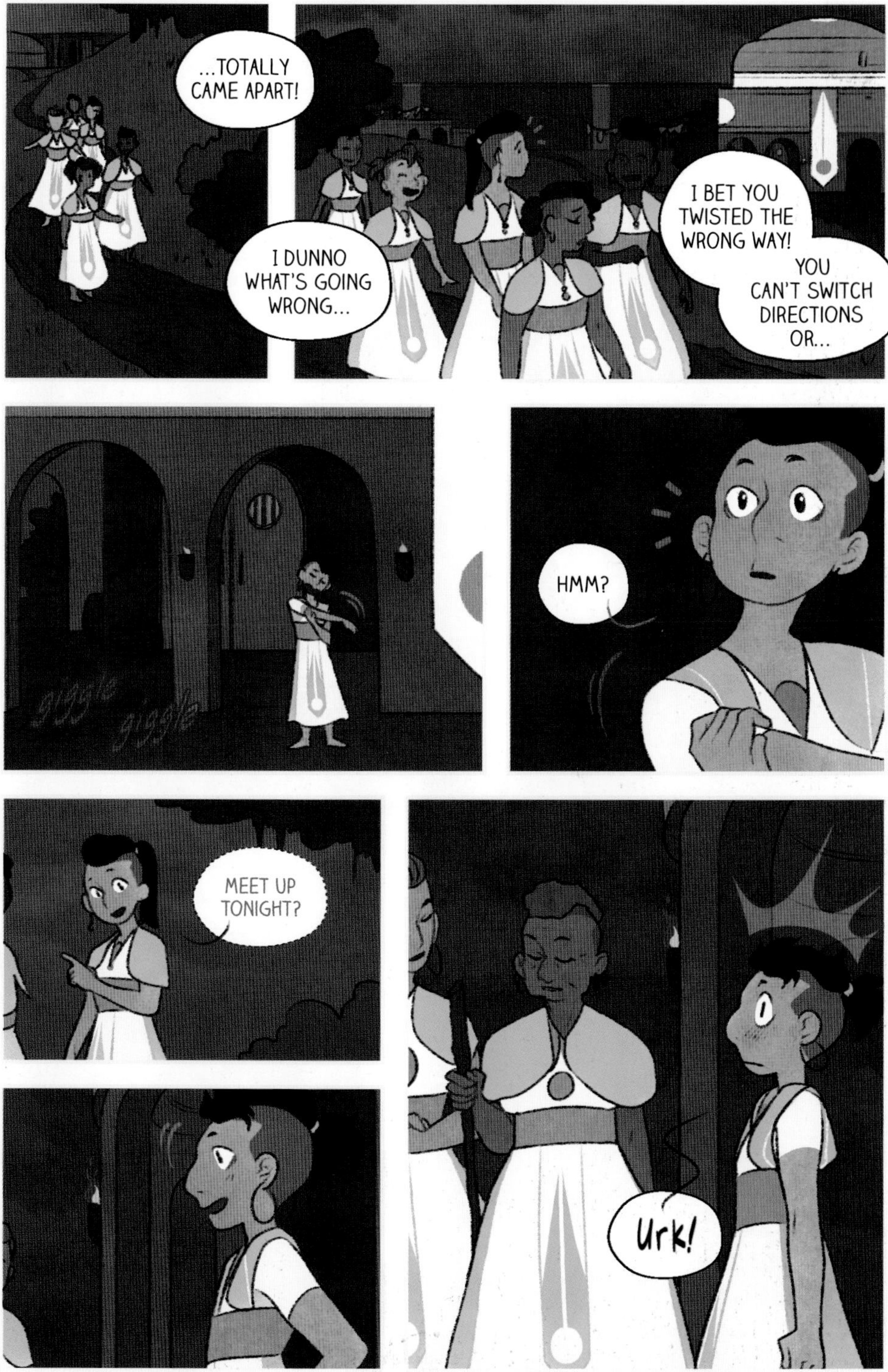
...TOTALLY CAME APART!
I DUNNO WHAT'S GOING WRONG...
I BET YOU TWISTED THE WRONG WAY!
YOU CAN'T SWITCH DIRECTIONS OR...
giggle
giggle
HMM?
MEET UP TONIGHT?
Urk!

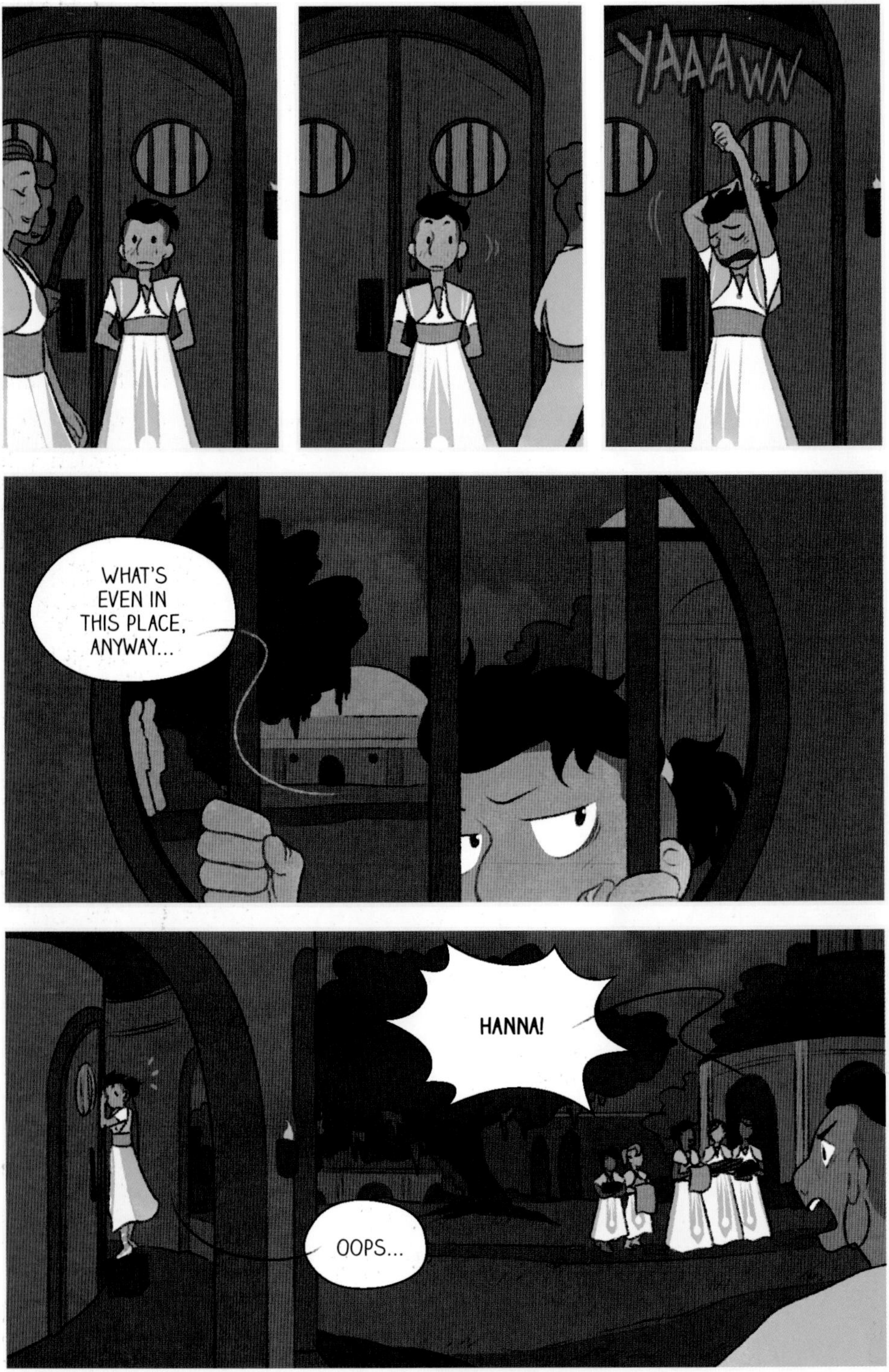
YAAAWN
WHAT'S EVEN IN THIS PLACE, ANYWAY...
HANNA!
OOPS...

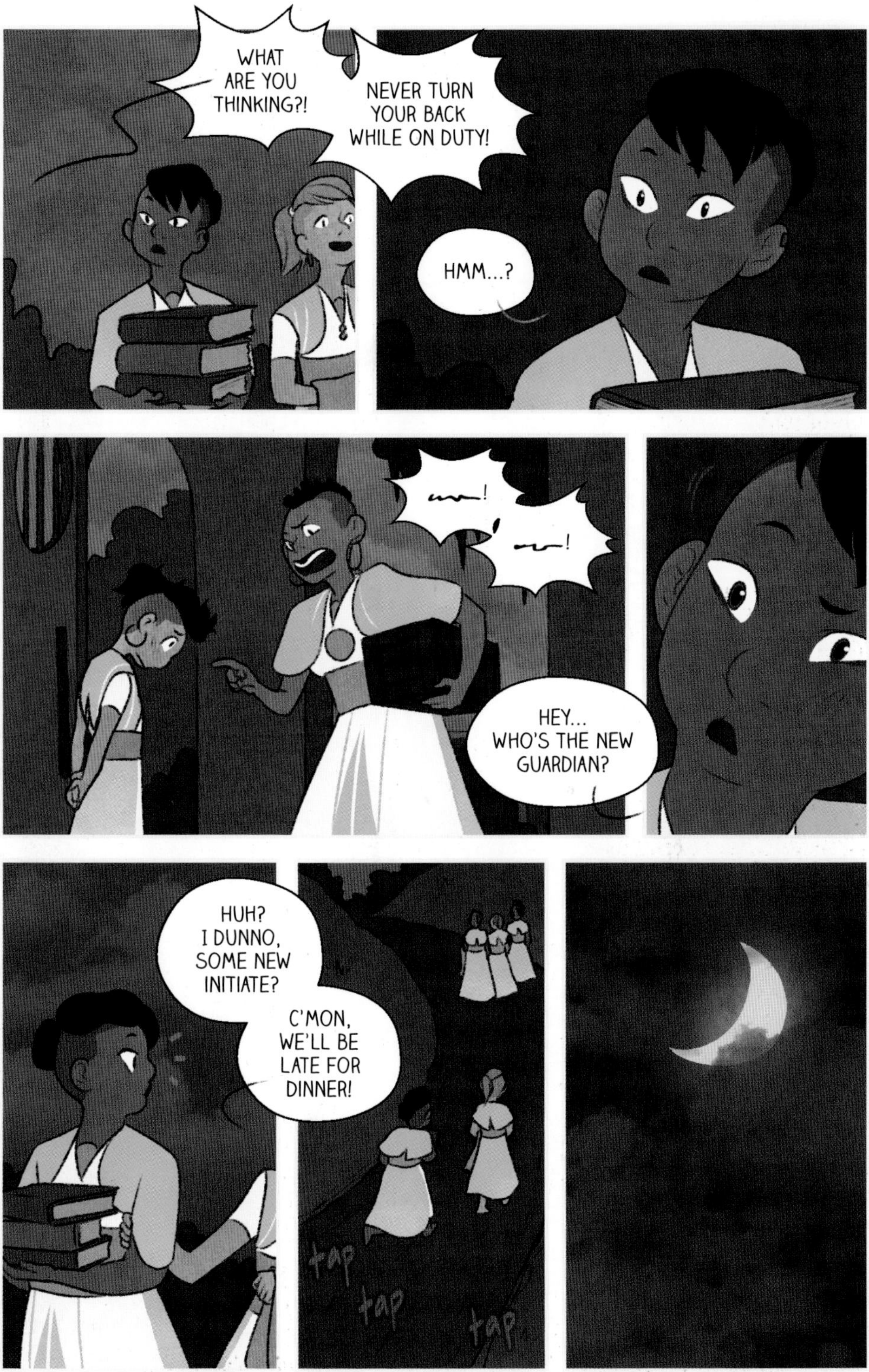
WHAT ARE YOU THINKING?!
NEVER TURN YOUR BACK WHILE ON DUTY!
HMM...?
HEY... WHO'S THE NEW GUARDIAN?
HUH? I DUNNO, SOME NEW INITIATE?
C'MON, WE'LL BE LATE FOR DINNER!
tap
tap
tap

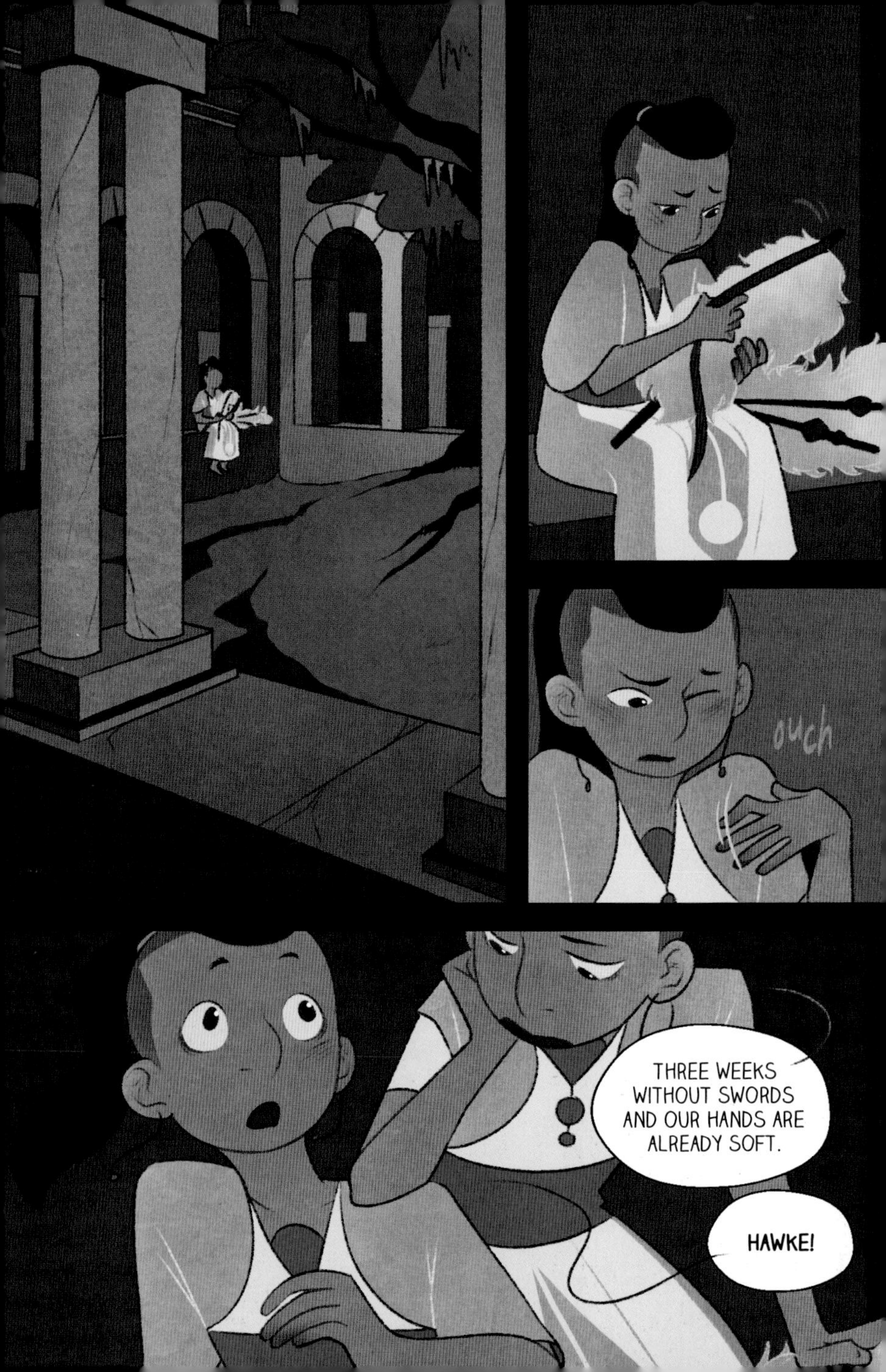
ouch
THREE WEEKS WITHOUT SWORDS AND OUR HANDS ARE ALREADY SOFT.
HAWKE!

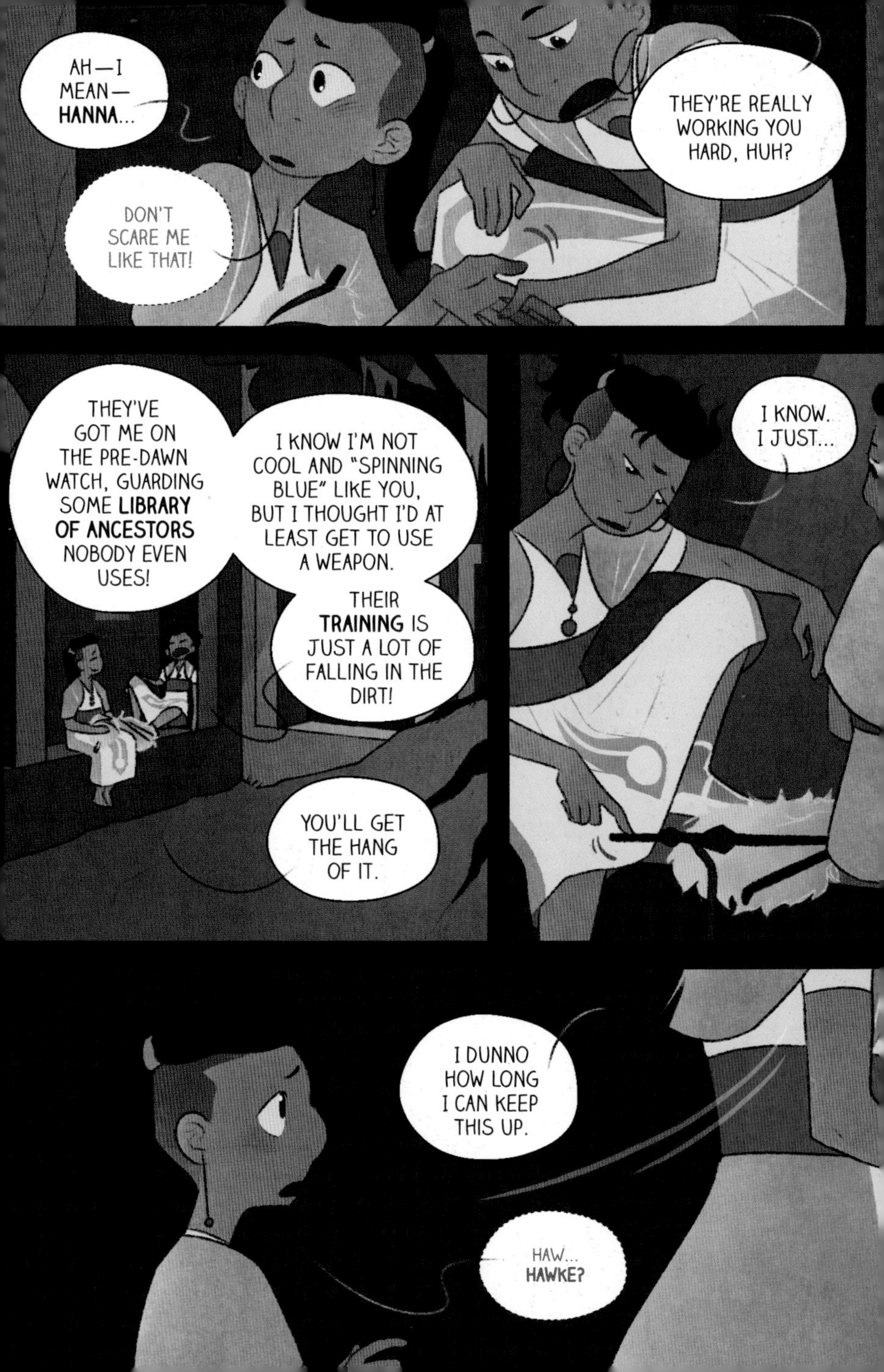
AH—I MEAN—**HANNA**...
THEY'RE REALLY WORKING YOU HARD, HUH?
DON'T SCARE ME LIKE THAT!
THEY'VE GOT ME ON THE PRE-DAWN WATCH, GUARDING SOME **LIBRARY OF ANCESTORS** NOBODY EVEN USES!
I KNOW I'M NOT COOL AND "SPINNING BLUE" LIKE YOU, BUT I THOUGHT I'D AT LEAST GET TO USE A WEAPON.
THEIR **TRAINING** IS JUST A LOT OF FALLING IN THE DIRT!
YOU'LL GET THE HANG OF IT.
I KNOW. I JUST...
I DUNNO HOW LONG I CAN KEEP THIS UP.
HAW... **HAWKE?**

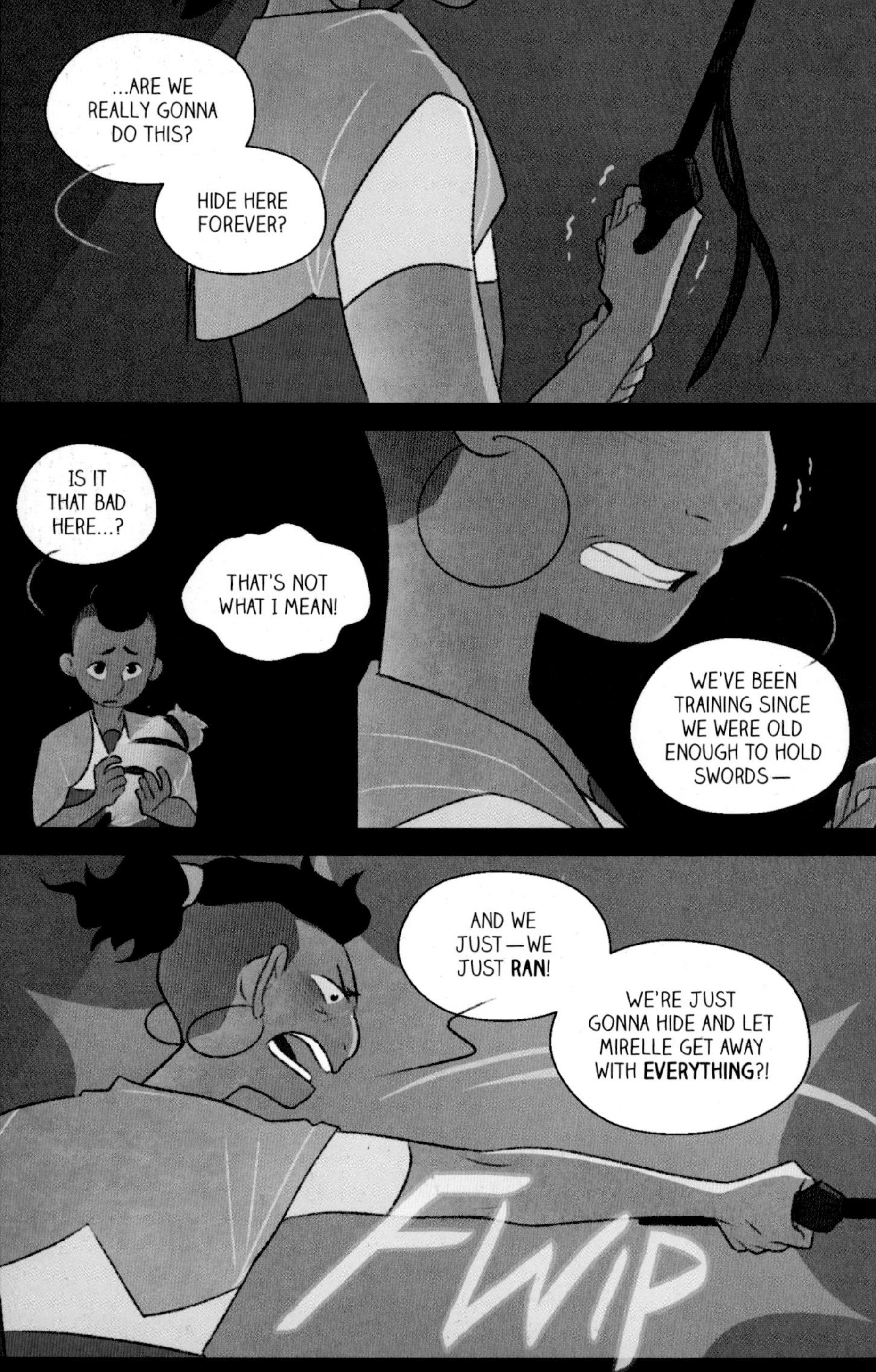
...ARE WE REALLY GONNA DO THIS?
HIDE HERE FOREVER?
IS IT THAT BAD HERE...?
THAT'S NOT WHAT I MEAN!
WE'VE BEEN TRAINING SINCE WE WERE OLD ENOUGH TO HOLD SWORDS—
AND WE JUST—WE JUST **RAN**!
WE'RE JUST GONNA HIDE AND LET MIRELLE GET AWAY WITH **EVERYTHING**?!
FWIP

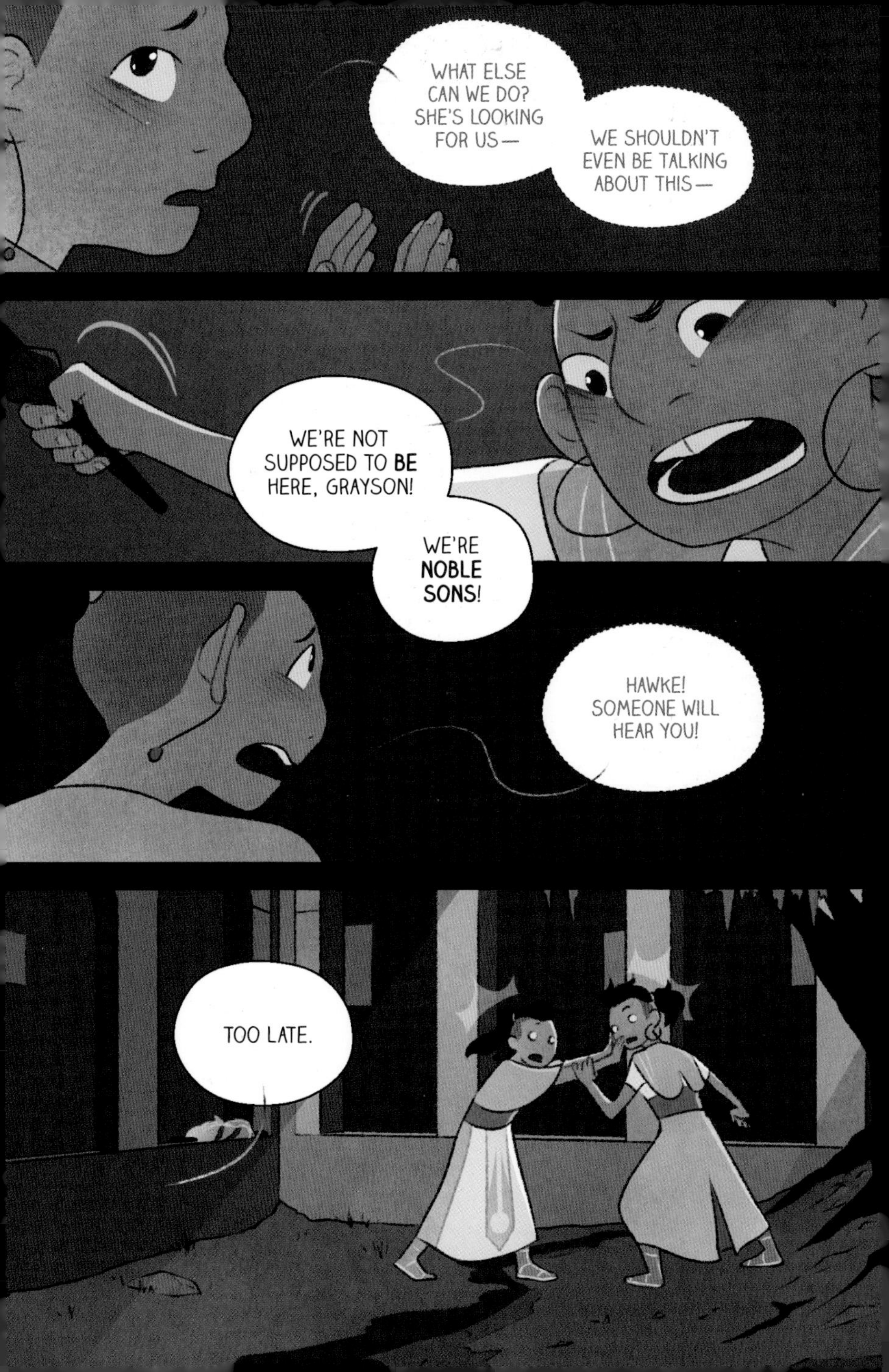
WHAT ELSE CAN WE DO? SHE'S LOOKING FOR US—
WE SHOULDN'T EVEN BE TALKING ABOUT THIS—
WE'RE NOT SUPPOSED TO **BE** HERE, GRAYSON!
WE'RE **NOBLE SONS**!
HAWKE! SOMEONE WILL HEAR YOU!
TOO LATE.

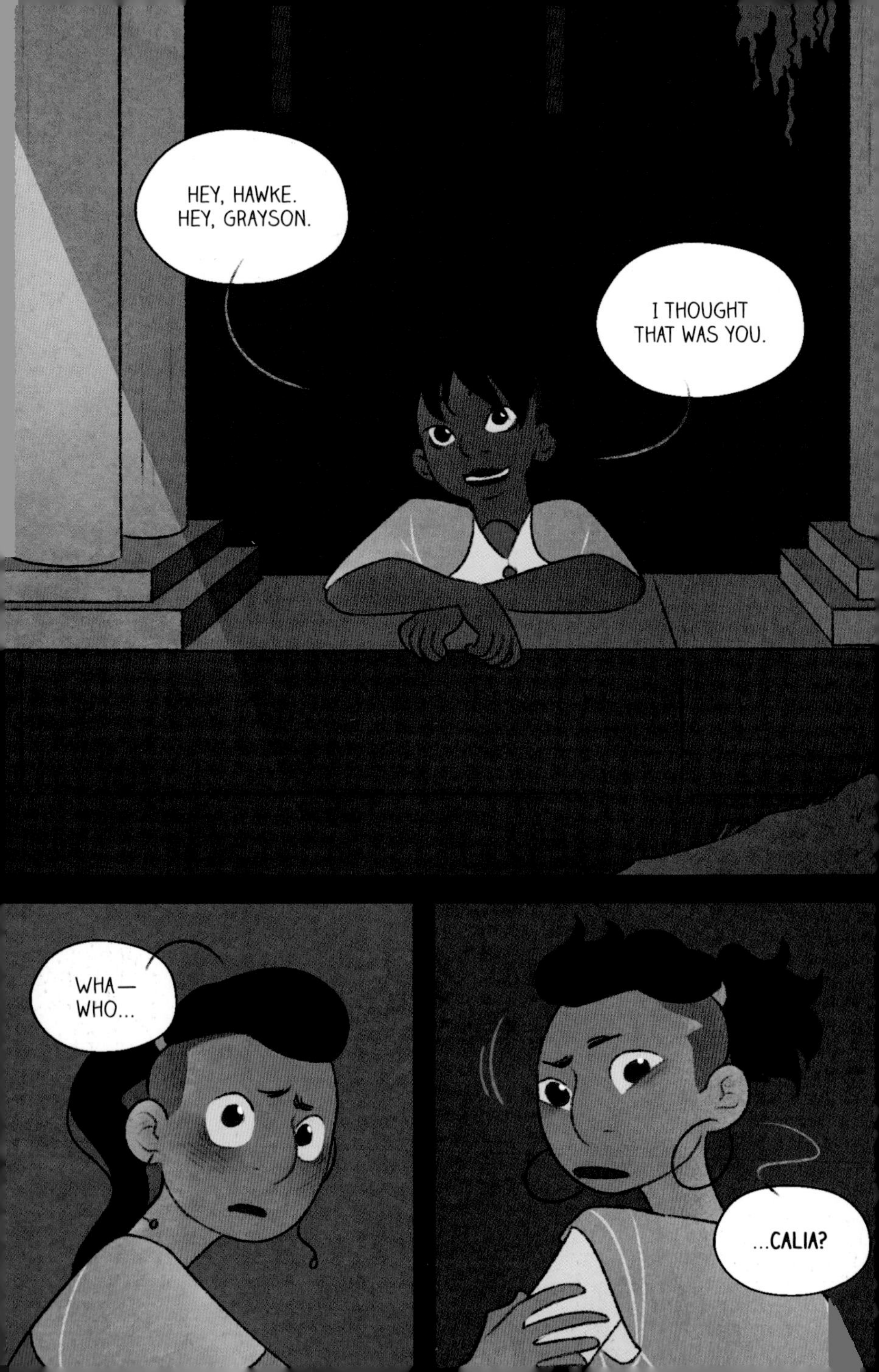
HEY, HAWKE.
HEY, GRAYSON.
I THOUGHT
THAT WAS YOU.
WHA—
WHO...
...CALIA?

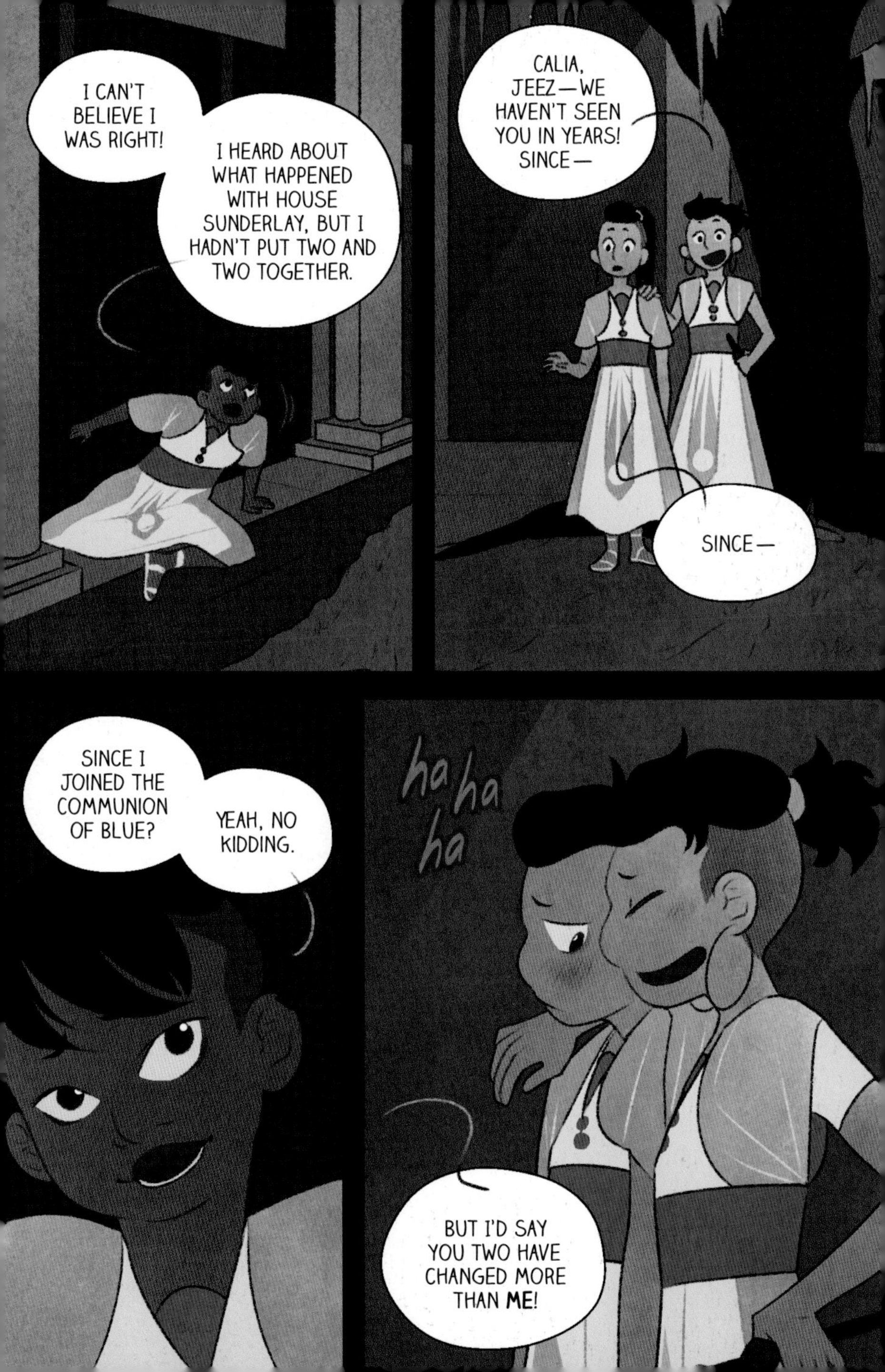
I CAN'T BELIEVE I WAS RIGHT!
I HEARD ABOUT WHAT HAPPENED WITH HOUSE SUNDERLAY, BUT I HADN'T PUT TWO AND TWO TOGETHER.
CALIA, JEEZ—WE HAVEN'T SEEN YOU IN YEARS! SINCE—
SINCE—
SINCE I JOINED THE COMMUNION OF BLUE?
YEAH, NO KIDDING.
ha ha ha
BUT I'D SAY YOU TWO HAVE CHANGED MORE THAN **ME**!

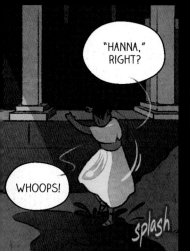

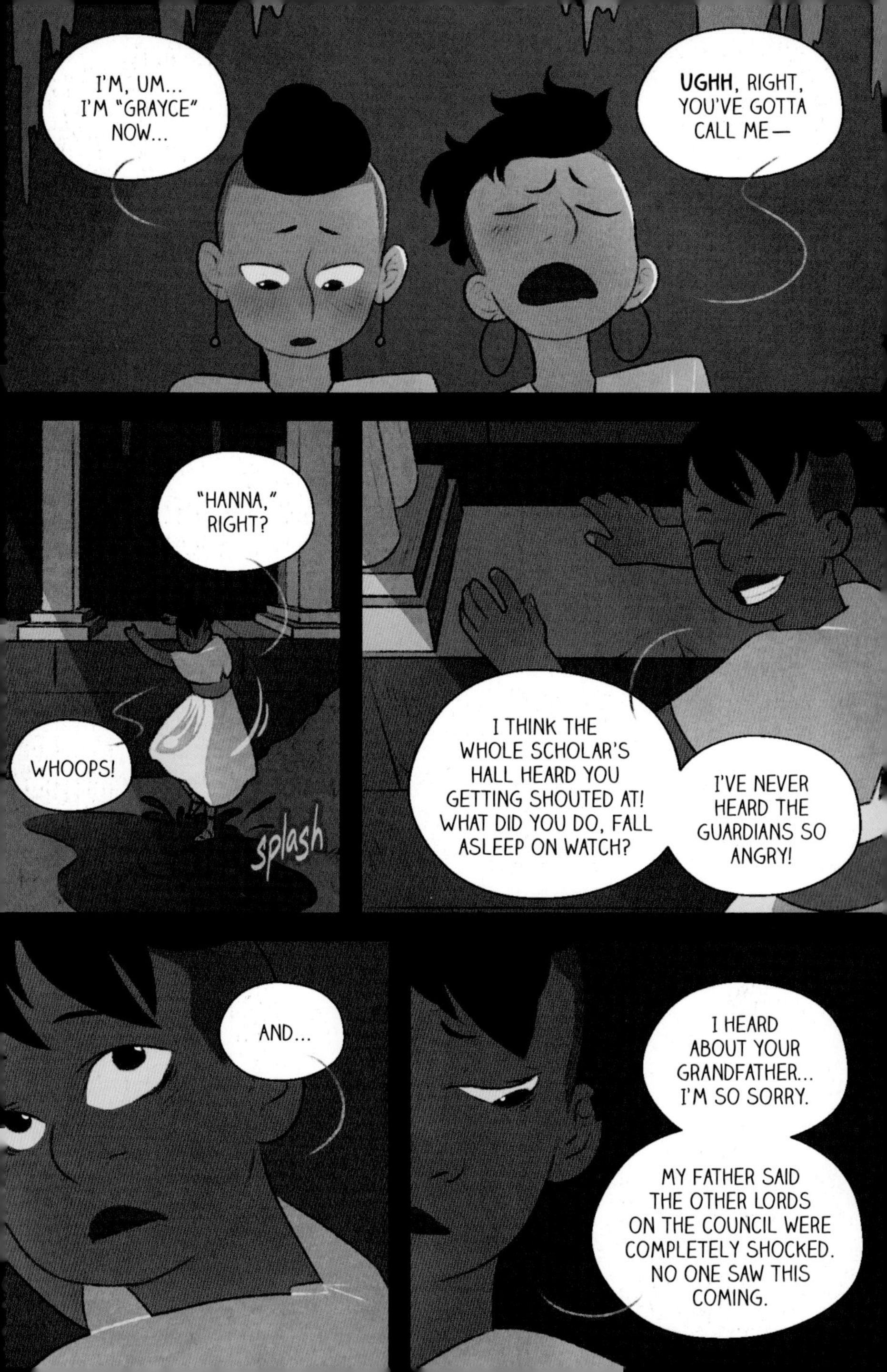
I'M, UM... I'M "GRAYCE" NOW...
UGHH, RIGHT, YOU'VE GOTTA CALL ME—
"HANNA," RIGHT?
WHOOPS!
splash
I THINK THE WHOLE SCHOLAR'S HALL HEARD YOU GETTING SHOUTED AT! WHAT DID YOU DO, FALL ASLEEP ON WATCH?
I'VE NEVER HEARD THE GUARDIANS SO ANGRY!
AND...
I HEARD ABOUT YOUR GRANDFATHER... I'M SO SORRY.
MY FATHER SAID THE OTHER LORDS ON THE COUNCIL WERE COMPLETELY SHOCKED. NO ONE SAW THIS COMING.

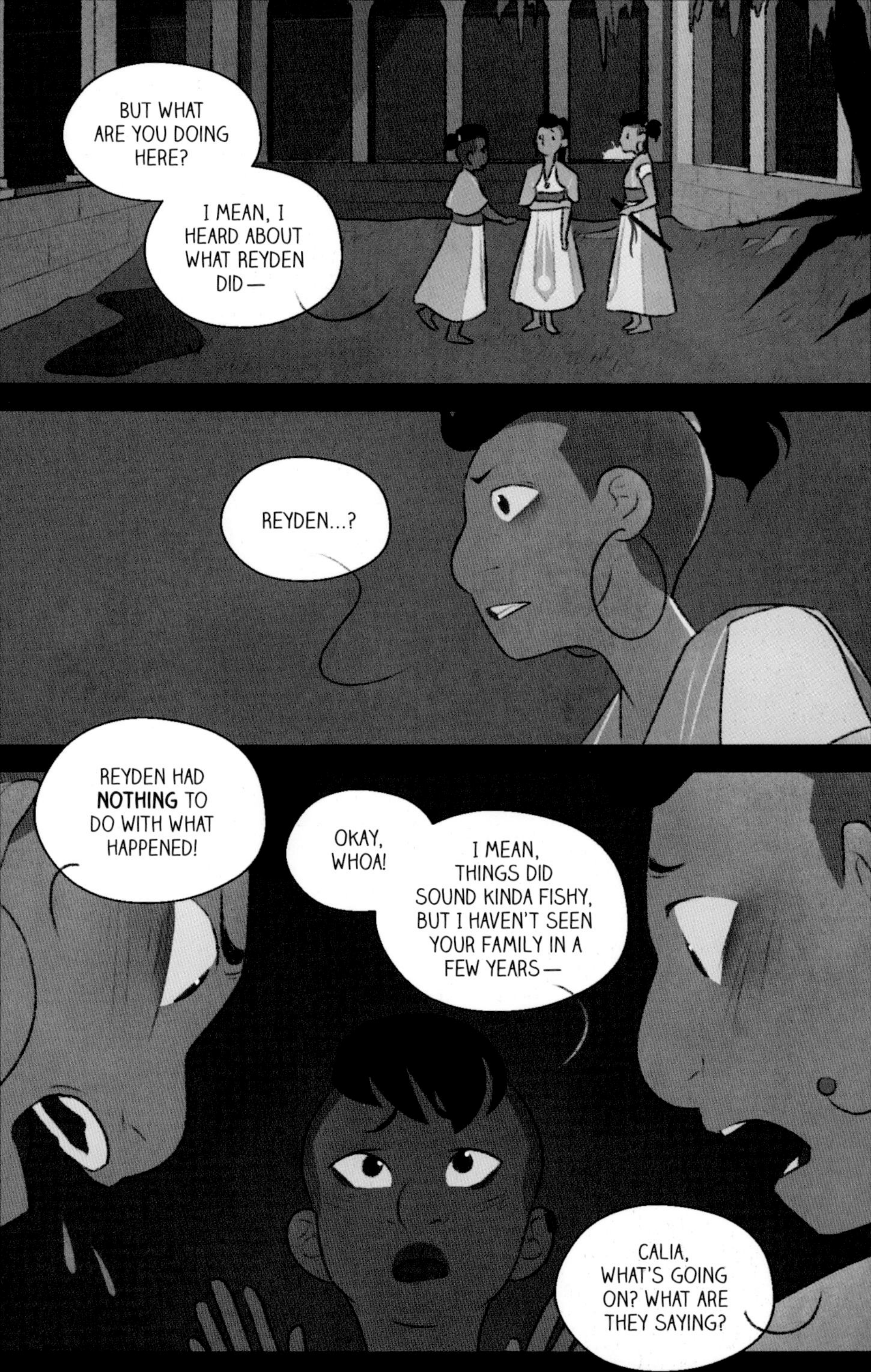
BUT WHAT ARE YOU DOING HERE?
I MEAN, I HEARD ABOUT WHAT REYDEN DID—
REYDEN...?
REYDEN HAD **NOTHING** TO DO WITH WHAT HAPPENED!
OKAY, WHOA!
I MEAN, THINGS DID SOUND KINDA FISHY, BUT I HAVEN'T SEEN YOUR FAMILY IN A FEW YEARS—
CALIA, WHAT'S GOING ON? WHAT ARE THEY SAYING?

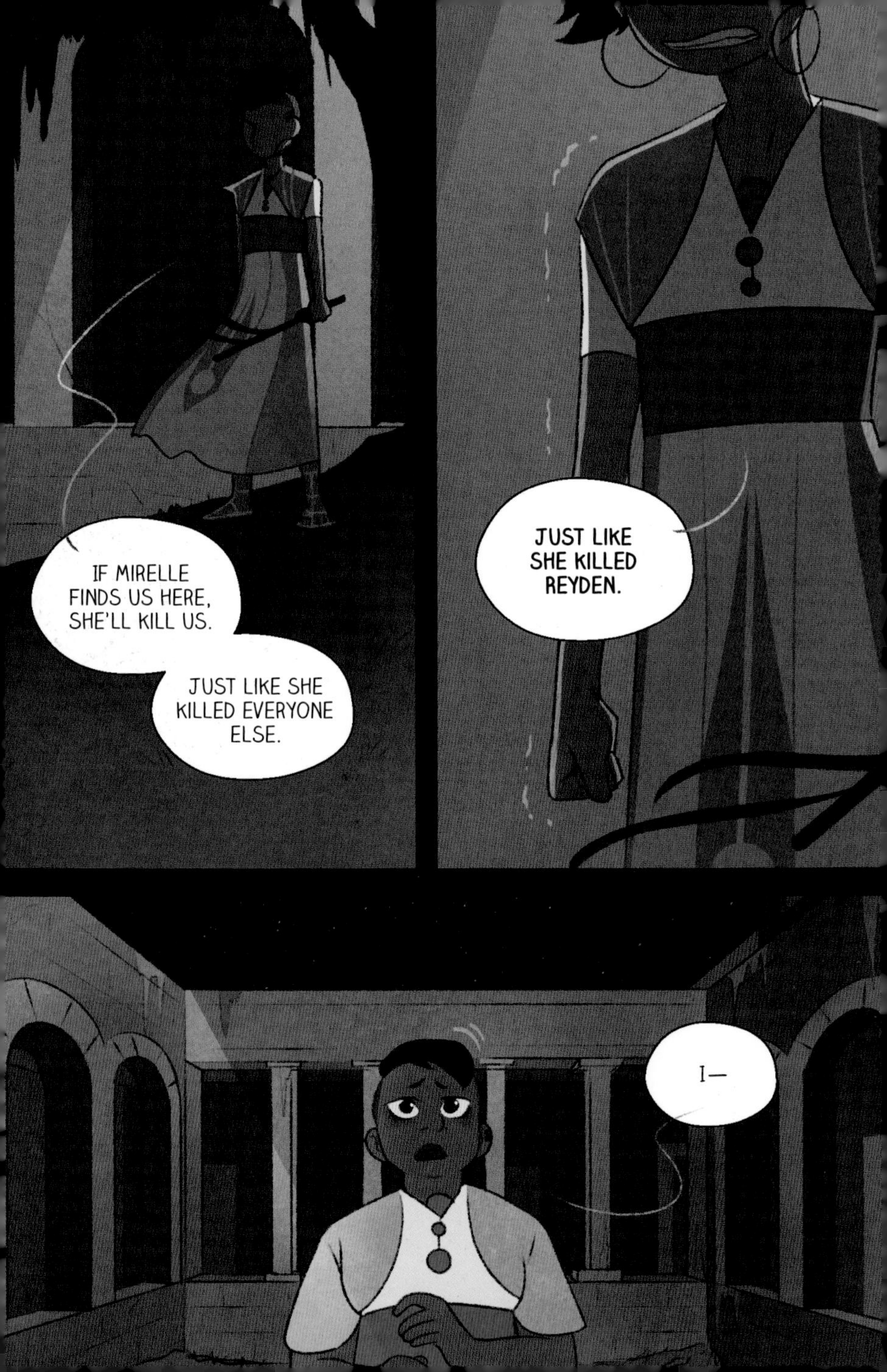
IF MIRELLE FINDS US HERE, SHE'LL KILL US.
JUST LIKE SHE KILLED EVERYONE ELSE.
JUST LIKE SHE KILLED REYDEN.
I—

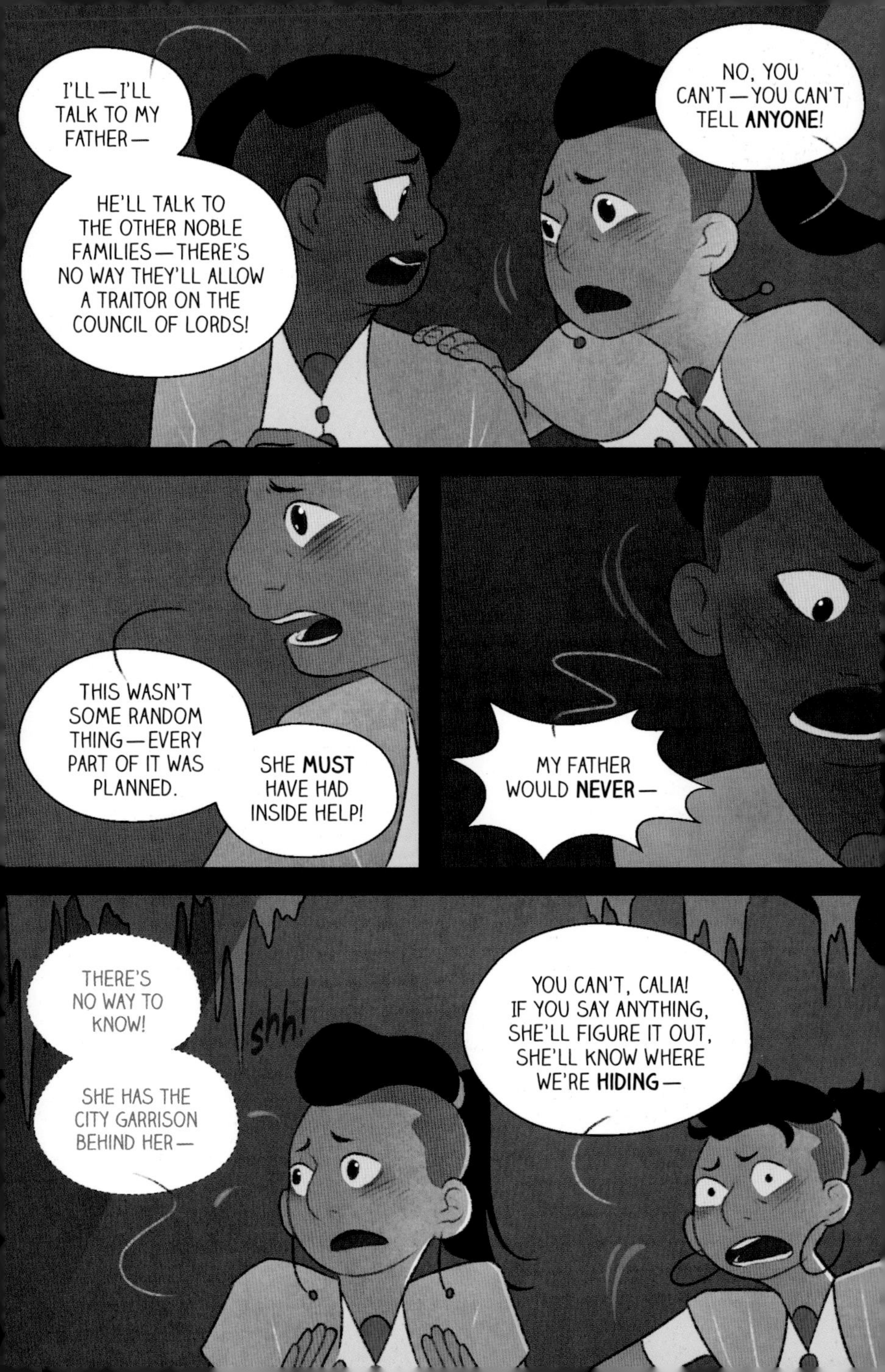
I'LL—I'LL TALK TO MY FATHER—
HE'LL TALK TO THE OTHER NOBLE FAMILIES—THERE'S NO WAY THEY'LL ALLOW A TRAITOR ON THE COUNCIL OF LORDS!
NO, YOU CAN'T—YOU CAN'T TELL **ANYONE**!
THIS WASN'T SOME RANDOM THING—EVERY PART OF IT WAS PLANNED.
SHE **MUST** HAVE HAD INSIDE HELP!
MY FATHER WOULD **NEVER**—
THERE'S NO WAY TO KNOW!
SHE HAS THE CITY GARRISON BEHIND HER—
shh!
YOU CAN'T, CALIA! IF YOU SAY ANYTHING, SHE'LL FIGURE IT OUT, SHE'LL KNOW WHERE WE'RE **HIDING**—

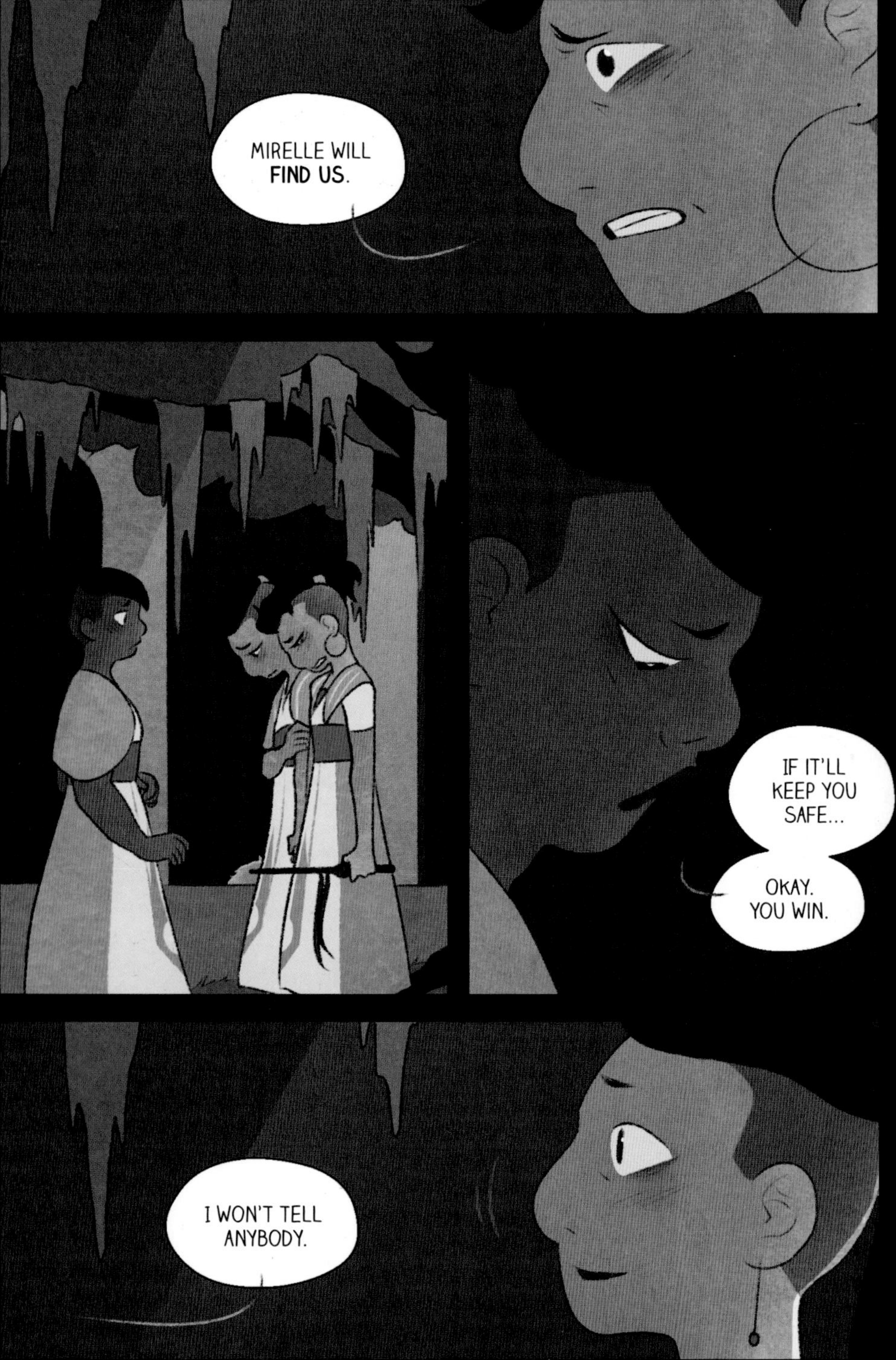
MIRELLE WILL FIND US.
IF IT'LL KEEP YOU SAFE...
OKAY. YOU WIN.
I WON'T TELL ANYBODY.

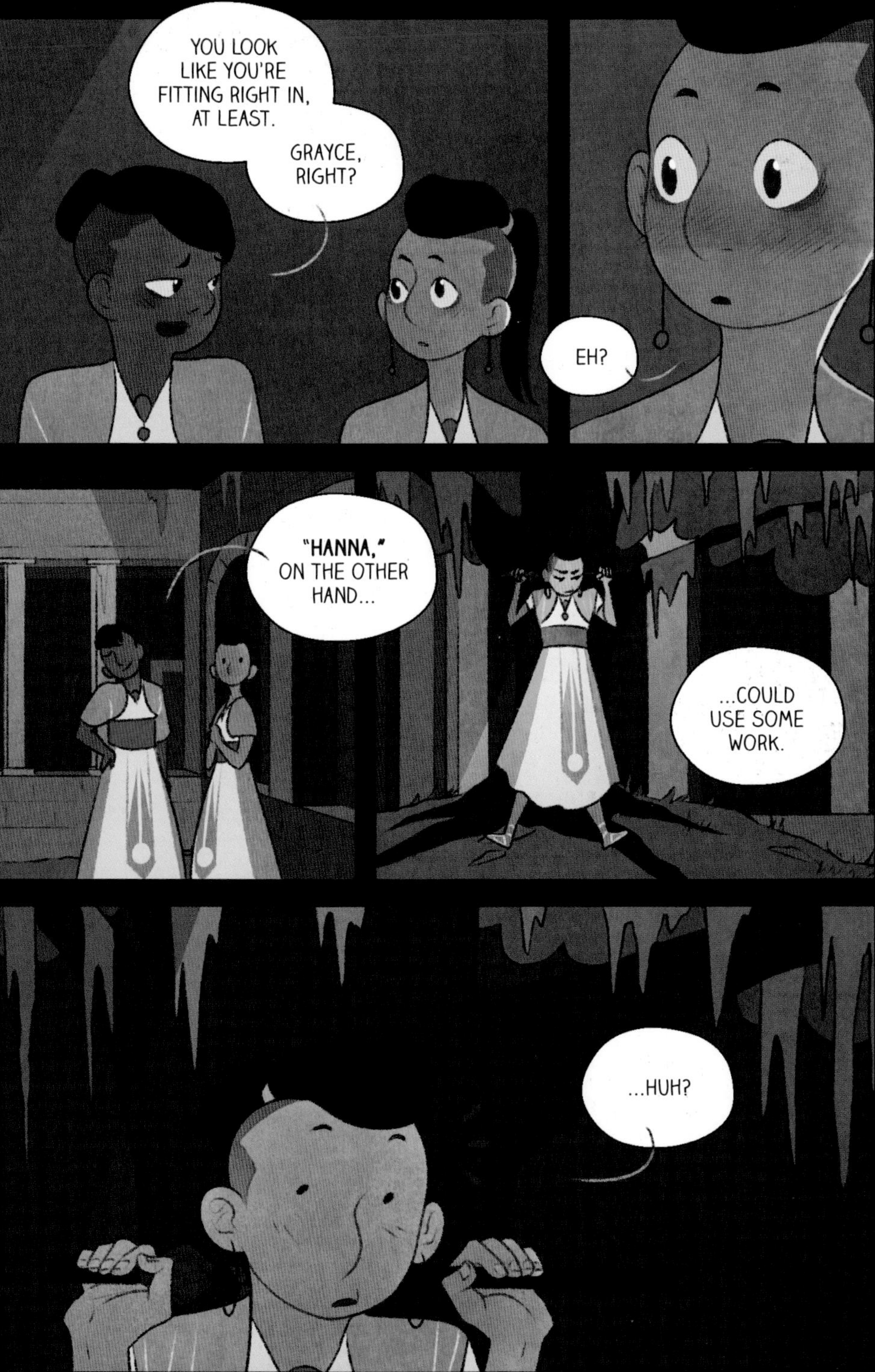
YOU LOOK LIKE YOU'RE FITTING RIGHT IN, AT LEAST.
GRAYCE, RIGHT?
EH?
"HANNA," ON THE OTHER HAND...
...COULD USE SOME WORK.
...HUH?

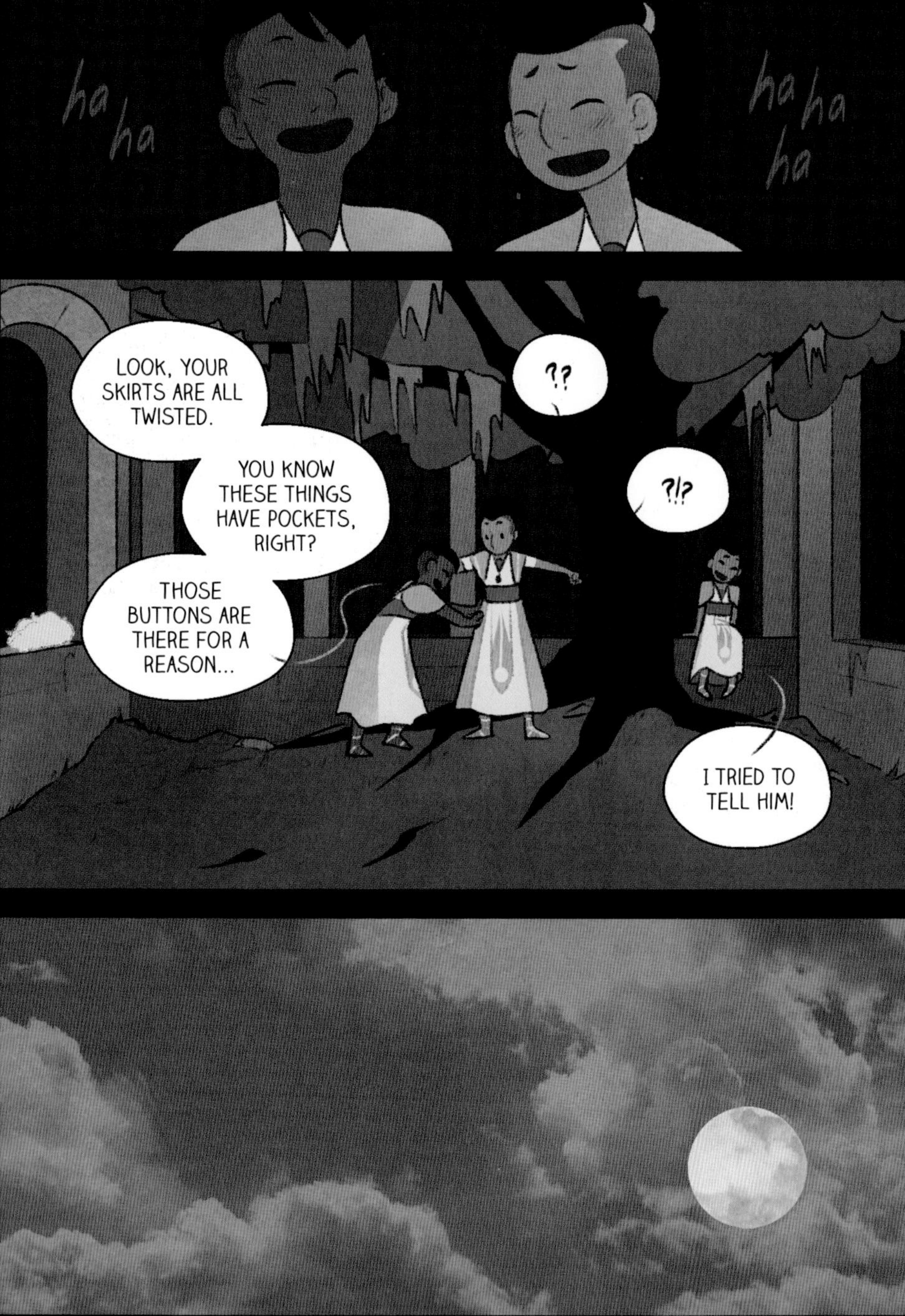

ha ha
ha ha ha
LOOK, YOUR SKIRTS ARE ALL TWISTED.
??
YOU KNOW THESE THINGS HAVE POCKETS, RIGHT?
?!?
THOSE BUTTONS ARE THERE FOR A REASON...
I TRIED TO TELL HIM!

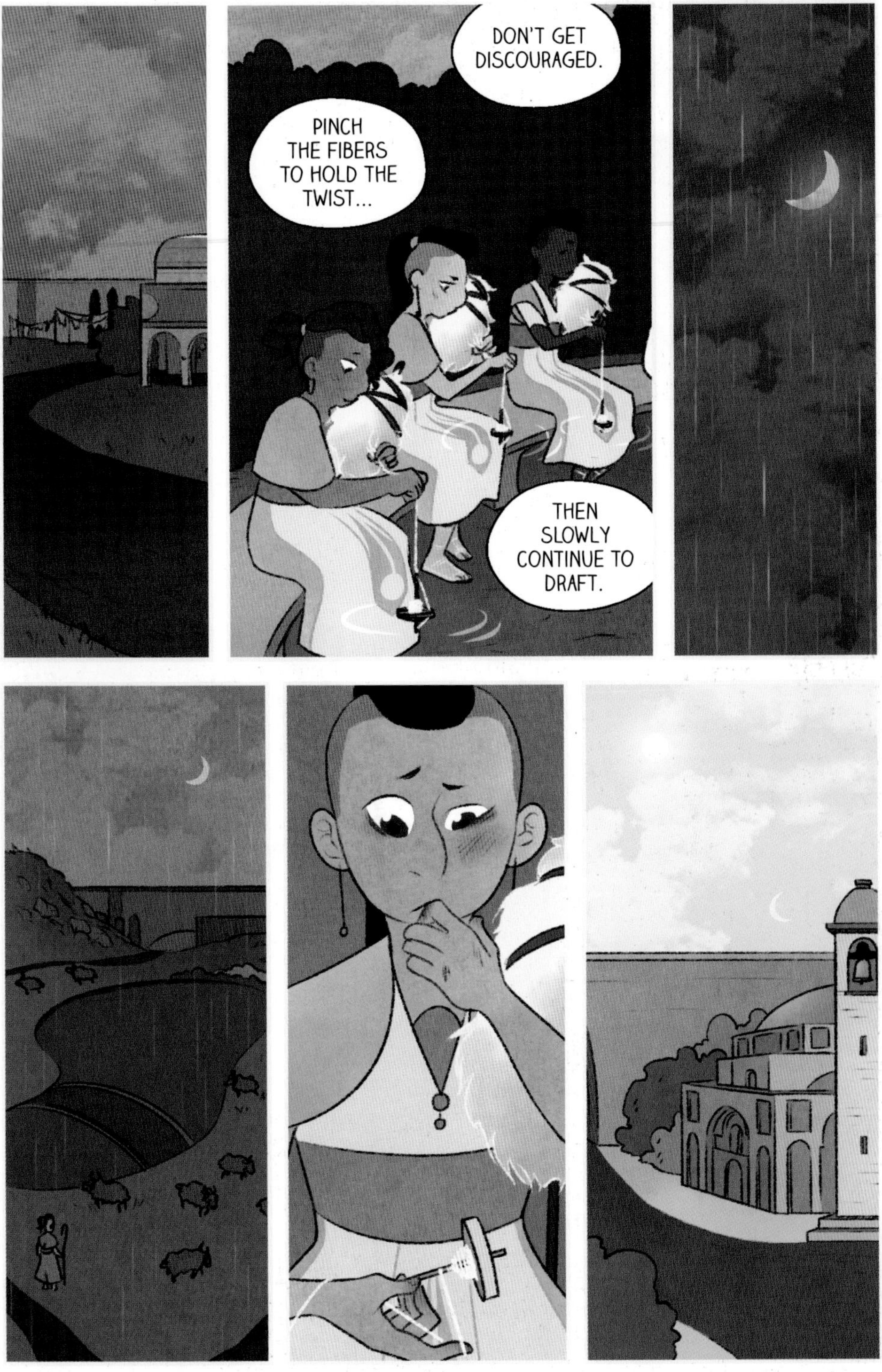
DON'T GET DISCOURAGED.
PINCH THE FIBERS TO HOLD THE TWIST...
THEN SLOWLY CONTINUE TO DRAFT.

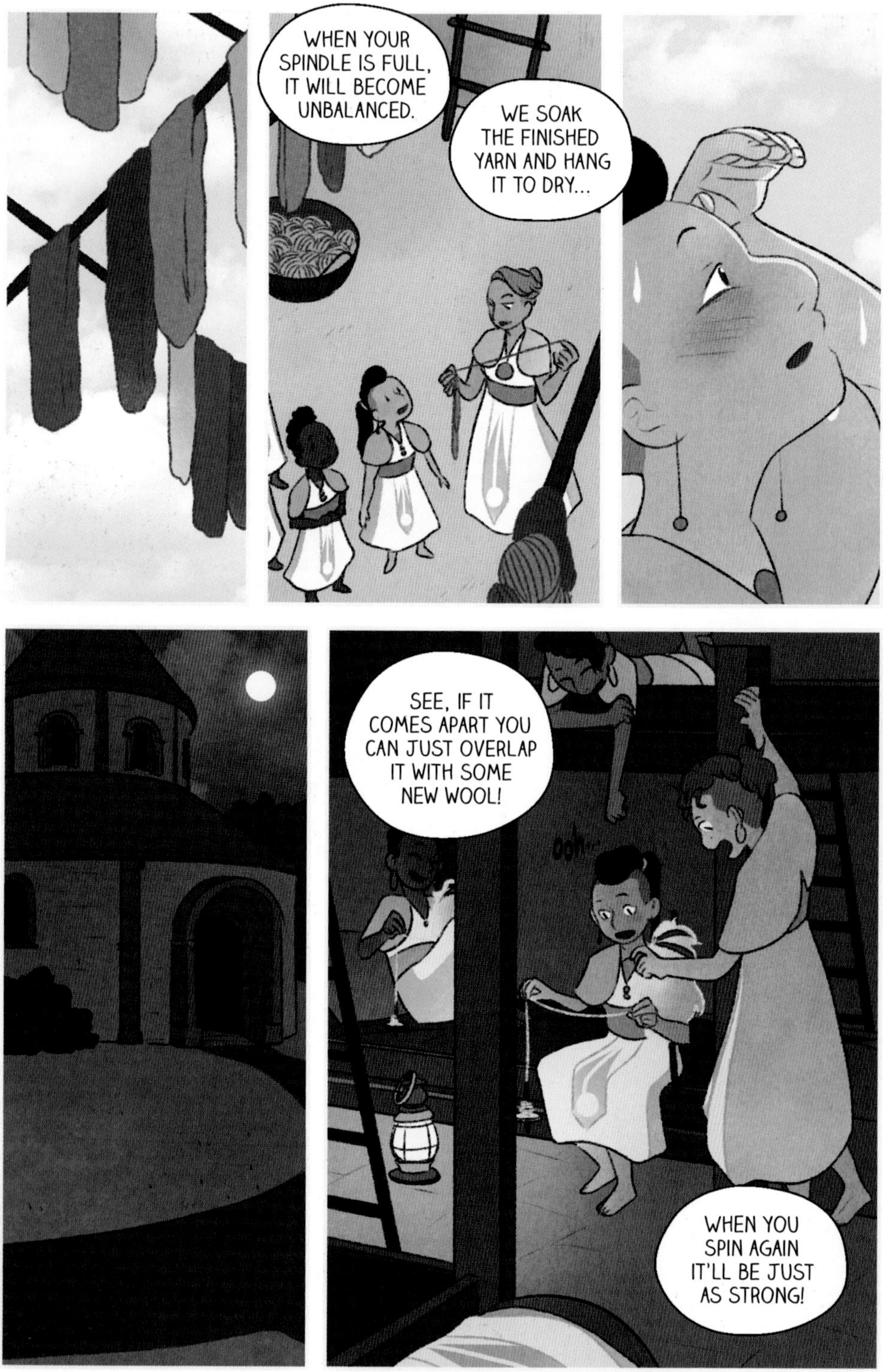
WHEN YOUR SPINDLE IS FULL, IT WILL BECOME UNBALANCED.
WE SOAK THE FINISHED YARN AND HANG IT TO DRY...
SEE, IF IT COMES APART YOU CAN JUST OVERLAP IT WITH SOME NEW WOOL!
ooh...
WHEN YOU SPIN AGAIN IT'LL BE JUST AS STRONG!

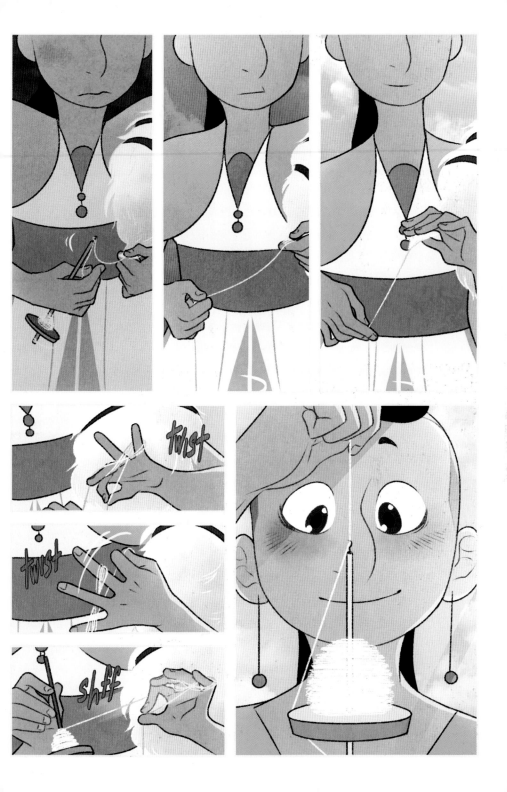

twist

twist

shff

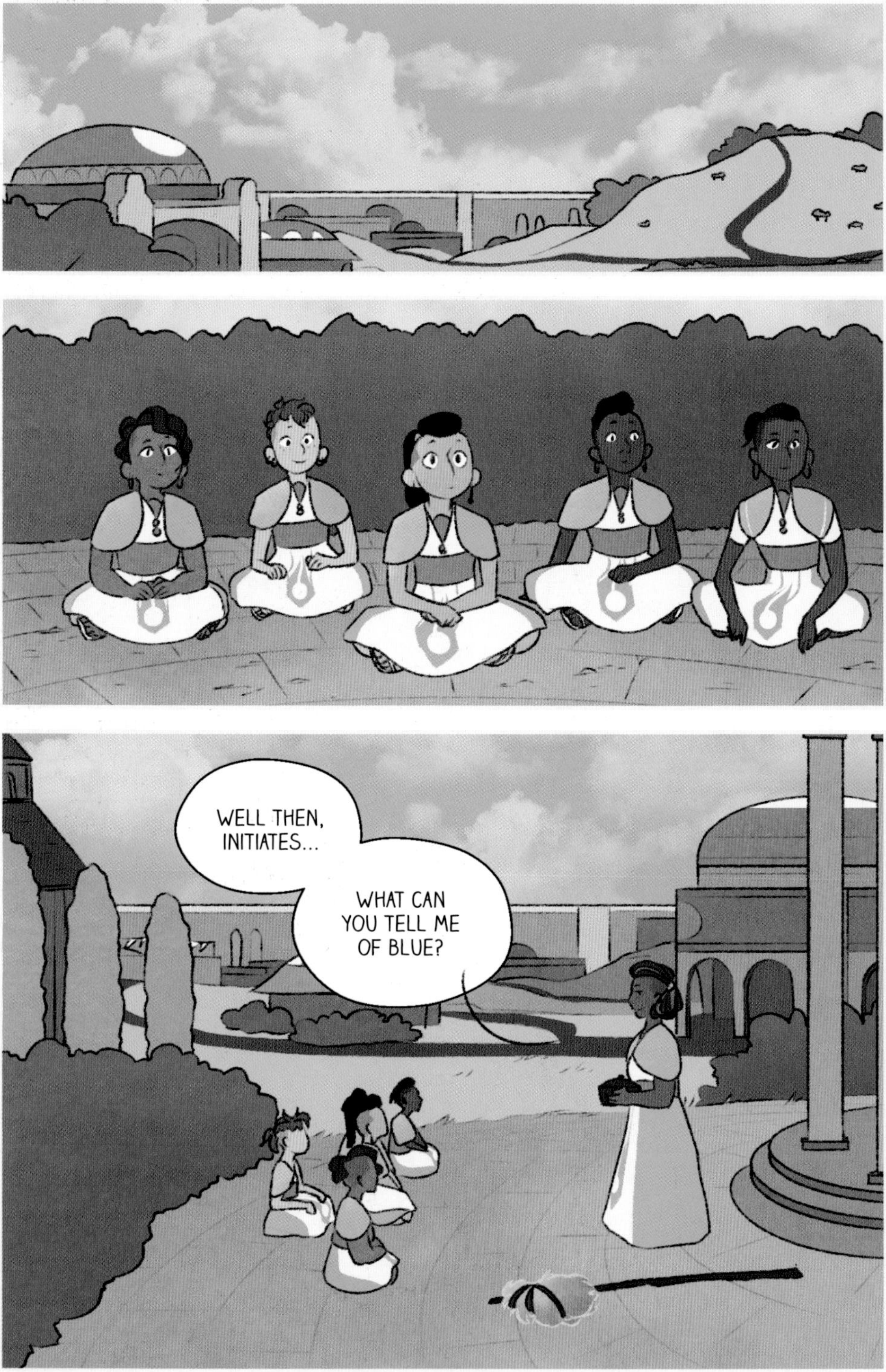
WELL THEN, INITIATES...
WHAT CAN YOU TELL ME OF BLUE?

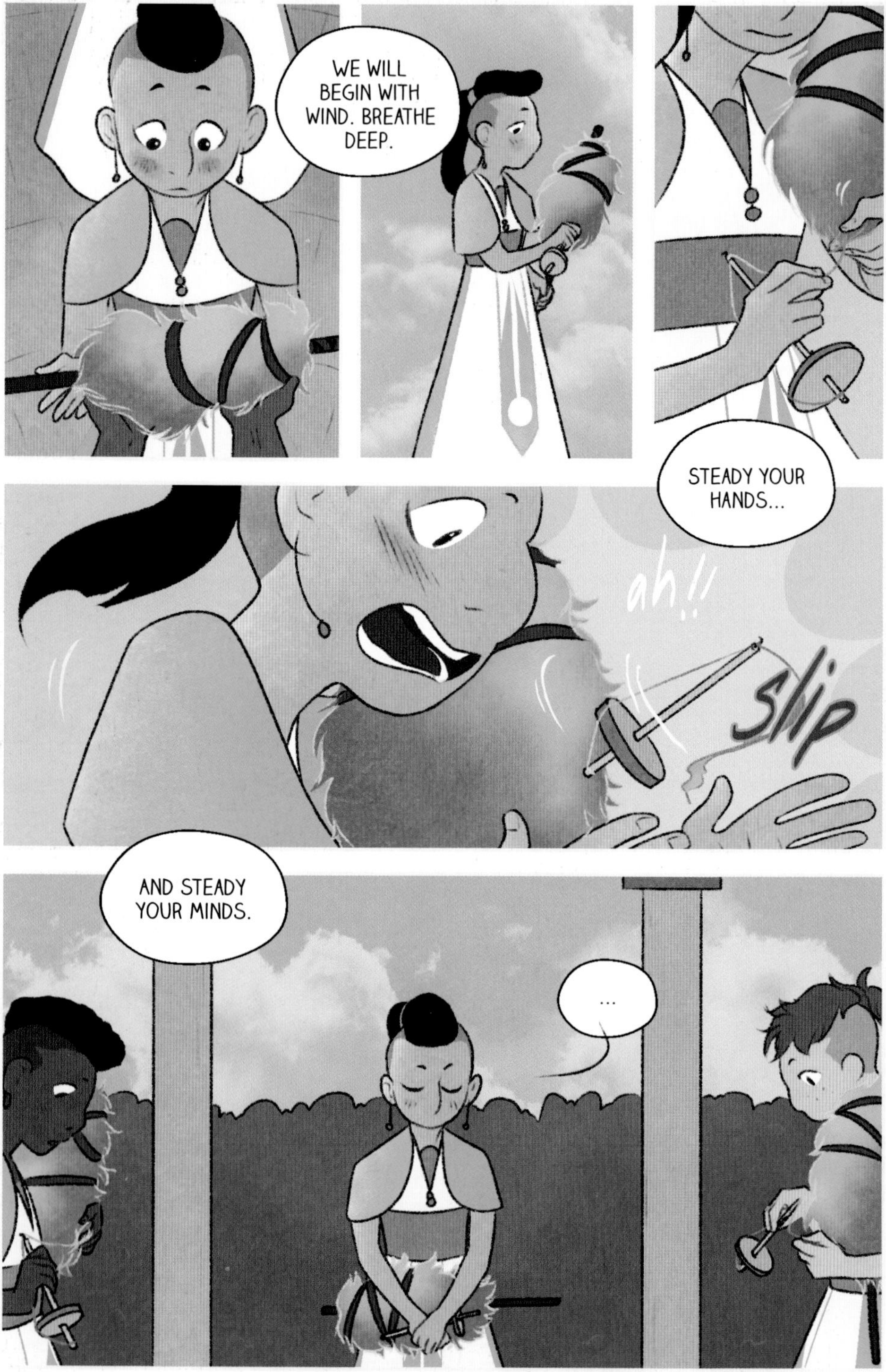

WE WILL BEGIN WITH WIND. BREATHE DEEP.
STEADY YOUR HANDS...
ah!!
slip
AND STEADY YOUR MINDS.
...

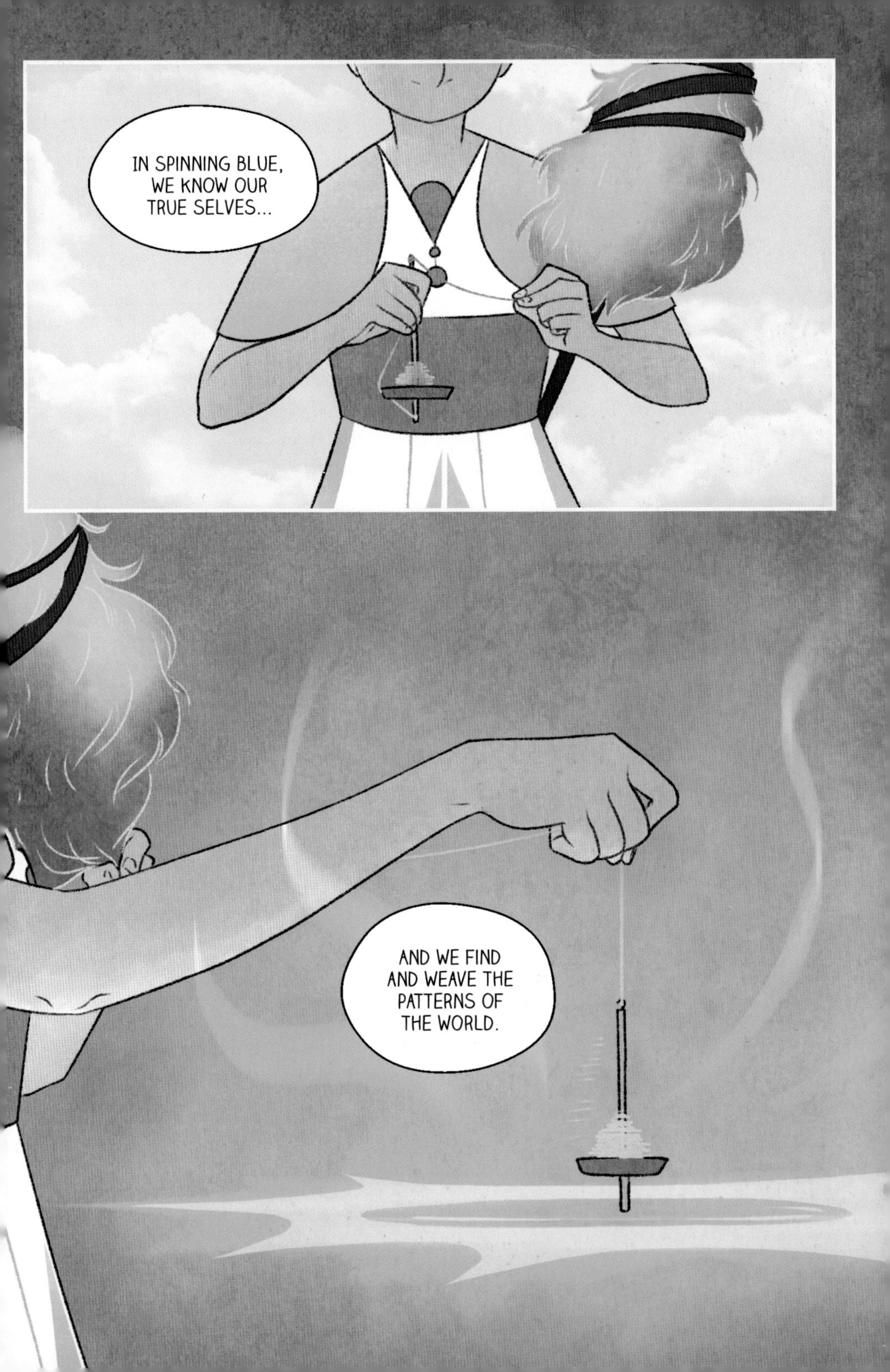
IN SPINNING BLUE, WE KNOW OUR TRUE SELVES...
AND WE FIND AND WEAVE THE PATTERNS OF THE WORLD.

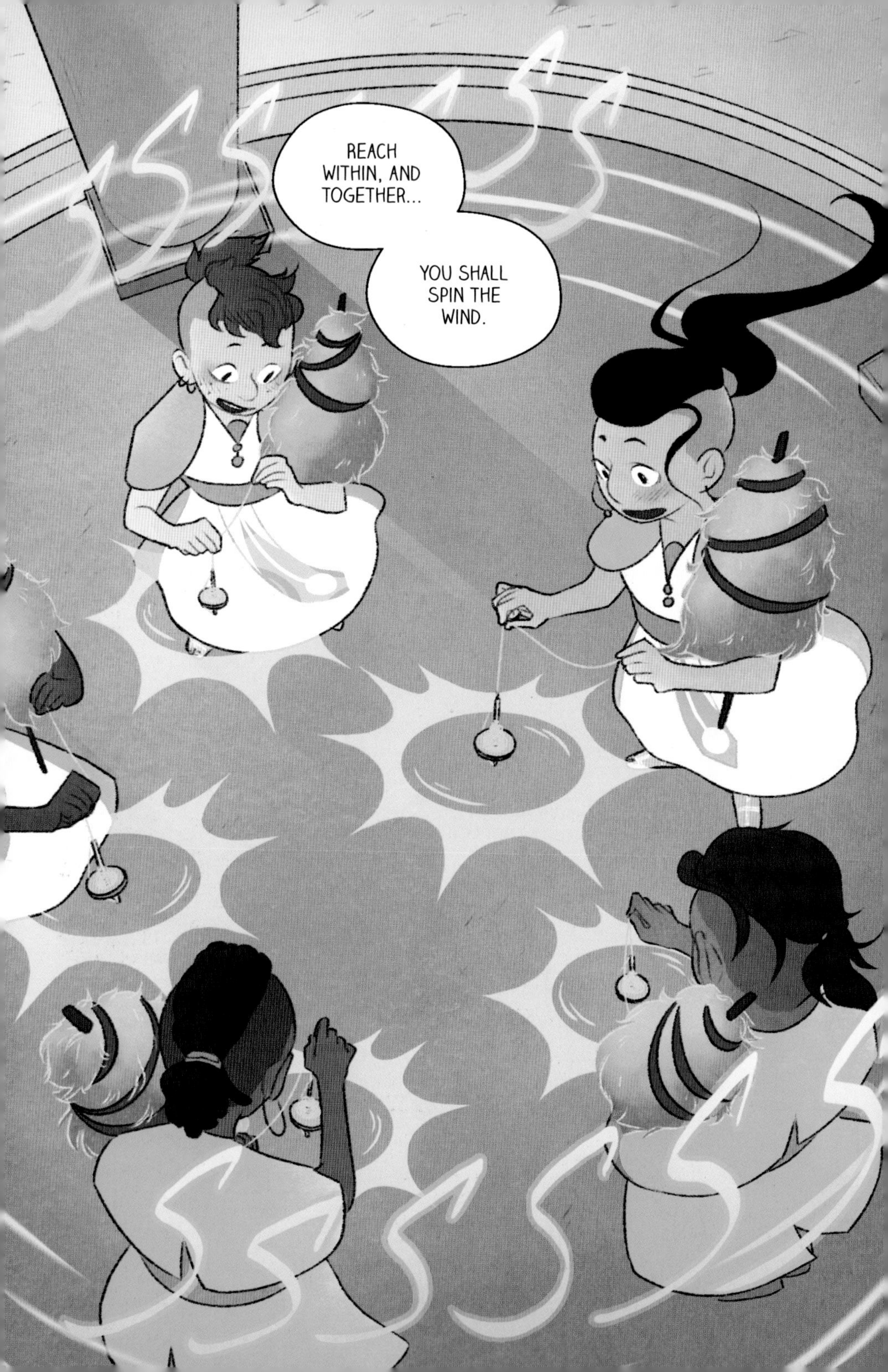
REACH WITHIN, AND TOGETHER...
YOU SHALL SPIN THE WIND.

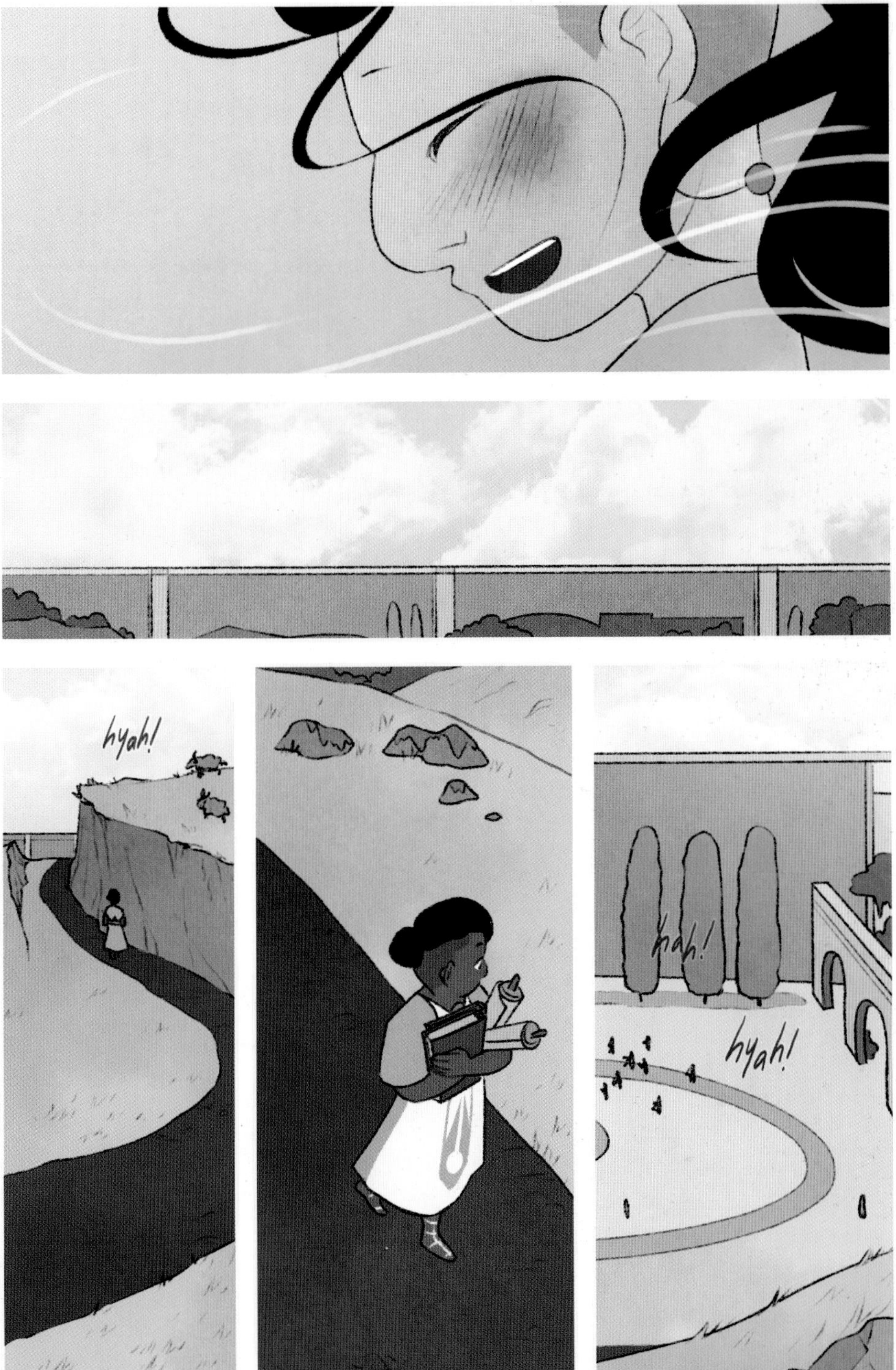
hyah!
hyah!
hyah!

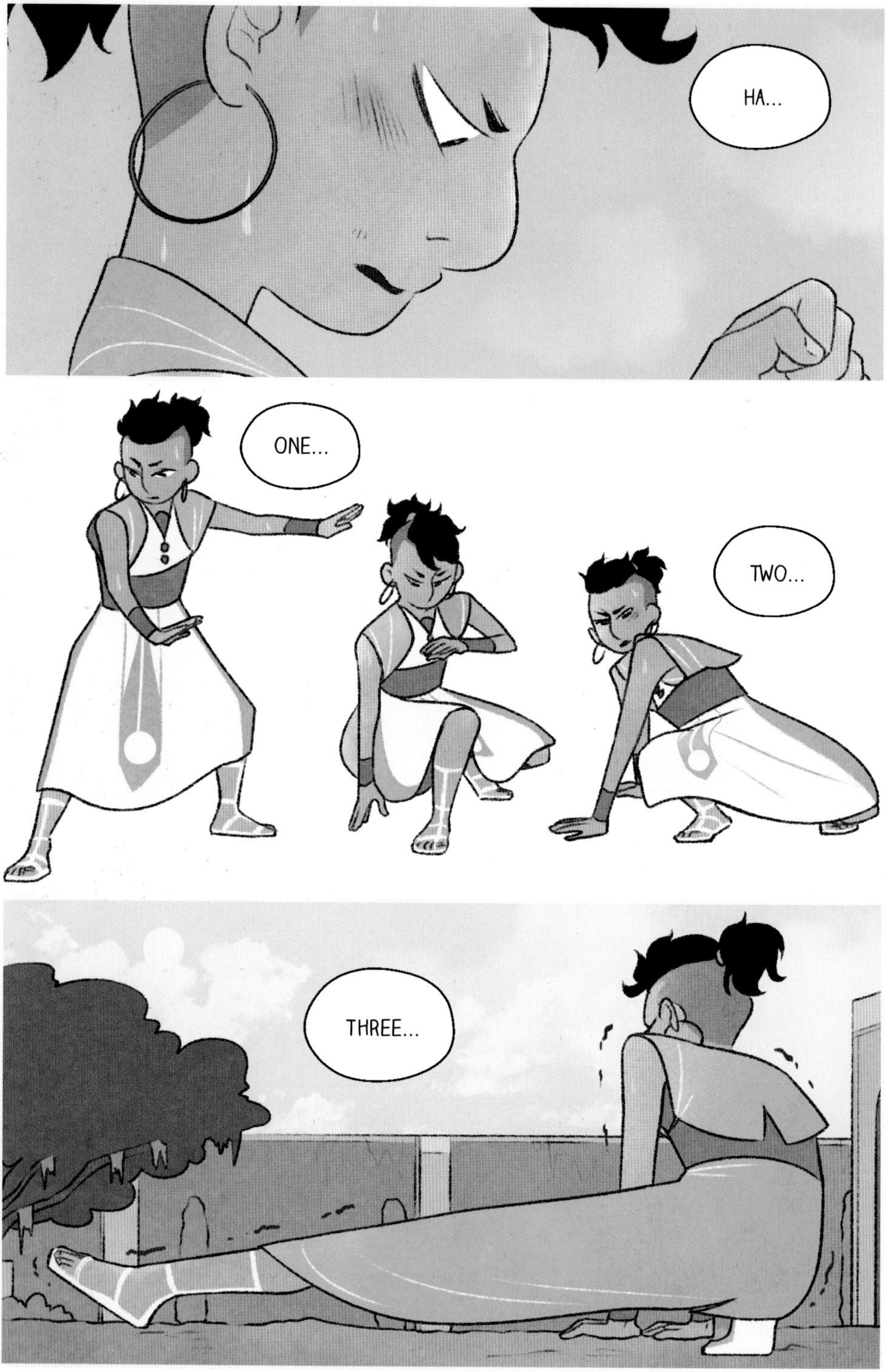
HA...
ONE...
TWO...
THREE...

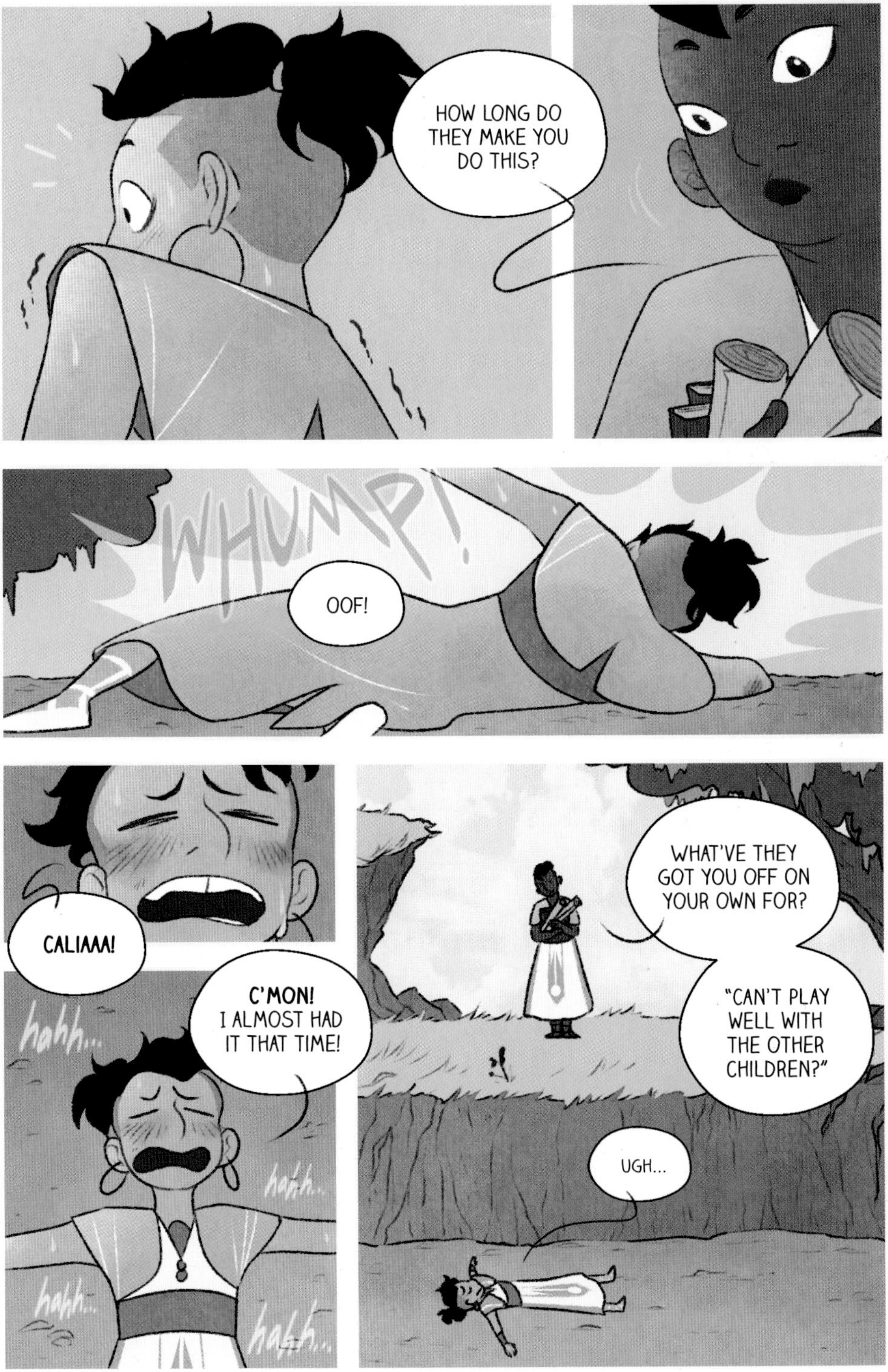
HOW LONG DO THEY MAKE YOU DO THIS?
WHUMP!
OOF!
CALIAAA!
C'MON! I ALMOST HAD IT THAT TIME!
hahh...
hahh...
hahh...
hahh...
WHAT'VE THEY GOT YOU OFF ON YOUR OWN FOR?
"CAN'T PLAY WELL WITH THE OTHER CHILDREN?"
UGH...

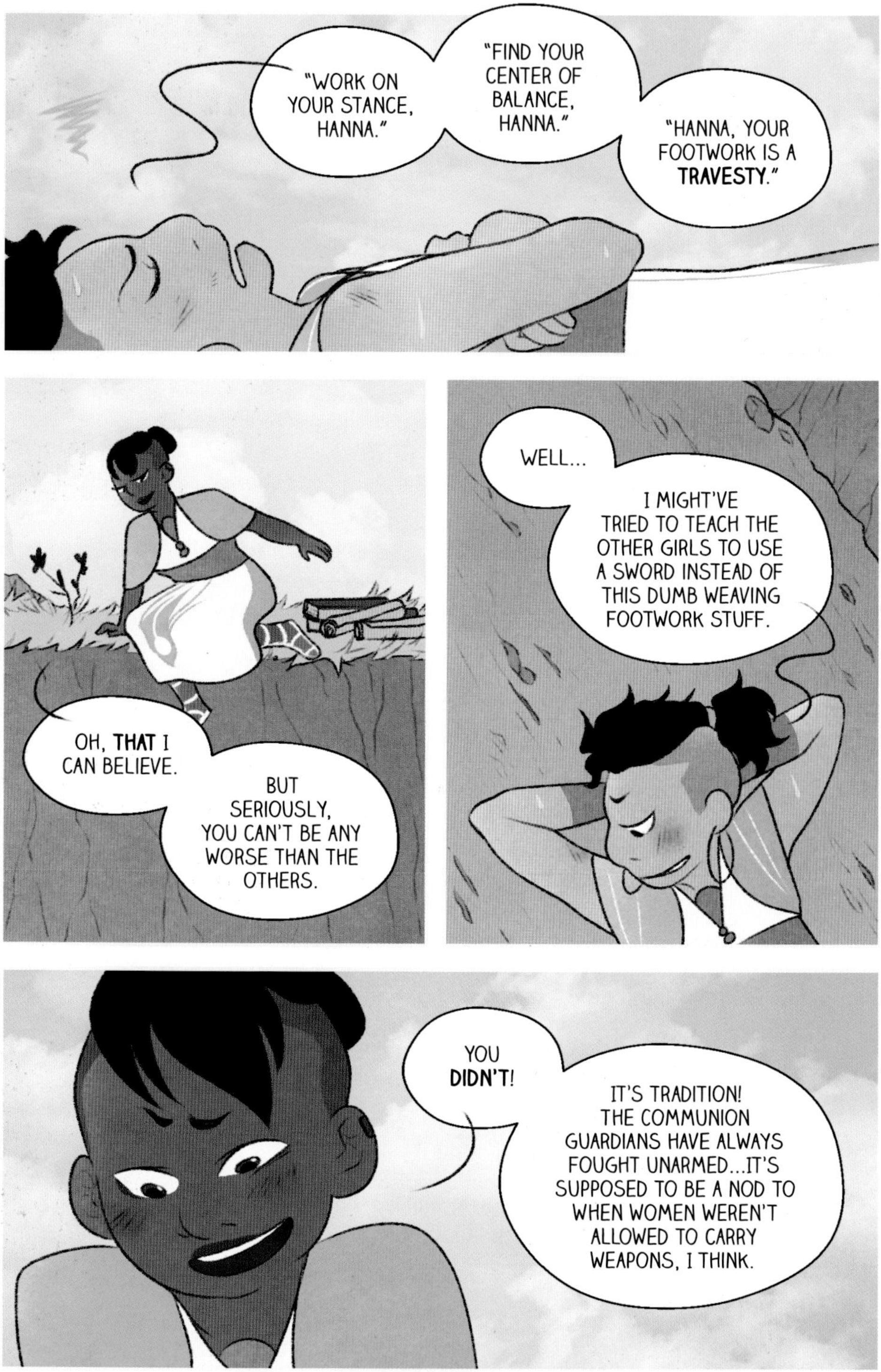
"WORK ON YOUR STANCE, HANNA."
"FIND YOUR CENTER OF BALANCE, HANNA."
"HANNA, YOUR FOOTWORK IS A **TRAVESTY**."
OH, **THAT** I CAN BELIEVE.
BUT SERIOUSLY, YOU CAN'T BE ANY WORSE THAN THE OTHERS.
WELL...
I MIGHT'VE TRIED TO TEACH THE OTHER GIRLS TO USE A SWORD INSTEAD OF THIS DUMB WEAVING FOOTWORK STUFF.
YOU **DIDN'T**!
IT'S TRADITION! THE COMMUNION GUARDIANS HAVE ALWAYS FOUGHT UNARMED...IT'S SUPPOSED TO BE A NOD TO WHEN WOMEN WEREN'T ALLOWED TO CARRY WEAPONS, I THINK.

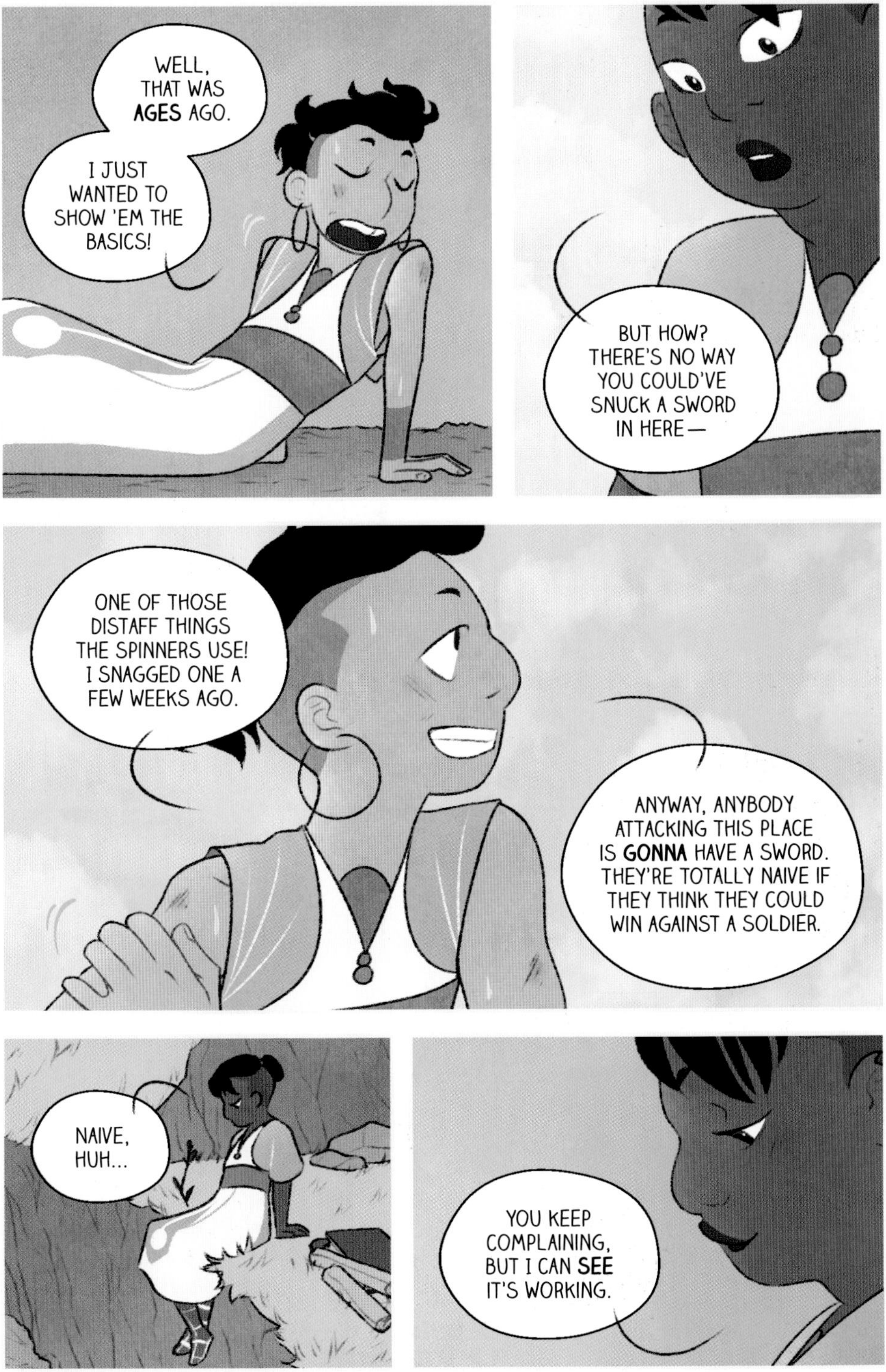
WELL, THAT WAS **AGES** AGO.
I JUST WANTED TO SHOW 'EM THE BASICS!
BUT HOW? THERE'S NO WAY YOU COULD'VE SNUCK A SWORD IN HERE—
ONE OF THOSE DISTAFF THINGS THE SPINNERS USE! I SNAGGED ONE A FEW WEEKS AGO.
ANYWAY, ANYBODY ATTACKING THIS PLACE IS **GONNA** HAVE A SWORD. THEY'RE TOTALLY NAIVE IF THEY THINK THEY COULD WIN AGAINST A SOLDIER.
NAIVE, HUH...
YOU KEEP COMPLAINING, BUT I CAN **SEE** IT'S WORKING.

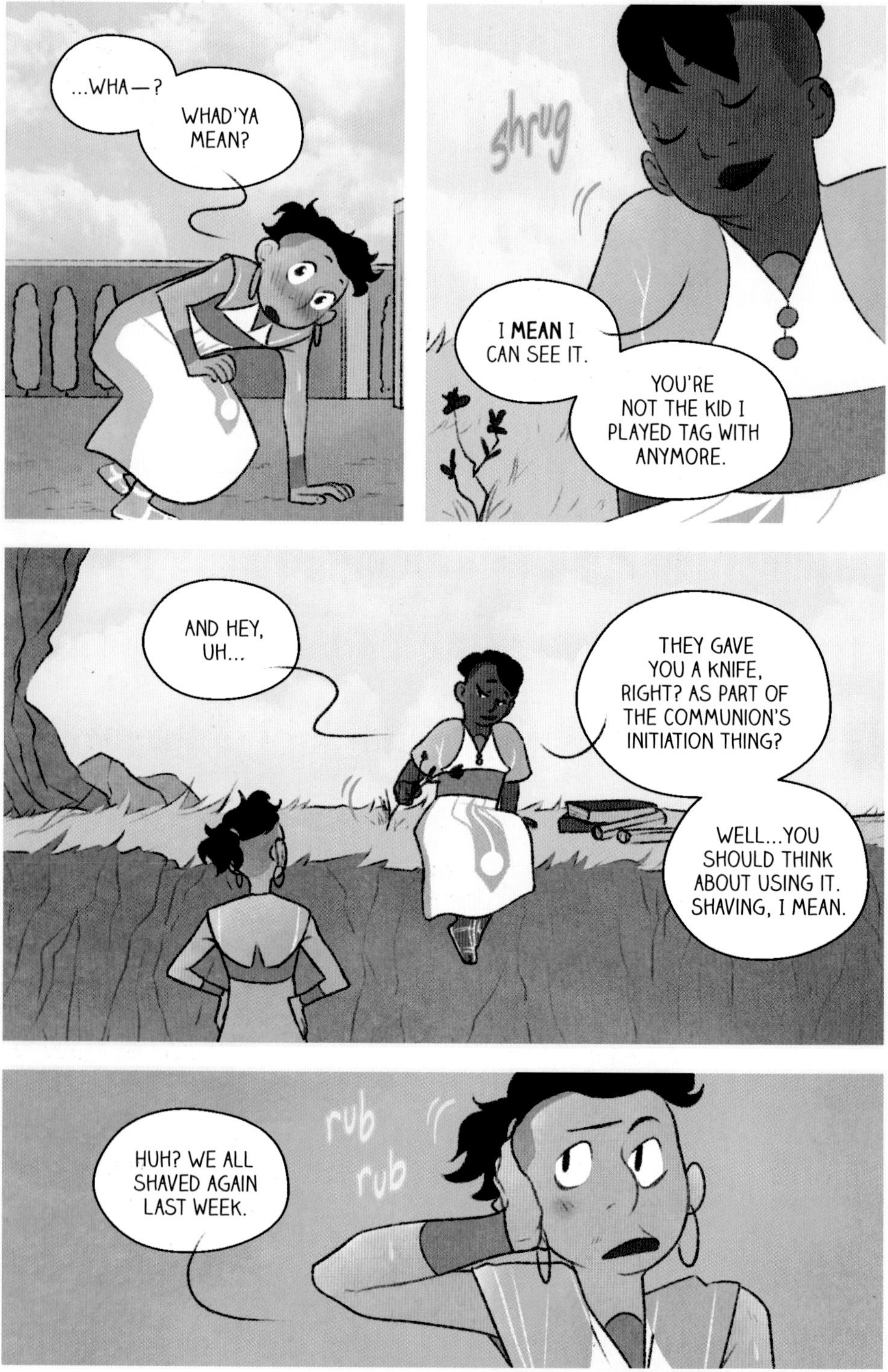
...WHA—?
WHAD'YA MEAN?
shrug
I **MEAN** I CAN SEE IT.
YOU'RE NOT THE KID I PLAYED TAG WITH ANYMORE.
AND HEY, UH...
THEY GAVE YOU A KNIFE, RIGHT? AS PART OF THE COMMUNION'S INITIATION THING?
WELL...YOU SHOULD THINK ABOUT USING IT. SHAVING, I MEAN.
rub rub
HUH? WE ALL SHAVED AGAIN LAST WEEK.

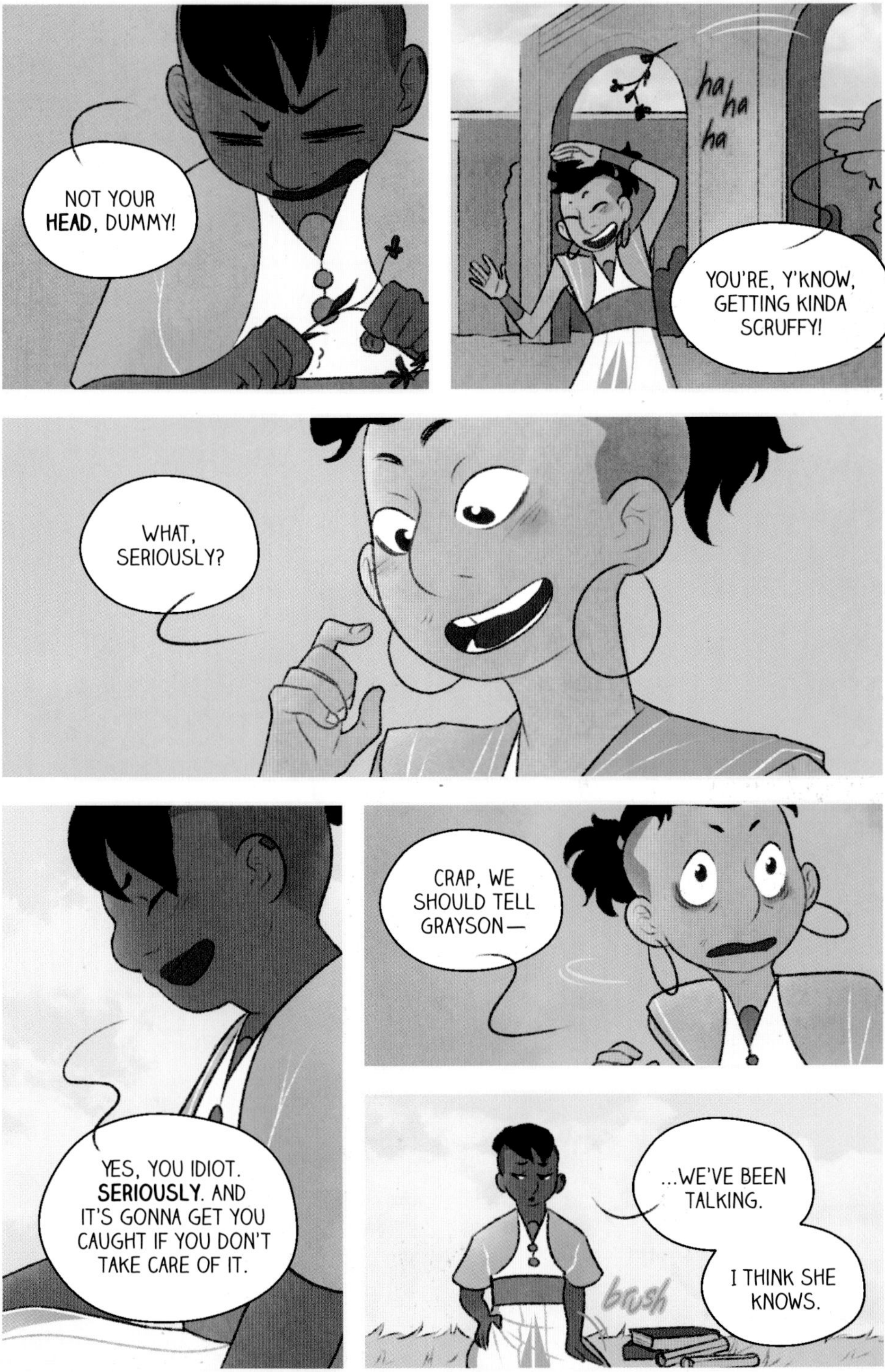
NOT YOUR **HEAD**, DUMMY!
ha ha ha
YOU'RE, Y'KNOW, GETTING KINDA SCRUFFY!
WHAT, SERIOUSLY?
YES, YOU IDIOT. **SERIOUSLY**. AND IT'S GONNA GET YOU CAUGHT IF YOU DON'T TAKE CARE OF IT.
CRAP, WE SHOULD TELL GRAYSON—
...WE'VE BEEN TALKING.
I THINK SHE KNOWS.
brush

CHAPTER III

HOME

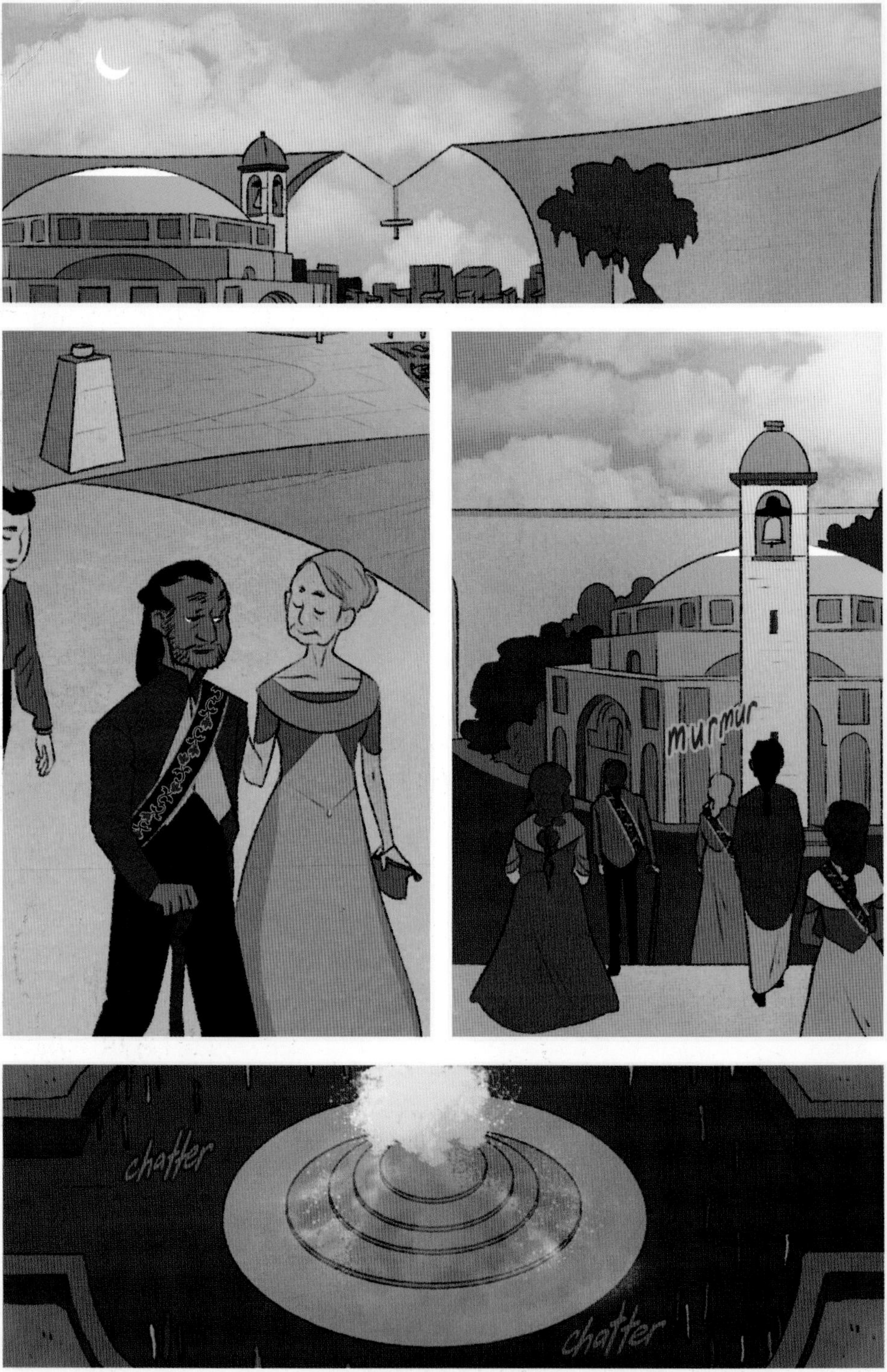
murmur
chatter
chatter

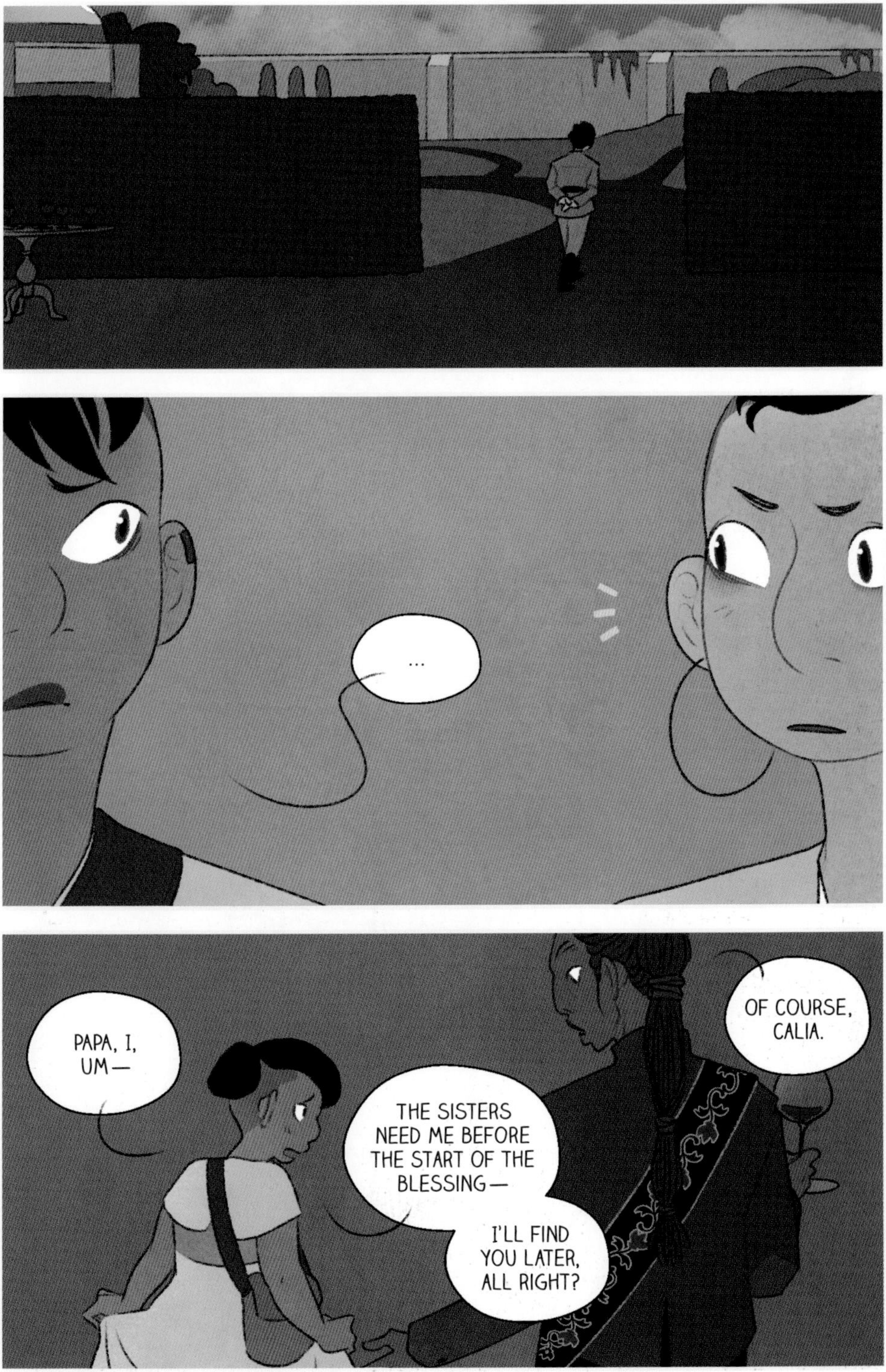
...
PAPA, I, UM—
THE SISTERS NEED ME BEFORE THE START OF THE BLESSING—
I'LL FIND YOU LATER, ALL RIGHT?
OF COURSE, CALIA.

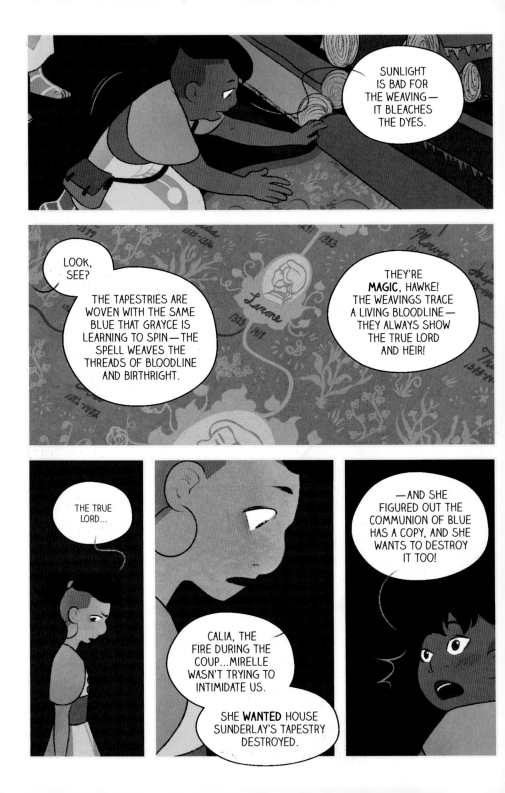

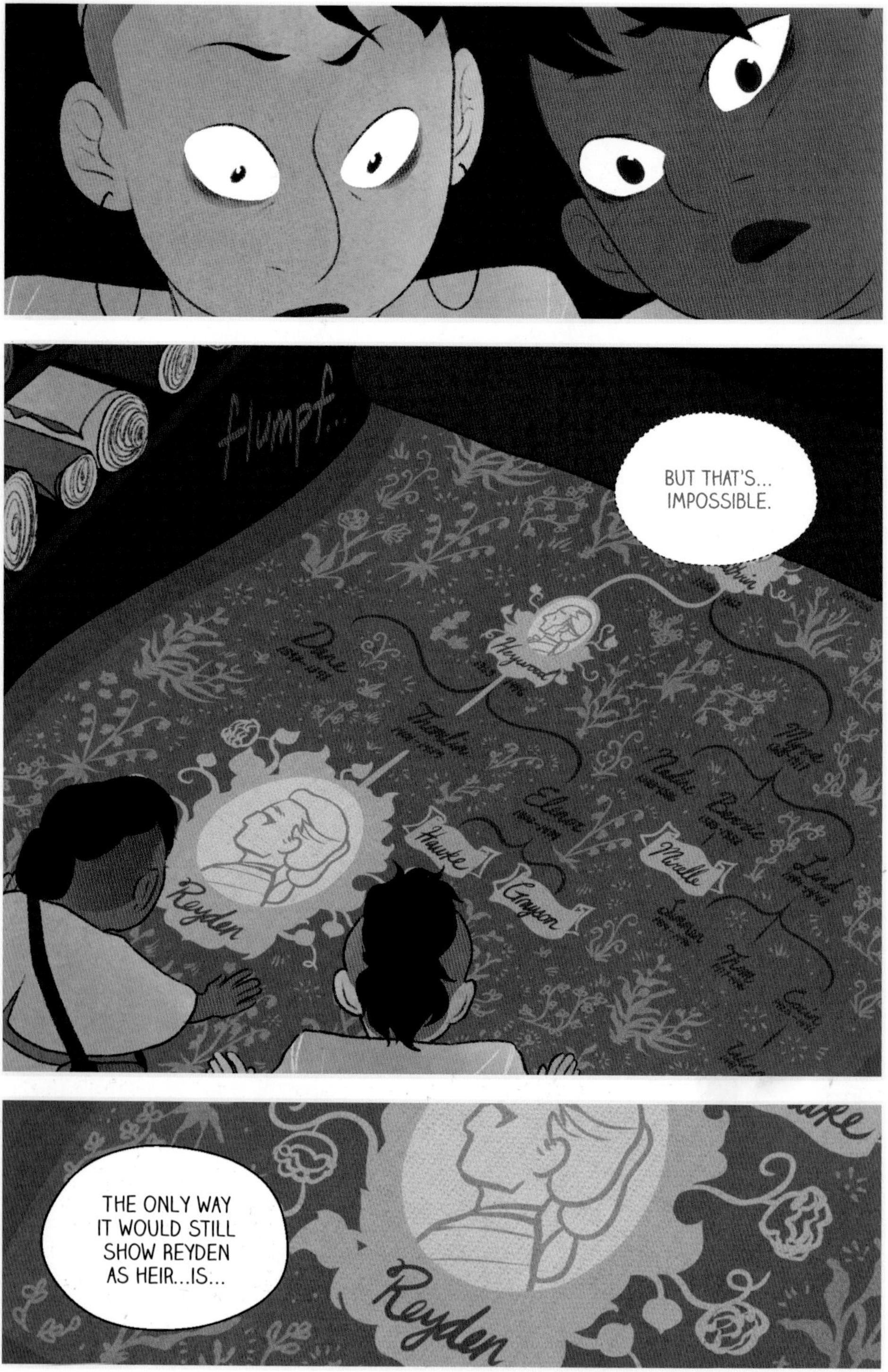
flumpf...
BUT THAT'S... IMPOSSIBLE.
Heywood
Reyden
Hawke
Grayson
THE ONLY WAY IT WOULD STILL SHOW REYDEN AS HEIR...IS...
Reyden

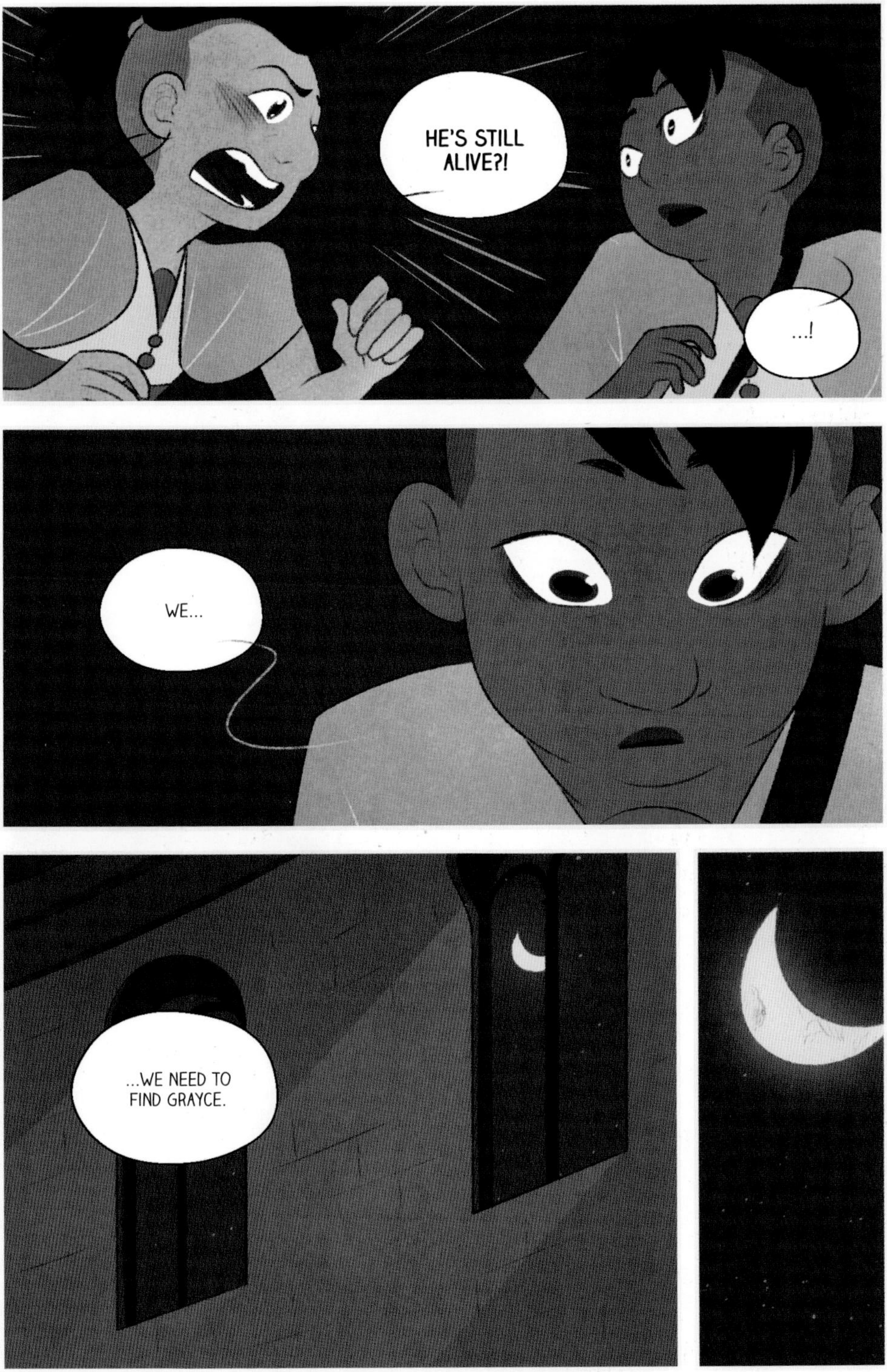
HE'S STILL ALIVE?!
...!
WE...
...WE NEED TO FIND GRAYCE.

THE CORONATION'S AT DAWN, AND SUNRISE ISN'T FOR HOURS.

EVERYONE'S STILL AT THE BLESSING — THEY WON'T NOTICE YOU'RE GONE.

...IF YOU GO NOW, YOU CAN MAKE IT.

BUT HOW WOULD WE GET IN...?

THE MANOR IS CRAWLING WITH MIRELLE'S SOLDIERS.

WE'D NEVER MAKE IT IN OVER THE WALLS. WE BARELY MADE IT **OUT!**

WE DON'T GO OVER THE WALLS...

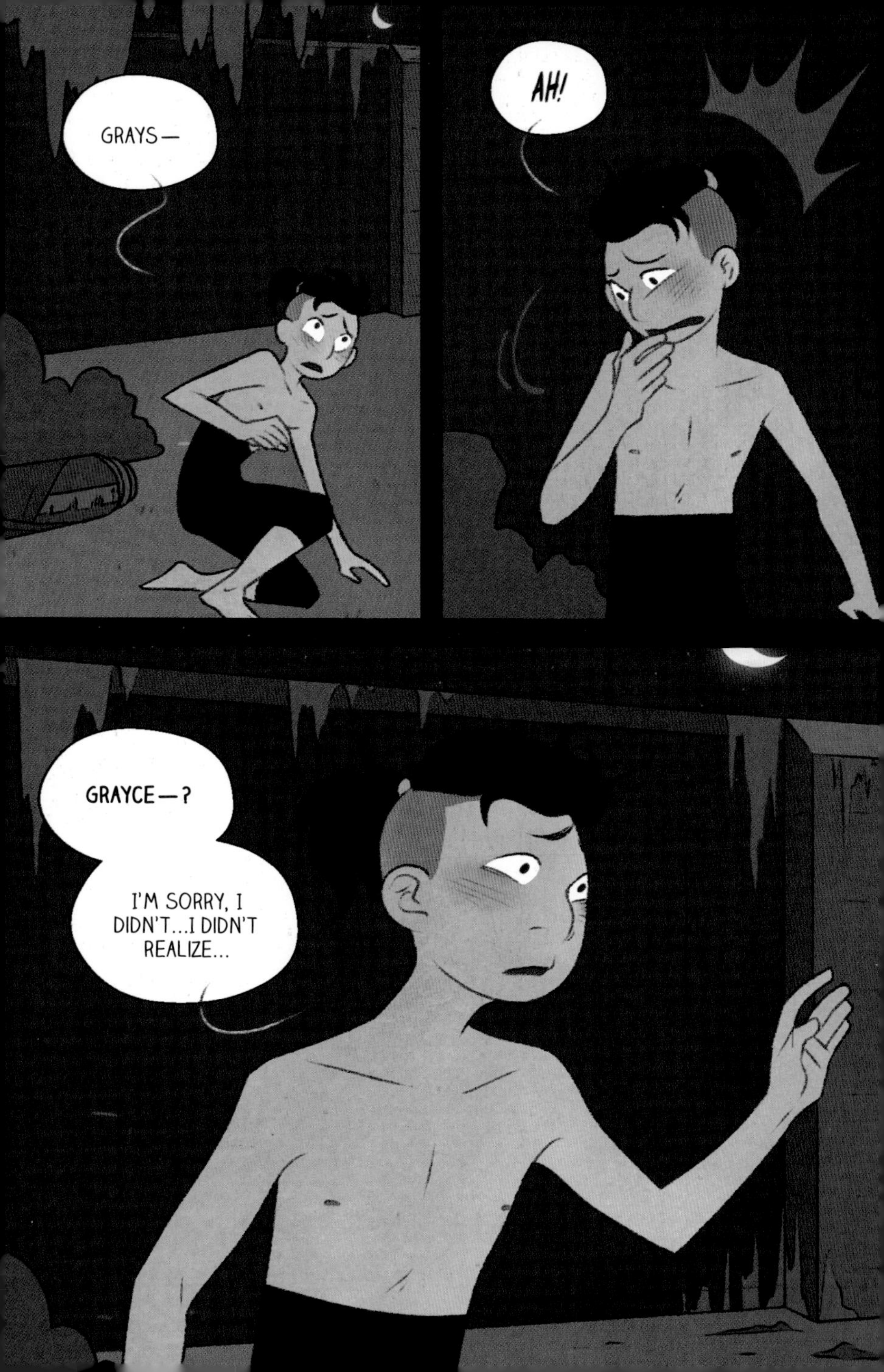
GRAYS—
AH!
GRAYCE—?
I'M SORRY, I DIDN'T...I DIDN'T REALIZE...

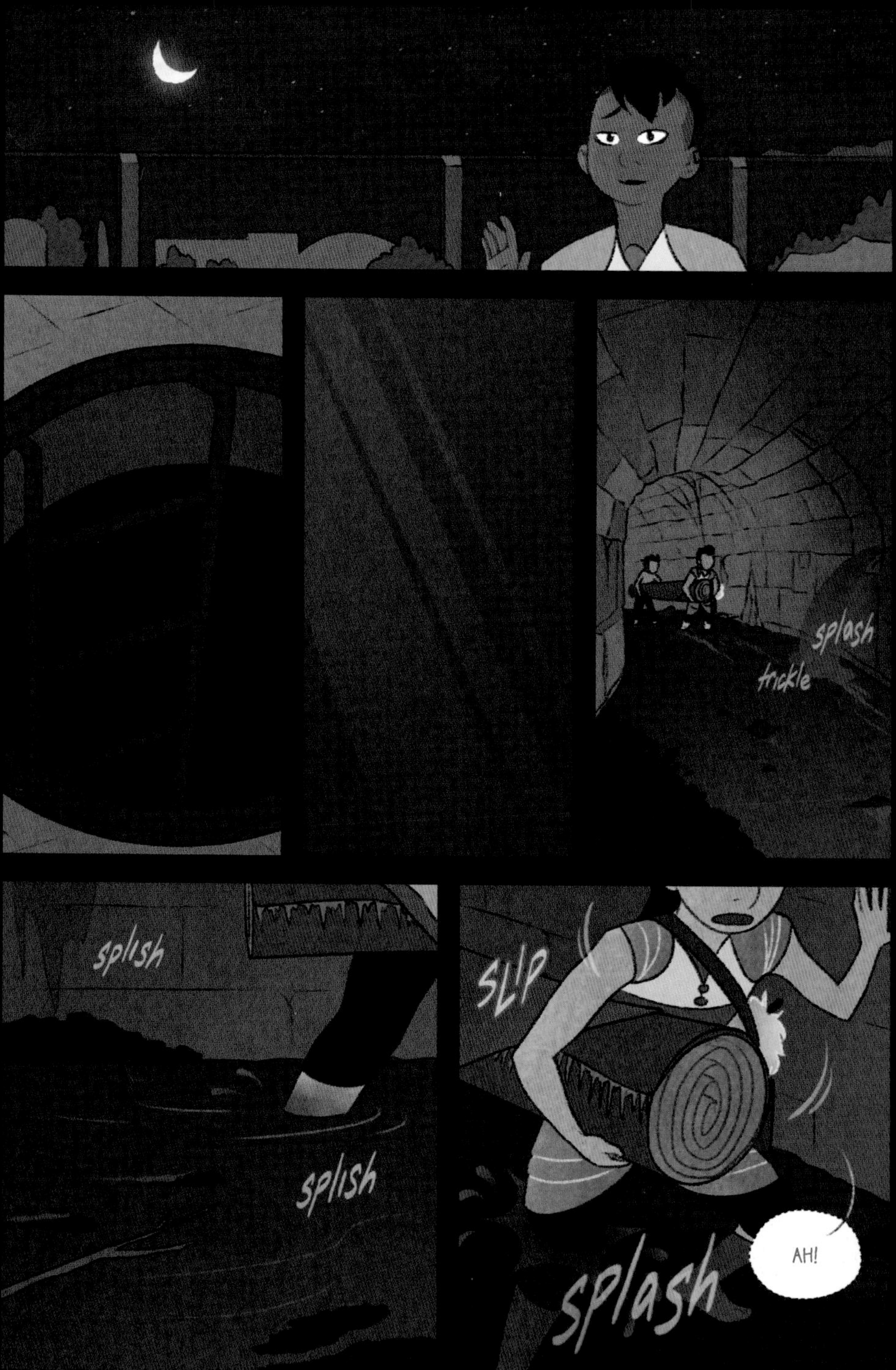
splash
trickle
splish
splish
SLIP
AH!
splash

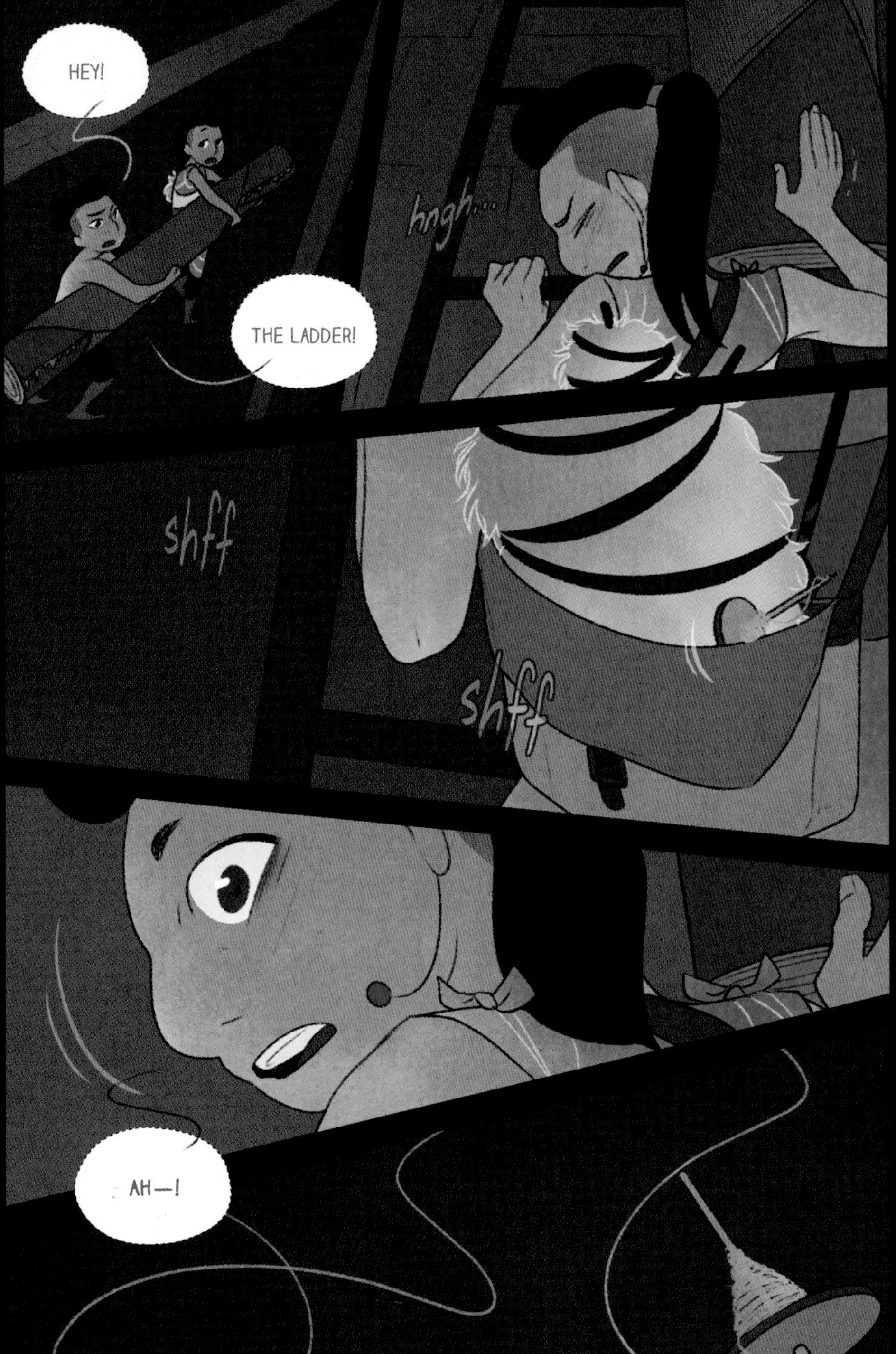
HEY!
THE LADDER!
hngh...
!
shff
shff
AH—!

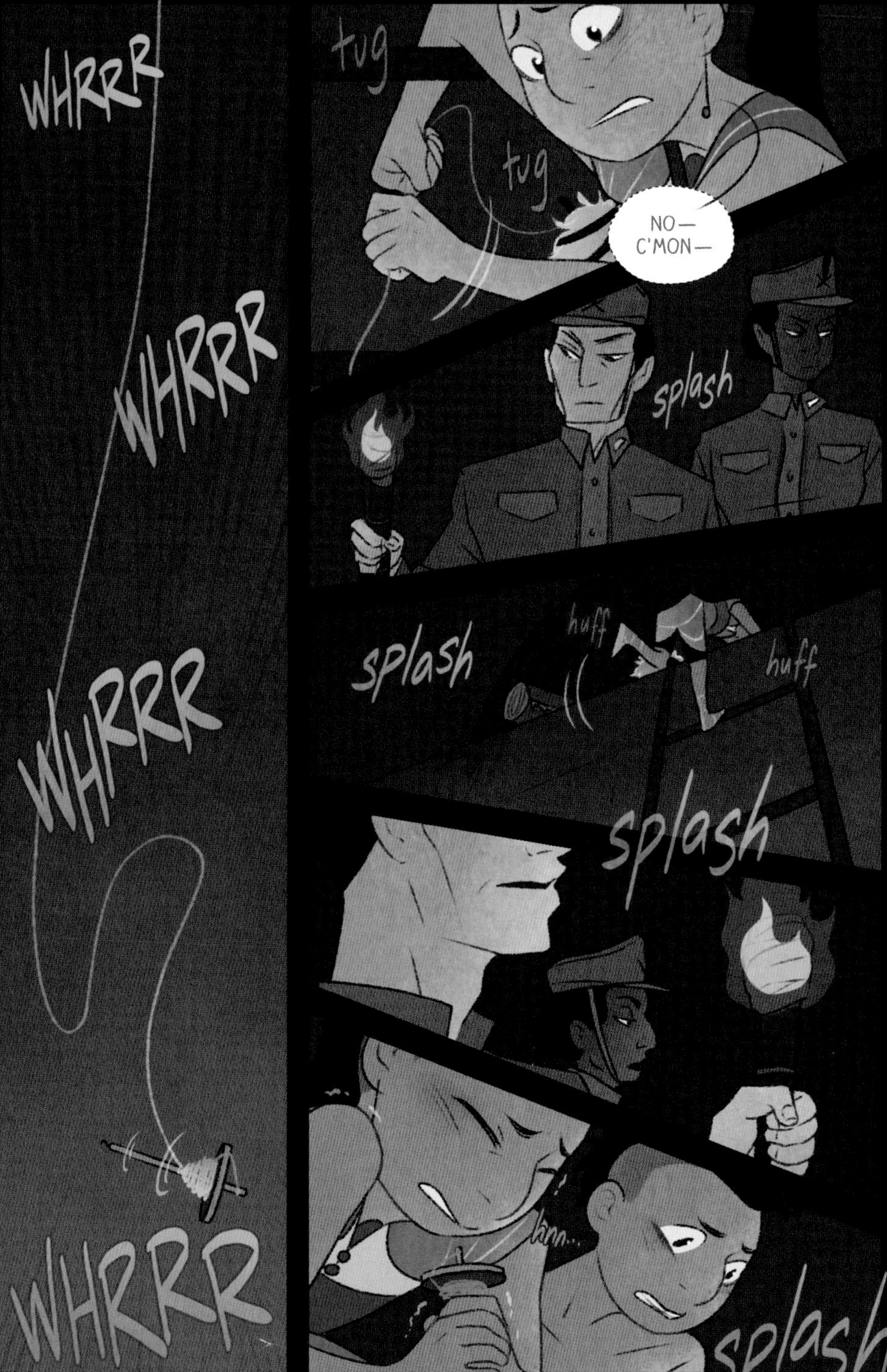

WHRRR
tug
tug
NO—
C'MON—
WHRRR
splash
splash
huff
huff
WHRRR
splash
hnn...
WHRRR
splash

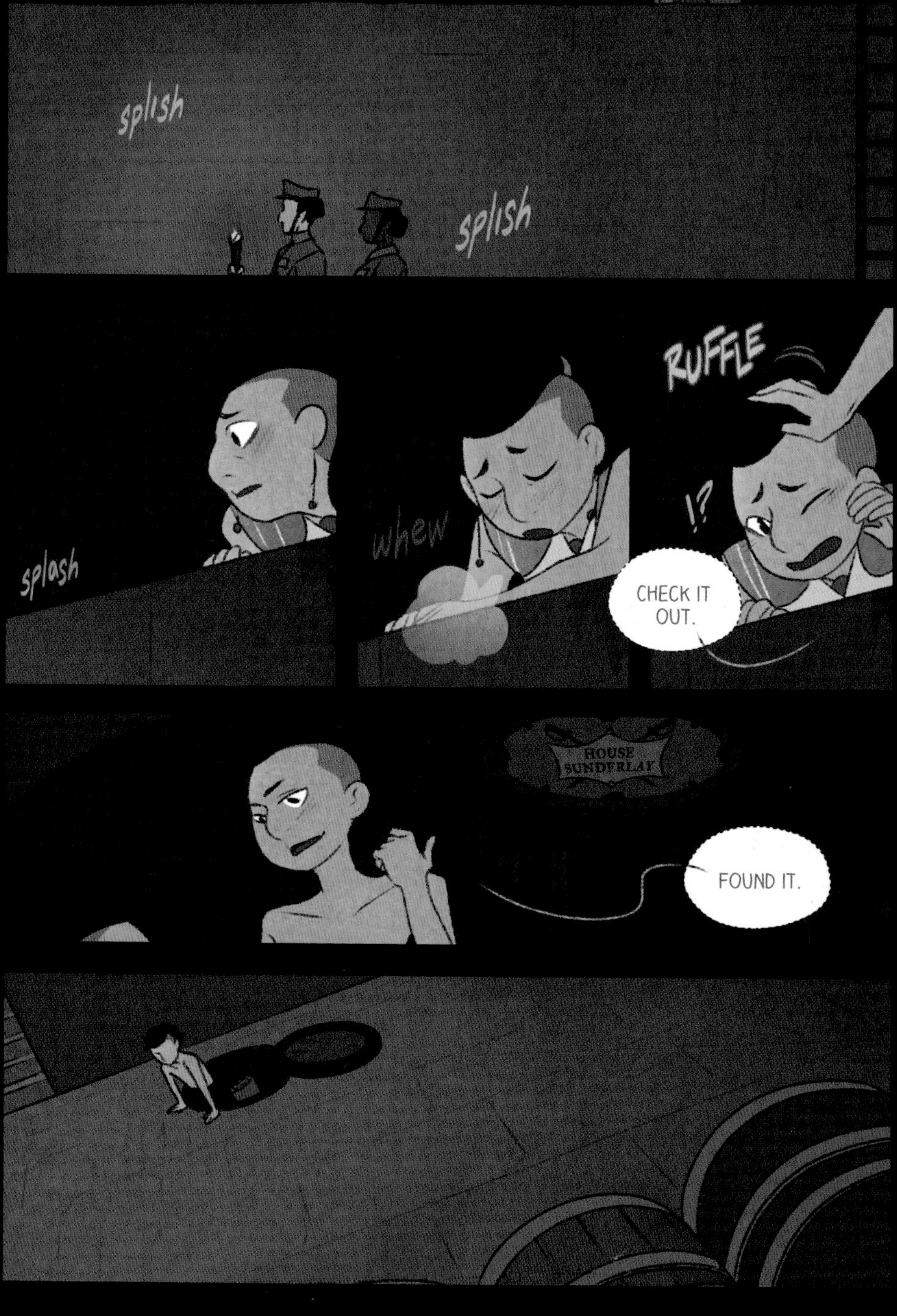
splish
splish
splash
whew
RUFFLE
!?
CHECK IT OUT.
HOUSE SUNDERLAY
FOUND IT.

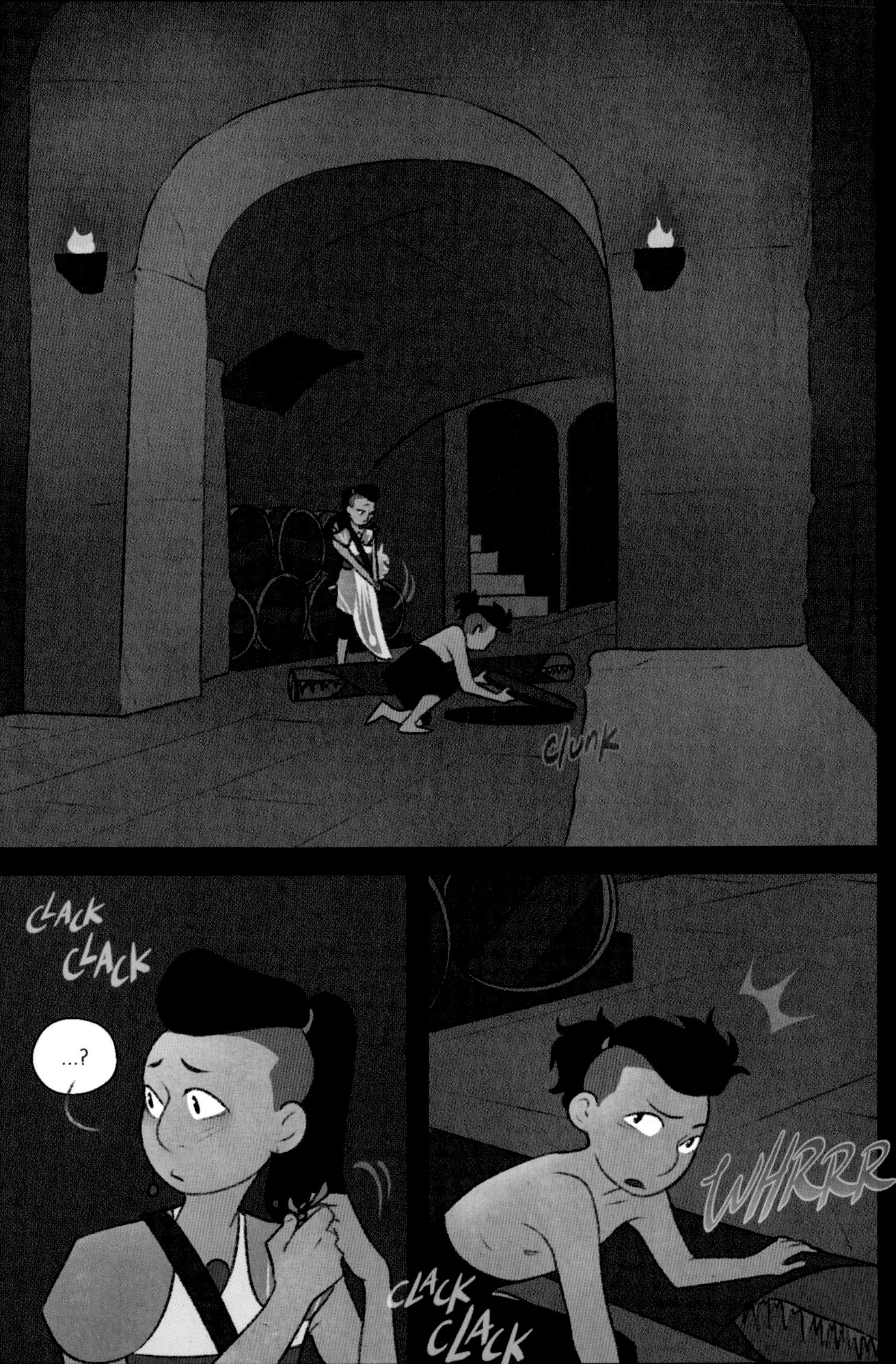
clunk
CLACK
CLACK
...?
WHRRR
CLACK
CLACK

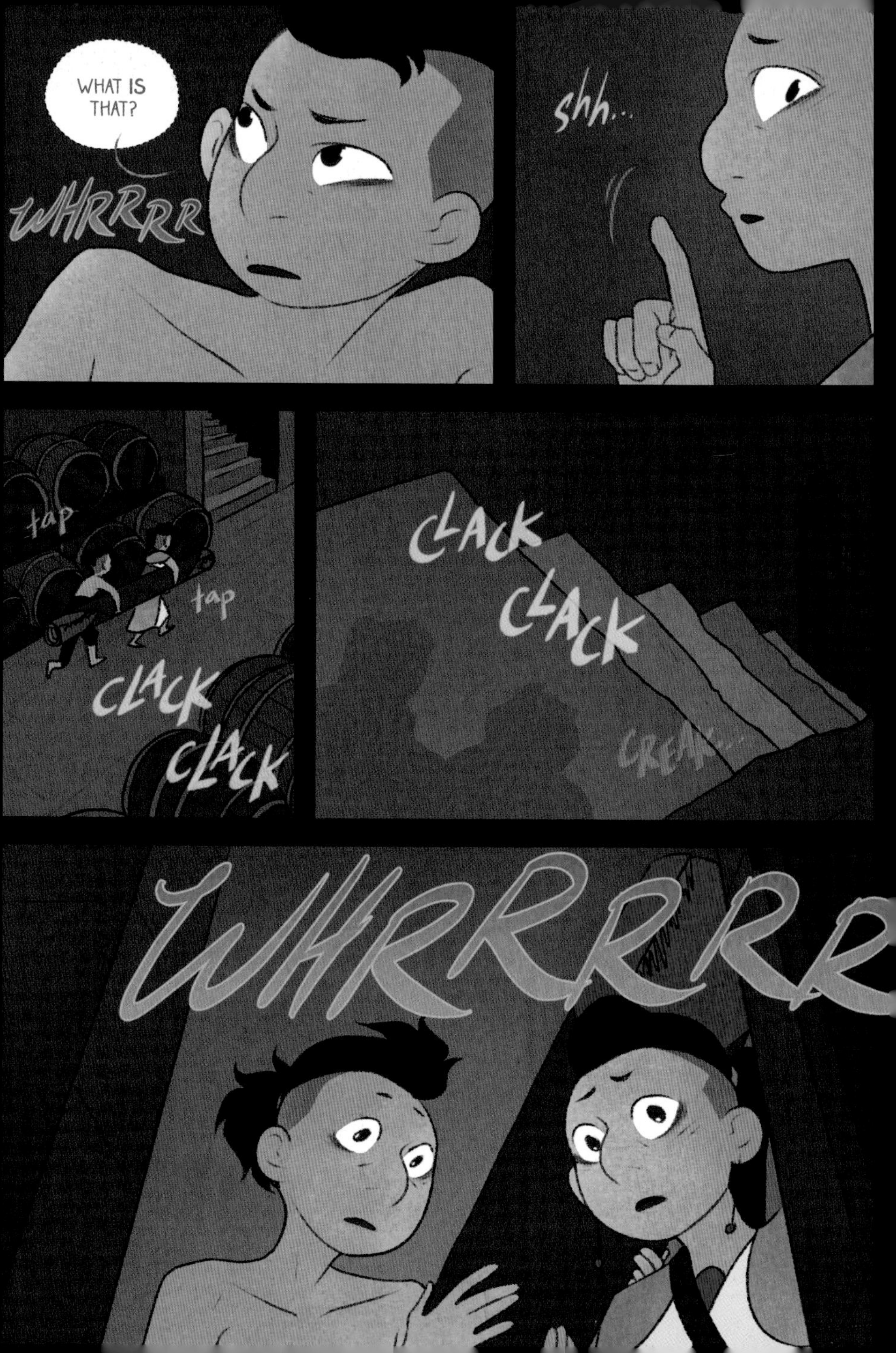
WHAT IS THAT?
WHRRRR
shh...
tap
tap
CLACK
CLACK
CLACK
CLACK
CREAK...
WHRRRR

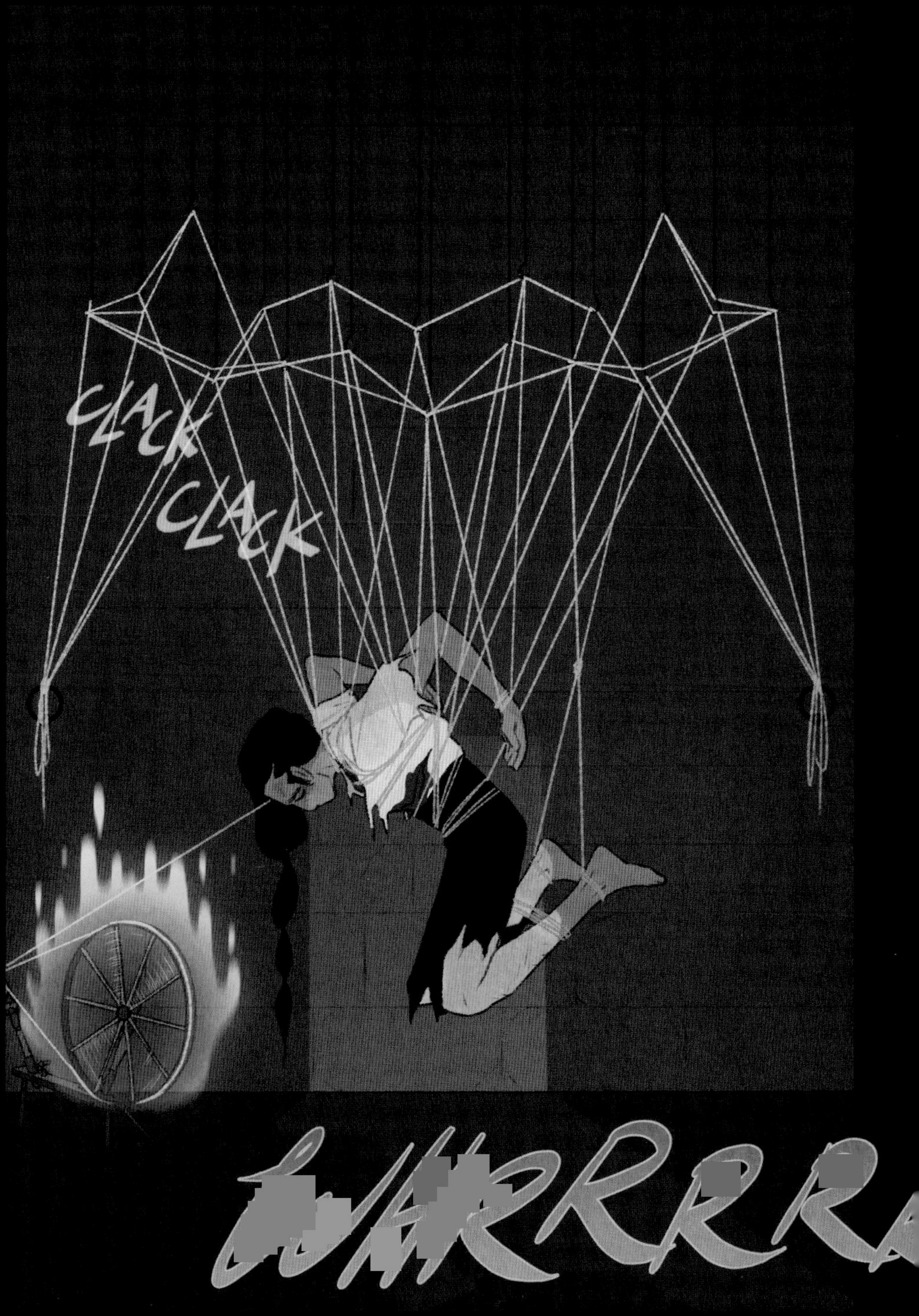
CLACK
CLACK
WHRRRR

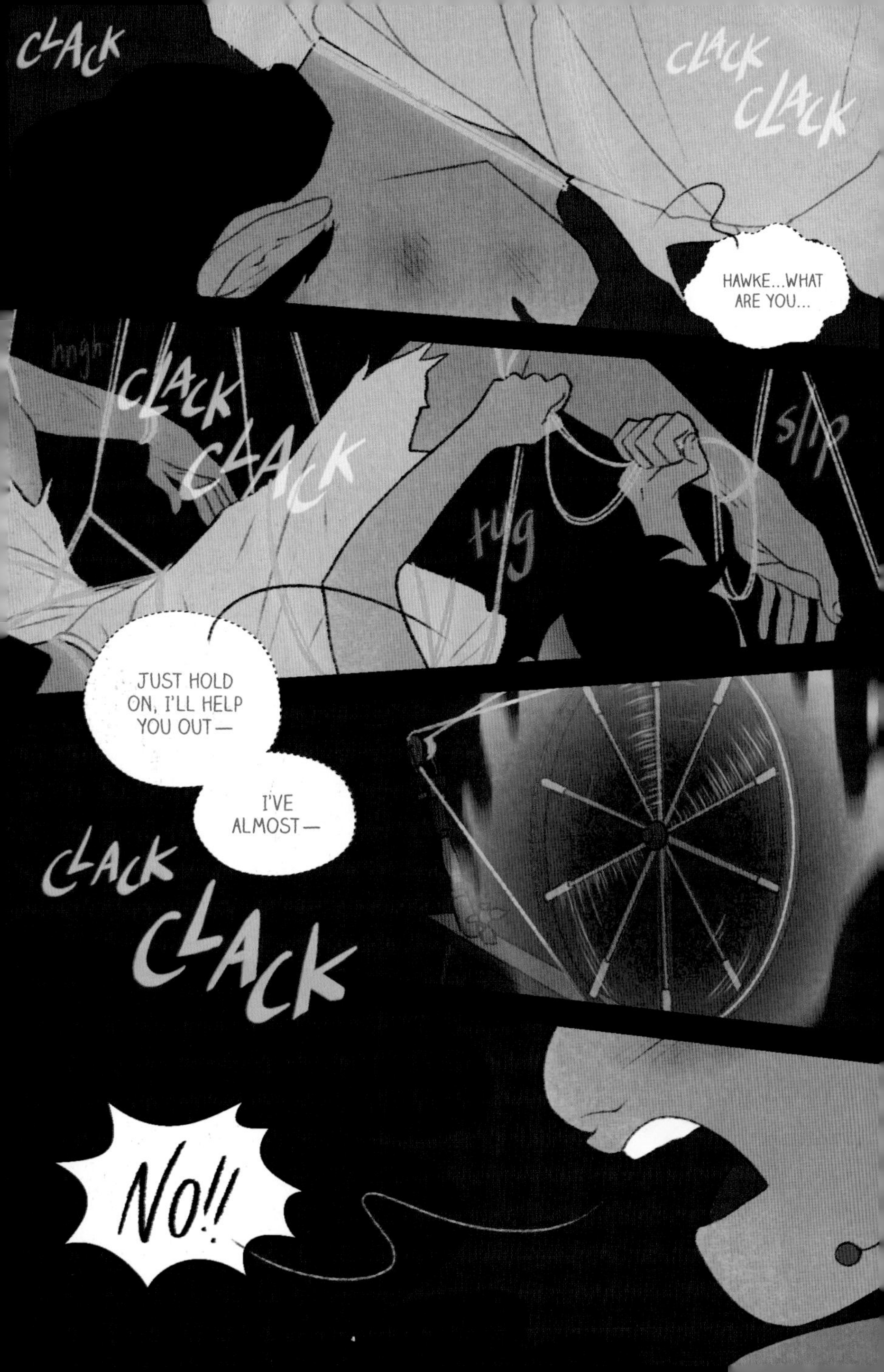
CLACK
CLACK
CLACK
HAWKE...WHAT ARE YOU...
hngh
CLACK
CLACK
slip
tug
JUST HOLD ON, I'LL HELP YOU OUT—
I'VE ALMOST—
CLACK
CLACK
NO!!

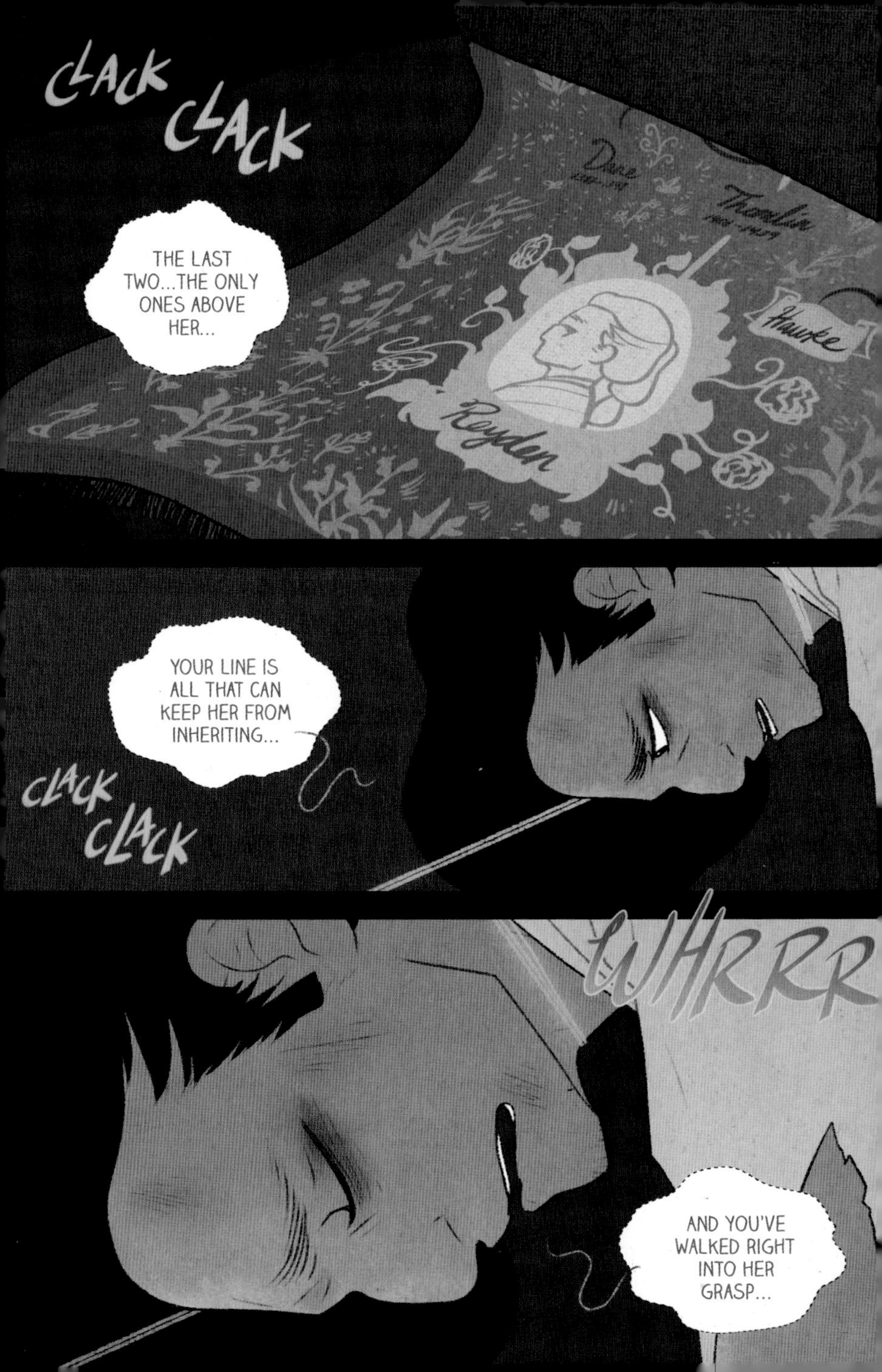
CLACK
CLACK
Dane
Hawke
Reyden
THE LAST TWO...THE ONLY ONES ABOVE HER...
YOUR LINE IS ALL THAT CAN KEEP HER FROM INHERITING...
CLACK
CLACK
WHRRR
AND YOU'VE WALKED RIGHT INTO HER GRASP...

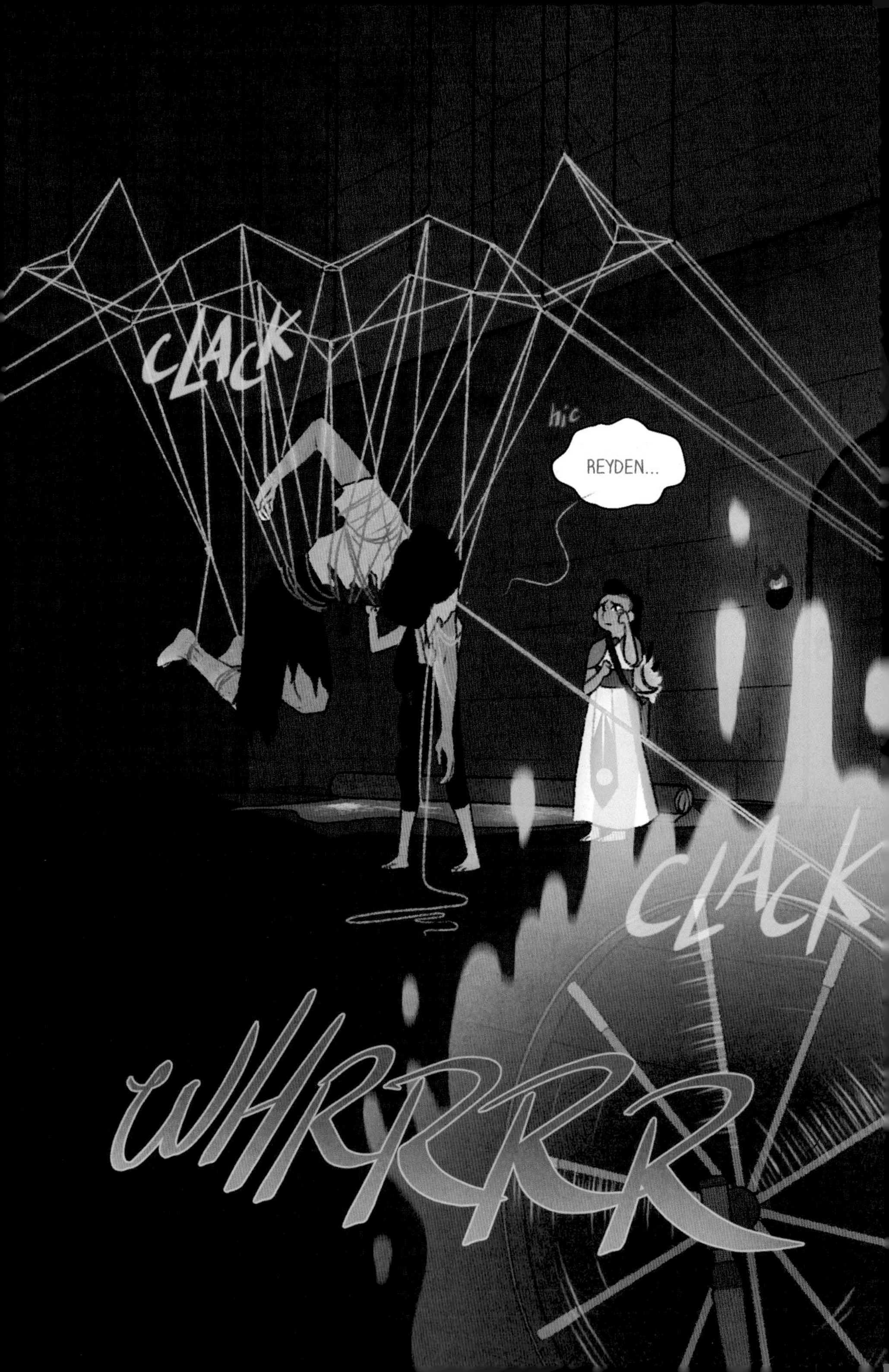
CLACK
hic
REYDEN...
CLACK
WHRRR

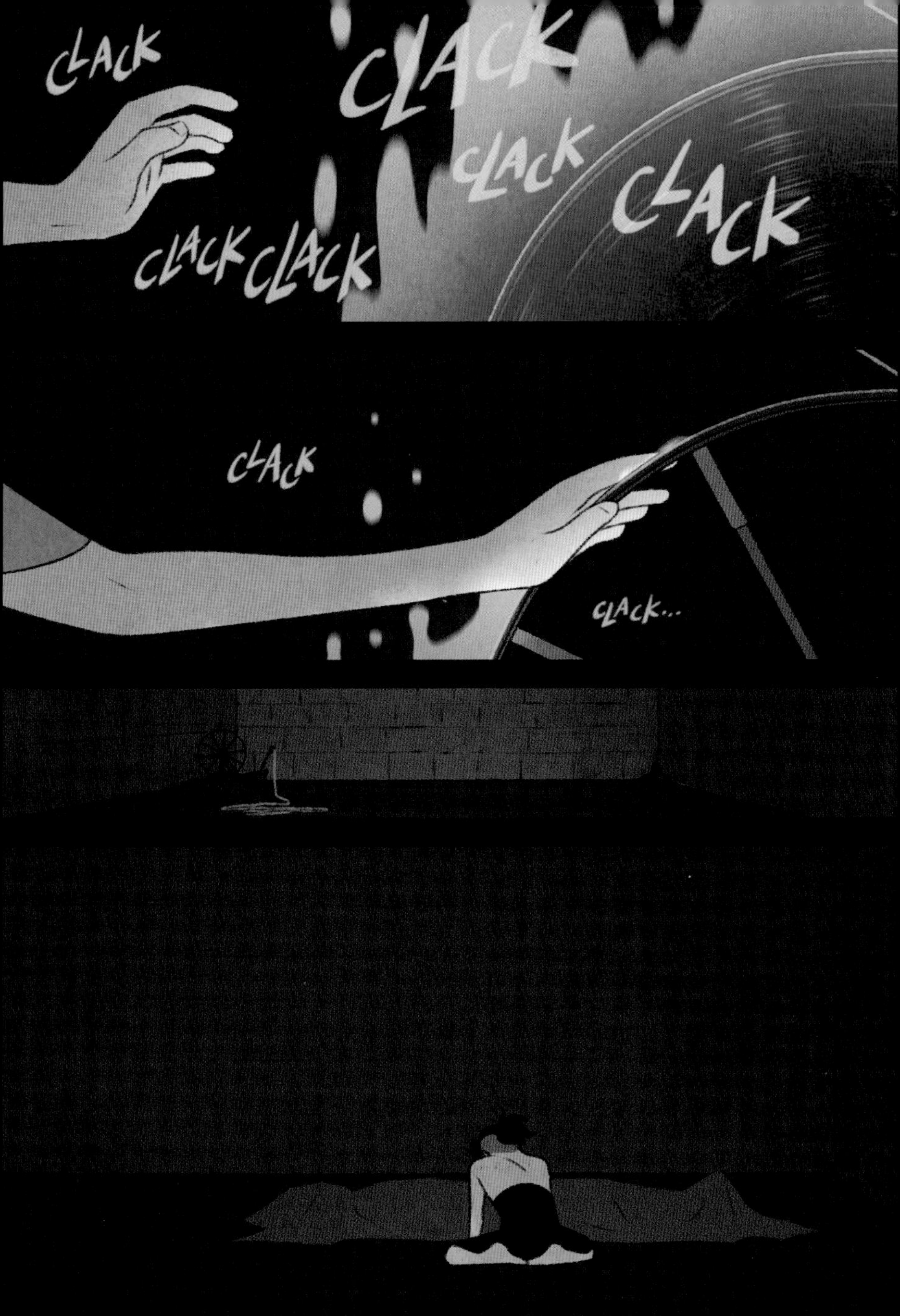
CLACK
CLACK
CLACK
CLACK
CLACK CLACK
CLACK
CLACK...

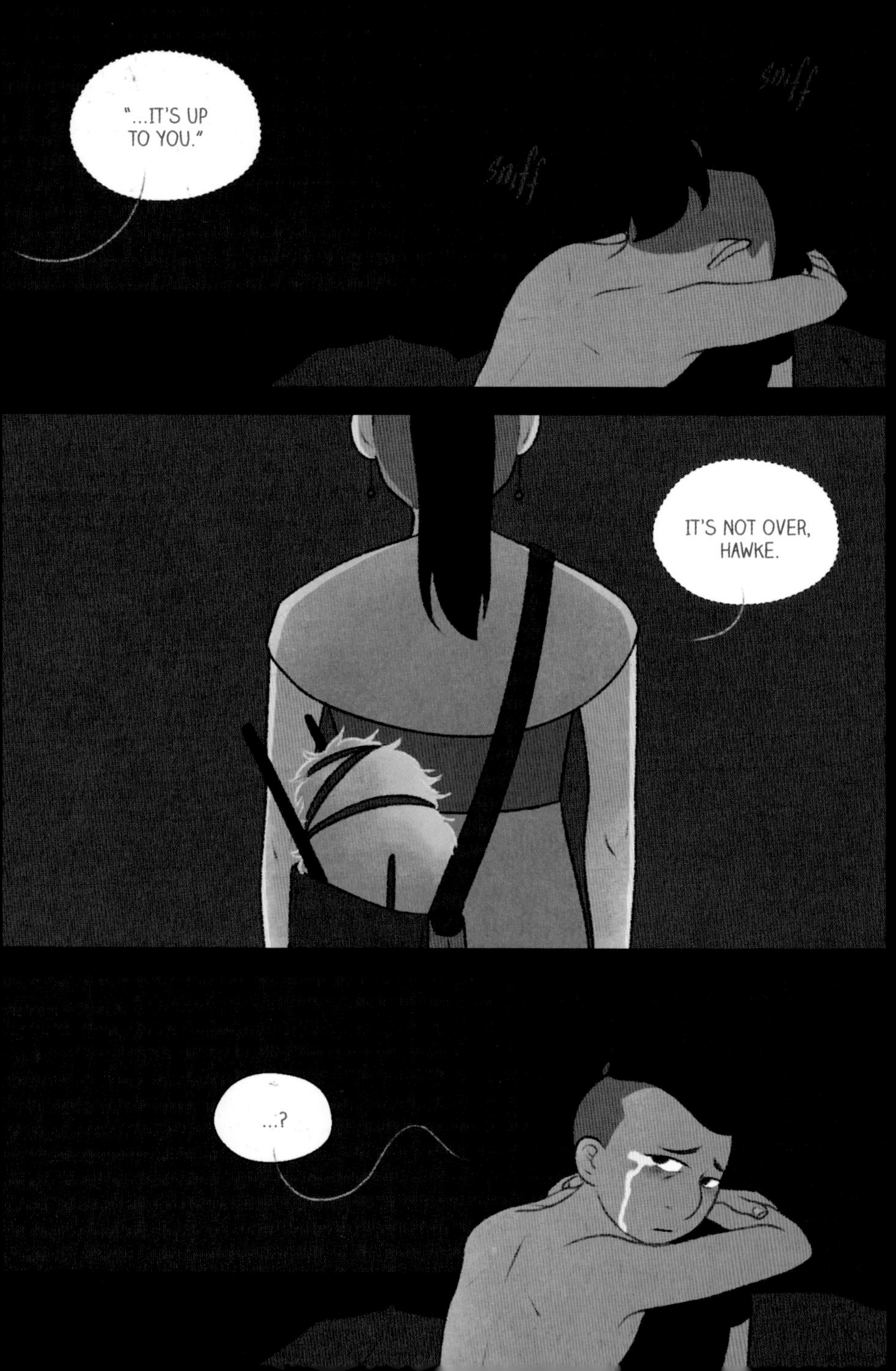
"...IT'S UP TO YOU."
sniff
sniff
IT'S NOT OVER, HAWKE.
...?

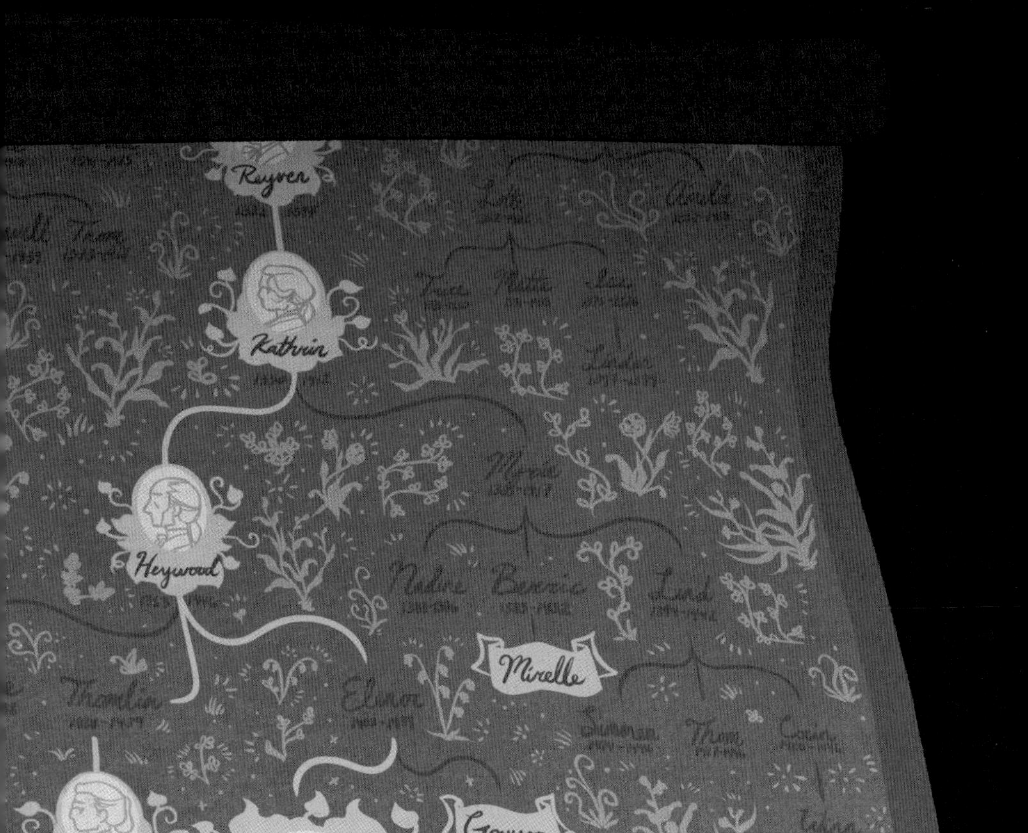
Reyven
Kathrin
Heywood
Mirelle
Grayson
Reyden
Hawke

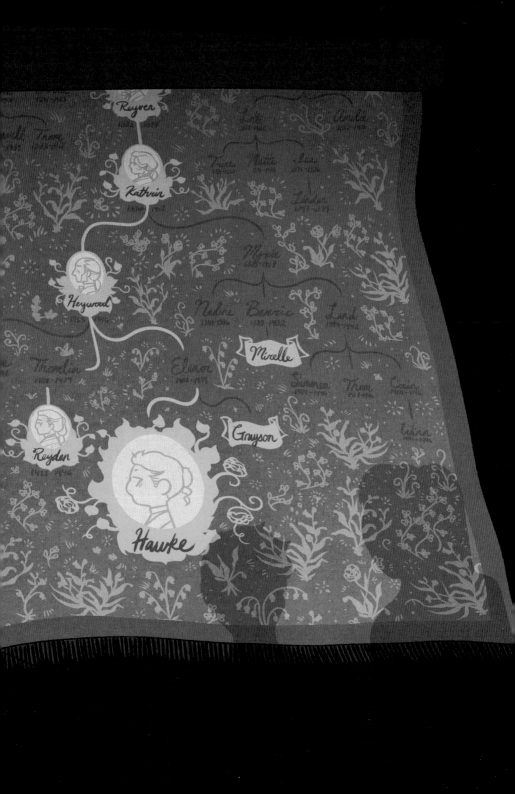

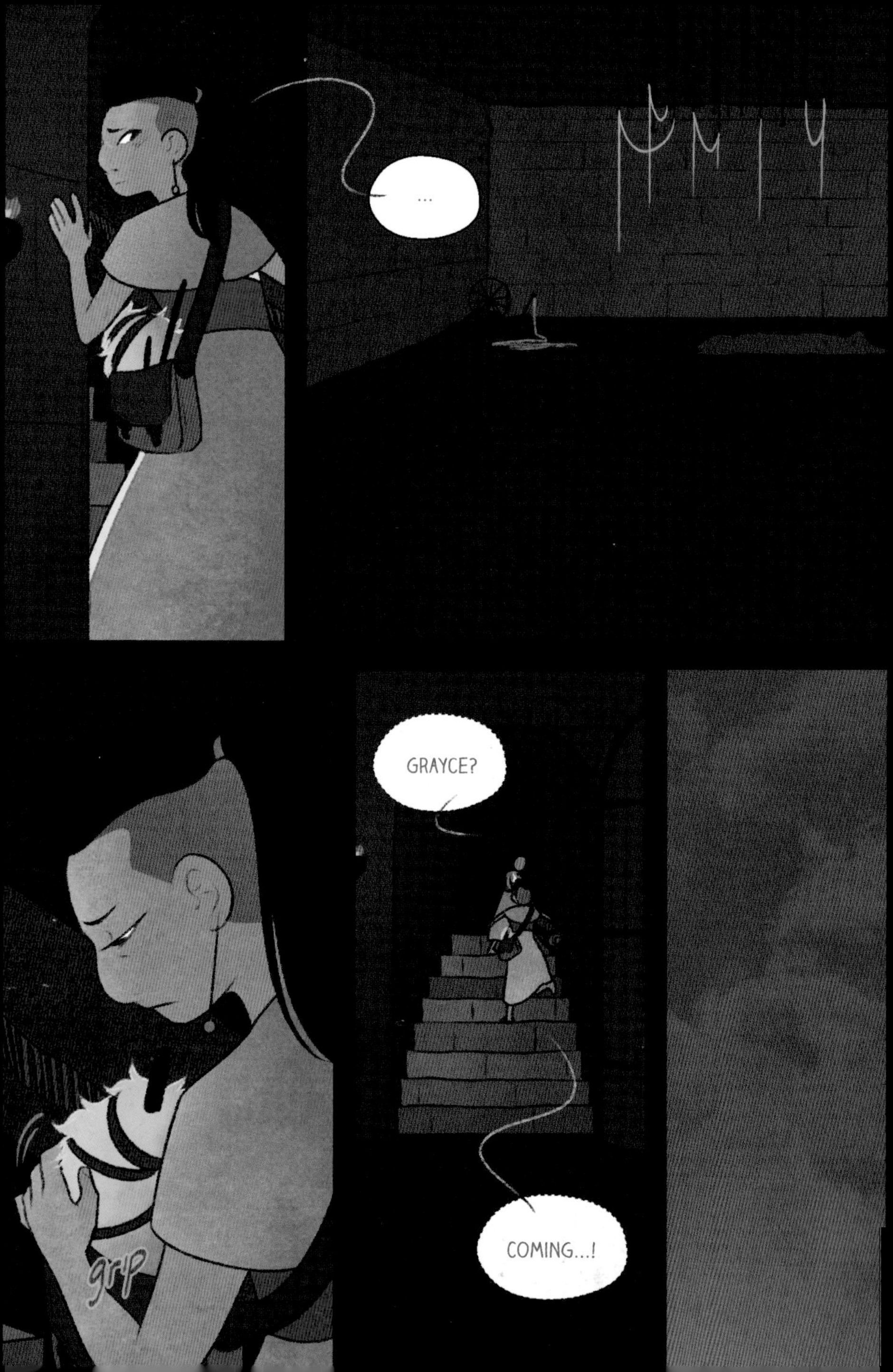
...
GRAYCE?
COMING...!
grip

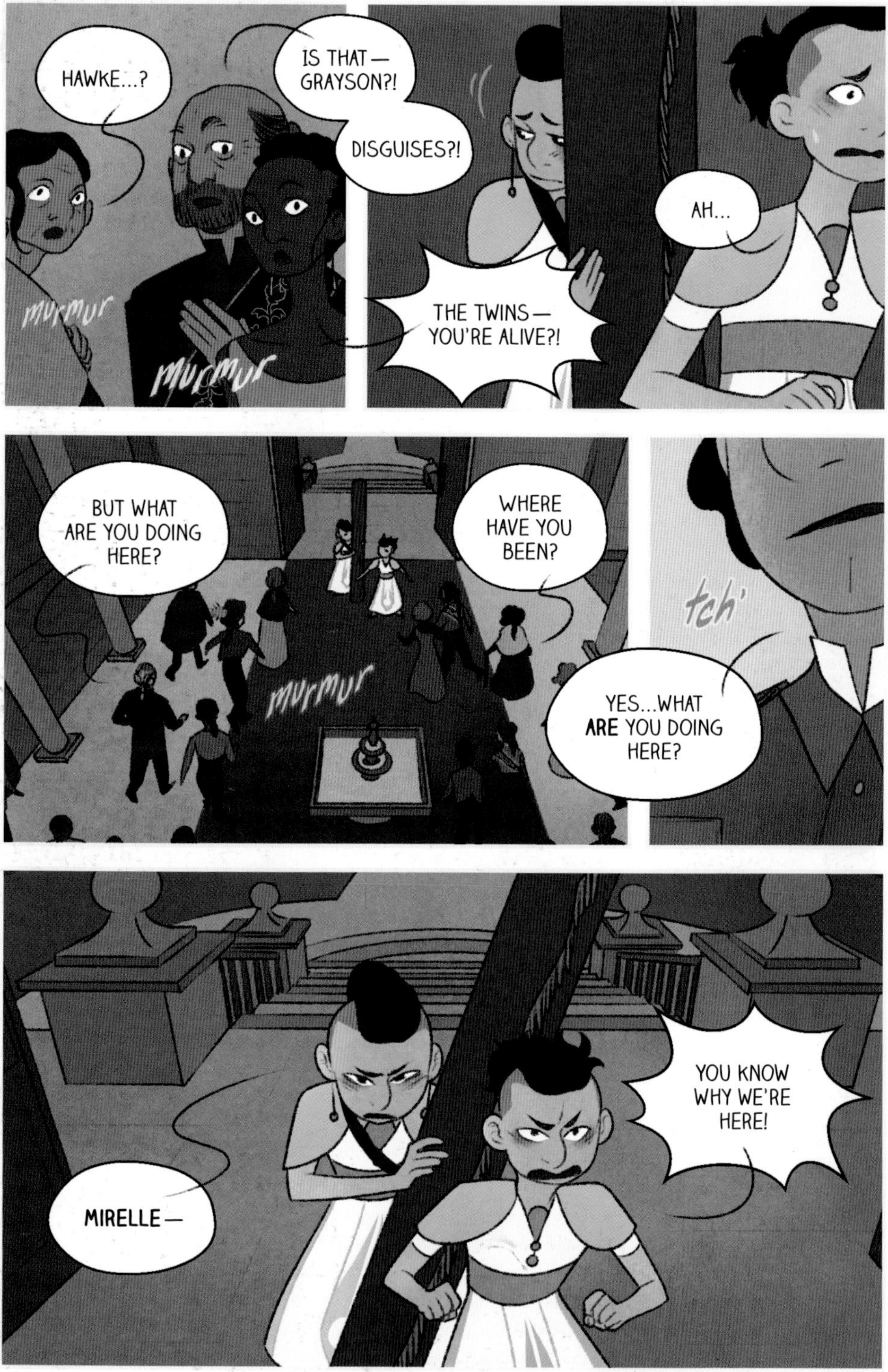
HAWKE...?
IS THAT—
GRAYSON?!
DISGUISES?!
murmur
murmur
THE TWINS—
YOU'RE ALIVE?!
AH...
BUT WHAT
ARE YOU DOING
HERE?
WHERE
HAVE YOU
BEEN?
murmur
tch'
YES...WHAT
ARE YOU DOING
HERE?
YOU KNOW
WHY WE'RE
HERE!
MIRELLE—

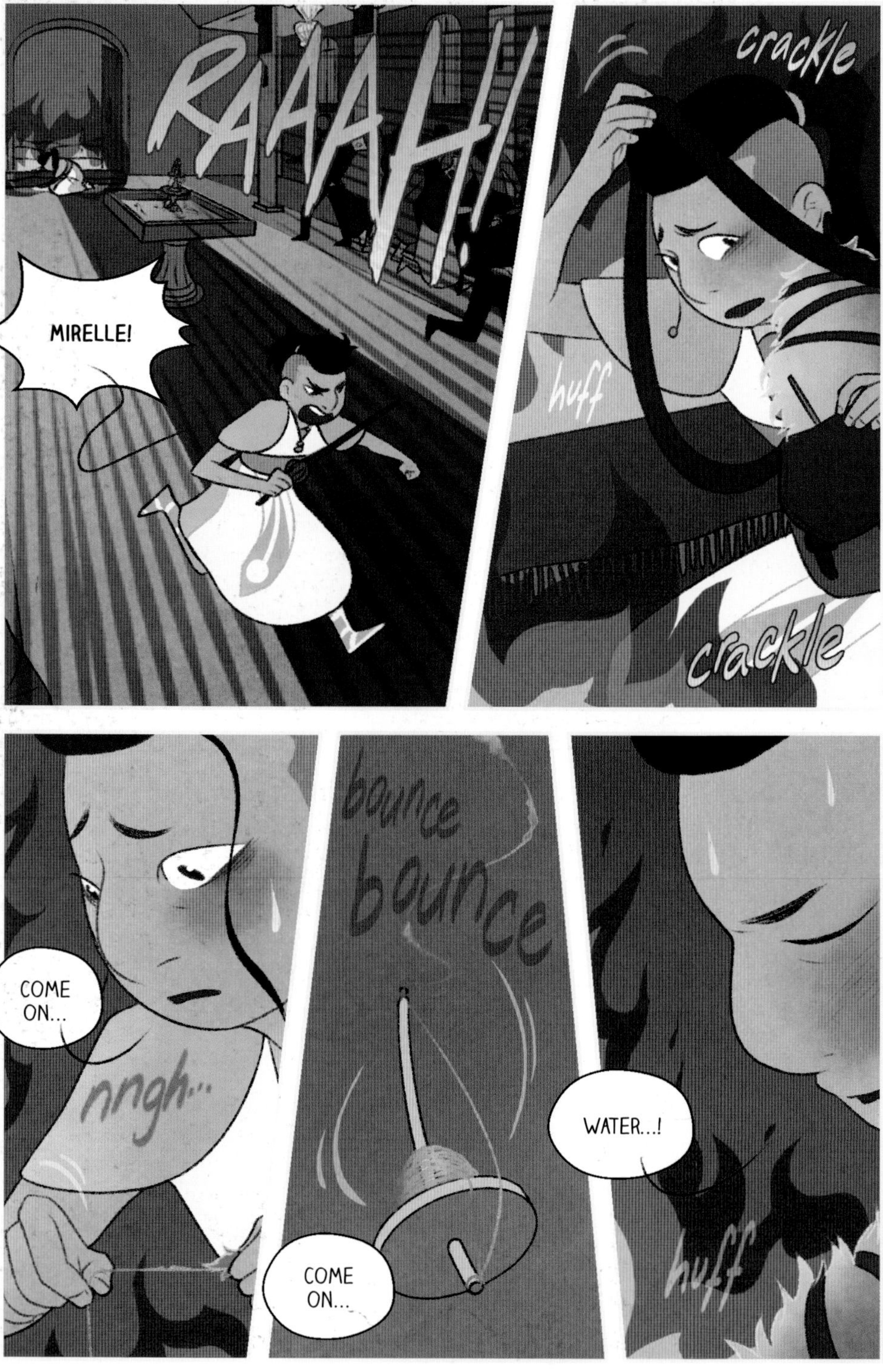
RAAAH!
MIRELLE!
crackle
huff
crackle
COME ON...
nngh...
bounce
bounce
COME ON...
WATER...!
huff

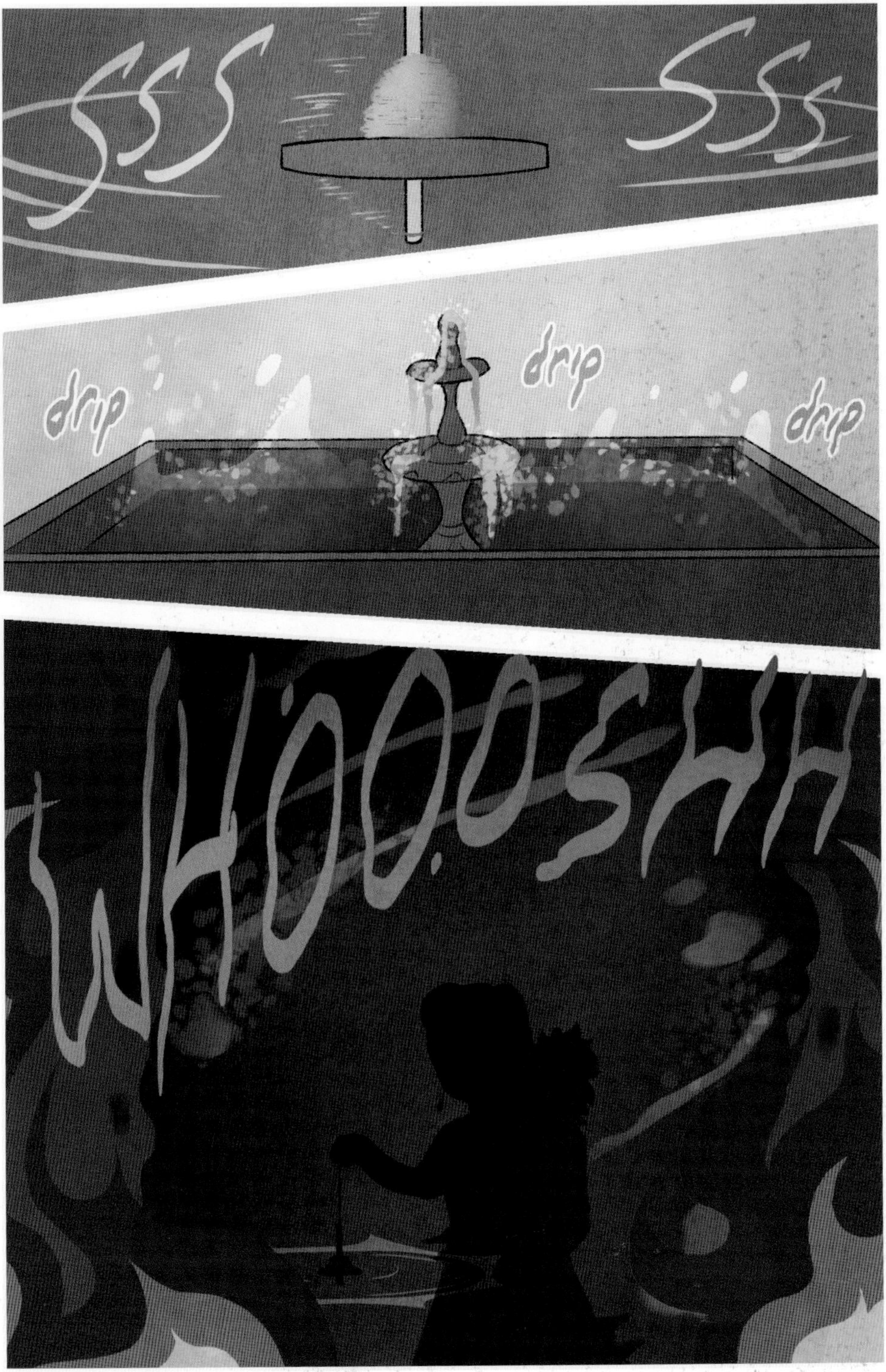
SSS
SSS
drip
drip
drip
WHOOOSHH

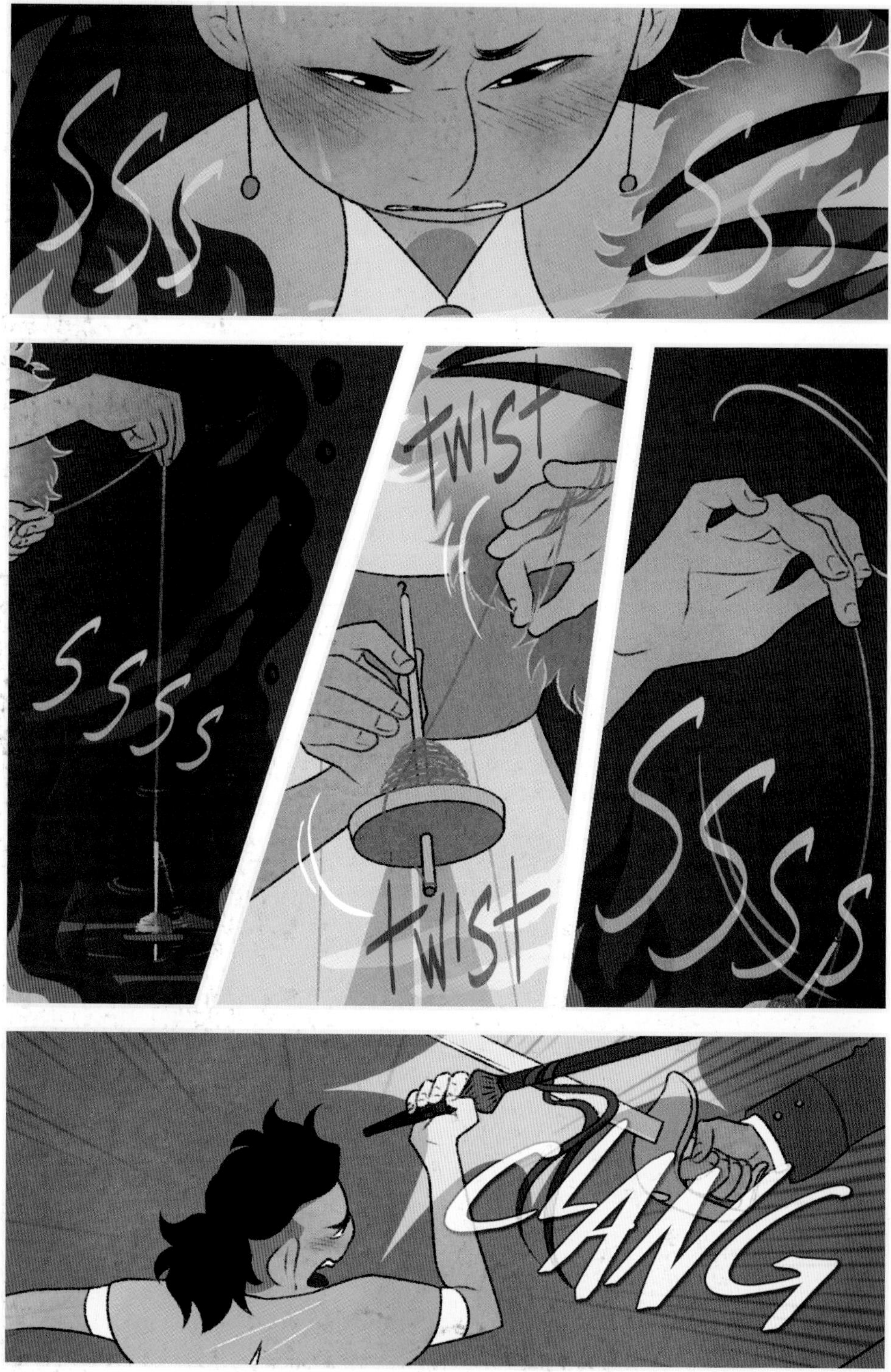
SSSS
SSSS
SSSS
TWIST
TWIST
SSSSS
CLANG

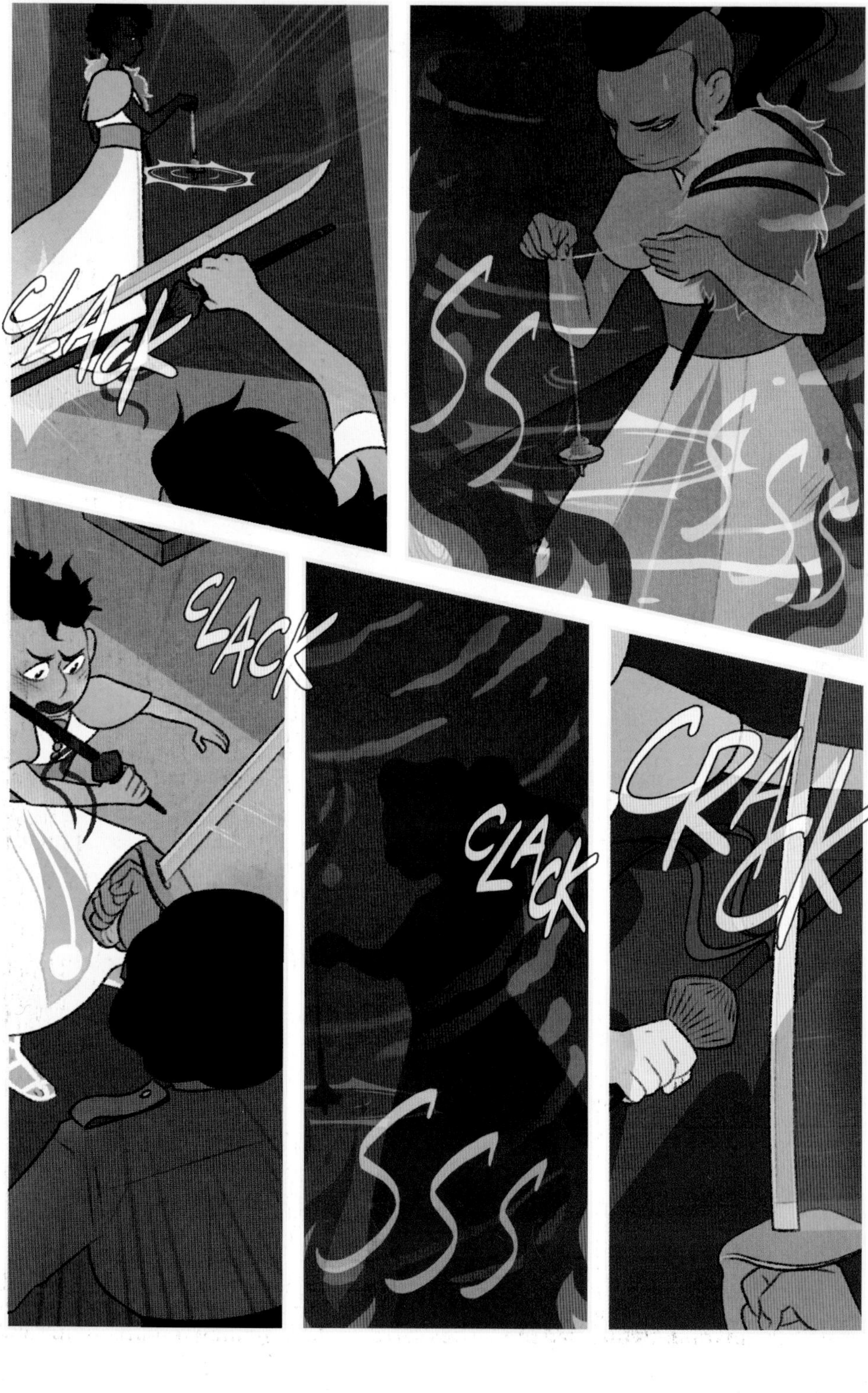
CLACK
SSSSSS
CLACK
CLACK
SSS
CRACK

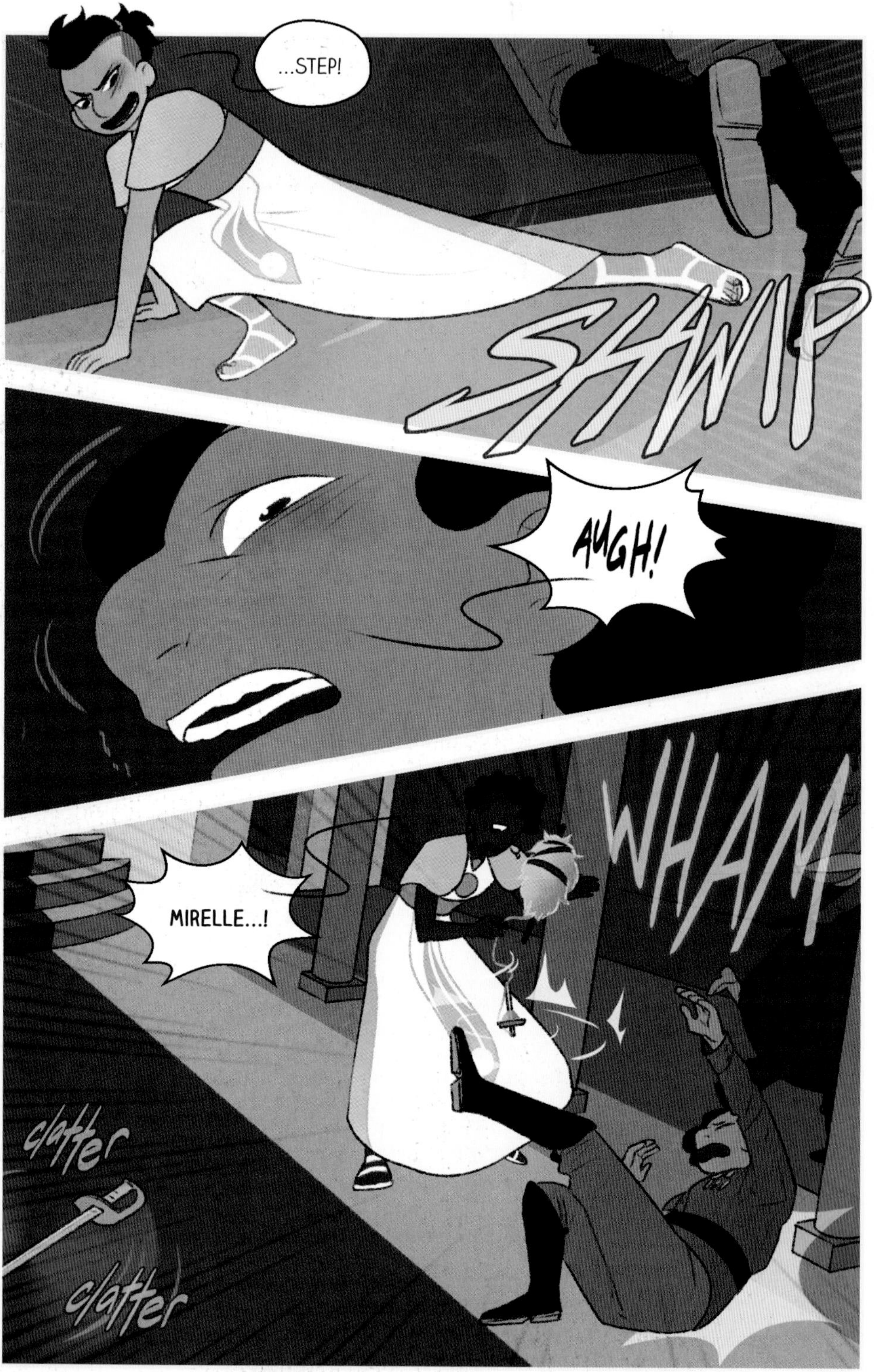
...STEP!
SHWIP
AUGH!
WHAM
MIRELLE...!
clatter
clatter

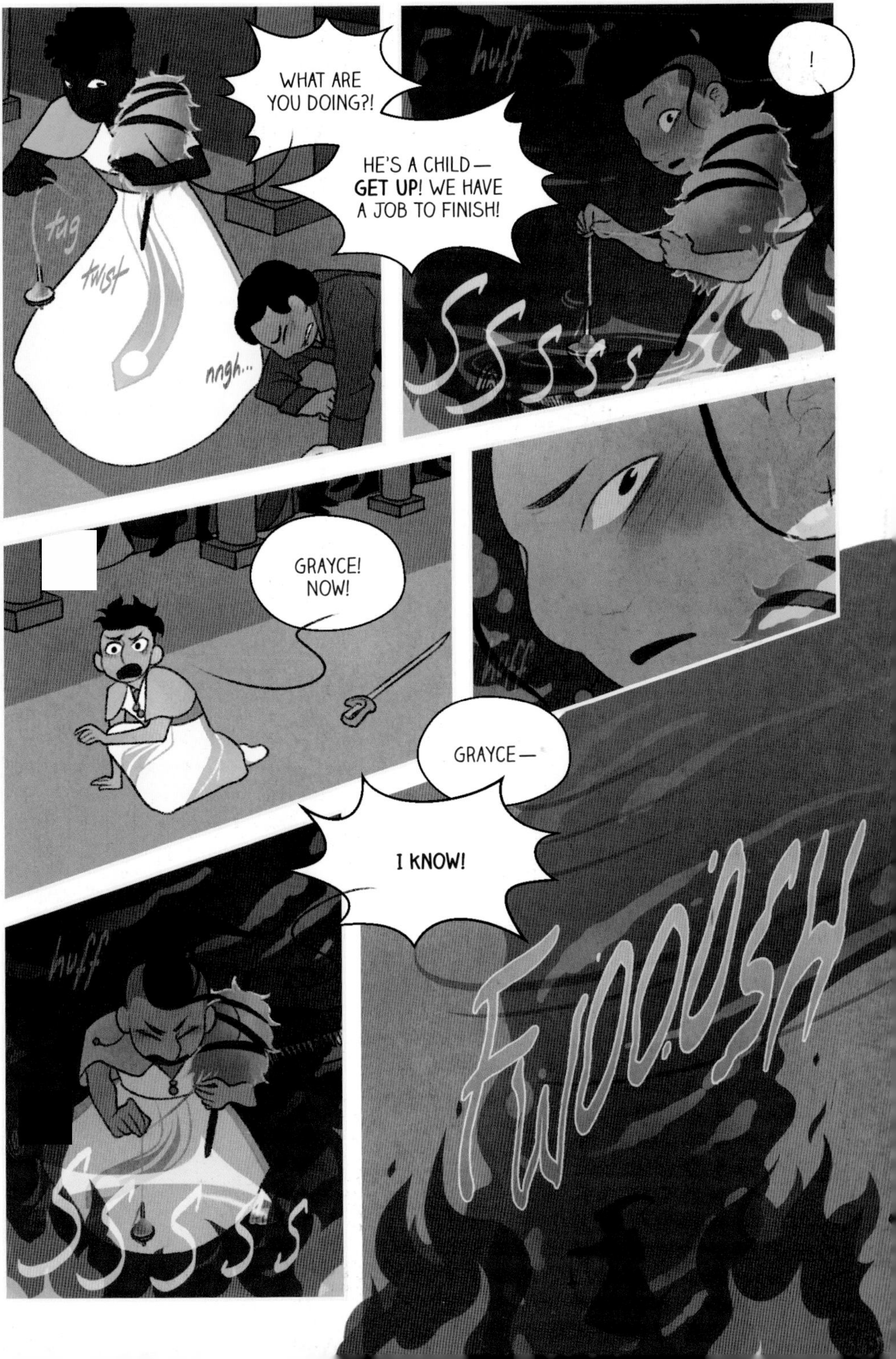
tug
twist
nngh...
WHAT ARE YOU DOING?!
HE'S A CHILD— **GET UP**! WE HAVE A JOB TO FINISH!
huff
!
SSSSS
GRAYCE! NOW!
huff
GRAYCE—
I KNOW!
huff
SSSSSS
FWOOOSH

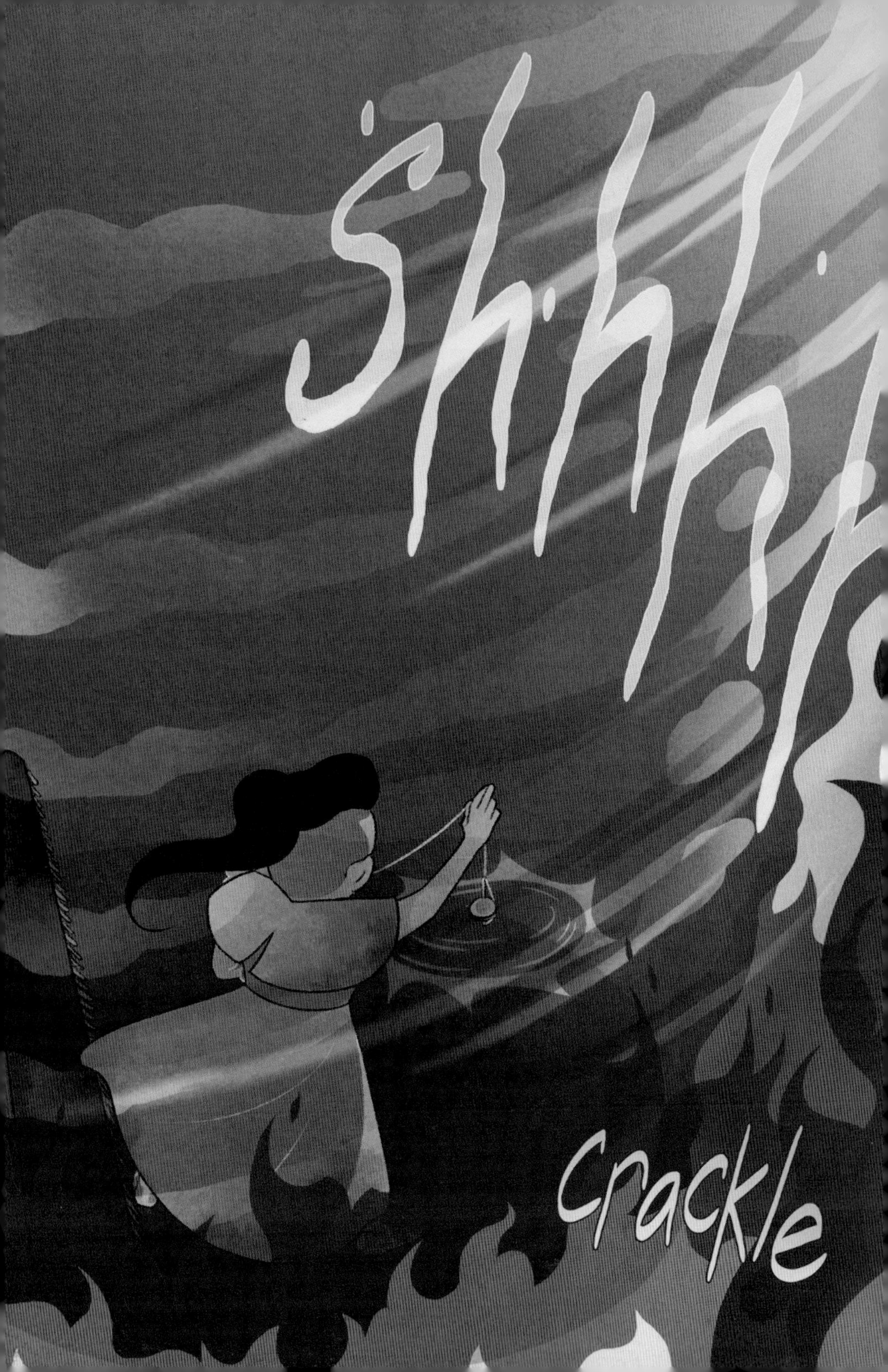
Shhhh
Crackle

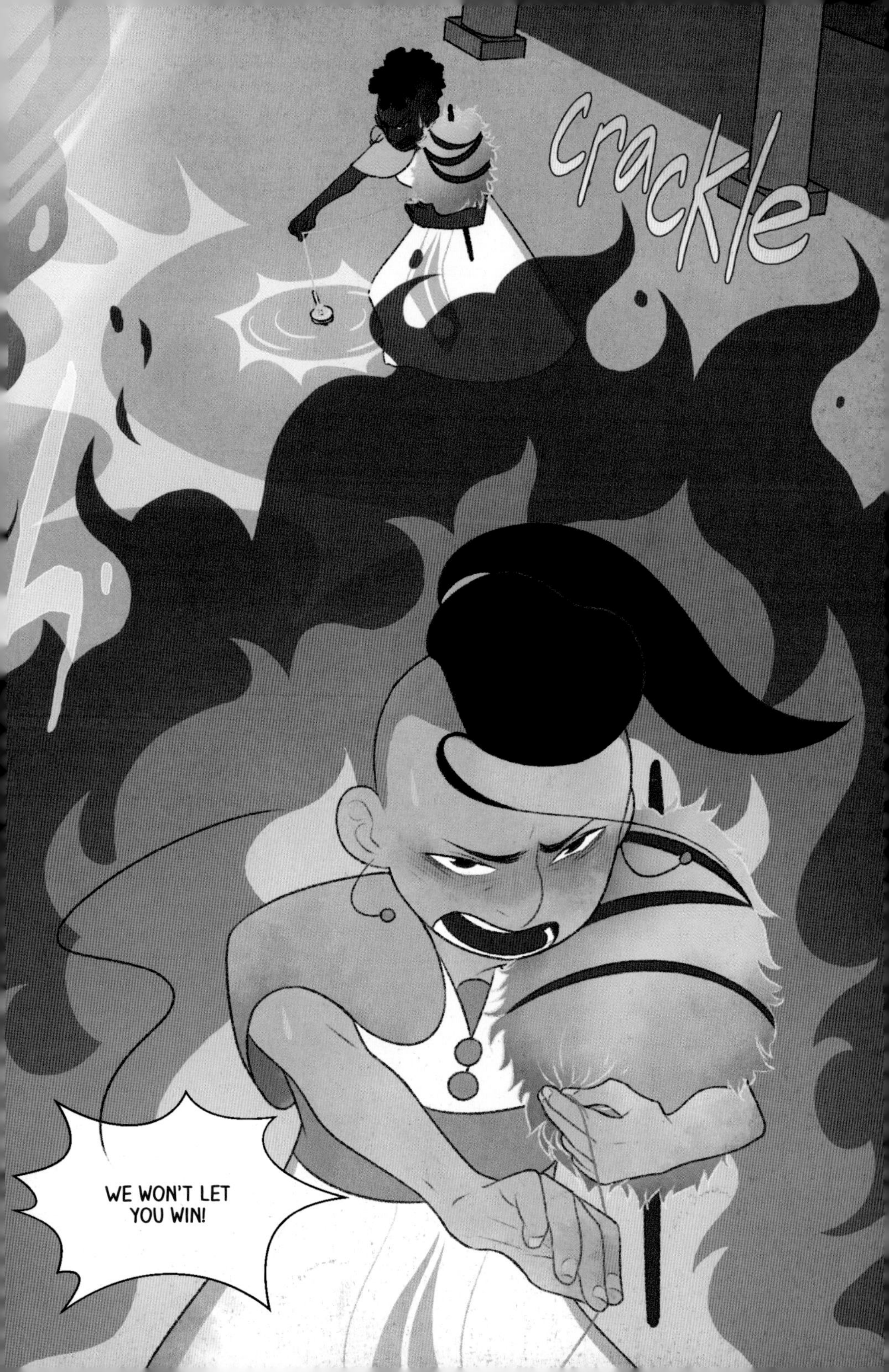
crackle
WE WON'T LET YOU WIN!

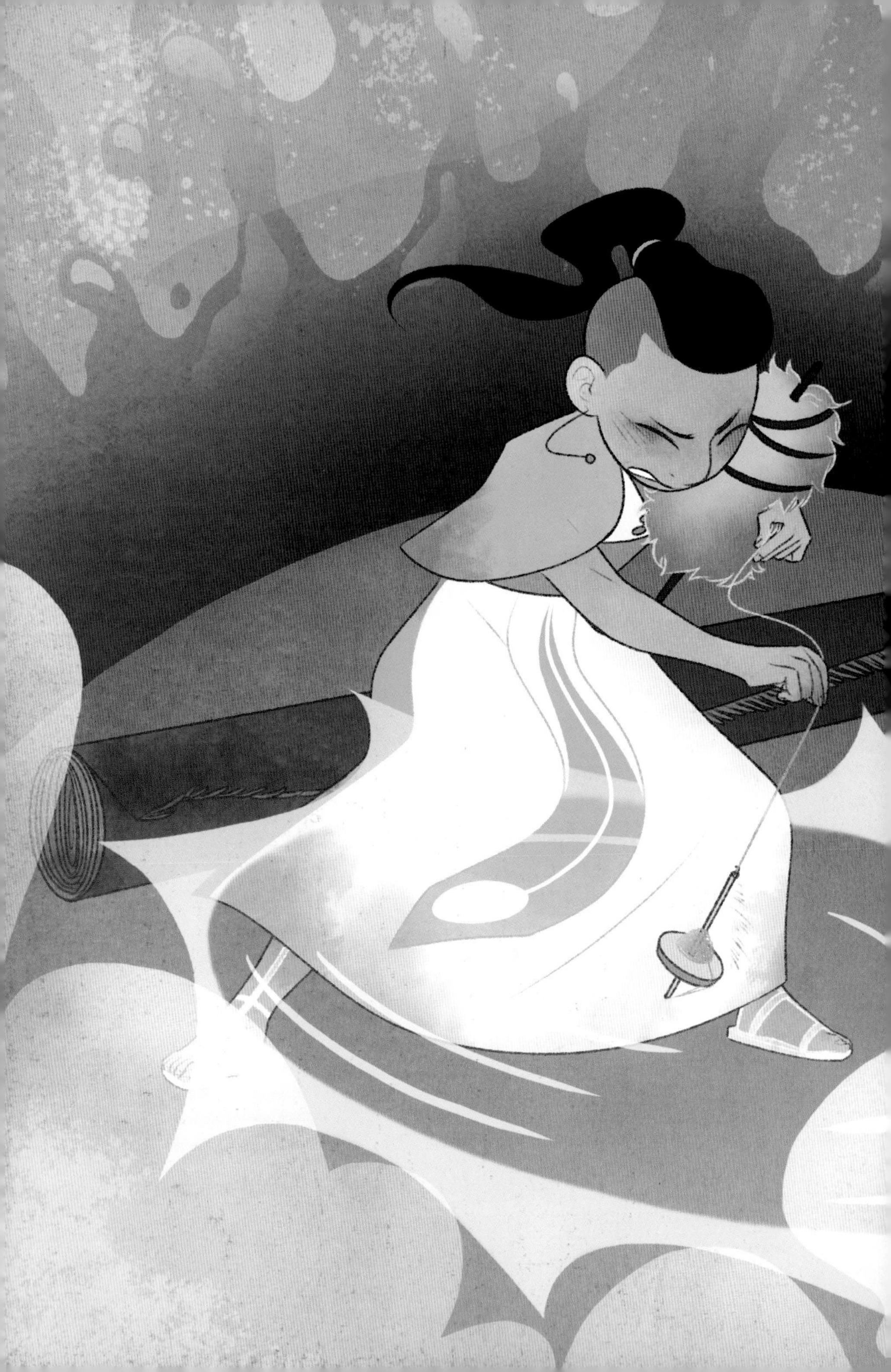

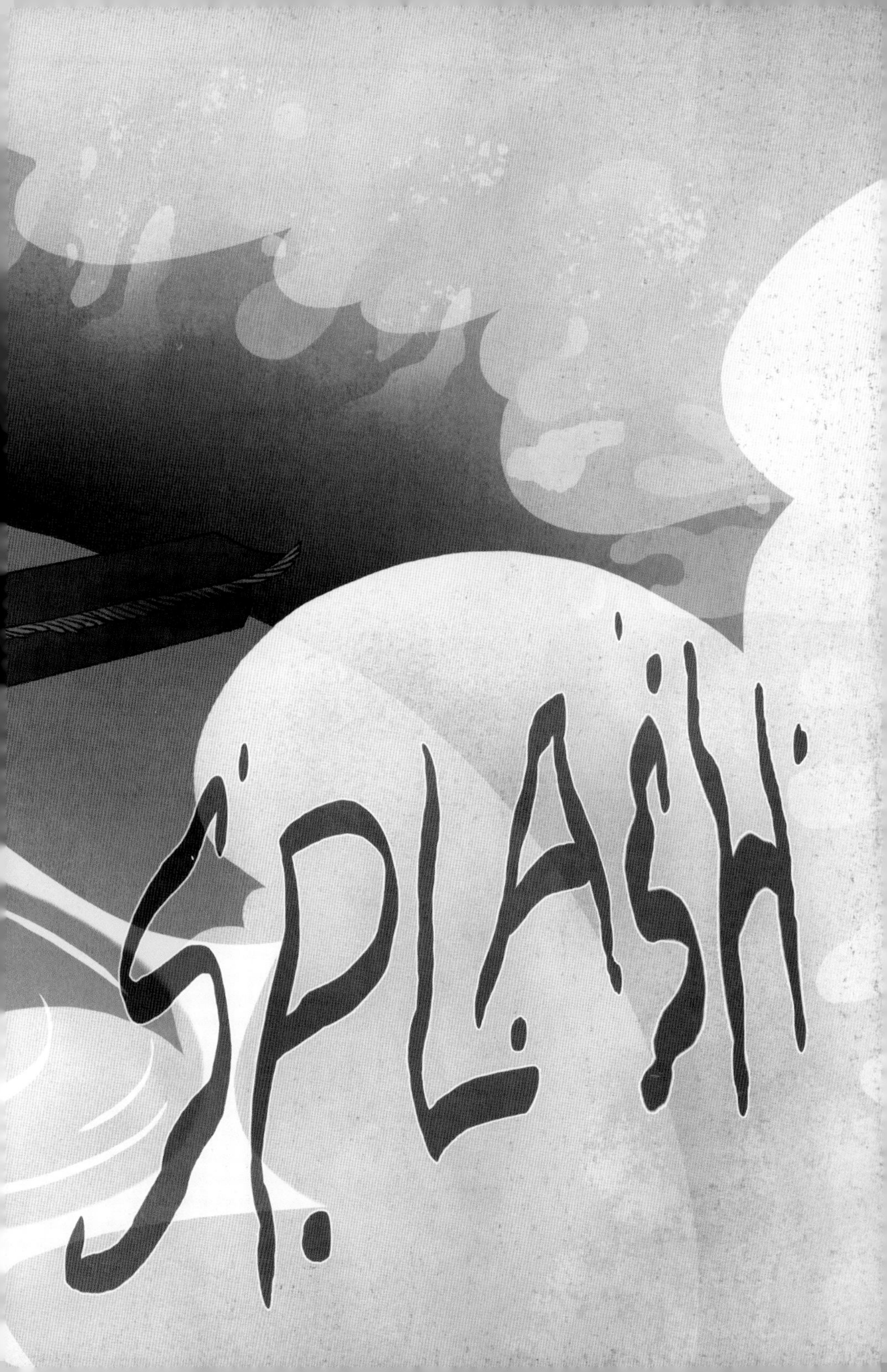
SPLASH

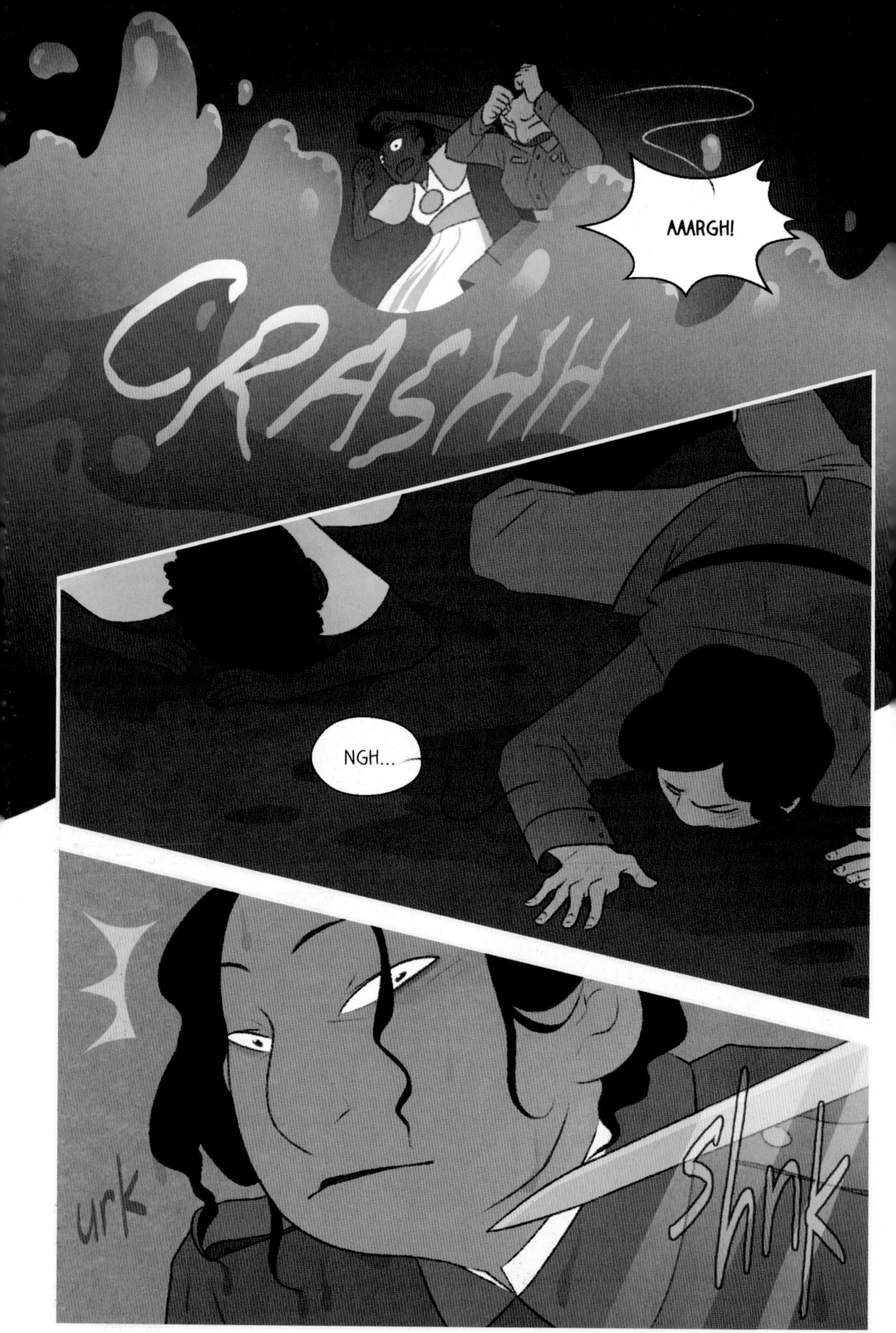
AAARGH!
CRASHH
NGH...
urk
shnk

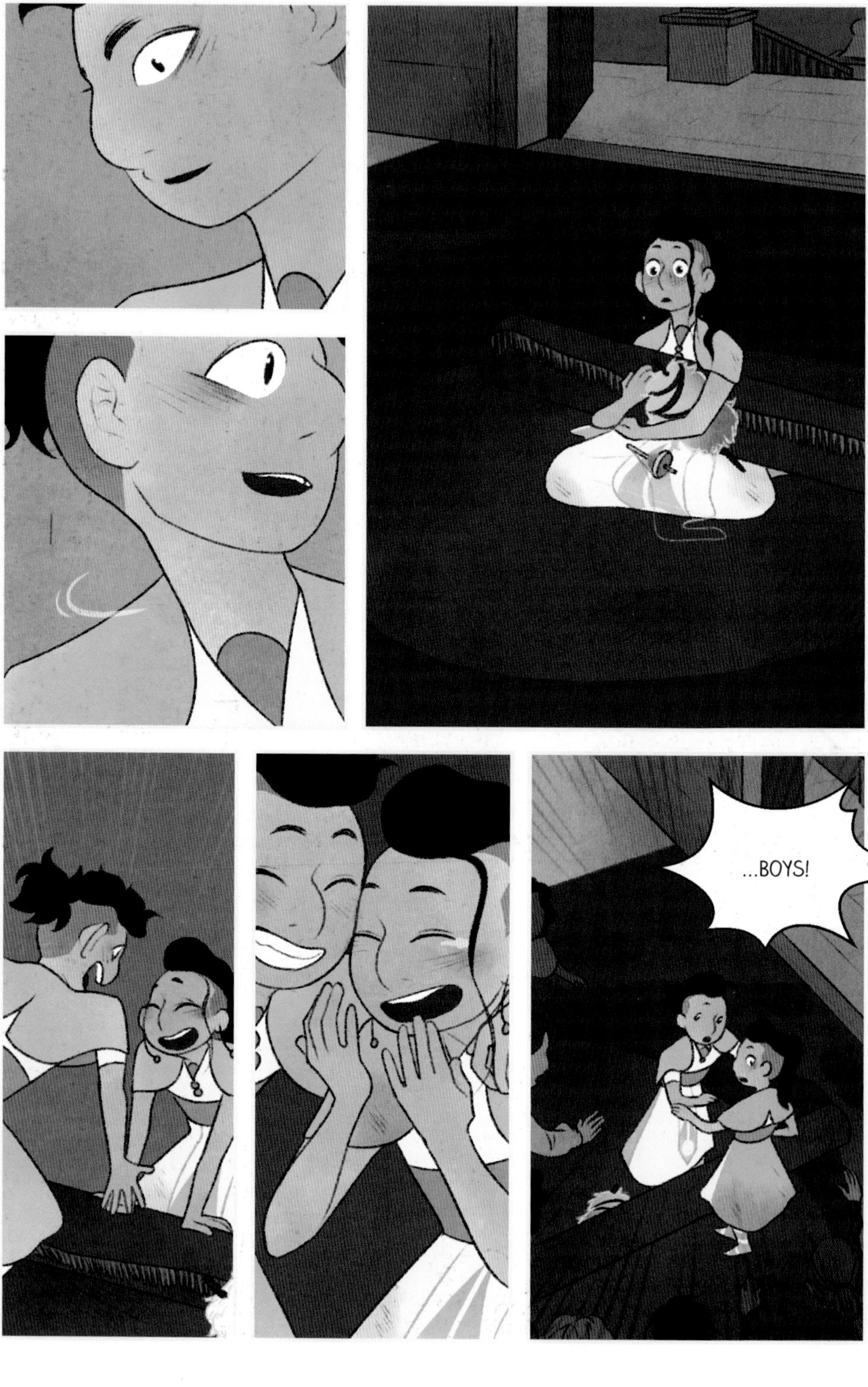
...BOYS!

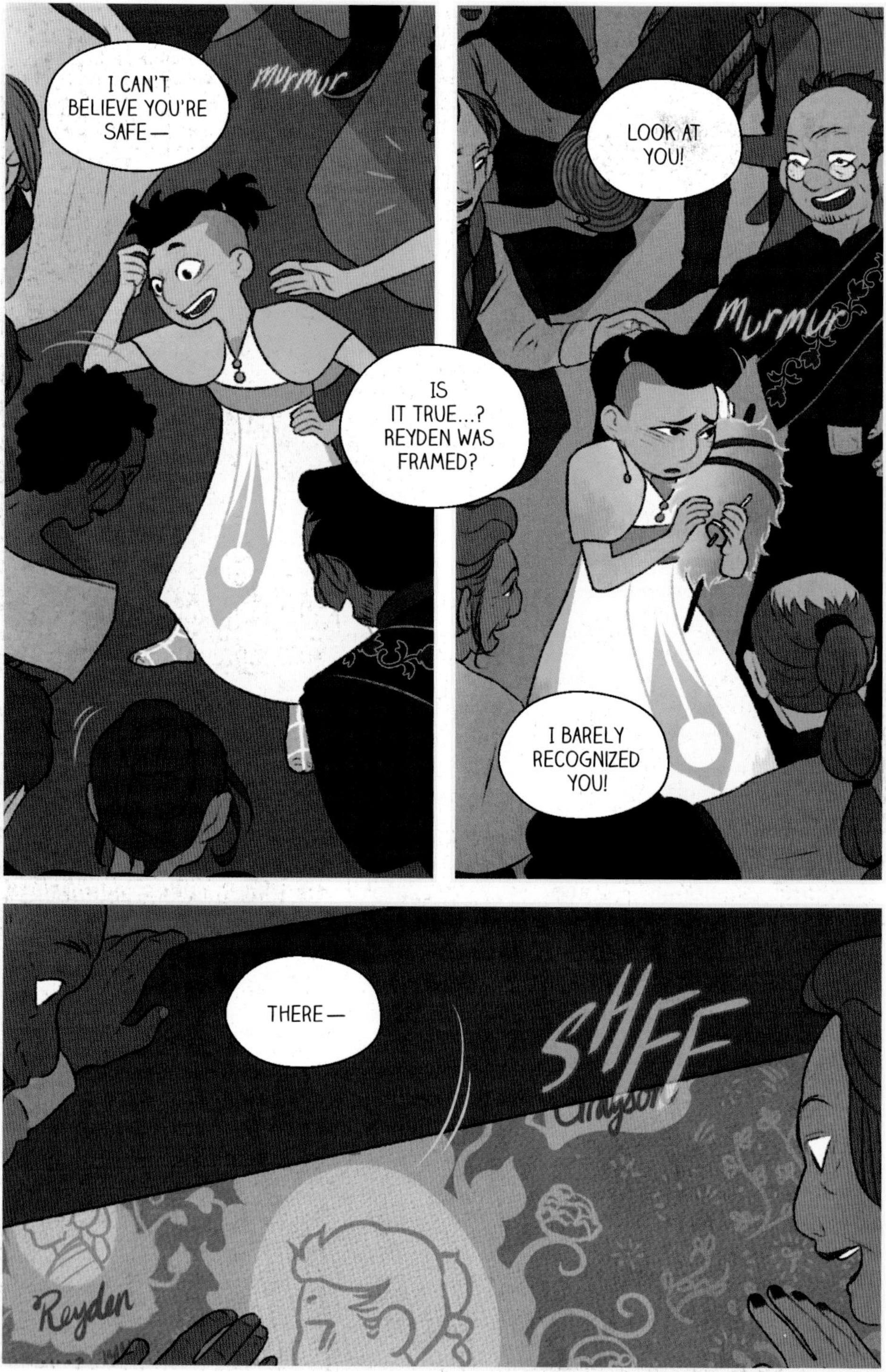
I CAN'T BELIEVE YOU'RE SAFE—
murmur
IS IT TRUE...? REYDEN WAS FRAMED?
LOOK AT YOU!
murmur
I BARELY RECOGNIZED YOU!
THERE—
SHFF
Reyden

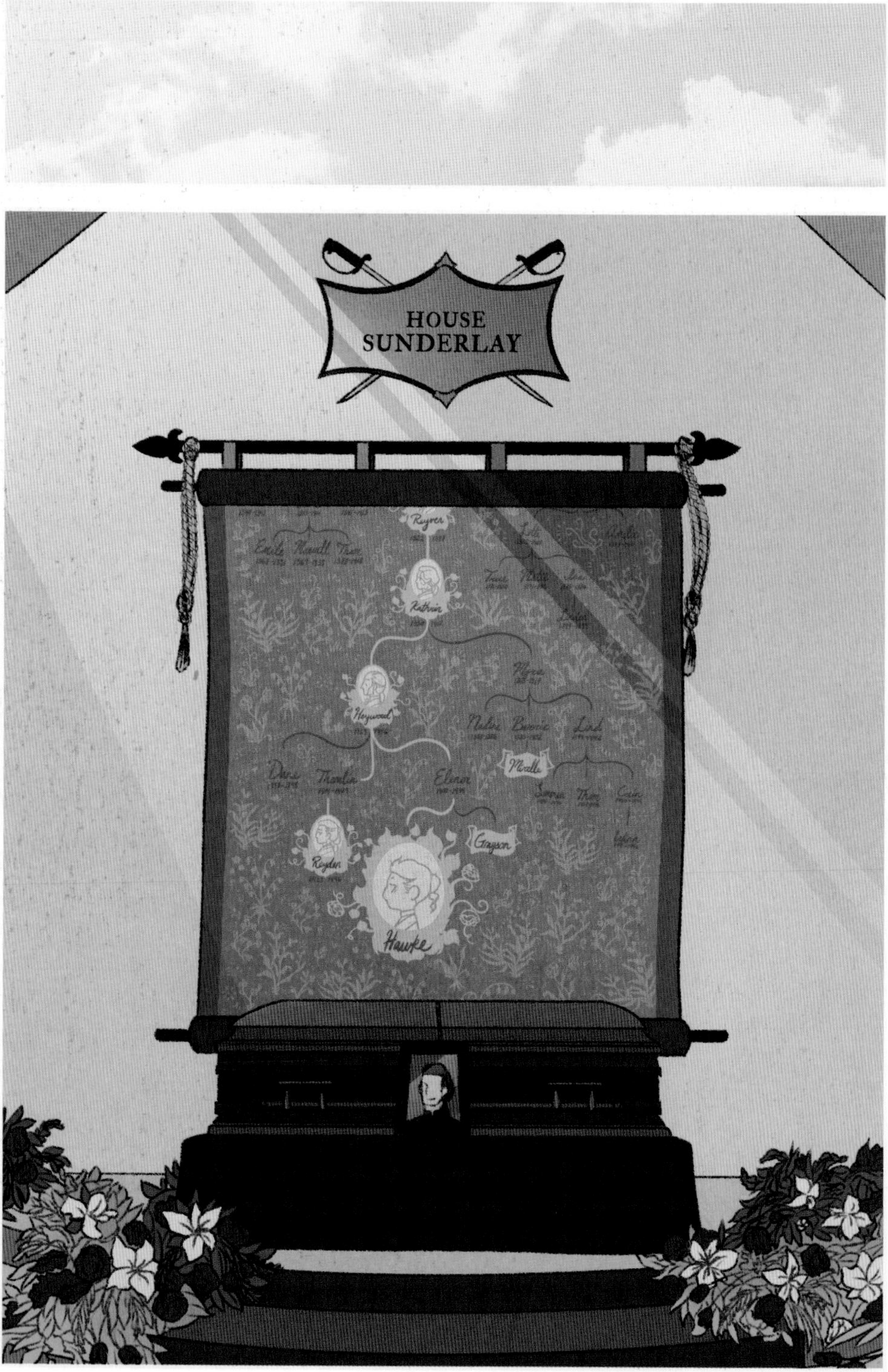
HOUSE SUNDERLAY
Rayner
Kathrin
Heywood
Dane
Elenor
Royden
Grayson
Hawke

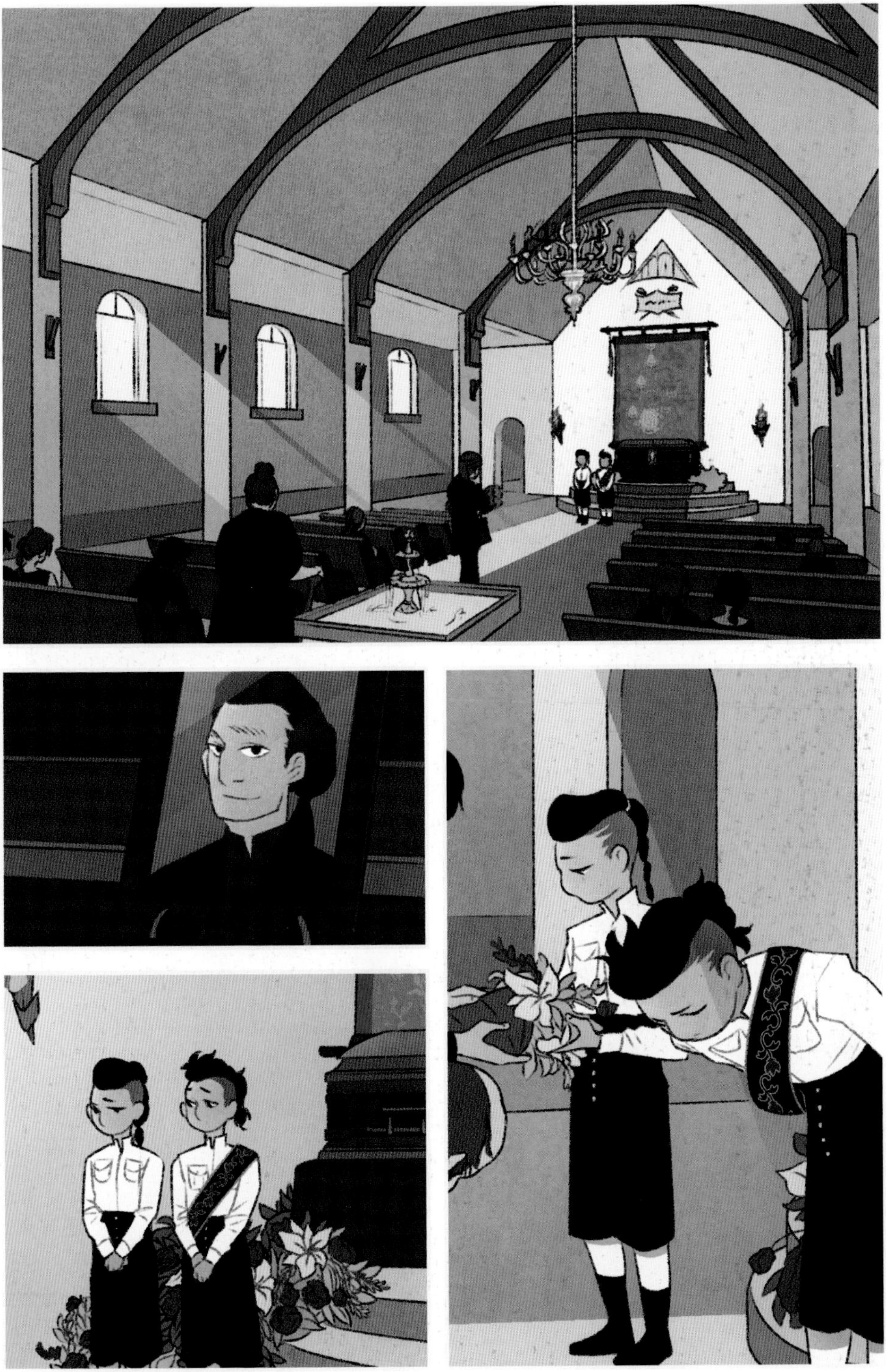

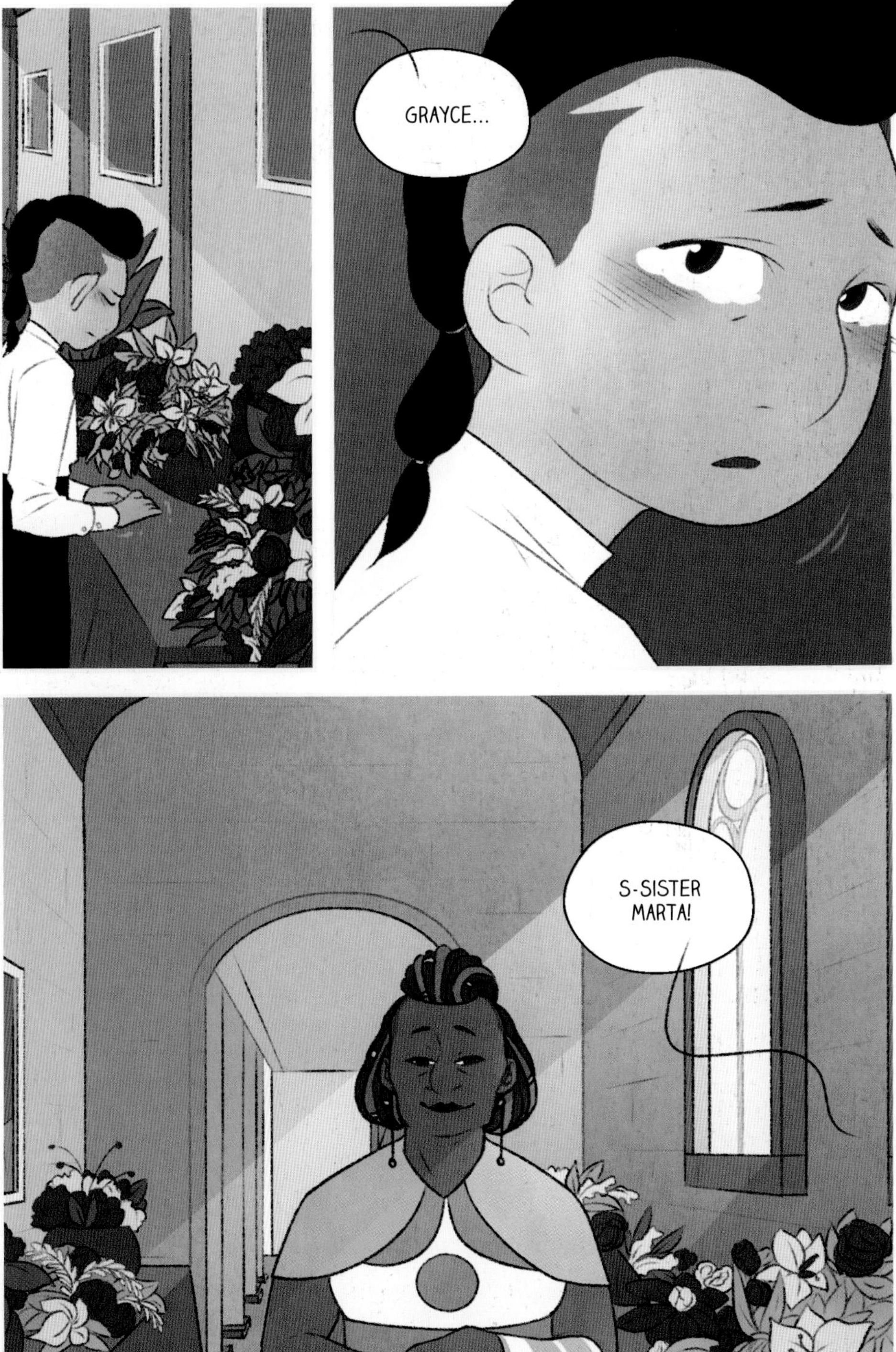
GRAYCE...
S-SISTER MARTA!

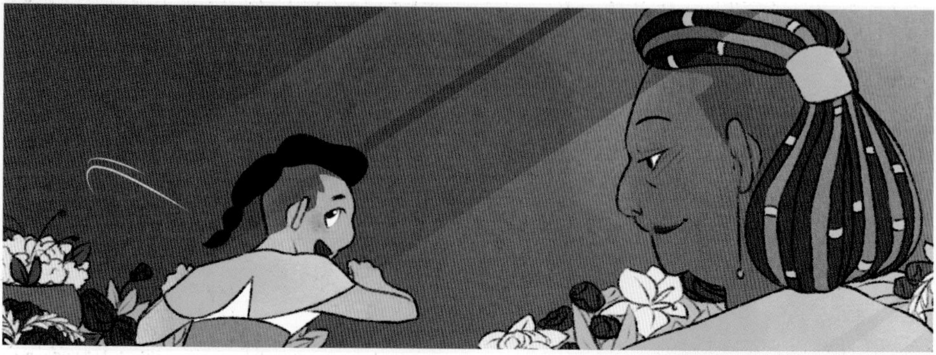

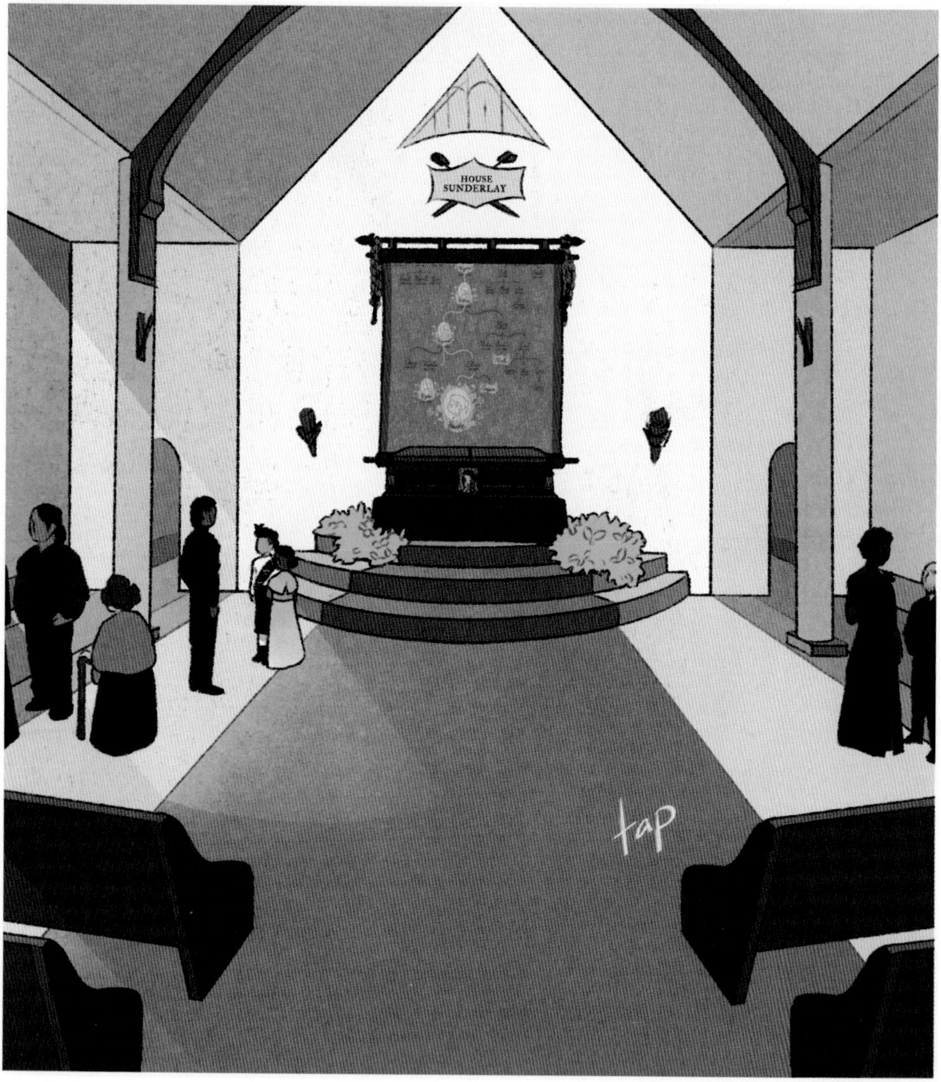
HOUSE
SUNDERLAY
tap

THE END

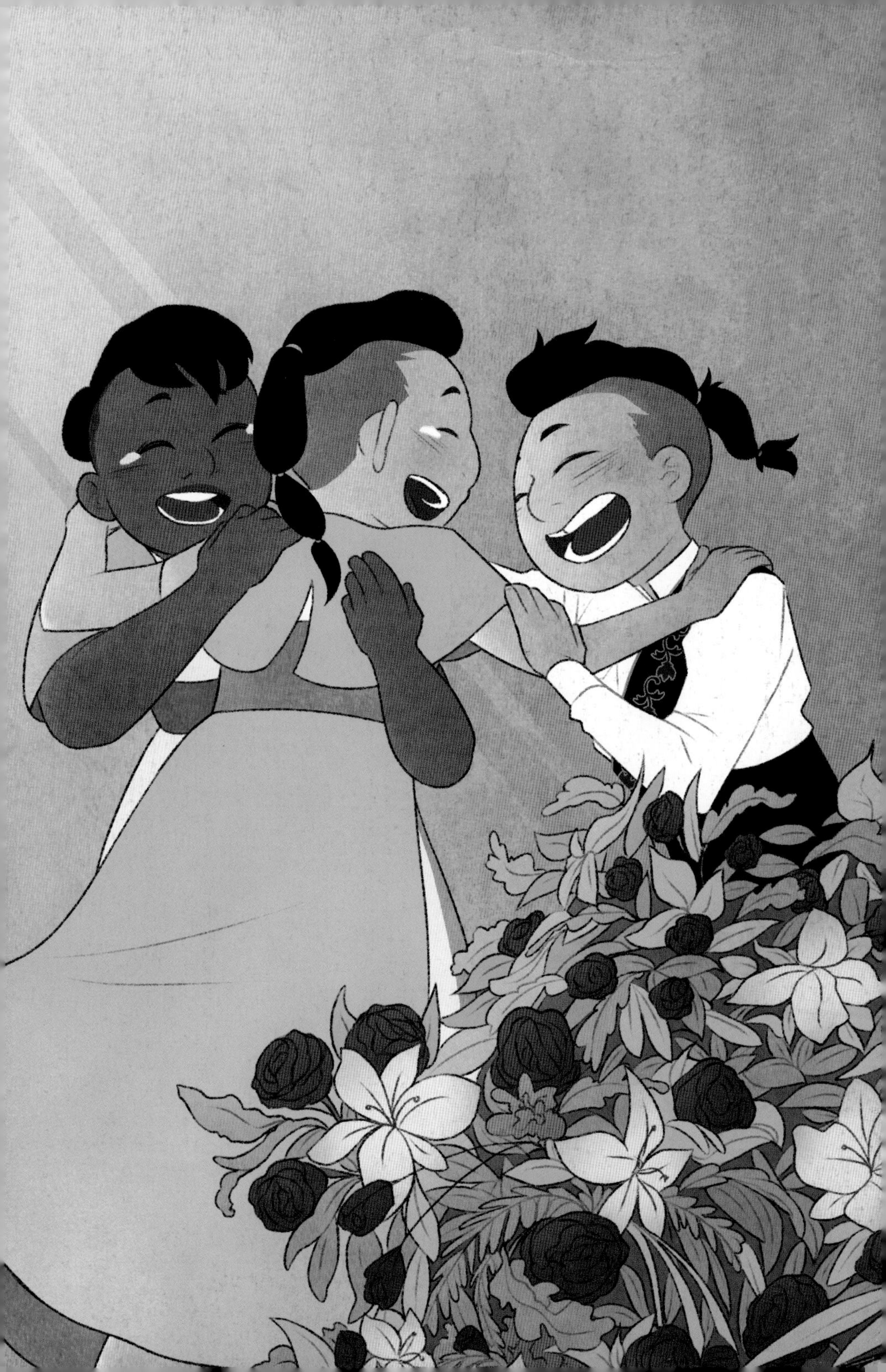

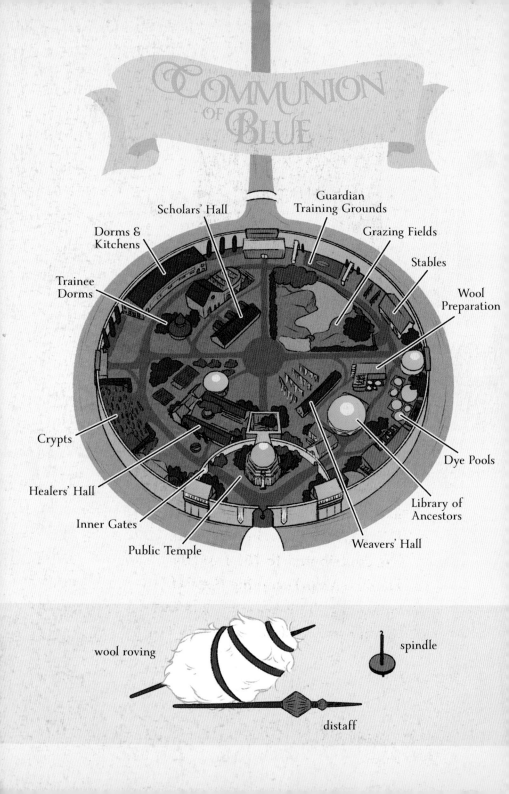

COMMUNION
OF
BLUE

Scholars' Hall

Guardian
Training Grounds

Dorms &
Kitchens

Grazing Fields

Stables

Trainee
Dorms

Wool
Preparation

Crypts

Healers' Hall

Dye Pools

Inner Gates

Library of
Ancestors

Public Temple

Weavers' Hall

wool roving

spindle

distaff